Praise for Federico Moccia and the Rome Novels

"A deep, passionate romance that transcends time and age. Readers will appreciate this highly intense coming-of-age story that shows how much some are willing to risk for love. *One Step to You* has been aptly compared to the novels of Nicholas Sparks and John Green and will appeal to readers of those highly emotional tales."

—*Booklist*, starred review, on *One Step to You*

"Capture[s] the turbulent passion of teen love."

—*Publishers Weekly* on *One Step to You*

"Federico Moccia has touched the romantic heart of a whole generation." —*Il Giornale* (Italian newspaper)

"Federico Moccia is the romance king of the Mediterranean bestseller." —*Woman* (Spain)

"Federico Moccia knows how to get straight to the heart of all young readers. His words always hit the right spot."

—*TTL* (Italian newspaper)

"With his novels, the writer Federico Moccia has revolutionized young people." —*Glamour*

"Federico Moccia is an author who writes about love, and he wins the hearts of a broad and diverse audience—the teenagers of today and the teenagers of yesteryear."

—*la Repubblica* (Rome newspaper)

"Federico Moccia is a household name for millions of readers." —*Revista Universitarios* (Spain)

"The Roman writer has managed to connect with an audience who have become dedicated fans and who are eager to read his novels, great romances with vital teachings."

—*El Pais* (Spain)

"His novels of young love are sold by millions around the world." —*El Mundo* (Spain)

"Italian writer Federico Moccia brings the reader an updated version of the classic tale of star-crossed lovers, separated by differences in social class and learned attitudes. A tautly paced novel with intense action and unpredictable twists and turns." —*5 o'Clock Books* (Romanian TV show) *two chances with you*

One Step to You

two chances with you

FEDERICO MOCCIA

TRANSLATED BY ANTONY SHUGAAR

GRAND
CENTRAL
PUBLISHING

New York Boston

Copyright © 2006 by Federico Moccia
English language translation copyright © 2021 by Hachette Book Group by agreement with Pontas Literary & Film Agency

Cover design and lettering by Kathleen Lynch/Black Kat Design
Cover photo: man on bridge © CollaborationJS/Trevillion Images; sky by Jerry Lin/Shutterstock; woman by Oleh Slobodeniuk/E+/Getty Images
Cover copyright © 2021 by Hachette Book Group, Inc.

Grand Central Publishing
Hachette Book Group
1290 Avenue of the Americas, New York, NY 10104
grandcentralpublishing.com
twitter.com/grandcentralpub

Originally published in 2006 by Giangiacomo Feltrinelli Editore in Italy as *Ho Voglia di Te*
First U.S. Edition: October 2021

Grand Central Publishing is a division of Hachette Book Group, Inc. The Grand Central Publishing name and logo is a trademark of Hachette Book Group, Inc.

The publisher is not responsible for websites (or their content) that are not owned by the publisher.

The Hachette Speakers Bureau provides a wide range of authors for speaking events. To find out more, go to www.hachettespeakersbureau.com or call (866) 376-6591.

Library of Congress Cataloging-in-Publication Data
Names: Moccia, Federico, author. | Shugaar, Antony, translator.
Title: Two chances with you / Federico Moccia ; [translator: Antony Shugaar].
Other titles: Ho voglia di te. English
Description: First U.S. edition. | New York : Grand Central Publishing, 2021. | Series: The Rome novels ; 2
Identifiers: LCCN 2021023047 | ISBN 9781538732786 (trade paperback) | ISBN 9781538732793 (ebook)
Classification: LCC PQ4913.O23 H613 2021 | DDC 853/.92—dc23
LC record available at https://lccn.loc.gov/2021023047

ISBN: 978-1-5387-3278-6 (trade paperback), 978-1-5387-3279-3 (ebook)

Printed in the United States of America

LSC-C

Printing 1, 2021

For Gin.

Your smile told me this story.

For Nonna Elisa and Zia Maria,
who cooked so well and with such love.
And who came to see me, that day,
long ago . . .

Chapter 1

I feel like dying." That's what I thought the day I left. When I caught the plane, that day just two years ago. I really wanted to end things. There was a thunderstorm, and everyone was tense and frightened. Not me. I was the only one still smiling. That's right, the best thing that could have happened would have been an ordinary, unremarkable accident. That way, it wouldn't have been anyone's fault, I wouldn't have had to live with the shame, no one would have had to delve into the reasons why...I remember that the plane lurched and jolted the whole way.

When you're depressed, when the whole world looks dark, when you have no future, when you have nothing to lose, when...every instant is a burden. Immense. Intolerable. And you heave an endless succession of sighs. All you want to do is get rid of that load. In whatever way necessary. In the simplest way, in the most cowardly fashion, without putting off till tomorrow this thought: She's not here anymore. She's gone now.

And so, very simply, you wish that you were gone too. That you could just vanish. Poof. Without complications, without bothering anyone. Without anyone taking the trouble to say: "Oh, did you hear? That's right, him, that's who I'm talking about . . . You won't believe what happened to him . . ." Exactly, that guy is going to tell the story of your end on earth, embroidering it with who knows which and how many lurid details, inventing absurdities, as if he'd known you all your life, as if he were the only one who really knew the depth and nature of your problems. How weird . . .

And to think that even you never had the time to figure out what they were. And there's nothing you can do to stop this appalling word-of-mouth legend from spreading. What a pain in the ass. Your memory for all time will be a plaything in the hands of just any old asshole who happens along, and there's nothing you'll be able to do about it.

In fact, I wish I could have run into one of those strange wizards that day. They throw a cape over a dove that's just made its appearance and, poof, suddenly it's gone. It's gone, and that's that. And you leave the theater, delighted with the show. But one thing is certain. You'll never again wonder what became of that dove.

But that's not the way things work. We can't disappear that easily. Time has gone by. Two long years. And now I'm sipping a beer. When I think back to how I longed to be that dove, a smile comes to my face, and I feel slightly ashamed.

"Care for another?"

A flight attendant stands next to his drinks cart, giving me a big smile.

"No, thanks."

I look out my window. Pink-tinged clouds make way for the plane as it sails through the sky. Those clouds are soft, light, and infinite. There's a sunset in the distance. The sun sinks with one last wink. I can't believe it. I'm coming back.

A27. That's my seat number aboard this flight. Right-hand row, just behind the wings, central aisle. A flight attendant smiles at me again as she walks past. A little too close. She leaves a faint trail of perfume; her uniform is perfect. Up and down the airplane's aisles she goes, with that smile.

"Ladies and gentlemen, please fasten your seat belts."

The woman is struggling beside me. And she's not struggling in silence. "Darn it, I never seem to be able to find the seat belt in these planes." Observant, with a cheerful smile, her eyes are hidden behind the thick lenses of her eyeglasses.

I help the woman to find it, as she's literally sitting on top of it. "Here you are, signora, it's right down here."

"Thanks, even if I can't imagine what good it would do. It's not going to be able to hold us in place."

"Ah, certainly not, it can't do that."

"I mean, after all... I'm just saying, if we crash, it's not like being in a car."

"No, not like being in a car, certainly not... Are you nervous?"

"Very nervous, deathly nervous." She looks at me and appears to regret using that phrase. She seems so worried.

I take a long slurp of my beer while I notice, out of the corner of my eye, that she's staring at me.

"Please, just tell me something."

"Exactly what, signora, what do you want me to tell you?"

"Distract me, don't make me think about what could..."

She grips my hand tightly.

"You're hurting me."

"Oh, excuse me." She loosens her grip, but she doesn't let go entirely.

I start to tell her some story. Little jumbled flashes from my life, as they occur to me. "All right, do you want to know why I left Rome?"

The woman nods. She can't seem to talk.

"Well, okay, but it's a long story . . ." I feel as if I'm talking to a friend, with my old friend . . . "His name was Pollo, okay. Strange name, right? I mean, Chicken, what a name."

The woman doesn't seem to know whether to say yes or no.

"Right, so he's the friend I lost more than two years ago. He was inseparable with his girlfriend, Pallina. She's just incredible, a great person, bright eyes, always laughing, hilarious, sharp and funny and really witty . . ."

She listens in silence, her eyes curious.

Sometimes you feel more comfortable with a person you don't know at all. It's easier to talk about yourself. You really open up. Maybe because you don't care about how they judge you.

"Whereas I was with Babi, who was best friends with Pallina." I tell this stranger everything. How I met Babi, how I started to laugh, how I fell in love, how I lost her . . .

You can only see the beauty of a true love after you've lost it. I think while I speak, with little pauses every so often.

The woman is amused and curious, more relaxed now. She's even let go of my hand. She's forgotten about the impending airline disaster. She's taking an interest in my own personal disaster. "So this Babi, have you talked to her since?"

"No. Every so often, I talked to my brother. And now and then, my father."

"Did you feel lonely in New York?"

I answer with something vague. I can't bring myself to say it. I felt less lonely than I did in Rome. Then, inevitably, I make a reference to Mamma. I just plunge right in. My mother cheated on my father. I caught her in bed with the guy who lived across the street from us.

The passenger can hardly believe it. The airplane? She doesn't even remember that she's riding in an airplane. She asks me a thousand questions. I practically can't keep up with her. Why on earth do people love to wallow in other people's misery so much? Spicy topics, forbidden details, obscure acts, salacious sins. Maybe because, when you're just listening to them, you don't get dirty.

The woman seems to relish and suffer at every twist and turn of my story. So I tell her everything, and I do so without reluctance. My violent assault on my mamma's lover, my extended silences at home, the fact that I never told my father or my brother a thing about what happened. And then, the trial. My mother sitting there, right in front of me. She sat in silence. She never had the nerve to admit what she'd done. She could have used her betrayal as a justification for my rage and violence.

The woman stares at me, mouth agape. She understands. Suddenly she turns serious.

So I try to cut the drama. "As Pollo would say, I don't give a flying fuck about *The Bold and the Beautiful*!"

Instead of being scandalized, she laughs. "And then what happened?" she asks, itching to hear the next installment.

I explain to her about the reason I went to America, why

I wanted to run away and bury myself in a graphics course. "And seeing how easy it is to run into each other, even in a big city...so much the better to move to a new one entirely. Only new experiences, new places, new people, and most important of all, no memories. A year of the challenge of conversation in English, with the aid of the chance presence of the occasional passing Italian. All of it quite amusing, a reality filled with colors, music, sounds, traffic, parties, and new things.

None of what people talked about to you had anything to do with Babi, none of it could evoke her, bring her back to life. Useless days in an attempt to bring rest to my heart, my stomach, and my head. The total impossibility of retracing my steps, finding myself in the blink of an eye downstairs, looking up at Babi's apartment, or running into her on the street. No danger of that in New York.

No room in New York for Lucio Battisti and his melancholy music. "And if you hark back in your mind, it's sufficient just to think that you're not there, that I'm suffering pointlessly because I know, I know it, I know that you'll never come back."

The woman smiles for one last moment. Stah-tuh-*thump*. A flat, metallic noise. A sharp movement and then the plane lurches ever so slightly.

"Oh my God, what was that?" The woman seizes my right hand.

"It's the landing gear, don't worry."

"What do you mean, don't worry! Does it have to make so much noise? It sounds like the landing gear fell off..."

Not far away from us, the flight attendant and the other crew members all sit down in the unoccupied seats, as well as a few odd side seats next to the exits. The passenger does her best to distract herself. She lets go of my hand in exchange for one last question. "So why did it end?"

"Because Babi found another boyfriend."

"She did what? Your girlfriend? After all the things you told me?"

It seems like now she's enjoying herself, sticking her thumb into my psychic wound. The airplane and the imminent landing procedures have faded into the background. And in fact, now she's pelting me with questions, right up to the very last moment. Caught up in her excitement, in fact, we've exchanged names and moved on to a first-name basis. And she's not holding back. "Since you broke up with her, have you had sex with any other women? Would you get back together with her? Is forgiveness an option? Have you talked about it with anyone?"

Either the beer is having quite an effect on me or it's her and her questions that are making my head spin. Or else it's the pain of that not-yet-forgotten love affair. I'm confused at this point. Utterly bewildered. I can only hear the roar of the spinning jet engines and the backthrust of the landing maneuvers. The woman looks out the window, frightened at the airplane and its wings that seem to brush the ground and wobble indecisively. She seizes my right hand and glances out the window again. Then she slams her head back into her headrest and jams her legs against the footrest with all her might, as if she were trying to use her own feet on the brakes of the plane. She digs her fingernails into the flesh of my hand. With a few gentle bounces, the airplane touches down. Immediately, the plane's turbine engines go into reverse thrust, and that enormous mass of aluminum and steel shivers crazily, including all its seats and the woman beside me. But she doesn't surrender. She squints and shudders, taking it all out on my hand.

"This is the captain, ladies and gentlemen. I'm pleased to inform you that we have landed at Rome's Fiumicino Airport. The temperature outside..."

A ragged attempt at a round of applause rises from the back of the plane, dying out almost immediately.

"Well, we made it," I say.

The woman sighs. "Thank God!"

"Maybe we'll fly together again someday."

"Oh, I hope so. It was a real pleasure to speak with you. But are all those stories you told me really true?"

"As true as the fact that you held my hand." I hold up my right hand and show her the fingernail marks she left.

"Oh, I'm so sorry."

"Don't think twice."

The occasional cell phone starts ringing. Nearly everyone stands up to open the overhead bins, pulling down shopping bags full of gifts brought back from America, collections of items that are all more-or-less useless, ready to file up the aisle and reach the exit as quickly as possible. After the hours of sitting, immobilized, in the airplane, where you're forced to consider the balance of all the years of your life that have passed thus far, we return to the hasty rush of *not* thinking, fake thinking, the race to the last finish line.

"Arrivederci."

"Thanks, buonasera."

Flight attendants say goodbye at the airplane door. Then I head down the steps.

Warm wind. September. Sunset, it's just eight thirty

in the evening. Right on time. It's nice to walk again after an eight-hour flight. We all climb aboard the shuttle bus. I look around at the other passengers aboard. A few Chinese travelers, a big, heavyset American, a young man who hasn't once stopped listening to one of those Samsung digital audio players that I'd seen all over New York. Two girlfriends on holiday together who are no longer speaking, perhaps thoroughly sick of their extended cohabitation. A happy, loving couple. They laugh, constantly chatting about matters of only minor interest. I envy them or, really, I just enjoy watching them.

My traveling companion, the woman who now knows everything about my life, walks over to me. She smiles as if to say, *Well, we made it, didn't we?*

I nod. I almost regret having told her so much. Then I relax as I realize that I'll never see her again.

Passport check. Here and there German shepherds on short leashes pace nervously back and forth, in search of a modicum of cocaine or grass. Frustrated dogs on endless rounds look up at us with kind eyes, probably exhausted from the relentless training to which they're subjected.

An immigration officer distractedly glances at my passport. Then he focuses in. He skips a page. Then he turns back and gazes more carefully. My heartbeat accelerates slightly. But then, nothing. I'm of no interest to him. He hands me back the passport, I shut it, and I put it back in my backpack.

I go to the luggage carousel. And then I walk out of the airport, a free man, back in Rome. I spent two years in New York, and it feels as if I left just yesterday.

I walk briskly toward the exit. I cross paths with people

dragging their luggage, a guy running breathless to reach an airplane that he may be about to miss. On the other side of the partitions, relatives await someone who doesn't seem to be arriving. Beautiful young women, still bronzed from the summer, stand waiting for their sweethearts.

"Taxi, do you need a taxi?" A fake taxi driver comes hurrying toward me, pretending to be the real deal: "I'll give you a low price to the city." I say nothing. He realizes I'm not a good prospect and turns away.

I look around. Nothing. No one. How stupid. But of course. What else did I expect? Who am I looking for? Is this why you came back? Then you haven't understood a thing. I feel like laughing, and I feel like an idiot.

~

"He should have landed by now..."

Concealed behind a pillar, she speaks to herself under her breath. Maybe it's just to cover the pounding of her heart, which is actually racing at two thousand miles a minute. Then she gathers her nerve. A deep breath, and then she emerges from behind the pillar. "There he is. I knew it, I knew it!" She practically jumps up and down, though both feet remain firmly planted on the floor.

"I can't believe it... Step. I knew it, I knew it, I was sure he was returning today. I just can't believe it. Mamma mia, no doubt about it, he's lost so much weight. Still, he's smiling. Yes, it seems as if he's doing well. Can he be happy? Maybe he had a good time living abroad. Too good of a time.

"What's the matter with me? I let myself get swallowed

up by jealousy. After all, what right do I have? None. Well? Look at what a mess I am. Seriously, I'm just a wreck, a complete wreck. I mean, I'm just too happy. Too happy. He's back, I can't believe it. Oh my God, he's looking this way!"

She quickly dodges back around, hiding behind the column. A sigh. She shuts her eyes, squeezing them tight. She leans back, her head resting against the cold white marble, hands splayed against the column. Silence. A deep breath. Exhale. Inhale...Exhale...

She opens her eyes again. At that very instant a tourist walks by, glancing at her in bafflement. She tries to put on a smile in order to reassure him that all is perfectly normal. But it's not. No doubt about it.

"Oh, crap, he spotted me. I can tell. Oh, God, Step saw me. I'm sure of it."

She sticks her head out again. No one's there. Step went by as if he hadn't seen a thing.

"Oh, of course, what an idiot I am. And after all, what if he had?"

⌒

Here I am, back again. I'm home. I walk toward the exit. The glass doors slide open, and I emerge onto the side-walk. Right at the taxi stand. But at that exact moment, I have a strange sensation. I feel as if someone's watching me. I whip around. Nothing. No one. There's nothing worse than thinking you're going to see something...and nothing's there.

Chapter 2

Stefano!" Right in front of me, in the middle of the road, is my brother.

I smile. "Ciao, Pa." I'm happy to see him. I'm almost touched, but I manage to keep it from showing too much.

"Well, how are you? You have no idea how often I've thought about you."

He hugs me tight. He gives me a squeeze. For a fleeting second, I remember the last Christmas we spent together. Before I left.

"Well, here you are... Did you have fun down there in America, huh?"

He takes one of my suitcases out of my hand. Naturally, the lighter one.

"Yes, I had a great time in America. But why do you refer to it as 'down there'?"

"I don't know. It's just a manner of speech."

My brother, using manners of speech. No doubt about it, things have changed. He looks at me happily. He's relaxed. He actually does love me. But we don't look a bit alike.

I take a closer look at him. Dressed to the nines, a new shirt, perfectly pressed, a pair of lightweight trousers, brownish in color with cuffs, a checked blazer, and finally...

"Hey, Paolo, what happened? Did you misplace your necktie?"

"No, I just don't wear a tie in the summer. Why, does it look bad?"

He doesn't even wait for an answer. "Here we are, this is the car. Look at what I got for myself..." He waves his hand, showing off what constitutes, to his mind, a magnificent new vehicle. "Audi A4, the latest model. You like it?"

How could I say no in the face of such unbridled enthusiasm? "Very nice, not bad."

He pushes the button on the remote in his hand. The alarm stops after a couple of beeps, and the double blinkers disappear. Paolo opens the trunk. "Come on, put your suitcases in here."

I toss in the two duffel bags, next to the small one that he's already neatly placed. "Hey, take it easy," my brother warns.

His warning immediately sparks an idea. "Hey, can I try driving it?"

He looks at me. His expression changes. His heart is clearly torn. But his brotherly love wins out. "Sure, of course, here." He makes a small effort to smile and tosses the keys to me. Crazy. You should never trust a brother like me. Especially not if that brother asks you for an Audi A4 like that one.

I get behind the wheel. It smells new, an impeccable car. I turn the key in the ignition, and the engine turns over.

"Just think. I'm still breaking it in..." He looks at me with some concern and fastens his seat belt.

And I, maybe because of the fact that I've just come back to Rome, my desire to shout, oh, I don't know, the fact that

I'd like to free myself of these last two years of silence, of my rage, living so far away, I suddenly jam my foot down on the gas. The Audi screeches, fishtails, protests, rebels, and screams, its tires sliding against the hot asphalt.

Paolo clamps both hands tight on to the handle over the car window. "There, I knew it. I knew it! Why does it always end up like this with you?"

"What are you talking about? I only just got in the car!"

"I meant that a person can never relax around you," my brother says.

"Okay..." I downshift, taking the curve, and I jiggle the steering wheel just enough so that I'm practically grazing the guardrail. "How'm I doing now?"

Paolo leans back, adjusting his blazer.

"Come on, you know perfectly well I was just needling you. Don't get so damn worried. I'm different now. I've changed."

"Again? Just how changed are you?"

"That I can't say. I've come back to Rome to find out."

We drive in silence.

"Okay if I light a cigarette in here?" I ask.

"I'd rather you didn't."

I stick a cigarette in my mouth, and I push in the lighter.

"Wait, what are you doing? Lighting it anyway?"

"It's the 'rather you didn't' that screwed you."

"You see? You've changed. For the worse," he says.

I smile and look over at him. I love my brother. And maybe he's changed, too, come to think of it. He seems more mature, more of a man. I take a drag on the Marlboro Medium and start to hand it to him.

"No, thanks." In response, he cracks his window open.

Then he cheers up again. "You know what? I've got a girlfriend."

My brother is seven years older than me. It's incredible, there are times when he seems like a little kid. He likes confiding in me, and it's a delight. I decide to give him the satisfaction. "So what's she like? Is she cute?"

"Cute? She's gorgeous! She's tall, a honey blonde. You've got to meet her. Her name is Fabiola, she's an interior decorator, she only likes to go to certain places, and she has great taste..."

"Okay, got it. I understand, sure, sure..."

"Okay, okay. That response from you is an obvious wisecrack. In fact, it's a dumbcrack. You like that? It's something she always says!"

"Sounds a little dubious, don't you think? She needs to be careful, when she says it. Anyway, now I understand why you two get along so famously."

"Yeah, no doubt about it. We're really in tune."

Very much in tune. But what is that even supposed to mean? Being in tune is something that has to do with music. Love is something else, when you can't breathe, when you miss her, when it's beautiful even if it's off tune, when it's all madness... When the sheer idea of seeing her with someone else would be enough to drive you to chew your way across the ocean.

"Well, if you're really in tune, that's the important thing. And then there's another thing..." I try to give it a good final flourish. "Fabiola is a pretty name."

An obvious, unremarkable conclusion. But I couldn't come up with anything else. Fundamentally, I couldn't care less, but Paolo needs everybody else's good opinion. Which is the stupidest thing a person can do. And after all, who do you mean by everybody? Not even our parents were one hundred percent in favor of *us*.

He seems to practically read my mind: "Plus Papà has a girlfriend. Did you know that?"

"How am I supposed to know that if nobody told me?"

"Her name is Monica, and she's a good-looking woman. She's turned his apartment upside down and inside out. She's made it look less old-fashioned. She's spruced the place up."

"What about Papà? Did she do the same for him?"

Paolo laughs like an idiot. "That's just great, too much."

My brother and his enthusiasm. Was he like this before I left? When you get back from a trip, everything seems different.

"They're living together. You have to meet her."

What's that supposed to mean? I don't have to do anything. I jerk the steering wheel to one side to get around a car. The driver doesn't seem to feel like getting out of the way. Move it, buddy! I flash my lights, but nothing doing. I hit the gas; I upshift. The car screeches to the right to get around him.

Paolo pushes both feet into the floorboard and grabs the armrest between the two of us.

Then I ease back to the left and reassure him. "It's all okay. In America, I could never drive like that. They're always clocking you to the last inch."

"So, you came back here to have fun with my new car, is that it?"

"How's Mamma?"

"Fine."

"What do you mean by fine?"

"And what do you mean by 'how is she'?"

"Oh, what a pain in the ass you're being. Is she happy? Is she seeing anyone? Do you talk to her? Does she see Papà? Does she talk to him?"

I can't bring myself to ask him the last, unasked question: Has she asked about me?

"She asks me about you all the time." It's the only question he answers. "She wanted to know if I'd talked to you on the phone from New York, how your classes were going, and so on and so forth."

"So what did you tell her?"

"I told her the little I did know. That your classes were going well, that strangely you didn't seem to have gotten into any fights with anyone, and then I invented a few other things."

"Such as?"

"That you'd been dating a girl for two months, but that she's Italian. If I'd said she was American, she would have figured out immediately that I was making it up because you wouldn't have been able to understand each other."

"Ha, ha. Let me know when it's time to laugh. Was that one of your 'dumbcracks'?"

"Then I told her that you were having fun, that you went out every night, but you weren't doing drugs, and you had a bunch of friends down there. In other words, you had no intention of coming back but that you were doing fine. How'd I do?"

"More or less."

"Namely?"

"I dated two American girls, and we understood each other perfectly."

He doesn't even have a chance to laugh, I downshift and veer off to the right, down the exit ramp. Off the beltway, I accelerate into the curve as the tires screech, and an old car honks behind me. I continue into the curve nonchalantly, and I pull into the straightaway.

Paolo sits upright again. He pulls his jacket down and into place. Then he tries to point something out. "You forgot to use your turn indicator."

"Right."

I drive for a while in silence. Paolo looks out the window frequently and then again toward me, trying to catch my attention.

"What is it?"

"What ever happened with the trial?"

"I was granted a pardon."

"How is that?" He looks at me, curiosity aroused. I turn and meet his gaze for a while. He remains silent. He looks at me calmly. Untroubled. I don't think he's lying. Or else he's a formidable actor. Paolo is a good brother, but I can't say that among his finer qualities I can think of anything that qualifies as formidable.

I turn my eyes back to the road. "Nothing, just that I was granted a pardon, period. Full stop."

He smiles. "You know, I've been wondering for a long, long time now why you would have wanted to beat up a guy who lived across the street from us."

"And yet you've managed to survive with this agonizing doubt gnawing at you all this time?"

"Sure, but I had other things to do with my time."

"In America, you wouldn't last a single day. There's no time to wonder about things."

"Okay, but since I was living in Rome, between a cappuccino and aperitif, I thought about it. And I even came to a conclusion."

"How wonderful! And what was your conclusion?" I ask.

"That our neighbor must have been harassing Mamma somehow, rude flirtations or one too many insults. I don't know, somehow you found out about it and, wham-bam, you sent him to the hospital..."

I sit in silence. Paolo stares at me. I try to avoid his gaze.

"Still, though, there's one thing that I just don't get. I mean, listen, Mamma was there at the trial and she never said a word, she didn't tell the court what happened, what that guy could have said to her, or anyway, what made you react the way you did. If only she'd talked, then maybe the judge would have been able to understand."

So what does Paolo actually know? I look at him for a second before turning my eyes back to the road. White stripes on the pavement, one after another, pass placidly under the body of the Audi. One after another, here and there slightly sloppy, the paint going over the line. The sound of the road. Ba-dum, ba-dum, the Audi, running along gently, rising and falling at each little bump. The seams between sections of that piece of road can be felt, each as it goes under, but none of them really annoying.

Is it right to tell the truth? Present one person under a different spotlight to another person? Paolo loves Mamma the way she is. Or he loves her the way he thinks she is. Or maybe the way he chooses to believe she is.

"So, Paolo, why are you asking me this?"

"I don't know, just to find out..."

"It doesn't really add up for you, does it?"

"Well, no, not really."

"And for an accountant like you, that's a nightmare."

So our neighbor's name was Giovanni Ambrosini, something I only discovered during my trial. Actually, no, that's not true. I found out his surname before that. When I rang his doorbell, it was written right next to it.

He came to answer the door dressed in nothing but a pair of boxer shorts. When he saw me, he quickly tried to slam the door. I'd only stepped in to talk to him. To ask politely whether he'd turn down the music.

Then my heart raced. In the narrow gap where the door stood ajar, framed by that door jamb, her face. That glance, a glance that joined us and divided us for all time. I'll never forget it. Nude like I'd never seen her before, beautiful as I'd always loved her...My mamma. Between the bedsheets of another man. I don't remember anything else except for the cigarette she had in her mouth. And her eyes. As if she were hungry for something else to devour after him, that cigarette. Listen, my son, this is reality, this is life.

And then I yanked Giovanni Ambrosini out his apartment door by the hair on his head. I knocked him to the floor. I broke both his cheekbones when I kicked him in the head. His face got wedged between the uprights of the stair railing, and I kept bringing my heel down hard on his right ear, his face, his ribs, the fingers of his hands, until I'd shattered them. Shattered the hands that had touched her. And then enough. Enough was enough. Please, enough. I can't take anymore. Those memories that just won't quit. Ever.

I look at Paolo. One deep breath. Calm. A second, longer breath. Calm and lies. "Sorry, Paolo, but sometimes things just don't add up. I didn't like that asshole, and that's all there is to it. Mamma had nothing to do with it. I mean, come on."

He seems satisfied. He likes this version just fine. He looks out the car window. "Ah, there's something I didn't tell you."

I give him a worried look. "What?"

"I've moved. I still live in the Farnesina, but now I have a penthouse."

At last, a piece of decent news. "Is it nice?"

"It's great. You've got to see it. You're sleeping at my place tonight anyway, aren't you? My telephone number is still the same. I managed to keep it by asking a friend who works at Telecom."

He smiles with satisfaction at this tiny moment of power of his. Damn it, I hadn't even thought about that! I'm just lucky he kept the same number. It's the number I put on my business card.

Corso Francia, Vigna Stelluti, and up, up, up toward Piazza dei Giuochi Delfici. I pass by Via Colajanni, the cross street that leads to Piazza Jacini. A scooter stops suddenly at an intersection. A young woman. Oh, sweet Jesus. It's Babi. Long, ash-blond hair, spilling out from under the helmet. She's also wearing a baseball cap. She has a sky-blue iPod and a light jacket, also pale blue, just like her eyes. It really, truly does look like her.

I slow down. She's nodding her head in time to the music, and she smiles. I stop. She takes off. I let her drive past. She veers cheerfully past the front of our car. She thanks me silently so I can read her lips...

My heart slows down again. No, it isn't her. But a

memory surfaces. Like when you're in the water, at the beach, early in the morning, and it's cold out. Someone calls your name. You turn, you wave. But then, when you turn back to continue your walk, a wave suddenly crashes over you. And then, without even wanting to, I find myself back there, shipwrecked unexpectedly on the beach of a day just two years ago. A day, or, really, a night.

Her folks were out. Babi had called me. She told me to come see her. *I climb the steps. The door is open. She left it ajar. Slowly, I open it. "Babi? Are you there? Babi…"*

I don't hear a thing. I shut the door behind me. I walk down the hallway on tiptoes toward the bedrooms. The faint sound of music comes from her parents' bedroom. That's strange; she'd said they were at Monte Circeo. From the half-shut door comes a faint light. I step closer. I open the door.

Suddenly she appears to me, next to the window. Babi. She's wearing her mother's clothing, a light, sand-colored silk blouse, translucent and unbuttoned. Underneath I see an ivory white brassiere. Then a long skirt with a paisley pattern. Her hair is pulled up, intricately braided. She seems older. She wants to be older.

She smiles. In her hand, she's holding a glass of champagne. Now she's pouring another one for me. She sets the bottle down in an ice bucket that stands on a side table. All around are candles and a scent of wild roses that slowly envelops us.

She puts one foot up onto a chair. The slit skirt slides open and falls to one side, revealing an ankle boot and her leg, sheathed in a stocking in honey-colored fishnet. Babi stands there, waiting for me, with the two champagne flutes in her hands, and her eyes suddenly change. As if she'd suddenly grown up.

"Take me, as if I were her…Her, even though she doesn't want you, even though she sucks the life out of me every day

that goes by, doing her best to separate us..." She hands me the glass. I toss it back, all in a single gulp. It's chilly, it's delicious, it's perfect. Then I give her a kiss, as intense as the desire I'm experiencing. Our tongues taste of champagne, sleepy, lost, tipsy, anesthetized...Suddenly they come to life. I run my hand through her hair, and I'm caught, a helpless, happy prisoner of tight, intricately worked locks. I hold her head like that, lost in my hands, helplessly, hopelessly mine, while her kiss grows steadily more greedy. It's as if she wants to climb into me, devour me, reach all the way down to my heart. Wait, what are you doing? Stop. It's already yours.

Then Babi pulls away and looks at me. And I'm scared at the intensity that I sense, that I had never glimpsed before. Then she takes my hand, she lifts her skirt a little to one side, and she guides my hand in. Then she leads me, up, farther up...up her legs. She lets her head fall backward. Her eyes shut. A smile on her face. A hidden smile. A sigh escapes her, loud and clear. My hand, she guides it farther up. Without haste, until it reaches her panties. There they are. She gently pulls them aside, and I lose myself with my fingers in her pleasure.

Now Babi is sighing louder. She undoes my trousers and yanks them down, quickly, eagerly again, like never before. And gently she finds me. She stops. She looks into my eyes. And she smiles. She licks my mouth. She bites me. She's hungry for me. She leans against me, she pushes, she presses her forehead against mine, she smiles, she sighs, she starts moving up and down on my hand, hungrily losing herself in my eyes, as I do in hers...

Then she slips off her panties, she gives me one last light kiss, and she caresses me under my chin. She gets up on all fours on the bed, and she pulls the skirt aside, uncovering herself from behind. She lays the skirt across her back and turns her head to look at me.

"Please, Step, take me forcefully, hurt me. I'm begging you. I swear it, I'm dying for it."

It strikes me as incredible but I do as I'm told. I obey, and she starts moaning like she's never done before, and I practically faint with pleasure, desire, the love I could never have thought possible. I'm still panting with pleasure just in remembering it, and it almost takes my breath away.

"Hey, Step!"

"Yes?"

Suddenly I'm back. It's Paolo.

"What's going on? You just stopped in the middle of the road."

"Huh?"

"You're surprising me. Have we suddenly become courteous? I've never seen you do anything like it, let a young woman cross when she doesn't even have the right of way! Incredible. Either America has really done you good or else you've changed. Or else..."

"Or else?"

"Or else that young woman reminded you of someone else."

He turns to look at me.

"Hey, don't forget that we're brothers."

"In fact, that's exactly what I'm worried about. And that's a 'dumbcrack,' in case the fact escaped you."

Paolo laughs. I start driving again, reaching out for some sense of self-control. And I find it. Then one long breath. Another, longer one. And the pain of knowing that that high tide will never leave me.

Chapter 3

Here we are, Step. It's number 237. Wait just a second, let me open the gate. Now park here, number 6, that's mine." Paolo is clearly proud. We get out my bags. "The elevator runs directly from the garage." He's proud of that detail too.

We ride up to the sixth floor. He opens the door as if it were a bank safe. Burglar alarm, two different locks, heavy armored door. On the door is his name. PAOLO MANCINI, a little printed card set in a small gold-framed holder. Horrible, but I don't tell him that.

"You see? I put one of my business cards in the name-plate. It's even got the phone number. Good idea, right? But why are you laughing? You don't like it, do you?"

"Of course I do. But why on earth do you always assume I'm lying to you? Seriously, I like it, trust me."

He smiles back, a little more relaxed, and shows me in. "Okay, come on, now take a look. Here it is . . ."

The inside of the apartment isn't bad at all, new hardwood floors, white walls.

"It still needs some furniture, but just think, I had the whole place renovated. Just look, I had dimmers put in, so you can have the lights as bright or soft as you want, you see?" He goes over to one of the switches and turns the lights up and then down. "Cool, right?"

"Super cool." I stand by the front door with my bags in hand.

Paolo smiles happily at his brilliant idea. "Let me show you to your room." He throws open the door to a bedroom at the end of the hall. "Pampadapah!" He mimics a trumpet fanfare with his lips. Paolo stands in the doorway, beaming.

"Huh..." There must be some surprise awaiting me. I walk in.

"I got your things and brought them over. A few sweaters, your T-shirts, your sweatshirts. And look here..." He shows me a painting hanging on the wall. "There was still one panel by Andrea Pazienza. This is one you didn't burn."

He reminds me, inadvertently, of that Christmas two and a half years ago. Maybe he realizes it and regrets it a little. "Well, I'm going into my room. You get yourself settled the way you like."

I put my bag on the bed, unzip it, and start pulling clothing out. An Abercrombie track jacket. Faded jeans, Junya brand. A khaki-colored Vintage 55 sweatshirt. Well-pressed Brooks Brothers shirts. I hang them all up in a white armoire. There are plenty of drawers. I open my other suitcase as well and fill them all. At the bottom of the duffel bag is a gift-wrapped package. I pull it out and go to the other room. Paolo is in his bedroom, lying down on the bed, his feet poking out.

"Here," I say as I toss the package onto his belly. He folds in two as if I'd just punched him in the stomach and then places the package next to him on the bed.

"Thanks. Why did you do that?" He always seems to want an explanation.

"It's the latest American fashion."

He unwraps it and lays it out to look at it. He seems a little baffled.

"It's a New York City Fire Department jacket. Down there, people who've really made it like to wear these jackets."

Now that he's been told, he obviously likes it better. "Let me try it on!" He puts it on over his jacket and takes a look at himself in the mirror.

I do my best not to laugh.

"Hell, that's great!" That doesn't really sound much like him. He really likes it. "You even got the size right."

"Take care of it. It's worth as much as a room of your apartment."

"Did it really cost that much?"

"Hey, sure, but your bedroom is nicer. It's bigger."

"Yes, I know that, Step, but..."

"Paolo...I was just kidding."

Paolo heaves a sigh of relief.

"No, seriously though, you've really got this place looking nice."

"You can't imagine how much it cost me." Here we go, the accountant rears his head again.

I go back to my bedroom and start getting undressed. I want a shower.

Paolo comes into the bedroom. He's still wearing his jacket with the tag hanging from the neck and has a package in his hand. "I have a surprise for you too." He starts to toss it to me but then he thinks better of it and just hands it to me. "I shouldn't throw it. It's breakable."

I open it, my curiosity aroused.

"It's for your birthday." He manages to embarrass me. "I mean, actually, it's for the birthday you had while you were in America. All we could do was call you."

"Yes, I heard the message on my answering machine." I continue to unwrap the gift. I try not to think back to that day. But I can't do it. *July 21. Staying out all day intentionally to avoid waiting pointlessly by the telephone. Then coming home to see the answering machine blinking. One message, two, three, four. Four messages, four calls received. Four possibilities. Four hopes. Let's hear the first. "Hello, ciao, Stefano, it's your papà. Happy birthday! You thought I'd forgotten, didn't you?" My father. He always has to throw in a little extra humor in everything he does.*

I push the button and fast forward. "Happy birthday to you. Happy birthday to Step . . ." My brother. My brother, no less, singing birthday wishes to me over the telephone. What a nut!

Two messages left. "Ciao, Stefano . . ." No. It's my mother. I listen to her in silence. Her voice flows softly, slowly, full of love, perhaps sounding weary, a little bit. So I squint my eyes. I clench my fists. And I choke back those tears. Successfully. Today is my birthday, Mamma. I want to be cheerful, I want to laugh, I want to feel good, Mamma . . . Yes, I miss you too. There are so many things I miss. But today I'd rather not think about them. Please. "Best wishes to you again, Stefano, and seriously, call me when you can. Kisses."

Now there's just one message left. The green light blinks soundlessly. I look at it in silence. Slowly, it lights up and blinks out. That green light could be the best birthday present of my life. Babi's voice. The idea that she might miss me too. That I might be able to go back in time for a moment, back to then, to start over.

I go on dreaming for a moment. Then I push the button. "Ciao, living legend! How are you doing? Oh, such an absurd pleasure to hear your voice, even if it's only on an answering machine. You can't imagine how I miss you. It's killing me. Rome is empty without you. But you recognized my voice, right? It's me, Pallina. Certainly, by now I have something more of a woman's voice. All right, well, I've got an ocean full of things to tell you. Where should we begin? Well, let's see... After all, I can take my time, my folks are out. I'll call you from home, and I'll make the call as long as I want, whatever the cost, seeing that they pissed me off. So I'll punish them a little. Why not?" She makes me laugh, she warms my heart. I listen to her with a smile.

But I can't lie, not to myself. That wasn't the phone call I was hoping for. It's not a birthday without Babi's voice. I don't feel as if I was ever really born. And yet, now, after more than two years, here I am, back again.

"Well, what do you say? Do you like it?"

I finish unwrapping it, and then I pause to look at the box.

"Hey, listen, it's the latest model, a fantastic Nokia."

"A cell phone?"

"Nice, isn't it? It's got great reception everywhere. Just think, I got it thanks to a friend of mine, because it's not even in stores yet. It's an N70. It's got everything, and it's even tiny. It fits right in your jacket pocket." He slips it in his pocket to show me how true that is.

"You certainly have some busy friends, don't you?"

"Et voilà, you see? And then this is how you open it and you can even turn the sound off and just let it vibrate for notifications. Here."

He didn't even hear my joke. He's just waiting to see

what I think of it. "Thanks" is the only thing I can manage
to get out. "I really needed a cell phone."

"And you already have your own number, 335-808080.
Easy, right? Again, thanks to my friend over at Telecom."

He's even more satisfied now. My brother and his friends.
Now I have a number. I'm tagged. Identified. Reachable.
Maybe.

"It's beautiful, but now I really absolutely need to take a
shower." I toss the cell phone onto the bed.

Paolo leaves the room, shaking his head: "Wait and see,
that cell phone won't last long if you treat it like that."

My brother. There's nothing I can do about it. He's such
a bore. And yet we were both born from the same seed, or
at least I hope so.

I turn on the radio, there on the nightstand, and tune
to a station. As I undress, I start laughing, all on my own.
My mother who brought Paolo into the world, the son of
another man. That would be too much. At least I'd have an
explanation. But I'm going to have to rule that out. Those
were other times. Times of love.

I like this song. I start humming something.

━

I'm downstairs from Paolo's apartment. I've seen the
lights turning on. I know that this is his brother's new
apartment.

There, now I see him. Step walks in front of the window.
That must be his bedroom. Hey, wait, he's undressing. And
he must be singing something. I put in my earbuds. I turn
on the radio on my cell phone. I change stations until I

think I find what Step must be humming. I look at the station. Ram Power 102.7.

I look at the time. It's late, I'd better get home. My folks must be waiting for me.

⌐

"Paolo, do you happen to have a towel?"

"I already put towels and washcloths in the bathroom. You'll find them, arranged by color, light blue for your face, dark blue for the bidet, and then a dark blue bathrobe hanging on the door."

I walk out in front of the door.

"Damn, you're looking good. Have you lost weight?"

"Yes. In America, they train differently in the gym. Lots of boxing. In my first matches, I found out just how slow we are here in Rome."

"You've got some nice muscle definition."

"Since when have you learned these sorts of technical terms?" I can hear my rougher Roman accent coming to the surface.

"I'm going to a gym now."

"I can't believe my ears. It's about time! Just think, you used to give me such a hard time about it. 'Why are you wasting time in the gym, what do you care about your physique' and all that...So now you're going yourself?"

"Well, Fabiola talked me into it."

"Ah, there you go. You see, I'm already starting to like this Fabiola."

"She said that I spend too much time sitting down

and that a man has to decide who he is physically by age thirty-three."

"By age thirty-three?"

"That's what she said."

"Then you still had two years to do as you please."

"I didn't want to be a perfect case study."

"Well, good for Fabiola." I go into the bathroom. "So which gym are you going to?"

"The Roman Sport Center."

Silence. I stick my head back out the door. "And was that Fabiola's decision too?"

"No." He smiles. "I just...well, actually, truth be told, she was already a member there."

"Ah, I see..." I go back into the bathroom and shut the door. I can't believe it. There couldn't be anything worse than going to the gym with your woman. There you are, thinking of her lifting weights too, checking to see who comes over and talks to her, what they say, some guy who doesn't know what he's doing pretending to teach her the right move. Just terrible. Every once in a while, I see those couples. A kiss at the end of each set. And then, when they're done working out, the standard question, "What do you want to do tonight?"

I turn the shower faucet and get in. Cold water. Now the water splashes off, a little warmer. Then I tilt my head back, mouth half open, and the water suddenly changes its course. A small impetuous river that finds curves and hiding places between my eyes, between nose and mouth, between teeth and tongue. I spit the water out of my mouth as I breathe.

My brother who goes to the Roman Sport Center. My

brother with his new Audi A4. My brother who works out with his girlfriend, between laughs and deciding what to do that night. Now it's all clear. He is Papà, beyond a shadow of a doubt. The older he gets, the clearer the photocopy becomes.

I step out of the shower. I put on the bathrobe and dry my hair with the light blue towel, just as he wants me to. I scrub my short, newly cut hair good and hard, and in a minute, it's dry. I leave the towel on my head and go to my room.

Paolo sees me. "Amazing how much you look like Mamma. Call her. You'll make her happy."

"Sure, later on." Today I don't feel much like making anyone happy.

Chapter 4

Paolo is there, watching TV while he talks on the telephone, stretched out on his bed, his legs sticking out a little and his thumb dancing over the buttons of the remote control, looking for something that interests him more than whoever's on the other end of the line.

"Ciao, I'm going out."

"Where are you going?"

For once, I look at him without smiling. "Just to get some air."

He already regrets asking me and immediately scrambles to make amends.

"The extra copy of the house keys is there in the kitchen inside the cabinet on the left right before the door, in a little terra-cotta pot." His usual precision. Then he explains to whoever's on the other end of the line what he's doing, for who, and why. I'm the brother who's just come back from America. Then he shouts at me from a distance. "Did you find them?"

I put the keys in my pocket, and then I go by him again. "Found them."

He smiles. He's about to go back to talking when he

suddenly covers the receiver with his left hand, tense as a violin string: "But do you want me to lend you my car?" He's visibly worried as he says it, sorry to have suggested it, desperate at the thought I might say yes.

I let just a few seconds go by. And I enjoy it. After all, it wasn't me who asked. "No, don't worry about it."

"Ah, okay, okay." He heaves a sigh. Now he's more relaxed. In any case, he still does his best to solve the issues of my life. "Did you see, Step? I brought your motorcycle over, and it's parked downstairs in the garage."

"Yes, I saw it, thanks." But the issues of my life aren't all that easy to solve.

I take the elevator, and I head down to the garage. Under a gray tarp, all the way back at the far end of the courtyard, I see a wheel poking out. I recognize it. Slightly worn but still alive, a little dust and lots and lots of miles under its tread.

With a move befitting a toreador, I whisk the tarp away. And there she is. My metallic dark blue custom Honda VF 750. I run my hand over the gas tank. My fingers paint a soft sign in the dust sleeping atop that paint job.

Then I lift the seat, attach the cables to the battery terminals, and I lower it again. I climb on. I pull the keys out of my jacket pocket and insert the ignition key into the lock down below. Next to the engine. The keychain dangles lightly, swinging, bouncing every now and then, clicking against the cool engine. Farther up, a faint green and red light illuminates the ignition display. The battery is dead. I give it a try, just for fun, but there's no way on earth it's going to turn over. I push the red button with a finger of my right hand. Vain hopes now confirmed. Nothing doing. I'm going to have to give it a push.

I emerge from the garage with the motorcycle sloping to one side, leaning against my body on my right, pressed against my legs. My quadriceps strain. One after another, light footsteps, faster and faster. The beat of my footsteps alternates with the sound of the gravel, one, two, three. I emerge from the courtyard and push it down the street. Faster now. Just a few more steps.

The bike is already in second gear. I'm holding the clutch handle tight with my left hand. Okay, this is the moment. I release the clutch handle. The motorcycle stops practically dead. But I continue pushing, and the bike starts to grumble. I grab the clutch handle and then release it again. And the bike sputters.

Once again, pushing harder still. I'm starting to sweat now. One last push, I can feel it. And in fact, this time, it turns right over. It lurches forward. I clench the clutch handle with my left hand, and I rev the engine with my right hand. The engine comes fully to life and roars in the night, up to the windows, filling the dark street with noise.

I rev it again. Old smoke pours out of the mufflers, huge clouds that cough out the past, the long months of sleep. I give it more gas. I climb on and turn on the lights. Then I release the clutch and tear off, into the nocturnal wind.

I dry the sweat off my body as I race away toward the Farnesina. I shoot under the overpass. I take the curve, leaning into it as I downshift without braking. I let up a little on the gas and then twist the handle again midcurve and lean into the acceleration. The motorcycle fishtails. I give it more gas and, like an obedient dog, the bike roars away with me toward Ponte Milvio, past the church, the Pallotta, the thousand pizzas I ate there, the Gianfornaio on the left and that florist's shop right next to it. Fuck, all the flowers I sent from that florist's, the florist who offers more discounts than anybody else. Lots of flowers, all of them different, but all for the same *her*. I don't even stop to think about her, I don't want to think about her.

Then there's Pistola, the watermelon vendor, standing out front. I honk twice, and he looks over at me. I wave but he doesn't recognize me. I'll go pay a call on him later on and remind him of who I am.

I just keep on going, indifferent right now, and I slide away into the night. Fuck... Rome is so beautiful. I missed you, city of mine.

I twist the throttle again, and off I go, down the Lungotevere, the riverfront avenue. I zip around the cars. Right, left. And then I swerve wide, zipping along down the far edge of the road. I brush past the pine trees of the Foro Italico. There are a few prostitutes out for business, next to their steel can fires, not yet burning. One prostitute, either actually educated or faking it, is reading a newspaper. She laughs, mouth hanging open, at some idiotic witticism found in those pages. Another prostitute is already sitting in a small folding chair, and in one hand, she's holding the crossword puzzle, filling it in rapidly with a pen.

I rev the engine again and, at the same time, downshift. Fifth gear, fourth, third, tight curve on the right. I brake to a slower speed a little farther on, in front of the multiplex cinema. I put down the kickstand, and I get off the motorcycle.

Groups of young women laugh heartily as they smoke

cigarettes, unseen by some deluded parent. A blonde with short hair and excessive makeup looks at me, elbowing her friend. A brunette, with hazel eyes and a pageboy haircut, sitting with her legs crossed on a petroleum gray SH 50, stares at me in astonishment, and her jaw drops.

I reach back and touch my short hair on the nape of my neck. I'm bronzed and skinny. I smile. I feel good. I'm relaxed. I want to drink a cold beer and watch a movie. I want something else, to be honest, but I know I can't have that.

"Step, I can't believe it!" The brunette gets off her SH 50 and comes running toward me, screaming like a lunatic.

I look at her, trying to focus. Then all of a sudden, I recognize her. Pallina. I can't believe it. Pallina, my best friend's woman. Pollo, my buddy who was there the first time I got drunk, the first time I had a woman, my companion of a thousand fucked-up pranks, laughter and fistfights, wrestling on the ground, in the rain, in the mud, in the nights, in the cold, in the heat, on all the vacations of my life. And cigarettes by the carton and hundreds of quarts of beer. That's right, Pollo of the thousand motorcycle races, and then that last one...

"Pallina." She throws her arms around my neck, hugging me tight with a strength that reminds me of him, my friend who's no longer with us. I try not to think about it. I hug her tight, tighter and tighter, and I inhale through her hair, trying to catch my breath, to get back to the present, to my life. "Pallina."

She pulls away and stands there, gazing at me, her eyes glistening. I have to laugh. "Fuck, you've turned into a complete babe on me, here!"

"Oh, you finally figured it out!" She laughs happily, laughing and crying, as usual, crazy as she is, and beautiful as she's become.

Then she wipes away her tears with the back of her hand and sniffs loudly.

"Who would even have recognized you!"

She spins around in front of me, her eyes filled with loving warmth. "So how do I look? Do you like my hair short like this? What do you think? Do you know this hairstyle?"

"No, absolutely not."

"What the fuck? Come on, this is the very latest! I mean, you've just been to America and you don't know about it?" She laughs like crazy. "I'm the height of fashion right now! I copied it from *Cosmopolitan* and *Vogue*. You know Angelina Jolie and Cameron Diaz? Well, I just mixed them together and then outdid them!"

The most difficult moment is past. She punches me in the shoulder. "Oh, I missed you, Step." And she gives me a hug.

"I missed you too."

"Hey, you look fantastic yourself. Let me take a look at you. You've lost weight. Do you still have these?" She reaches out to touch my T-shirt and runs her hand over my abs. "Oh, I'll say you do . . . Better than ever!"

She tickles me.

"Hey, no, stop."

She laughs. "Damn, you're in shape. Come here, let me introduce you. This is my friend Giada."

"Ciao."

"He's Giorgio, and she's Simona." We exchange glances and nod hello. My gaze lingers a little too long on Giada's face, and she blushes, giving that last tiny touch of rouge to her cheeks, already too made up.

Pallina notices. "Oh, great. You've only just landed, and already you're slaying the ladies."

Giada turns away, letting her hair fall over her face. She conceals herself, smiling, her green eyes poking from between her blond locks.

Pallina shakes her head. "Oh, no. There she is. She's gone. We should go too, come on. Let's go in and get a beer. Oh, if you feel like it, you can catch up with us, okay? We need to talk about old times."

I don't even get a chance to say goodbye before Pallina's dragging me away. "Christ, there are a thousand things I need to tell you. Oh, if you'd bothered to drop me a line, a short letter, even a postcard. Do you even remember my phone number?"

I recite it for her. Then I give myself away. "That's where I'd call to reach Pollo." Fuck, I wish I hadn't said it. Luckily, we're already at the entrance. Pallina saves me. Either she didn't even hear me or else she's pretending she didn't. She says hi to a skinny-looking bouncer. "Ciao, Andrea. What do you say, can we get in?"

"Of course, Pallina, are you alone with your friend?"

"That's right, but do you know who he is?"

Andrea says nothing.

"Come on, this is Step. You remember, I told you all about him . . ."

"Of course." He smiles. "Fuck, are all the stories I've heard about you really true?"

"Cut it down to about sixty percent, and there might be something good in there."

Pallina shakes her head, pulls on my arm, and heads in. "He's just being modest." Pallina slaps him on the shoulder: "Thanks, Andrea."

I follow after her, laughing. "Certainly, times have changed . . ."

"Why?"

"Is that the way they're hiring bouncers these days?"

Pallina looks at Andrea, who's following our progress with an uncertain glance. Maybe he has his doubts as to whether I'm *the* Step he's heard so much about.

"Oh, hey, listen, Step. He's serious about his work."

"Okay, serious about his work. What is that supposed to mean? Back in the good old days, before they'd let you stand on a door, they'd beat you silly to see whether or not you could pull it off. You know that, once, at the Green Time, they told me to take the money down to a room at the far end of the club. I went in, and there were three of them. They all jumped me at once." I start telling the story. Pollo was there too. This time, though, I manage to keep him at bay. I convince Pollo to stay quiet, to stay in his place, wherever that is. I just hope that he's listening, and that he's smiling at this memory.

"Anyway, no way was I going to let them get that money. I whipped off my belt and boom! In the face of all three of them. I got one with the buckle and shattered his cheek-bone. The other two, nothing much. But I let them have it with blows to the face. And after that day, I worked four months running on the door at the Green Time. Pulling down a hundred a night. It was a dream come true, and you picked up chicks like it was a dream."

"Pollo had a mark on his face right under his left

cheekbone. He told me it was a belt mark." She misses nothing.

"Maybe it was his father."

She looks at me and smiles. "Liar. You haven't changed a bit."

We sit down at a plastic table with white chairs and remain silent. I turn and look around. Behind us, there's a sort of patched-up rubber dinghy that serves as a swimming pool. People of all sorts splash and yell in it.

"So how are you?"

"Just fine. How about you?"

"Fine. fine." We sit in silence for a while, embarrassed about a time that's long gone. Luckily, from the speakers scattered all over the place come the notes of a song, "The Lion Sleeps Tonight." And who knows which of us is the lion here, among us. And, more importantly, whether he's actually sleeping. A waiter comes to take our orders.

"Wait, let me guess. A Corona with a slice of lemon," Pallina says.

I smile. "No, strictly Bud these days."

"Oh, right, I love Bud too. Two Buds, thanks."

Who knows if she really meant it.

"You know, I thought about you lots while you were down there... in New York, right?"

"Right." I have to laugh because Pallina hasn't changed a bit. She talks in machine gun bursts and sometimes just for the fun of it. Fuck, Step, it's Pallina. Let her be. She's the girlfriend of your old friend Pollo. Don't judge her, too, don't be analyzing her words continually. Come on, cut it out.

I slap my forehead. "That's right, in New York. And I had the time of my life."

"I bet you did. You were right to get away. It's all been so difficult here." The Buds arrive. We raise them in a toast. We know what we're about to drink to.

"Here's to him..." I say it in a low voice.

And she nods. Her eyes are glistening with love, memories, the past. But here she is present. And the Buds slam into each other violently.

Then I chug that Bud down, ice cold, just fantastic. I want to keep drinking and never let go, but halfway through the bottle, I put on the brakes and catch my breath. I set the Bud down on the table. "Good."

I look in my jacket. Pallina beats me to it. She pulls out a pack of Marlboro Lights from her light green shirt with military shoulder straps and zip-up pockets. She extracts a cigarette for herself and hands me the pack. I pull out one for me and notice that there is no "lucky cigarette" in this pack. The one you turn upside down before smoking any others. Does that mean she thinks her luck is finished? Her dreams have ended? A wave of sadness washes over me.

I shut the lid of the pack and hand it back to her. I put the cigarette in my mouth. Then she extends a lighter, no, wait, she insists on lighting mine. Her hands are cold but she smiles. "You know, since then, I haven't even been with another man."

I take a drag and swallow it, heavy and full. "Man? Boy!" I say, trying to deflect.

"Okay, whatever, you know what I mean." Maybe it's the Bud, or the cigarette, or the noise and the mess, all the filth around us. We laugh. And everything goes back to the way it once was, easy, no problems. We tell each other all sorts of things, memories, our news, the news about other people. All the usual bullshit. But we're happy. She tells me all the latest Roman news. "Hey, come on. You know who I mean. You remember her, don't you? You can't imagine what she's turned into!"

"Hot?"

"A knockout." Laughter.

"You know what, though, Frullino is back behind bars."

"No, not seriously!"

"Yes, he got in a brawl with Papero because he got together with his girlfriend and so Papero turned him in to the cops."

"I can't believe it. Doesn't anybody believe in Jesus anymore?"

"I'm telling you, it's the solemn truth."

We both laugh.

"The Bostini brothers opened a pizzeria."

"Where?"

"Flaminio."

"And how is it?"

"It's great. You can run into just about everyone, but also lots of new people. The food is really fantastic, and it's not expensive. So Giovanni Smanella still hasn't graduated from high school."

"No, I can't believe it. What's wrong with his brain?"

"Well, just think, this last winter he wouldn't leave me alone."

"Get out of here. What a piece of shit!"

The good old days come back to the surface. Pallina looks at me, worried now. "Hey, no, he was just being nice. We'd become friends, and he was keeping me company. He'd talk about Pollo all the time."

"No kidding!" I say. Then we sit in silence.

"Fuck, Step"—Pallina takes a long slug of beer—"you haven't changed a bit!"

I'm still tense, but I let it drop. Oh, well, what the hell. He didn't really do anything wrong. After all, life goes on.

"I've changed." I smile.

"Okay, that's a relief. Well then, can we talk about other sensitive topics?" She smiles and gets a cunning, unforgettable look on her face. "Ouch..." It's obvious that my expression changes. "Here we go. Here comes some sorrow. Well, you asked for it." She drains the last sip of beer. "Well...have you talked to Babi at all? When's the last time you heard from her? Did you try calling her at all while you were away?"

She's clicking away like a typewriter. She never seems to stop.

"Hey, calm down, for fuck's sake. I feel like I'm getting grilled by the cops here!" I try my best to seem relatively indifferent to the whole subject. But I don't know if I'm successful. "No, never talked to her once."

"Not once?"

"Not once."

"Swear it!"

"I swear."

"I don't believe you."

"What the hell? You think I'm lying to you? Then I talked to her."

"No, no, okay, I believe you. But I've seen her."

Then she pauses. A long pause. Too long. She doesn't say a thing. And she's doing it on purpose. She looks at me and smiles. She wants me to say something. She waits some more, too long now. But why? What a pain in the ass.

I can't take it. "All right, Pallina, enough. Come on. Spit it out. Let me hear the rest."

"Still cute as ever but..."

"But what?"

"Different. I couldn't tell you how. But she's definitely changed."

"Okay, that's no surprise. We've all changed."

"Sure, I know. But she's changed in a way...I don't know, but look, she's changed in a different way."

"You already said that! But what do you mean when you say different?"

"Listen, I couldn't tell you. She's just different, and that's all I can say. That's how it is, and I don't know anything more. Either you understand or you'd have to see her to get it."

"Well, thanks for that."

And then, I don't even know how I did it, but I ask the question. It comes out naturally. I thought it but I didn't want to say it. But I just blurt it out like that, without meaning to, as if it weren't even me asking. "So was she alone?"

"Yes. And you know where she was going? Shopping."

I can't help but laugh. I remember Babi, I imagine her, and suddenly I see her.

"Wait right here. Don't budge from this spot, Step. Don't disappear on me like you usually do. No, seriously, don't go because I want to get your advice..." Babi left me standing in front of a shop window. She went in, looked around, made her choice, and then called me. "Look, I've made up my mind, I'm getting this. Do you like it?" But she didn't even give me time to answer before she

thought it over and changed her mind. She tried on something else, and it looked good on her. Now she seemed to have made up her mind. She did a sort of runway presentation, and then she looked at me. "Well? What do you say?"

"I think it looks great on you."

She looked at herself in the mirror again. But then she found something about it that didn't work, something only she could see. "Excuse me, I just want to think it over some more."

Then she left the shop and gave me a hug. "No, no, I decided against it. Too expensive."

And after all, I bought it for her as a gift a few days later. It made her laugh. It had turned into a game. Babi, why did you have to stop playing? But I wasn't fast enough to find out the answer.

"Oh, did you know she's not dating that guy anymore?" Pallina asks.

"No, I don't know any such thing. I told you that I haven't talked to her. What, am I supposed to have a network of secret informants?"

"I don't think she's dating anyone." Pallina says it intentionally, with a smile on her face, thinking I'll be happy to hear it. "Well, I'm not interested in Babi."

She makes an incredulous face when she hears my response. "You what?"

"I'm not interested in her. Seriously. And anyway, a wise man once said that if you can make it in New York, you can make it anywhere. And I think I've made it there."

"I understand. It wasn't someone. It was *As Good As It Gets*. Okay, I believe you." She smiles and lifts an eyebrow.

I take another drink of beer. "Listen, I'm really not interested in her."

"Then why are you telling me again?"

I stand up and pick up the check.

"What are you doing, heading out?"

"Yes, but first I'm going to pay."

Pallina seems a little disappointed: "Are we going to see you one of these days, or are you leaving again right away?"

"No, I'm staying."

"Give me your number, that way I can track you down."

"I don't know it by heart."

She looks at me with her funny face. She tilts her head to one side, and she stares at me. She's more attractive, more of a woman. And I care deeply for her. But she doesn't believe me.

"All right then, I'll give you a call. Or else call my brother's house. Just call the old number, he kept it when he moved."

She relaxes. She stands up and gives me a kiss. "Ciao, Step. Welcome home." And she goes off to join her friends.

Chapter 5

The motorcycle starts up immediately. The battery has recovered without problems. First gear, second, third. In a matter of seconds, I'm riding along under the viaduct on Corso Francia. I'm reminded of something I want, and I make a U-turn.

I go to buy two slices of watermelon from an old friend at the Ponte Milvio. I hadn't seen him in forever so he gives them to me for free. He has the tastiest watermelons in Rome.

He asks me if I've come home because of a girl. There's nothing more amusing than trading details with a friend. Especially if the girl hasn't captured your heart. Not like back then. Not like with *her*. I've never told any other guy anything about Babi. Not even Pollo.

Nothing, there's nothing to be done. When the love you've lost comes back looking for you, it finds you easily. It doesn't bother to knock. It just barges in, rough and ready, rude and gorgeous as only love knows how to be. And in fact, in less time than it takes to think it, I'm lost in that color again, in the blue of her eyes. Babi. That day.

"Come on, get moving. It's taking you forever."

The beach at Sabaudia. The sea. The motorcycle, parked under a pine tree, near the sand dunes.

"Huh? Step, I don't understand you. Do you want gelato or don't you?"

I was bent over, locking my bike with the chain. "What do you mean, you don't understand? You're a real comedian. I told you, no, Babi. Thanks but no."

"No, of course, you do. I know you do." *Babi, sweet and stubborn.*

"Well, in that case, why do you even bother asking? Plus, what do you think, Babi, if I wanted it, don't you think I'd get some? It's cheap."

"There, you see what you're like. The first thing you think about is money. You're just a cynic."

"Huh? No, I wasn't saying it because a popsicle is cheap. What do you care, Babi? You can get it, and if you don't want it, you just throw it away."

Babi walked over with a couple of popsicles in her hand. "And sure enough, I bought two. Here, orange flavored for me, and mint flavored for you."

"But I don't like mint as a flavor at all."

"Come on now. First you didn't want one at all, and now you're complaining about the flavor! You really are a piece of work. Anyway, go ahead and try it. You'll see, you'll like it."

"Don't you think I know whether or not I like something?"

"Now you're just digging your heels in. Come on, I know you better than that."

She unwrapped my popsicle and gave it a couple of licks. Then she handed it to me, after tasting it for herself. "Yummm... Yours is delicious."

"Then why don't you just take mine?"

"No, now I want the orange-flavored one." *And she licked her popsicle, looking at me and laughing. And then she got a little risqué because her popsicle was melting fast, so she put the whole thing in her mouth. And she laughed.*

And then Babi was absolutely determined again to taste mine. "Come on, let me have just a little," and she said it like that on purpose, laughing, and she rubbed up against me, and we were leaning against the motorcycle, and I spread my legs, and she slipped in between them, and we kissed.

The popsicles started to melt, trailing along the palms of our hands and down our arms. And every so often our tongues darted to catch a bit of orange, a bit of mint. On our hands, between our fingers, down our wrists and all along our forearms. Soft. Sweet.

Babi seemed like a little girl. She was wearing a long, light blue beach wrap, dotted with a darker pattern. It was wrapped around her waist. She was wearing light blue sandals, too, and a two-piece swimsuit, also light blue. She was wearing a long necklace with round white seashells, some bigger and some smaller. They bounced and wedged themselves between her warm breasts. She kissed me on the neck.

"Ouch!" She had just intentionally laid her popsicle on my stomach.

"Poor little thing, ouch…" She laughed at me, mockingly. "What's wrong? Did I hurt you? Was it cowd??"

I stiffened my muscles, and then she was really enjoying herself. She slid her popsicle over my abs, one after the other. But I took my revenge. "Here, try a little minty freshness on your hips."

"Ouch."

And on we went, painting each other with daubs of orange and mint on our backs, the nape of our necks, our legs, and then right between her breasts. The popsicle broke. A piece slipped in under the hem of her swimsuit.

"Hey, you dummy, it's cold!"

"Of course it's cold. It's a popsicle!"

And we laughed. Lost in a chilly kiss under the hot sun. And in our mouths, orange met mint as we sweetly joined.

"Come on, Babi. Come with me."

"Come with you where?"

"Come with me..."

I looked first to the right and then to the left, and then I hurried across the road, pulling her after me, and she ran, practically tripping, yanking her sandals off the blisteringly hot asphalt. We left the sea and the road, and we climbed up and up, high up on the dunes. And we kept running inland. Then, not far from a campsite occupied by tourists, we stopped. There, concealed in the low underbrush, between the arid greenery, on the practically rarefied sand, beneath a peeping-tom sun, I lay down on her beach wrap. Then we were flat on the ground. And she lay down on me, out of her swimsuit, all mine now. And in the heat, drops of sweat slid down over us, conveyed by streams of ash-blond hair, vanishing over her already bronzed belly, lower and lower down still, among her darker curls, and farther down still, among mine...

And that sweet pleasure was all ours. Babi moved on top of me, up and down, slowly. Then she let her head fall back, smiling into the sun. Happy to be loved. Beautiful in all that light. Mint. Orange. Mint. Orange. Mint...

That's it. I'm out of there. Out of the memories. Out of the past. But I'm also out of my mind. Sooner or later the things you've left behind will catch up with you. And the stupidest things, when you're in love, are things that you remember as the loveliest ones. Because their simplicity is incomparable.

And I feel like screaming. In all this silence that's

torturing me. Stop. Enough. Leave me alone. Put it all back where it belongs. There. Lock it up. Double-lock it. At the bottom of your heart, tucked away, hidden around the corner. In that garden. A few flowers, a little shade, and then nothing but pain and sorrow. Put them there, well concealed, make sure of it, trust me, where they can't hurt, where no one can see them. Where you can't see them. That's it. Buried again.

There now. That's better. Much better. And I drive away slowly. Via Pinciana, Via Paisiello, straight toward Piazza Euclide. There's no one out on the streets. A police car is parked in front of the embassy. One cop's asleep. The other one's reading something.

I accelerate. I pass the stoplight, then go down along Via Antonelli. I feel the cool wind caressing my face. I shut my eyes for a moment, and it feels as if I'm flying. I take a deep breath. Nice. Sweet. Sweet as a watermelon. No, sweeter. I turn down Corso Francia. It's the middle of the night. I speed up along the viaduct. Now it's practically cold. A few seagulls rise up into the air from the Tiber. They peer over the bridge. And then, shyly, they seem to wave. Then they dive down again, down to the river water. They let out soft cries, a plea, a request. Tiny, suffocated cries, almost as if they were afraid of waking someone up.

I downshift and turn up Via di Vigna Stelluti. Then I start laughing to myself.

Chapter 6

Half-asleep, half-awake, I hear the sounds of my brother, Paolo, in the kitchen. He's moving things around, trying not to make any noise. I can tell from the way he sets plates down on the table and shuts the drawers. My brother is every bit as considerate as my mother.

My mother. I haven't seen her in two years. I wonder what her hair looks like now. She was constantly changing her hairstyle in that last year. She'd change with the fashions, the trends, her girlfriends' advice, a picture in a magazine. I've never understood why a woman should always be so obsessed with her hair. I think of a film I saw, with Lino Ventura and Françoise Fabian, *La bonne année*. 1973. He winds up in prison. She goes to see him. It's dark. You can just hear their voices.

"What's wrong? Why are you looking at me like that?"

"You've changed your hairstyle."

"Don't you like it?"

"No, it's not that. It's that when a woman changes her hairstyle, it also means she's going to change men."

I smile. My mother has seen that film plenty of times.

Maybe she's taken those words seriously. One thing is certain. Every time I see her, her hairstyle is different.

Paolo appears in the doorway, opening it slowly, careful not to let the hinges squeak. "Stefano, are you coming to have breakfast?"

I turn to look at him. "Did you make a good breakfast?"

He's momentarily stumped, and then he says, "Yes, I think so, yes."

"All right then. In that case, I'll come." He never understands when I'm joking. He's different from my mother as far as that goes. I put on a sweatshirt but just boxer shorts below.

"Jesus, you've lost weight," Paolo says.

"You've already told me that."

"I ought to move to America for a year." He touches a roll of belly fat, gripping it between his fingers. "Look here."

"Power and wealth bring a gift of a belly," I say.

"In that case, I ought to be skinny as a rail." He tries to make a joke of it. In this aspect, too, he's different from Mamma because he doesn't know how to do it.

"What are you thinking about?"

"That you're good at setting the table."

He sits down. "Well, yes, I like doing it." He hands me the coffee.

I take it, and I add a dollop of cold milk without even tasting it first, just eyeballing it. Then I bite into a large chocolate cookie. "Mmm, good."

"I got them for you. I don't like them. The chocolate is too bitter. Mamma always used to get them for me when we all still lived together."

I sit in silence and drink my caffè latte. Paolo looks at

me. For a moment, it seems as if he wants to add something. But he changes his mind and sets about making his cappuccino.

I finish drinking my caffè latte. "Ciao, Paolo, see you around."

"Lucky you, the way you are."

"What's that supposed to mean?" I ask.

Paolo stands up and starts putting things away and clearing the table. "You know, you're lucky you are the way you are, free as a bird. You can do what you want. You've gone out together, things are still loose, nothing is nailed down."

"Yes, I'm lucky." I leave. There are too many things I'd have to say to him. I'd have to explain to him in the kindest of terms that he's just uttered a huge, deplorable, terrifying load of bullshit. That you only dream of freedom when you feel like a prisoner. But I'm tired. Now I don't feel like it, I seriously don't feel like it at all.

I go into my bedroom, I look at the alarm clock on the side table, and I turn and walk out of the room, abruptly. "Fuck, you woke me up, and it's only nine o'clock?"

"Yeah, I have to be in the office soon."

"But I don't!"

"Sure, I know that, but seeing as how you're supposed to go see Papà…" He looks at me, puzzled. "Wait. Didn't I tell you?"

"No, you didn't tell me anything about that."

He continues to display a certain confidence. He's either genuinely certain that he told me or else he's a great actor. "Well, in any case, he's expecting you at ten o'clock. So it's a good thing I woke you up, right?"

"Of course, no two ways about it. Thanks, Paolo."

"Don't mention it."

Nothing. Zero sense of irony. Paolo continues putting the cups and the coffeepot into the sink, nice and tidy, only and exclusively the right-hand basin.

Then he goes back to the same subject. "Hey, aren't you going to ask why Papà wants to see you at ten o'clock? Aren't you curious?"

"Well, if he wants to see me, I imagine that he'll tell me when he sees me."

"Oh, right, of course."

I see that I've hurt his feelings a little. "Okay. Well then, so why does he want to see me?"

Paolo stops washing cups and turns to look at me, drying his hands on a dish towel. He's enthusiastic. "I shouldn't tell you because it's supposed to be a surprise." He must realize that I'm starting to lose my temper. "But I'm going to tell you anyway because I'm so pleased about it. I think he's found you a job! Aren't you happy?"

"Overjoyed." I'm getting better though, I have to admit it. I manage to fake it, even in the face of a question like that.

"Well, what do you think?"

"That if I keep chatting with you, I'm going to be late."

I go to get dressed.

Are you happy? The hardest question of them all. "It takes courage to be happy," said Karen Blixen. Only my brother would think of asking a question like that.

Chapter 7

It's a minute before ten when I look at my last name written on the intercom. But this is my father's apartment. The name is written in pen, in shaky handwriting, without imagination and warmth, and utterly devoid of joy. In America, it would have been completely unacceptable.

But what does that matter? We're in Rome, in a small piazza of Corso Trieste, near a shop that sells fake, wannabe-classy clothing. The shopkeeper stacks it up in the window at a price of 29.90 euros. As if any jerk in off the street could believe that this disgusting dreck should set him or her back thirty euros.

I ring the bell.

"Who is it?"

"Ciao, Papà. It's me."

"Right on time. America has changed you." He laughs.

I'd love to turn around and go straight back home, but by now I'm here. "What floor are you on?"

"Third floor."

I walk in and shut the front door behind me. I push three.

The elevator opens, and Papà is standing in the doorway, waiting for me. "Ciao." He appears to be thrilled, and he hugs me tight. Too long, way too long. I get a little lump in my throat, but I brutally shove it aside. I don't want to think about it.

He gives me a gentle punch in the shoulder. "Well, how's it going?"

"Great." I wrestle my voice back to normal. "How about you? How are you doing?"

"Great. What do you think of my nice little apartment? I've been here for six months already, and I like it. I furnished it myself."

I'm tempted to say, "And it shows," but I decide not to.

"Plus, it's convenient, it's not too big, it must be about eight hundred fifty square feet, but it's perfect for me, I'm almost always alone here anyway."

He looks at me. He believes or he hopes that that "almost always" is going to lead somewhere. But it doesn't. He smiles pointlessly and then continues. "I found this opportunity, and I went for it, but you know something? I've always thought that a third story wouldn't suit me but instead, it's better. It's better...insulated. It's nice and quiet."

Too many adjectives are almost always a sign that you're trying to justify a bad decision.

I'm reminded of something Sacha Guitry said: "There are people who talk, talk, and talk until, finally, they find something to say."

"Sure, I couldn't agree with you more."

He smiles at me. "Well?"

I look at him, ill at ease. Well? Well, I love my father. So I make an effort. "You can't imagine how happy I was in New York, super happy."

"Were there people there? I mean, were there Italians?" he asks me.

"Sure, lots of them, but all of them very different from the kind of people I'm used to meeting here."

"What do you mean, different?"

"Oh, I don't know. More intelligent, more self-aware. They all spout less bullshit. They circulate, they talk freely, they talk about themselves—"

"What do you mean, they talk about themselves?"

If only we were sitting down to dinner. After a good dinner, one can forgive anybody, even one's own relations. Who said that? I heard it in high school, and it made me laugh. Maybe it was Oscar Wilde. I don't think I know how to answer him. But I give it a try. "That they don't hide themselves. They face up to their lives. And then they admit that they're struggling. It's no accident that nearly all of them see a psychoanalyst."

He looks at me, suddenly worried. "Wait, why, have you gone to one?"

My father, always the wrong question at the right time.

I reassure him. "No, Papà, I haven't gone." I feel like adding, "But maybe I should have. Maybe that American psychoanalyst would have understood my Italian problems." Or maybe not. I'd like to tell him that, but instead I drop it.

I try to simplify. "I'm not American. And we Italians are too proud to ever admit we need help from anyone else."

He remains silent. He's worried, and I'm sorry to see it. So I try to help him out, to keep him from feeling that he's at fault in any way. "And after all, why would I do it, why throw perfectly good money away? Going to see a psychoanalyst and not even understanding what he says to you in English. Do that and you seriously do have something wrong with your head!"

He laughs.

"I preferred to spend my money on language lessons. I was wasting the money, but at least I didn't hope I would feel any better!"

He laughs again. But it seems forced to me. Who knows what he'd actually rather hear me say.

"Anyway, sometimes we're not really capable of even telling ourselves what our problems are."

He turns serious. "That's certainly true."

"It's the same reason that I've read that there are fewer and fewer people going to confession in church."

"Right..." He's not convinced. "But where did you read that?"

Just as I suspected. "I don't remember."

"All right, let's get back to us," my father says.

Why, where did we leave us? What a thing to say. I'm starting to get pissed off.

"Did Paolo tell you anything?" my father asks.

"About what?" Lying to my father. I'm part of that article about going to confession. I don't go to church. Not anymore. "No, he didn't tell me a thing."

"Well..." He smiles at me, super enthusiastic. "I've found you a job."

I do my best to fake it. "Thanks." I smile. I should be an actor. "Mind if I ask what kind of job?"

"Oh, of course. How silly of me. Well, I thought, seeing that you've spent time in New York and you took a computer graphics course and a course in photography, right?"

Oh, this is promising. He's not even sure what it is that his son went to New York to do. And to think that he was the one paying for the school every month. "Yes, that's right."

"Well, the ideal thing would be for me to find you a job that had something to do with what you studied. And I found it! They'll take you on for a television program, in charge of computer graphics and pictures!"

He says it in a tone of voice that seems like an Italian translation of an American Oscars announcement: "And the winner is..." *Me?*

"Well, of course, you'd be the assistant, that is the person who works alongside the person who actually does all the graphic design on the computer and processes and edits all the various images, I think."

So I'm not the winner. I'm just a runner-up.

"Thanks, Papà. It seems like a really great thing."

"Or something of the sort. I really don't know how to explain it exactly."

Approximate and unclear. Close to the truth, or something of the sort. My father. I mean, did he ever really understand what happened with Mamma? I doubt it. Sometimes I wonder what part of him I have inside me.

The intercom buzzes. "Ah, that must be for me." He hastily gets to his feet, faintly embarrassed. Well, of course, who else could it be for?

Papà comes back but he doesn't sit down. He stands there, moving his hands nervously. "You know, I don't quite know how to put this, but there's a person I'd like to introduce you to. It's a strange thing to say to your son, but let's say it, man to man, okay? It's a woman." He laughs to take the edge off.

I'm not interested in making this any harder for him than it has to be. "Certainly, Papà, there's no problem at all. We're both men."

I sit there in silence. He stands there looking at me. I don't know what else to say. I can see that he's avoiding meeting my eyes. There's a knock at the door, and he goes to answer it.

"Here we are. This is Monica."

She's a good-looking woman. Not very tall. She's wearing strong perfume, a formal dress, hair with too much of a permanent, and too much lipstick. I get to my feet the way my mother taught me, and we shake hands. "A pleasure to meet you."

"Your father's told me so much about you. You just got back to the country, didn't you?"

"Yesterday."

"How did you like it, overseas?"

"Fine, just fine."

She sits down calmly and crosses her legs. Long legs, shoes with a bit of wear. It's the shoes, I've read, that can really tell you everything about a person's sense of style. I read lots of things, but I never remember where. Oh, now I remember, it was an issue of *Class* on the airplane. It was an interview with a bouncer. He was saying that it's the shoes that help him decide whether to let someone into his club or not. He wouldn't have let her in.

"So how long did you live in New York?"

"Two years."

"That's a long time." She smiles, with a glance at my father.

"Oh, time flew by. It wasn't a problem."

I hope she doesn't ask any more questions. Maybe she understands that because she stops. She reaches into her bag and pulls out a pack of cigarettes. Diana Special Blend Blue.

When it comes to the cigarettes, the bouncer would have some misgivings too. Then she lights it with a colorful BIC lighter, and after her first drag, she looks around. She does it strictly to send a message, not actually looking for anything.

"Here, Monica." And my father rushes to her side with an ashtray grabbed on the run from a side table behind her.

"Thanks," she says, and tries to tap some ash into the ashtray. But it's too early. She's printed the shape of half her mouth on the cigarette in red lipstick, with all the wrinkles and indentations.

"Well, I'd better get going. See you around."

"Ciao, Stefano. It was a pleasure to meet you," and she smiles a little too broadly. And she watches me go as I walk away.

"Wait. I'll see you to the door." My father walks me to the door. "We've known each other for a few months. You know, after all, it's been four years since I last went out with a woman." He laughs. Every time that he tries to get out something that strikes him as difficult, he laughs. Plus, he justifies himself too much. It always seems as if he's trying to convince himself of the choices he makes.

"You know, she's really nice..."

I can see that he's talking and talking and talking about her. But I think about other things. I remember when I was little and my mother joked around with him in the dining room. Then she started running, and he went right after her, down the hallway, chasing her all the way to the bedroom door, and I ran after Papà, shouting "Yes, let's get her, let's catch her!" Then they wrestled a little bit in the doorway. Mamma laughed and tried to lock herself in, and instead he tried to force his way in.

In the end, Mamma let go of the door and ran toward the bathroom. But then he caught her and threw her on the bed and Papà laughed because she started tickling him. I laughed, too, that day.

Then Paolo arrived. So Mamma and Papà shooed us both out of their bedroom. They told us that they needed to talk, but they were laughing while they said it. So Paolo and I went into our room to play. Then, a little later, the two of them came to our room too. But they talked slow and softly. It was as if their faces had softened. I remember them in a different light, as if they were luminous. Even their hair, their eyes, their smiles. And they started playing with us, and Mamma hugged me and laughed and neatened up my hair. She'd brush it back, somewhat forcefully, to uncover my face. It annoyed me, but I let her do it. Because she liked doing it. And because she was my mamma.

"Excuse me, Papà, but I really have to run..." I cut off any further conversation.

"But you did hear me, right? You understand? At two o'clock, at Da Vanni. Signor Romani expects you for that TV show." So that's what he'd been talking about.

"Sure, of course, I understand. Signor Romani, two o'clock, at Da Vanni." I heave a sigh. "Excuse me, eh?"

Then I hurry down the steps. I don't even stop to look back. A few minutes later, I'm on the motorcycle. I really want to get as far away as possible. I shift gears, and the speed is more welcome than usual.

Chapter 8

Paolo hasn't come home. Maybe he won't be back in time for lunch. The apartment is perfectly tidy. Too tidy. I pack my bag. Socks, T-shirt, shorts, a sweatshirt, and underwear. Underwear. Pollo used to make fun of me because of the words I used. My mother must have influenced me somehow. I told Pollo that once. He started laughing. "What a woman you are," he kept telling me, "you have a woman inside you." And my mother laughed when I told her about it.

I zip up my bag. I miss you, Pollo. I miss my best friend. And there's nothing I can do to bring you back. I'll never be able to see you again.

I pick up my bag, and I leave. I look at myself in the mirror as the elevator descends. I start singing an American song. I can't remember all the words. It was the only song I used to listen to all the time in New York. An old Bruce song. Fuck, singing makes you feel better. And I want to feel better.

I set out of the elevator with my bag over my shoulder. I start to sing, "Needs a local hero, somebody with the right style..." Yeah, that's not right, but it was something sort of like that. It doesn't matter. Pollo is gone now. Little hero that he was. "Lookin' for a local hero, someone with the right smile..." I wish I could talk to him but it's not possible. My mother lives somewhere not far, but I don't want to talk to her. I try singing it again. "Lookin' for a local hero." I never learned that song at all.

⌒

Flex Appeal, my gym, our gym. It belongs to us, to our friends. I get off my motorcycle. I'm deeply moved. What will have changed in there? And who will I run into?

I stop for a moment in the little piazza outside the front door. I peer through the plate glass windows, fogged up by straining muscles and sweat. There are girls dancing to an American song in the big exercise room. Among them are just two men who are desperately trying to keep up with Jim's Bodywork. That's the name I read on the sheet of paper posted by the door advertising the special class. They're wearing shoes, leotards, exercise suits, and skimpy tops, nearly all of them designer brand names. How the fuck could two men not be ashamed of that pathetic attempt at gymnastics? In the middle of all those women, just to make things worse. Tight, colorful bodysuits, perfect makeup, black leotards, skin-tight workout outfits or hotpants...and then a couple of men in baggy shorts. They leap around, uncoordinated, panting, desperately trying to catch up to the rhythm. But they can't find it. In fact, someone must have concealed it from them scrupulously ever since childhood.

I walk past and go in. At the front desk, there's a young man with an uneven dye job in his long hair and a bronzed face. He's speaking in a subdued voice on his cell phone with a hypothetical woman. He sees me, and for a little while, he continues chatting. Then he looks up and excuses himself with a certain "Fede"—short for Federica, no doubt—on the phone. "Can I help you?"

"I'd like to get a membership. For the whole month."

"Have you ever been here before?"

I look around, and then I look down at him. "Isn't Marco Tullio around?"

"No. He's out. You can find him here tomorrow morning."

"Okay, then I'll join tomorrow. I'm a friend of his."

"As you prefer..." He doesn't seem to care. After all, that money doesn't go to him.

I head for the locker room. Two guys are getting changed before working out. They're still laughing and joking around while I head off to work out.

"Hold on to my keys for me. I'll leave them right here." I put the keys I used to shut the locker in a pencil holder on the counter.

The guy at the front desk tilts his head in my direction and goes on chatting on his cell phone. Then he has a second thought. He puts his hand over his cell phone and decides he needs to tell me something. "Hey, buddy, you can work out today, but starting tomorrow, you're going to have to get a membership."

He looks at me, smug with his wise-ass expression, along with a bit of a tough-guy scowl. Then with a moronic grin, he goes back to his conversation. He turns around, his back to me now. He boasts. He laughs. I hear his last words, "You understand, Fede? This guy shows up and already acts like he's at home."

He doesn't even get a chance to finish his sentence. I grab him by the hair. A nice, fat handful of hair. I practically lift him bodily out of his chair. He stands to attention with his head bowed slightly in my direction. When you yank a handful of somebody's hair, it hurts like hell. I know that. I remember all too well. But now it's his hair.

"Shut your damned cell phone, asshole."

He blurts out a quick, "Let me call you back, okay, sorry." And he ends the call.

"All right, just for starters, this *is* my house. And then another thing . . . " and I yank harder on his hair.

"Ouch, ouch, you're hurting me."

"And another thing, and I want you to listen closely. Don't you ever dream of calling me *buddy* again as long as you live. Do you understand me?"

He tries to nod his head but he can only produce a tiny, faint movement. I yank harder to be certain. "I didn't hear that. Do you understand?"

"Ouch, ouch . . . Yes."

"I still didn't hear."

"Yes," he practically bellows in pain. He has tears in his eyes. I almost feel sorry for him. I let him go with a gentle shove. He collapses in the chair. He immediately starts massaging his scalp.

"What's your name?"

"Alessio."

"Okay, now put a smile on your face," and I give him two light slaps on the face. "You can call her back now if you want, go ahead and tell her that you fought back, that you kicked me out of the gym, even that you beat me up. Tell her whatever you want, but do not forget. Never call me *buddy* again."

Then there's a voice from behind me.

"'Cause you really ought to know his name anyway. It's Step."

I turn around in surprise, even slightly readying my defense. I hadn't expected to hear my name. I hadn't seen any of my friends, no one who could have known my name. But instead, there *is* someone. This guy. He's skinny, in fact, incredibly skinny. Tall, with long arms, hair cut in a pretty standard way, slightly thick eyebrows, meeting at the center above a long nose that juts out over the narrow lips of a broad mouth. Maybe it's broader than usual because he's smiling. Self-confident, relaxed, his hands in his pockets and a look of bemusement on his face, he's wearing the pants of a tracksuit and a ragged worn sweatshirt, a faded red hue. Over that he's wearing a light blue Levi's jean jacket. I can't place him.

"You don't remember me, do you?" No, I don't remember him. "Take another look at me, maybe I've grown." I look again, more closely. He has a cut over his forehead, hidden by his hair, but nothing serious. He notices what I'm looking at. "It was the car crash. Come on, you even came and visited me while I was in the hospital."

Fuck, how could I have forgotten. "Guido Balestri! It's been a lifetime. We were in middle school together."

"Right, and we were in high school, too, for the first two years at least. Then I quit school."

"Did you flunk out? I just can't remember all the details."

"No, I went to work with my father."

Ah, of course. Naturally! Balestri. His father is some big deal, someone who's always in the middle of all those things, stocks and bonds or that kind of financial stuff. He was always traveling around the world.

"Well, how are you doing?"

"Fine, how about you?" I ask.

"I'm fine too. It's great to see you again. I've heard all about you, Step. Here in Vigna Clara you're basically a legend."

"Well, I wouldn't say that."

I look over at Alessio. He's filing some papers, and he pretends not to hear. He can't stop touching his hair.

Guido laughs. "We all still talk about those epic brawls. I remember when you boxed with Il Toscano behind Villa Flaminia in the woods."

"We were just kids..."

Guido looks a little disappointed. "I heard that you went to New York."

"Yeah, I lived there for two years."

He says so long and takes off. What on earth is he coming to the gym for? He hasn't gained a pound. He's skinny as ever, as even my most faded memory. That's his fucking business. But I like him.

⌒

There. I knew it! I knew that Step was coming here to work out at the gym. I was positive of it. And I was certain that it would be this gym, and no other! I'm just too smart. And he's just too conservative. A creature of habit. Too much so. I hope that at least something about him has changed! All right, well, time for me to go. He didn't see me. But I heard everything I needed to hear.

⌒

I start off on the first exercise machines. I warm up fast, machine gun bursts of reps, to stretch and soften my muscles. I don't overload, just the bare minimum I can get away with.

I see a young woman leave in a hurry, wearing an orange baseball cap pulled halfway down on her head. I have to tell you, there are some really weird people in this world.

I smile and think about my abs. First, I do a series of a hundred sit-ups.

Second series of a hundred. I look up at the ceiling without stopping, one after the other, hands behind my head, elbows neatly aligned, tense, wide open. One after the other. Harder still. I can't take it anymore, the pain is starting to make itself felt.

I think about my father, and his new girlfriend. I continue without stopping. *Eighty-eight, eighty-nine, ninety.* I think about my mother. *Ninety-one, ninety-two.* How long it's been since I last saw her. *Ninety-four, ninety-five.* I need to call her, I ought to call her. *Ninety-eight, ninety-nine, one hundred.* All done.

Chapter 9

Anyone who's never been to Da Vanni can't begin to understand. I park my motorcycle out front and get off. It's a sort of modern casbah of colorful individuals. Everyone's chatting loudly, the occasional customer orders a frozen yogurt, and young people astride their scooters prepare for the evening ahead. The occasional Maserati cruises past, searching for a parking spot. A Mercedes decides to double-park. Everyone greets everyone else; everyone knows everyone else.

I take a look around. I'm here to meet someone powerful, at least I imagine him to be powerful from my father's description. He told me I'd be meeting an extremely cultivated man, tall, well-dressed, slender, and always impeccably groomed, with long hair, dark eyes, a striped tie, and at least one of his collar wings unbuttoned. My father insisted stubbornly on that point. "The loosened collar has a genuine meaning, Step, but no one has ever managed to figure it out."

I'm guessing that no one ever bothered to ask him, for that matter. There's no one in sight who matches up with my understanding of the "powerful."

But then I spot the man in question. There he is. He seems practically extraneous to everything that's happening around him. He's sitting alone at a small round table, sipping something light colored with an olive floating in it. His hair is long. As in the description, he's wearing a dark blue linen suit and a white shirt, impeccably pressed. A tie with black-and-blue stripes lies softly down his chest, coming to a rest beyond his belt, there, between his crossed legs. Just below the cuffs of his trousers are a pair of Top-Siders, neither too new nor too old, as worn as necessary to be in line with the belt of his trousers. In case I'd had any lingering doubts, that shirt collar, unbuttoned only on one side, would have eliminated them instantly. It's him. "Hello there."

He gets to his feet. He seems happy to see me. "Oh, buongiorno. Are you Stefano?" We shake hands. "Your father had only good things to say about you."

"What alternatives did he have?"

He laughs. "Excuse me." His cell phone is ringing: "Ciao. Certainly, don't worry. I've already told them everything. I've already taken care of everything. Everything is going to work out. Wait and see, they'll sign."

A powerful man who's in love with the word "everything."

"Now, if you'll excuse me, I'm in a meeting. That's right, ciao. But of course. But of course I'm delighted. I told you that." He ends the phone call. "What a pain in the neck." He smiles. "I hope you'll excuse me, eh? So what were you telling me?"

I start talking again and I tell him about the course I took in New York.

"So 3D graphics."

"Yes."

"Perfect." He nods contentedly. He seems to really know the business. His cell phone rings again. "Please, excuse me, today is really just crazy."

I nod, feigning empathy. I imagine every day is like this for him. I remember that I have a cell phone myself. Stupidly, I come close to blushing. I pull it out of my jacket and power down. Maybe he notices. Or maybe he doesn't.

The telephone call comes to an end. "All right, let me turn mine off too. That way we can chat without interruptions."

He noticed.

"All right then. You'll serve as assistant to the full-time graphic designer. His name is Marcantonio Mazzocca. He's excellent. You'll meet him soon. He's on his way over. That was him on the phone just now."

I hope it wasn't the guy on the first phone call because he called the other guy "a pain in the neck."

"Just think, he's an aristocrat. He owns vast hillsides covered with vineyards up north. In Verona, that is, and his father owns them. Then he became a painter, doing canvases. He moved down here to Rome and started circulating, in the clubs, and you know, designing invitations to parties and concerts, little jobs like that, right? Then he gradually started specializing in computer graphics, and finally, I hired him."

I listen. Certainly, to quote a great film, *Along Came a Spider*, "You do what you are." But I decide not to say it. First I want to meet him, this Mazzocca.

The guy takes a sip of his aperitif. He greets someone he knows who happens by. Then he wipes his mouth with a paper napkin. He smiles. He's obviously proud of the power he enjoys, his decisions, the fact that he was able to hire an aristocrat just to work as a graphic designer on his television productions. "Well, I hope you'll enjoy working with him. Now, no question, he's certainly a bit of a pain in the neck..."

So he was the guy from the first phone call.

"But he's very scrupulous and precise in the work he does." Romani finishes his aperitif. "Here he is. He's arriving. It's Marcantonio."

A strange hybrid of Jack Nicholson and John Malkovich comes walking along toward us, smiling and smoking a cigarette. Receding hairline, with short hair, cut above the ears, and long sideburns caressing his cheek and curling at the end like a comma. A handsome smile, a cunning glance. He flicks the cigarette away into the distance and then practically pirouettes as he spins to sit in an unoccupied chair next to us. "Well, how's it going? I was a bit of a pain in the neck on the phone, wasn't I?"

He doesn't give Romani a chance to reply.

"But it's my strongest asset. Squeeze the life out of people, slowly but relentlessly. Chinese water torture, drip drip drip, until it corrodes even the hardest metal. It's all just a matter of time, as long as you're not in a hurry, and I never am." He pulls out a sky-blue pack of Chesterfield Lights and sets it down on the table with a black BIC lighter on top of it. "Marcantonio Mazzocca, a penniless aristocrat well on the way to restoring the family fortune."

I shake his hand. "Stefano Mancini. I think I'm your assistant."

"Assistant, what an ignoble term they've come up with, just to pigeonhole us, each and every one."

Romani interrupts him: "You may find it ignoble, but he's going to be your assistant. Well, time for me to leave you two. Explain everything clearly to him because he's starting work next Monday. We're on the air in just three weeks. And everything is going to have to be perfect!"

"Oh, it's going to be perfect, boss! I brought a logo for the credits, if you'd be so courteous as to give it the once-over..." and he hands him a small file folder that's appeared as if by some miracle from an inside pocket of his lightweight jacket.

Romani opens it.

Marcantonio watches him, relaxed, appearing confident of the work he's done.

Romani is pleased, but then he notices. "Um, I think the logo should be a slightly lighter color, and then...Get rid of these flourishes, these arrows, here. I want everything lighter, cleaner!" Then Romani walks off with the file folder under his arm.

"He always wants to put in his own two cents. It makes him feel more important. And we just play along," Marcantonio says. He lights another cigarette. Then he relaxes, slumps back in his chair, reaches into his pocket and pulls out another file folder. He opens it. "Et voilà."

It's the same design, with the logo a little lighter and without the arrows, just like Romani asked.

"You see? Already done!"

Chapter 10

"How did your meeting go?"

No sooner do I walk in the door than Paolo is bothering me with his curiosity.

"I think it went well."

"What do you mean, 'I think it went well'?"

"I mean that I think it went well, that maybe I made a good impression."

"By which you mean what?"

"That I start next week!"

"Perfect, that's how I like to see you! We need to celebrate. Let me make you a fabulous dinner. I've become a wizard in the kitchen. You know, while you were away, I took a cooking course at Costantini..."

"Not tonight, I can't."

"Why not?"

Now I'm to my bedroom, and he appears in the doorway. "Look here." He has a clear plastic bag in his hand. He looks at me in surprise. "Wait, what, don't you recognize them? They're morselletti! Those cookies that Mamma always used to make you, with honey and hazelnuts. Come on, how could you have forgotten them? She always used to put them on the radiator for us, to soften them, and then we'd eat them like crazy when she let us stay up to see the Monday night movie." He pulls one out. "Come on, I can't believe you don't remember them."

I walk past, bumping him as I go. "Sure, I remember them, but I don't want one now. I'm going out to dinner."

Paolo is disappointed. He stands there with the morselletto in one hand, watching me put on my jacket and grab my keys.

"Come on. I'll eat one tomorrow morning for breakfast, okay?"

"Okay, as you prefer." Paolo watches me get ready to leave and then focuses his attention on the morselletto and tries to bite into it. "Ouch, it's hard."

"Warm them up in the oven," I tell him before I go.

I'm in the elevator, and I button up my jacket. What a pain in the ass. I run my hand through my short hair, mussing it up a little, as much as I can. Morselletti are the best cookies in the world. They're not too sweet, they're hard to chew at first but then...They seem like a kind of chewing gum, just a little harder than that, they take on a taste all their own, and now and then you bite into a hazelnut.

Mamma. I remember her there in the kitchen. "Mix up the honey in the pot, stir and stir it and, every once in a while, take a taste..." She'd lift the very tip of a long wooden spoon to her mouth and then roll her eyes, half shutting them, to concentrate better on the flavor. "This needs a little more sugar. What do you think?"

Then she'd invite me to join the game, sampling a little with the wooden spoon. I would nod. Always in agreement with her, with my mamma. Then she'd sing, "Makes the medicine go down, the medicine go down." She'd take off the red lid of the sugar jar and shake it ever so slightly with her wrist, sifting a little into the pot. Just enough, at least, according to her. Then she'd put the lid back on the jar, set it down, rub her hands on her flowered apron, and come over to me to see how it was going. "If you finish studying early, I'll give you one morselletto more than Paolo...after all, he'll never know." And we'd laugh together, and she'd kiss me on the back of my neck while I hunched up my shoulders, shivering at the tickle...

It's hard to forget nice things.

I zip away fast on my motorcycle. The wind is pleasant and warm on this September evening. There are very few cars out on the road. I turn up Corso Francia off of Vigna Stelluti, and I arrive at the traffic light. Then I turn and take the Via Flaminia. I twist the throttle and accelerate. The traffic light at the end of the street is green so I accelerate harder to make it through before it turns red. It's colder here, and a shiver runs through me. It's the greenery along the edge of the road, through the higher hills, with the occasional concealed cavern and tall trees that occasionally hide the moon.

The motorcycle slows down all on its own. I'm down to my reserve tank now. Strange. I'd filled up recently. Maybe the carburetor is fouled. That would explain why it's consuming more fuel than usual.

I twist the throttle again, and without shifting, I reach down to the left of the tank until I find the lever. I push it down to start the reserve tank. I need to stop for gas. I go past the big Centro Euclide shopping center on the right, and just a short distance past that, I spot the lights of a self-service gas station. I pull to a halt next to the pump. It's working.

I kill the engine and put the key in the lid of the gas tank. Then I stand up and pull my wallet out of my jeans pocket. Still holding the motorcycle steady between my legs, I pull out two ten-euro notes and slide them into the slot. The second ten-euro note is rejected, and the machine spits it out. I slide it back in, and as the slot pulls at it, I slam the heel of my hand into the side of the pump. A few more seconds and then a mechanical quack informs me that the second bill has been digested too.

I wheel the motorcycle back a short distance and reach out for the pump handle. Fuck, this just can't be. Impossible. There's a padlock on the gas hose. I can't use it. And it's not the usual kind of padlock they have at gas stations. This one is bigger. Big enough to block the button to get the receipt. This is a con game! A trick some fucking jerk has pulled so he can fill his tank on my twenty euros. That bastard basically just held me up...

Fuck. Fuck. Fuck. I don't have time. I have to get to dinner. This is the last thing I need. I shut the gas tank, put the keys back in the motorcycle's ignition, and take off, furious, engine roaring.

The gas pump stands there, all alone now, in the silence of the night. The occasional car goes racing past, heading out for who knows what magical weekend or else, more prosaically, a cheap dinner out somewhere around Prima Porta. A cat creeps across the asphalt of the gas station. Suddenly it stops as if it had heard some strange noise. It stands there motionless in the shadows, its head turned, its neck twisted, its eyes half-shut. As if it was searching for something. But there's nothing to be found. The cat relaxes and continues on its way, heading who knows where.

A few clouds scud past overhead. A light breeze occasionally uncovers the moon. From behind the daytime station attendant's little building, a car pulls out. It's a dark blue Nissan Micra, with only its running lights glowing. It rolls slowly toward the gas pump. It parks, the motor switches off, and someone gets out, not too tall, wearing a somewhat feminine black hat and a dark Levi's denim jacket. The person looks around. Then, seeing no one, they pull the key to the padlock out of their pocket and open it.

But before they can lift the pump handle, I'm on them, slamming them on the hood of their car, climbing on top of them. "Like fucking hell are you going to fill your tank with my cash!"

I grab them by the neck but they're struggling to get free. In the struggle, the hat flies away. A cascade of long dark hair spills out over the car hood. I pull my right fist back, ready to punch them in the face, but a pale shaft of moonlight suddenly illuminates their face. "You're a woman!"

She tries to wriggle free. I hold on to her a little while longer as I slowly lower my right arm. "A woman, a fucking woman."

I let her go. She gets up off the car hood and adjusts her jacket. "Okay, so I'm a woman. So what? What the fuck do you have to laugh about. You want to fight? I'm not afraid of you."

This woman is pretty cool. I take a better look at her. Her legs are spread wide, a pair of low-rise jeans and a pair of Hi-Tec sneakers. She's wearing a black T-shirt under her dark denim jean jacket. This gal has style. She picks up her hat and shoves it in her back pocket. "Well?"

"Well, what? Listen, you're the one who was trying to steal my money."

"So?"

"This again? So nothing." I climb into the Micra and pull the keys out of the dashboard. "That way, we can avoid the whole car chase." I put the keys in my pocket. Then I continue walking. I emerge a moment later with my motorcycle. I had circled back around behind the hedge with my engine off. I start the engine, and in a second, I'm right in front of her. I kill the engine, and I unscrew the lid on the gas tank. "Hand me the pump."

"Wouldn't dream of it."

I shake my head, grab the pump myself, and start filling my tank. Then I get an idea, I put only ten euros' worth of gas in my tank and then stop. I walk around her Micra with the pump in my hand, I open her tank, and I put the other ten euros' worth of gas into her tank. She watches me. She's pretty with a kind of tough-gal demeanor. Maybe she's just pissed that she got caught. Her eyes are big and dark, and she has a nice smile, from what little I can see of it.

She makes a strange grimace of curiosity. "Now what are you doing?"

"I'm filling your tank."

"Why?"

"Because we're going out to dinner together." I roll the motorcycle away and put the lock on it behind the gas station.

"Not happening. Me going out to dinner with you? I have better things to do. I have a party, a rave. I'm supposed to meet my friends."

I act like a tough guy, but I'm struggling not to laugh.

"All right, let's put it this way. You wanted to enjoy your evening with my twenty euros, but you're much luckier than that. You're going to spend it with me."

"Listen to this guy."

"Or let's say that you spend the evening with me or else I'll report you to the police. Is that simple enough for you?"

The girl gives me a faint, sardonic smile. "Of course, I'll get in the car, or actually to be exact, I'll get in *my* car with a perfect stranger."

"I'm no longer a perfect stranger. I'm a guy who was basically about to be robbed by you."

She snorts in annoyance again. "All right, let's take a look at it from a slightly different point of view. I get in my car with a potential half-robbery victim, okay? So far, so good. But why shouldn't I assume that you'll take me to some godforsaken place and take advantage of me? Give me one good reason."

I stand there in silence. Fuck everyone she's worried about. Pieces of shit, you've ruined things for the nice guys. "Okay, okay..." I know that she has a point. "All right then, how about this? You see this cell phone?" I pull it out of my pocket. "Do you know how many 'advantages' much better than you I could have taken with just a simple phone call? So why don't you shut up and get in?" Finally, I find a situation where a cell phone turns out to be really useful.

She shoots me a look dripping with hatred and then steps toward me. She plants her feet wide and stands in front of me, and then she extends her arm, her hand wide open.

I throw my arm up in defense immediately.

"For the moment, I'm not going to slap you in the face. But give me the keys, I'll drive."

I smile, slipping into her car. "Not on your life."

"How on earth can you imagine that I'm going to trust you?"

"No, how can you think that *I'm* going to trust *you*? You're the one who started out by trying to rip me off!" I lean over and open the door for her. I give her a smile. "Am I right or am I right? Come on, get in."

She stands there, baffled, for a moment, and then heaves an annoyed sigh and climbs into the car, her arms folded across her chest and her eyes facing forward.

I drive for a while in silence.

"Hey, your car has a great ride."

"So is the idea that we're supposed to talk part of this deal?" We've just gone past Saxa Rubra.

"No, but now we can strike another deal. You see, I could drive away with your car and my tankful of gas. So try to be nice, enjoy yourself, smile. After all, you have such a nice smile."

"But you haven't even seen me smile yet."

"Exactly. So what are you waiting for?"

She fake smiles, gnashing her teeth. "Here you go. Happy now?"

"*So* happy." I extend my open hand in her direction.

She dodges to one side. "Hey, what do you think you're doing?"

"My God, so mistrustful. I'm just introducing myself, right? Like a well-mannered person, the kind that doesn't rip other people off. My name's Stefano, Step to my friends."

She ignores my extended hand, leaving it hanging in midair in the dim light of the car. "Okay. Ciao, Stefano. I'm Ginevra, Gin to my girlfriends. But to you, I'm still just Ginevra."

"Ginevra, nice, a name befitting a princess. And just how did your parents know in advance that they'd be bringing a princess like you into the world?"

I glance at her and lift my eyebrow, but then I can't hold back any longer and I burst into laughter. "Oh my God, excuse me, but I just can't help laughing, and I don't even know why. Princess."

I go on like that. I look at her and I laugh. She amuses me. There's something about her that I like. Maybe it's because she isn't pretty.

The car zips along at high speed. The streetlights abandon and then seize her face again. They daub it with light and then with darkness. And every so often, the moon gives her a kiss. She has high cheekbones and a small chin. Light eyebrows, like a vanishing point, flee toward her hair. She has intense, vibrant, cheerful hazel eyes, in spite of the fact that she's deeply annoyed. Yes, I really made a mistake. She's not pretty. She's gorgeous.

"Your folks were pretty cool. Excellent name they picked for you, Princess Ginevra."

She looks at me. "Stefano, my folks aren't around anymore. They're both dead."

My blood freezes in my veins. My expression changes. "I'm sorry."

We ride along like that for a while, in silence. The car tools along quickly. I look straight ahead at the road, trying to bury my stupid misstep under those fast white stripes. I hear her breathe, for all I know she's crying softly. I can't stand to turn around but I have to.

And I see her there in the corner, looking at me. Huddled up against the window. Sitting sideways. Then, all at once, she bursts out laughing like a lunatic. "Oh my God, I can't stand it anymore. What I told you was utter bullshit! So now we're even, okay? Truce." And just like that, she pops a CD into the stereo. "So that upset you, did it? You act like a tough guy but, deep down, you're just a big softie." Ginevra laughs and bounces along to the music of the Red Hot Chili Peppers. "All right then, where are we going to eat?"

I drive in silence. Fuck, she screwed me. Nice move, but a bit of a bitch. How can you kid around about something like that? I go on driving, staring straight ahead.

Out of the corner of my eye, I see her dance. She moves perfectly to the music, laughing as she sit-dances to "Scar Tissue." She swings her hair. She laughs every now and then, biting her lower lip.

"Oh, come on, you didn't really take offense, did you?" She looks at me. "Excuse me very much. You're driving my car. Okay, with your gas in the tank, I'll say that before you can bring it up again. You're taking a girl to dinner with your friends, right? Or something like that...So you really have no reason to be upset, do you? You said it yourself. Lighten up. Have fun. Smile! And I did it. So now why can't you?"

I continue to say nothing.

"Oh my God. He's holding a grudge. He's decided to pout. Would you have been happier if they really were dead? All right, then, let's try some basic conversation. How are *your* folks?"

"Excellent, they're divorced."

"Of course they are! Copycat. Mamma mia, you're so obvious. Can't you dream up anything better than that?" Ginevra asks.

"What can I do if it's true? You really are something. You see, it's all your fault. You undermined the credibility of anything we might have to say to each other."

"You're not seriously saying that—"

"Oh, yes I am. I already told you so."

Then she sits in silence for a while. She looks at me with a baffled expression. She studies me with a side glance. "It's not true."

"I told you it is."

She's still not fully convinced of what I've told her. As I drive, I turn to look at her. We ride along like that for a while, staring into each other's eyes. It's a sort of competition. Then she's the first to look away. She seems to be blushing. But the light is too dim to know whether or not that's true.

"Hey, eyes front, focus on the road. It might be your gas, but it's my car, okay? So try not to wreck it."

I smile without letting her see.

"You lied to me. That was bullshit, right? They're not divorced."

"Of course they are, and they have been for a number of years now."

"Well, if that's true, I'm sorry. Anyway, I read somewhere that more than sixty percent of all couples with grown children are divorced. So..."

"So?"

"So that's a statistic you can't use to act like a victim," Ginevra says.

"Who's trying to act like a victim? Not me. But listen to this..."

I'm tempted to tell her the whole story, maybe because she doesn't know anything about me or because she's showing some trust, or else for some other reason I don't even understand. But I don't, something holds me back.

"What are you thinking about? Your folks?"

"No, I was thinking about you."

"What were you thinking about me if you don't even know me?" she asks.

"I was just thinking how nice it is when you don't know someone, but you have them sitting next to you, and all the problems you don't have, how you can imagine them, you can just work on fantasy, and you go where you want to with your mind."

"And where did you wind up?"

I intentionally let a pause stretch out. "Far, far away." Even if it isn't true, it amuses me to say it to her.

"Actually, I thought it over, and I think you might have been right," I say.

"What do you mean?"

"I'm going to *take advantage*."

"You're just trying to worry me, aren't you? But it's not going to work, I'm sorry to tell you. I'm a third dan. Do you know what a third dan even is? Well, I'm happy to tell you."

She speaks in short bursts, and I listen to her, amused.

"It means that before you even had a chance to lay a hand on me, I'd already have destroyed you, get it? Third dan, in karate. And I've done kickboxing too. Just try laying a hand on me, and you'd be finished. Finished."

"Well, that's good. It means I'm safe."

Before I can even finish the sentence, the steering wheel whips out of my hand. The Micra swerves terrifyingly. I instantly countersteer and take my foot off the gas.

Ginevra lurches over against me. I guide the car gently to the right while she straightens up. The whole thing scared her. She punches me hard in the shoulder, in the same place as before. "You idiot, you scared me! You cretin!"

I laugh. "Ouch. Stop it. Listen, I had nothing to do with that. I think that was a blowout."

"What are you talking about? You did it on purpose!"

"I'm telling you I didn't." I get out of the car and bend over in front of the hood to get a look at the tires. "There, you see?"

She gets out, too, and sees the tattered tire. "So now what?"

"So now I just hope you have a spare tire."

"Of course I do."

"Excellent!"

We stand there for a while looking at each other.

"Well?" she asks.

"Well what? Go get it, why don't you?"

"Excuse me, but you were driving. So it's all your fault."

"Maybe so but the car belongs to you. So you change the tire."

Ginevra heaves a weary sigh and heads for the hood.

"It's in the trunk, in the back of the car!"

"I was just checking to make sure nothing was broken." She's lying.

"Sure, sure. Of course you were."

She opens the trunk and lifts the cardboard panel that covers the spare tire. "How do I get it out?"

"You see that big nut on the top? You unscrew that and then you pull the wheel toward you."

She follows my instructions and frees the wheel. She tries to pull it out, but when she gets it halfway out, the tire falls back in, bouncing as it does. She lacks the necessary strength. "Excuse me, but why won't you help me?" she asks.

"Why should I? Just pretend I'm not even here. You said that I wasn't expected as a part of your night out, didn't you? To say nothing of the whole issue of equality, plus there's something even more important."

She swings around to face me, hands on her hips. "Let's hear it. What else?"

"You said that you were a third dan, right? Just think if you lose against a wheel. Ha, ha, ha."

She looks at me, furious now. She practically lunges into the trunk, grabs the wheel, and arches her back. She makes a huge effort, and I head right over to her, ready to help, but she has the spare tire out of the trunk before I get there.

"I can do it. What are you worried about?" Then, as she passes by me, she hits me with her shoulder and shoves me aside, intentionally. "Get out of my way! Don't stand around, keeping people from working."

Chapter 11

I sit down by the side of the road, atop a low wall, and I light a cigarette. I just sit there, hidden in the darkness, watching Ginevra. Then I shout from a distance, "Nice work, good going. You're doing a great job."

She slides under the car to place the jack. She's bent over, with both hands on the ground, her fingers up in the air as she looks for the best place to slide in the jack. She starts to lift the side of the car with the jack, pumping up and down, making the car sway slightly.

"Let me know when you're done. Maybe I'll take a nap in the meantime."

I let myself slide back into a recumbent position on the top of the low wall. I watch the clouds scudding overhead in the dark sky. By now they're mixed up with the smoke that I let escape in plumes from my mouth. Transparent, bathed in hidden light, that higher moon, the one you can't see even though you know it's there.

I take a nice deep breath. I smile, and I turn to look at Ginevra. There she is, undoing the bolts. She puts all her strength into turning the lug wrench. She can't do it with the strength of her arms so she puts all her weight on it with one foot. The lug wrench attached to the bolt bounces off and clangs to the ground. She heaves a sigh of annoyance, and with the edge of her hand, to keep from smearing grease on herself, she pushes the hair out of her face. She's beautiful and overheated. She puts the lug wrench back on the bolt and gives it another shot.

A car is arriving. It has a dark paint job, and it goes by at moderate speed, flashes its brights, and honks its horn. Then I hear the screech of brakes from a short distance ahead, followed by the sound of tires backing up fast, typical of a knucklehead driver. It's a Toyota Corolla. It's in reverse but traveling at considerable speed, fishtailing as it comes. It half-curves in reverse. Then it comes to a halt right next to Ginevra's Micra. Some people get out. I sit up on the low wall. It's three guys. I flick my cigarette to the ground and sit there, watching the scene unfold.

"Hey, ciao. What are you doing here all alone at night?"

"Flat tire, huh? What lousy luck."

"What lousy luck for *us*, for a minute we thought you were a hooker."

They all laugh.

One of them coughs. They might be more or less twenty years old. They have buzz cuts. Maybe they're in the army.

Ginevra doesn't look in my direction. "Listen, do you mind very much? Could you help me change this tire?"

"Why, of course. We'd be delighted."

The shortest one gets down low and starts undoing the bolts with the lug wrench. "Damn, they're rusty."

"Yeah, I've never changed a tire on this car. This is the first time I've had a flat."

"Well, there's a first time for everything."

One of the three guys laughs in a raucous bark, and the other two follow suit.

"Hey, it's a good thing it happened to you tonight, when we just happened to be passing."

"Yeah, right, it's a good thing that you guys are here." This time Ginevra shoots a glance in my direction, and without letting herself be seen, she gestures with one hand as if to say, *Serves you right, you see? These guys are going to help me.*

The little guy changes the tire in the blink of an eye. He undoes all the bolts and sets aside the flat tire. He lets it fall to the ground nearby, so that it bounces and rolls, and immediately places the spare tire on the hub. He gets the holes aligned quickly and tightens all of the bolts. He gives them all a first tightening, one at a time without tightening too much, and then goes back over them for the final, decisive tighten-up. He must be a mechanic as a day job. He gives one last jerk to the lug wrench and gets to his feet. "Et voilà, all done. Taken care of, signorina!"

He cleans off his hands by smacking them against his jeans above the knee. The jeans are so dirty that his hands leave no marks.

"Thanks. I wouldn't have known what to do without your help."

There's just no two ways about it, I think to myself. She really is a princess. The right phrase at the right time. Or the wrong one. An ordinary and obvious attempt to get rid of them in an amiable manner. But just as I expected, it falls flat.

"Wait, what are you doing now? You're just going to send

us away like that?" The taller guy, who is also a little bigger than his two companions, takes the situation in hand.

"Well, I *said* thank you. It would have taken me a little longer, but believe me, I would have changed the tire just fine on my own. Trust me!"

The big guy looks at the other two and smiles. He's wearing a loose sweater, burgundy in color, with a tight neck and a black stripe across the chest. "Well, okay, but at least give us a little kiss."

"That's out of the question."

"Hey, it's not like I asked you to blow all three of us..." He laughs, delighted with his joke. "Come on, you're getting off easy with the kiss."

The guy just scoops Ginevra up and pulls her close. Ginevra looks stunned. He puts his arm around her waist and tries to kiss her. Ginevra instinctively draws her face back. The guy sort of licks her on the cheek and continues to try to stick his tongue in her mouth. Ginevra tries to wriggle free. The guy is strong, and he holds her tighter. Ginevra tries to hit him between the legs with a sharp blow of the knee, but he's on top of her, overpowering her. She can't do it. The little guy, the one who changed the tire, watches the whole scene in silence. In fact, he seems somewhat annoyed. The other one is off in a corner, laughing, rooting for his friend. "Good work, Pie. Stick your tongue in her mouth."

Pie, which I imagine is short for Pietro, can't seem to do it. In fact, Ginevra is wriggling and flailing so much that, before she's done, she's basically given him a sort of headbutt to the face.

"Ouch, damn your eyes." Pietro lifts his hands to his forehead.

"That'll teach you, asshole!" Ginevra straightens her hair, standing in the middle of the road not far from him, without running away, without calling me.

"You calling me an asshole? All right, now I'll teach you." The guy heads straight at her with determination. Ginevra lowers her head and wraps her hands around it protectively, curling up like a hedgehog. Pietro grabs her by the jacket.

It's time for me to take action. "Hey, you guys have been entertaining, but enough's enough."

Pietro lets go of her, and the other two turn in surprise when they see me emerge from the shadows. I head toward them.

"So who the fuck are you?"

"A guy who just happened to be passing by. How about you, who the fuck do you think you are?"

Pietro looks at me. He's weighing whether it's worth his trouble to answer me. In other words, whether or not he can take me on. He decides to go for it. "Oh, get the fuck out of my sight, why don't you."

Wrong answer. I let fly instantly with a straight punch, and it's perfect. He's not fast enough to even see it coming. I catch him with the edge of my knuckles, but still with plenty of oomph, just enough to smash in his nose. I see him wobble on both legs, and he desperately tries to get off a reaction.

I hit him again, with a left straight this time, square to the right eyebrow, and this time the impact is full and precise and nasty. He crumples to the ground with a dull thump. He doesn't have time to move before I catch him midway with a kick right to the face. Thump. As soon as

I pull my leg back, a puddle of blood starts to form. Lots of blood pours out from his nose to the asphalt, slow and gooey, in the dim light.

Pietro, or whatever the fuck his name is, is lying there openmouthed, and as he breathes, he's making strange little bubbles with that rivulet of blood that's catching on his lips. Every so often he spits out a few drops, mixed with saliva here and there. He's not laughing anymore.

"Okay, then." I look at Ginevra. "Come on, let's go. Otherwise we'll be late."

I take the flat tire, and I toss it into the trunk and shut the hatch. I walk past the little guy who changed the tire, and once I'm past him, I notice the other one, closer to the car. He's slow to figure things out. I smash his face in with a right straight. I find his ear somehow caught between my thumb and forefinger, and I grab it tight, twisting it angrily. I'd like to rip it off his head.

"Ouch, fuck, ouch."

"Get the hell out of my way, asshole." I give his ear one last brutal twist, and then I let him go. He stands there, bent over, his hands clasped in pitiful prayer over his ears as I get into the car. I wait for Ginevra to shut her door, and I take off, fast. I look at the three of them in the rearview mirror. By now they're far away, enveloped in the night that separates us from them.

"So, how are you doing?"

She sits in silence.

I try to make her laugh. "Those three don't know how lucky they were. If the third dan went to town on them, they'd be sorry now, wouldn't they?"

But I can't get her to laugh. She's not even going to

talk. I look at her. Her hair is hanging down, as if defeated, covering part of her face. Her lips, half open, look out from her hiding place, uncertain and undecided, trembling slightly.

"Come on, Ginevra. It's okay now."

"What the fuck do you mean, it's okay? Just think if I'd had a flat tire and I'd been alone."

"But you weren't."

"Still, it could have happened. What if those three had stopped, then what would have happened?"

"Maybe what could have happened is that I was passing by on my motorcycle, instead of them, and very simply I helped you to change your tire." I try to calm her down.

"I can't believe what assholes you men all are. The three of them, taking advantage of one girl, all alone, what pieces of shit!"

We sit in silence, and I continue to drive. Gin turns up the radio. "I really like this song. Do you know what the words mean?"

I try to listen to it but I can't lie to myself. I've learned perfectly well how to use a computer, how to do graphics, 3D and all the rest, but I've always struggled with English. "I get some of it..."

"It says, 'Don't know much about history, don't know much biology...'" Gin continues to translate, saving me from embarrassment.

I listen to her. "I like those words."

"It's a pretty song."

I don't know why, but it seems to have just happened along, perfect for the moment. "Yes, it's pretty."

And right away, another song starts on the radio. This

time, though, I don't have any problems. "You, dressed in flowers or headlights in the city, in the fog or in colors, picking roses barefoot and then..." I let myself go. I look out, into the dark of night. One of those strange coincidences, the right music at the right moment, a car that doesn't belong to you, a road without streetlights, without traffic, the infinite in front of you, a girl at your side. A very pretty girl, by the way.

She adjusts her jacket. "How long until we're supposed to be there?"

Just then we pass the exit right before the tunnel for Prima Porta. They're all there, Bardato, Manetta, Zurli, Blasco, and some other people besides. I also glimpse a few women. I zip past without stopping.

"No, we'll be there in a minute." I accelerate, but anyway I'm pretty sure they don't recognize me. They expect me to come on a motorcycle. And alone. Instead I'm in a car and with *her*. I go on driving as if nothing had happened. Gin looks out the window.

"You see that? There's a group right there, waiting for someone who's running late. What a ridiculous place to arrange to meet someone."

She looks at me right after she says it. My heart is pounding. I can't believe she's figured it out.

"Right, what a ridiculous place."

She continues looking at me. "This is a strange situation, isn't it?"

"What situation?" I hope she doesn't want to talk about the group again.

"Well, the fact that we're here in this car, you and me, two perfect strangers. And all sorts of things have happened. The minute we met we were already practically having a fistfight. And all over just twenty euros."

"Which you were trying to steal from me."

"True, but don't keep getting lost in the details. Then we have a blowout, and I have to change the tire."

"Go on. Don't you get lost in the details either."

Gin smiles.

"Three guys stop, one of them tries to come on to me, you beat them up, and now, just to end in glory, we're going to dinner with a group of your friends. We already seem like one of those typical couples. Just an ordinary night out, with a few unexpected twists."

"Right, except that we're not a couple."

"Okay, certainly."

I continue driving, but her statement sounds strange to me. "Well, that 'Okay, certainly' doesn't just mean *Okay, certainly*. There's a lot more behind it, right?" I look at her, waiting for an answer.

"Excuse me, eh, but what are we, an item, you and me?"

"Not at the moment, no."

"No, the correct answer in this case, seeing that we're even discussing it, should be clear and simple, just *no*, not 'no, not at the moment.' Is that understood?"

"Okay, certainly."

"So, we're not an item."

"No."

"Oh, great."

I wait a few seconds. "For the moment."

Gin looks at me with some annoyance: "You always want the last word, don't you?"

"Always."

"Well, let's put it this way. We're not a couple for now, and for sure not for the rest of the evening. And if you continue to argue, then I'll add other, much later dates. I could even stretch it out for months, is that clear?"

"Crystal clear." I smile. "I have learned one thing, which is that certainty, when it's too emphatic, is synonymous with insecurity. Should I make things even clearer?"

"Yes."

"It would have been better if you'd just said 'for now.'" I smile again.

Gin shakes her head. "For now I'm going to stop because I'm sick of this. And do you seriously think we should be sitting here arguing about the fact that we're not a couple?"

"True, usually people only argue when they already *are* a couple. It must mean that we got started backward."

"We haven't gotten started at all, in any way, shape, or form."

I slowly brake to a halt and pull over.

Gin looks at me with a hint of worry. "Now what are you going to do?"

"The plan was to meet here, but I don't see anyone. They must have left because we were running late."

"Then *you're* late."

"Okay. *I'm* late."

"And why on earth are you agreeing with me?"

"If we start arguing about every single thing like this, we're going to break up before we ever become an item."

This time Gin breaks into laughter. I laugh along with her. We look at each other, in the aftermath of an appointment that never existed.

The music is blasting, loud. They're playing a mixed sequence of golden oldies and new hits. "How great! This one is the best!"

Well, of course it is. They're playing the mythical "Love Me Two Times" by the Doors.

*"Love me two times, girl, one for tomorrow one just for today...Love me two times, I'm goin' away...*But I'm not going to translate that for you."

"I think I understand what it's saying."

All around us is darkness. But for now, maybe she's right. It's probably better to go.

"Where are you taking me?"

"We're going to dinner, just you and me. That'll mean that you meet my friends some other time."

ↄ

"What other time?" I look at Step, waiting for a reaction. I decide to accept the truce. "Well, if it ever happens."

"There, that's better. *If* it ever happens."

All satisfied, I turn up the volume on the radio, and I change the station, frantically searching for who knows what other song. Then, without letting him see me, in the dim light inside the car, out of the corner of my eye, I glance at Step.

I can't believe it. Me, Gin, in a car with him. *If my folks knew about this.* I don't know why, but it's always the first thing that pops into my mind. I mean, what if my folks knew that right now I'm in a car with a stranger, that is, with someone they think is a stranger, what would they say?

I can just imagine my mother. *"What, have you lost your mind? Ginevra, you should never put your trust in anyone. I must have told you a thousand times..."* Oh, there's no two ways about it, whatever it is, and I don't know why, but my mother always says that she must have already told me it a thousand times. Who knows? One thing is certain. She'd never expect this.

And after all, what could I tell her? You know, it was just to fill up my tank. How could I explain to her the way things really are? No, I don't want to think about it. I can't even believe it myself.

"You know who you reminded me of earlier?"

"When?"

"When I was changing the tire, and those three morons arrived."

"No, what did I remind you of?"

"Richard Gere."

"Richard Gere?" Step asks.

"Right, in that scene in *An Officer and a Gentleman*, when he and his friend go out with those two girls and they step into a bar. But at the door, there's a guy who starts hassling the girls, and Richard Gere does everything he can not to get into a fight, but in the end, it's more than he can put up with, so he punches the guy's face in."

"So was Richard Gere a third dan?"

"No, dummy. That was straight out of full-contact boxing."

"Wow, you know your way around this stuff."

"I already told you that. I've done kickboxing and taken a few full-contact lessons. Don't believe me? Sooner or later, I'm pretty sure I'll have a chance to prove it to you."

"Oh, that seems more than likely. And anyway, more than *An Officer and a Gentleman*, I think the reference we're looking for is a different one. Ezekiel 25:17: 'And I will strike down upon thee with great vengeance and furious anger those who attempt to poison and destroy my brothers and you will know my name is the Lord when I lay my vengeance upon thee.'"

"Oh, modest, aren't you? Anyway, you like *Pulp Fiction*."

"Yes."

"And you like it a lot, too, to judge from the way you took care of them!"

Step smiles and goes on driving. Who knows what he was trying to say with that line. Better not ask, I guess.

I watch him as he drives. His left elbow is resting on the sill of the car window, and his left hand is propping up his chin. His right hand is up high, at the top center of the steering wheel, gripping it firmly and accompanying the curves gently. He has a tattoo on his wrist, right next to a half-cuff gold bracelet. The tattoo seems to me to be a...I lean a little to take a closer look at it.

"It's a seagull."

"What?"

"It's a seagull, the tattoo I have on my wrist."

He smiles at me, taking his eyes off the road for a moment.

I can sense myself blushing, but I'm sure he doesn't notice. "Keep your eyes on the road."

"And you keep your eyes on your own tattoos."

"I don't have any tattoos."

"Wouldn't your folks let you get just one?" Step smiles in an obnoxious way, clearly mocking me.

"My folks don't have any say in the matter. It was my own decision."

"Ah, certainly, I understand..." He looks at me and lifts one eyebrow. "Your own decision."

"Yes, all mine."

We ride along for a while in silence.

Then, after a bit, I get annoyed. "Anyway, I lied to you. I have a tattoo, a beautiful one, but I doubt you'll ever get to see it."

"Is it well hidden?"

"That depends on your point of view."

"What do you mean?"

"Oh, you understood perfectly well."

"Sure, but I don't know how *perfectly well* I understood, or maybe I should say, *where* I understood."

"It's a small rose at the base of my spine, okay?"

"Better than okay. I love plucking flowers!"

"Then you should know that it's covered with thorns."

"You always have an answer on the tip of your tongue, don't you? But my hands are covered with calluses." He smiles back.

He has a nice smile. I can't deny that. But I can't tell him that either. He has a dimple on his left cheek. Oh, fuck it, I really like him. Plus, he's completely different from Francesco. I don't know why he should pop into my mind right now, of all times. Maybe because that whole thing with him cheating is still burning my butt. Francesco is the last boyfriend I've had. Actually, the only one.

Chapter 12

A curve appears ahead that comes in handy. Practically ninety degrees and sharply to the right. I reach around and grab the steering wheel from the bottom and steer with all my strength to the right. Gin lurches against me, as if catapulted in my direction. I slam on the brakes, screeching to a halt with Gin in my arms, and I kiss her on the mouth.

"At last," I mutter under my breath, and then I venture deeper into her mouth. "Ouch," as she bites down hard. I lift my hand to my mouth and let go of her.

Gin goes back to her seat. "Is that all? I was hoping for something better."

I run my fingers over my lips, looking for blood. None I can see.

Gin has assumed a defensive stance, both fists at the ready. "All right then, Stefano, or Step, or whatever the fuck you think your name is, are you ready to fight?"

I look at her with a smile. "You have some prompt reflexes, don't you?"

She punches me hard in the shoulder, one punch after the other, a series of impacts all to the exact same spot.

"I'm sorry, Gin. I didn't mean to do it. But it's just that

we're here, okay?" I hop out of the car fast, before she gets a chance to start hitting me again. "Shut the door, if you don't mind. Oh, hey, do whatever you want, after all, it's your car, right?"

Gin slams the car door and catches up with me. She looks up at the sign. THE COLONEL.

"Truce, okay? Come on, let's go eat a nice big steak."

"Okay. For the truce, we can do that, but for the dinner...it's on you, right?"

"That depends."

"On what?"

"On how things go after dinner."

"Here's what happens after dinner: I'm going to drive you back to your motorcycle and then we're done. Is that clear? Tell me so right away, otherwise I'm not eating so much as a crumb of the bruschetta. Of all things, trying to extort something for dinner. You make me sick!"

Gin walks into the restaurant. I follow her. We sit at a table reasonably far from the oven, which is putting out too much heat. I take off my jacket.

A waiter hurries over to take our orders.

"All right, guys, what can I bring you?"

"Well, the young lady will just have a plate of bruschetta. But I'll have a nice first course of tagliatelle with artichokes, and then a massive steak, make it a bistecca alla fiorentina, and a salad on the side." I look at her with a smile. "Or has the signorina thought things over and decided otherwise?"

Gin looks up at the waiter. "I'll have what he's having. Thanks. And could you also bring me a nice big beer?"

"A beer for me too."

The waiter jots it all down in a hurry and then walks away.

"If you want to go dutch, you're going to have to tell me where you live, and tomorrow I'll bring you the money, okay? That's just to make it clear that there's no dessert."

"Oh, there isn't? But if you look carefully, you'll see how wrong you are. They offer tartufo gelato, which I love, especially with an espresso poured over it. Affogati al caffè."

"Step, where are you? I couldn't see you for a second there. You'd just turned into a bourgeois bore like all the others."

Vittorio, the Colonel himself, comes over. "Hey, you've lost weight, you know that?"

"I was living in New York for two years."

"Oh, really? So that's why we haven't seen you around here. Is the food so bad there?" He laughs heartily at his own witticism.

"Ha ha, Vitto. You're always a funny guy! Have them bring us a bruschetta right away, could you?"

I set the keys to Gin's car on the table while Vittorio heads away. Older but still cheerful. He has the face of an overgrown child with apple-red cheeks, little tufts of silvery white hair over the ears, and a balding dome, invariably pink from the roasting heat of pork chops and massive Florentine steaks.

I look around. The place isn't packed, and the people are quiet, not fancy, not dressed up. They are probably recovering from a hard day's work, happy to have a nice plate of food set in front of them. A couple at a nearby table are eating without talking. He's gnawing away at a bone from a pork chop. She's just popped a fried potato into her mouth, and now she's licking her fingers. She meets my gaze and smiles. I smile back.

Gin goes on the offensive. "Let's get this one thing clear. Dinner's on who?"

"I'm paying for dinner."

"Oh, in that case, I'll stay for the meal."

Vittorio sets the bruschetta down on the table. "All right then, would the signorina care for one too?"

Gin rapidly grabs the bruschetta off my plate and takes a tremendous bite out of it, gobbling down the fresh tomatoes that Vittorio slices lovingly, not like those tomatoes chopped fine in the afternoon and left in a metal bowl in the refrigerator to chill.

"Bring me another one, Vit," I say.

"Yum, delicious." Gin puts a piece of tomato in her mouth and licks her fingers. "Good job, Step! I'd say the food is pretty good here."

Suddenly, I hear a couple of voices. "Over here, it's Step! I knew it. I told you that was him."

I can't believe it. They're all here, right behind me. Slipstream, Balestri, Bardato, Zurli, Blasco, Lucone, Bunny...Except for one, the best of them all: Pollo. I feel a stab of pain in my heart. I don't want to think about it, not now. I feel a shivery chill, and for a moment, I shut my eyes. No, not now, please.

Luckily, Schello throws his arms around my neck. "You turncoat, what are you doing, being a Bulgarian separatist?"

"American separatist, if anything."

"Oh, right, because he's been in the States. So why didn't you show up at the meet point? We were all there. Now he's having dinner with his woman."

"Okay, for starts, I'm not his woman."

"Second, look out boys. She's a third dan."

"Are you done with this thing about the third dan? You're becoming repetitive," Gin says.

"Me? You're the one who's pointed it out three times since we've met. And you're so completely third dan that I had to deck a guy just to defend you."

"Okay, Doubting Thomases. You asked for it." Gin gets up from the table, takes a long circuit around my friends and looks at them each for a second. Then, without a second thought, she whips around, grabs Schello by his jacket with both her hands, hoists him onto her hip, and then bends forward suddenly. Perfectly, without hesitating.

Schello's eyes bug out, and Gin bends her right leg and pushes upward, assisting herself with her shoulders. Schello flies away like a feather in the wind and is set down, on his back, directly on the silent couple's table. Now they'll have a better idea of what to talk about.

If for no other reason, Schello's sudden landing is going to become a story to tell, verging on the urban legend.

Schello gets to his feet, moaning with pain. "Ouch, what the fuck was that?"

"A third dan or thereabouts," Gin replies promptly.

Everyone laughs. "Hilarious." "She's too cool." "Yeah, your girlfriend is really something."

"I'm not his girlfriend!"

"Not yet," I say.

We all laugh, and then Vit luckily weighs in. "Hey, that's enough. Let me bring you a nice cool limoncello, come on. On the house."

Then he puts his arm around Schello and leads him back to the group. "You guys haven't changed a bit, have you?

I'm happy to see you, no doubt about it. I don't know why it is, Step, but when you're around, the evening out is never dull. Come on, all of you sit down now. Shall I get you a table for twelve?"

"Maybe Step wants to continue his romantic dinner."

I look at Gin. She throws her arms wide, helplessly. "We'll just have to do that some other time, right, honey?"

No doubt about it, she can be funny. "Why, yes, dearest, we'll do it next time. The next time your gas tank and your wallet are empty."

They all sit down, making a tremendous ruckus, shoving chairs aside, laughing, fighting over seating. Then the dinner sails along. Rapid chatter to bring me up to speed on all the latest minor news stories. "Hey, this is one you don't know, Giovanni broke up with Francesca. You'll never guess what she did to him. She hooked up with his best friend Andrea."

Guido Balestri takes up the narrative. "Oh, this piece of news is a bombshell. Alessandra Fellini finally put out! For Davide. Now they call him 'Er Goccia.' The Drop. And you know why, Step? It was four years of waiting, like Chinese water torture."

I watch them as they eat. Nothing. Not a single change. They're quite a show. They stuff their faces with the food as it arrives, as usual. They stab their forks into the air-dried, cooked pork lonza, the prosciutto, and the salami. They devour the cold cuts, talking spiritedly.

Then come the skewers bursting with savory meats and vegetables. Everyone grabs frantically to get theirs. They're still piping hot and steaming with sausages, bell peppers, fresh off the grill, and they're repurposed as aromatic swords for frantic fencing matches between Schello and Lucone.

Hook joins in with the two swashbucklers and the battle is on. The sound of clashing metal fills the room, occasionally muffled by bits of roast meat. Schello lunges, and Lucone promptly parries.

And there, in the fray, a sausage goes flying. Gin catches it midair with her right hand, sharp reflexes, and then to make it even better, she bites off a piece.

"Wow! Did you see the speed? I'll bet it reminded you of a movie, try to remember which..."

"It's true, it did remind me of something, a scene from a movie, right, but what movie?"

"Let me help you. Here's a hint. It's the story of a prostitute, or actually, really, more than the story. It's a fairy tale about a prostitute."

"It's *Pretty Woman*." She looks at me, raising an eyebrow.

Pretty Woman, of course, with Julia Roberts.

"Well, do you remember it, or not?"

I'm suddenly catapulted backward in time. Me and Babi, Hook and the Sicilian, all of us, who knows why or how, at the movies together. By intermission, Hook and the Sicilian had left. Then I could finally take Babi's hand and hold it for the rest of the film while she fed me popcorn.

"Yes, I remember."

But I don't tell her the full story of my time watching *Pretty Woman*.

"Come on, the scene where the waiter catches the escargot that Vivian has let fly. That's the name of the Julia Roberts character in the movie. She's trying to get the escargot out of the shell, and it flies across the room."

"Yeah, of course. In spite of all the lessons that the hotel manager gives her."

"You see that you remember it? Step acts like a tough guy, but deep down, he's just a big softy!"

"Way, way deep down."

"But I like to excavate. Who's in a hurry? When I was a little girl, I wanted to grow up to be an archeologist. And then I figured out that I suffer from claustrophobia, and I never would have been able to enter a pyramid anyway."

Just then Schello pulls out the boom box and quickly pushes play. "Every meal needs a good soundtrack." Out of the speaker of his Aiwa boom box, the theme from *Hair* starts up, full volume. Everyone starts dancing in their seats, waving their arms in the air in time to the music.

Then the most incredible thing happens. Gin climbs up onto her chair and lets loose, doing her best karaoke version of the legendary Treat Williams in *Hair*. She puts one foot up onto the tabletop and so on, one step after the other. Gin moves forward, dancing, letting her hair hang down in front and then whipping it back, uncovering her face again. Smiling, then sensual, then tough again, and the whole time, breathtakingly beautiful.

And everyone plays along. They move their now-empty plates aside, grabbing forks and glasses with every step she takes. Hook, Lucone, and Schello, even the other women are up for it. Everyone yanks back everything on the table in front of them. They pretend to be horrified by that outrageous Gin, just like the guests at that long banqueting table in *Hair*. Gin dances incredibly well.

Vit comes running in desperation. "For fuck's sake, what are you all, insane? Go on, get down off of there."

I reach up and grab Gin's arm and pull her down off the table. She's about to fall but I catch her in midair.

"What is it, what's wrong?" she asks.

"Nothing for the moment, but still, we'd better get out of here."

"Wait. Let me get my jacket," and she goes back and grabs her dark denim Levi's jacket and then takes off.

"Ciao, Vit. Sorry to eat and run, but we've got a party to go to."

"Sure you do. There's always a party for you guys, isn't there? I'd throw you a party!" He seems irritated, but he's actually amused, like always. He's standing there, resolute, at the door. He watches as we head out at a dead run, making a tremendous din.

Schello leaps in the air, clicking his heels together sideways like John Belushi, and the other guys laugh. Balestri trudges along. He looks weary, a little tipsy, and who knows what all else. Still, he smiles and spreads his arms as if to say, *That's just the way they are.*

"Just don't ever say I didn't buy you dinner," I say to Gin.

And so we run out into the night, following the others, hand in hand. And at that instant, in the night, I have just one thought. I'm happy that Gin robbed me of twenty euros' worth of gasoline.

Chapter 13

A little excessive but still hilarious and likable, your friends. Sometimes we women find ourselves going out with certain stiffs," Gin says from the passenger seat of her car.

"Who is *we women*?"

"Okay, then let's just say that sometimes *I've* found myself going out with certain stiffs. Is that better?"

"A little better."

"Okay then. So what else should I say? How about *Living legends, those friends of yours*! Is that better?"

"*Living legends.* What a horrible expression. Sounds like the title of a movie about Carlo Vanzini. You should just say that they're epic, maybe!"

Gin starts laughing. "Okay, touché." Then she looks at me and furrows her brow. "Oops, apologies. You don't know French, do you?"

"Of course I do. *Touché* means..."

I suddenly swerve into a super-tight curve, and Gin falls straight into my arms. "There, is that what *touché* means? Am I right?"

She tries to haul off and slap me, but this time I'm faster than she is. I block her hand.

"Oops, apologies. Or should that be, pardon! I didn't mean to '*touché*' you, mais tu es très jolie! So how does my French seem to you? Anyway, we've arrived. But that's something I don't know how to say."

I get out of the car. Gin is furious.

"So answer me this. If your friends are so *epic*, why did you pretend not to see them when we drove past them at the meeting place?"

Fuck. Nothing escapes her eye.

Gin gets back in her car, starts the engine, and takes off at top speed, tires screeching and fishtailing.

I run for my motorcycle. Another yard and I'm on it.

ﾍ

Would you just take a look at this asshole? He's so full of himself. Who the hell does he think he is?

"So, at least a little, you like him," I say, answering my own question.

"But if you like all these things about him, then tell me. Why did you steal the keys to his motorcycle?"

"Because no one can touch me without my authorization. Is that clear? And Step lacked authorization. And I'm just going to keep these nice keys as a reminder of the fact."

Oh, Christ, it's Step. He's on his motorcycle. How did he get it to start?

"I'm sure you were thinking about me. Pull over."

He must have hot-wired it. I slow down and finally stop.

"Well? Nice job, very amusing," Step says.

"What's amusing?"

"Ah, so you're even going to pretend you're clever? The keys."

"Oh, right, sorry. I just realized I had them. Maybe you got the wrong jacket and put them in my pocket. Or maybe I took them by mistake."

"Ah, if you're talking about mistakes, you definitely made a mistake. You took my house keys."

"No, seriously?"

"Oh, yes, I'm willing to swear to it," he says.

"I can't believe it."

"Well, believe it. Come on, get in the car, and I'll follow you home."

"No, don't bother."

"I *will* bother, thank you very much. You're one of those dangerous girls."

"What's that supposed to mean?"

"You have another flat tire, someone helps you to change it, and then you decide to trust them, you die a horrible death, and the last person you were seen with alive was me."

"Oh, is that the only reason?" I ask.

"People say that I like a quiet life, when I can get it. Oh, come on, just get in the car and stop causing trouble."

Gin heaves a sigh of exasperation and gets in the car. She starts the engine, but before taking off, she rolls down her window. "I know why you're doing it."

I pull up next to her on my motorcycle. "Oh, really, why is that?"

"That way you'll find out where I live."

"Your license plate reads *Rome R24079*. It would take me all of ten minutes and a phone call to a friend of mine at city hall to find out your address. And I'd have to do a lot less driving. Come on, get going!"

I take off, tires screeching. Jesus, Step knows my license tag by heart. I haven't even memorized it yet.

In a flash, he's right behind me. I see him in the rearview mirror. He's following me, but he doesn't pull up too close. How strange, he's cautious. I never would have expected that. Well, all things considered, I guess I don't know him all that well. Go figure!

⌒

I downshift and hang back at a safe distance. You never know, Gin might pull some prank like slamming her brakes on. That's the best way there is of putting a motorcyclist out of commission. If you're not paying close attention, you can't brake in time. You can kiss your front fork and motor-cycle goodbye. You smash into the car and you can forget about chasing them down.

Corso Francia, Piazza Euclide, Via Antonelli. She's show-ing off, conceited thing. She doesn't stop at any of the lights. She zips past the Cinema Embassy at top speed. She roars around the cars lined up at the red light and then goes straight and turns first right and then left, never once using her turn indicators. One sleepy driver honks his horn at her but far too late.

Via Panama. She stops just short of Piazzale delle Muse. Gin parks by whipping between two cars without touching them, in just one fell swoop. The product of practice and precision.

"Hey, you're good at parking."

"You say that because you haven't seen the rest."

"So do you ever let people say things without insisting on getting the last word with your little wisecracks?"

"Okay. Well then, thanks for dinner, I really enjoyed myself, you were fantastic, your friends are *epic*. I'm sorry about that little mistake with the keys, and thanks for seeing me home. How was that? Am I forgetting anything?"

"Yes, aren't you forgetting to invite me upstairs to your place?"

"What? No way in hell. I haven't invited any of my boyfriends upstairs, so you can just forget about me inviting *you*, a complete stranger. The very idea!"

"Why, have there been many boyfriends?"

"Lots of them.... Ah, buonasera, Signor Valiani."

I turn around to see who she's saying good evening to, but there's no one there. I hear the sound of the gate behind me.

"Ta-dah!"

I turn back around. Gin is on the other side of the gate, which is still quivering from being slammed. She shut it behind her. She was super quick.

Gin runs toward the street door. It only takes me a second. I vault over the gate, and I run toward her while she looks in her pocket for the key to the street door.

I wrap my arms around her from behind. "Ta-dah! When you were little, did you used to play red light, green light? You weren't fast enough to turn around before I caught you. Now you're mine."

Her hair is scented. But nothing sweet. Oh, God, I hate sweet-smelling perfumes. *Her* hair smells fresh, electric, cheerful, full of life.

I'm holding my cheek close to hers. Her check is smooth, soft, and cool as a magnificent peach. I open my lips and press them against that cheek. There's a faint evening breeze that brings the scent of jasmine from the garden.

"Knock, knock, Gin, can I come in?"

"You don't know what you might find there."

"I never walk into a place I don't know how to walk out of."

"What a striking phrase."

"You like it? I let the screenwriters for the film *Ronin* use it for free."

"You jerk."

While I embrace her, I hold her tight and rock her gently right and left. I sing her a little something under my breath. It's a song by Bruce Springsteen but I'm not sure if she recognizes it. The soft slow bars of music I sing are transformed into a warm breath that mixes with her hair and down onto her neck.

Gin lets her arms relax. I continue singing, slowly, moving my body. She follows my movements now. I see her mouth, and it's beautiful. It's partly open, dreamy, sighing, and it's shivering ever so slightly.

Slowly, gently, I caress her neck. I plant the palm of my hand on her cheek. Gin turns her face to relax against the door, her hair hanging forward and suddenly, half-hidden by that scented black river of hair, her mouth appears. Like a rose of love freshly opened, soft and wet. She sighs and sketches little clouds of mist on the glass of the door. Then I kiss her. And she smiles. She nibbles back at me, and it's wonderful. It's dramatic, it's comedic, it's heaven...No, it's better than that. It's hell.

"Gin, is that you?"

A man's voice behind me. Now of all times. No, I can't believe that we hadn't heard a thing. Dazed by desire. I whip around, ready to parry a blow rather than throw a punch. I look at him. This guy isn't too tall, and he's skinny.

"Sheesh, I can't believe it." The look on his face is one of amusement more than anger.

Gin smooths back her hair, and she's annoyed. "Well, believe it, or should we kiss again?"

I'm still standing there with my fists at the ready.

"Stefano, this is my brother, Gianluca."

I put down my arms and heave a faint sigh, but it's nothing to do about any worry over a fistfight. That's the least of my concerns. I have other thoughts. Which is perhaps the most worrisome aspect.

"Ciao." I extend my hand and smile. Certainly, this isn't the best way to make a brother's acquaintance. Getting caught making out with his sister.

"Well, now that you're in safe hands, I can go," I say.

I head off toward the gate and leave them behind me, brother and sister, framed in the front door. I start my motorcycle and take off, leaving in that redolent nocturnal bouquet of jasmine a kiss, only half-consummated.

⌒

Gianluca looks at me in amazement. "Seriously, Gin, I can't believe it!"

"Believe it. Your sister is just a female like any other, and if it's any consolation to you, she's not a lesbian, as you've had occasion to observe."

"No, you don't understand. What I can't believe is that you were actually smooching with Step!"

I've finally found the key, and I open the door. "Why, do you know him?"

"Do I know him? I'd like to know who doesn't know him in the city of Rome."

"Well, here I am. You have the living paragon right in front of you. I'd never heard of him."

Then I think to myself that it's just one lie, more or less.

"I don't believe you. It really isn't possible that you've never heard of him. Come on, everyone knows who he is. He even appeared in a newspaper on his motorcycle while he was pulling a wheelie, with his girlfriend riding on back, surrounded by cops. I can't believe it! My sister kissing Step." Gianluca shakes his head.

Together they step into the elevator.

"Anyway, I wouldn't want to destroy any of your myths, but the famous Step, rebel, performer of wheelies with women clinging to his back..."

"Right, right, I get it. So what about him?"

"He kisses exactly the same as all the other guys."

At that very same instant, I hit five, the button for our floor. Then I take a look at myself in the mirror. I'm blushing. That was another lie. An even bigger one. And I know it perfectly well.

Chapter 14

I'm racing down the street on my motorcycle at top speed. Piazza Ungheria, straight toward the zoo. I can't find a word to describe Gin. But I try, all the same. Likable? No. Cute as a bug? Oh, come on! Pretty, amusing, different. But why should I try to define her in the first place? Maybe she's all those things, put together. And maybe she's more than that. I don't want to think about it.

But something pops into my mind and it makes me smile. It was with Gin that I went by Piazza Euclide, following alongside her car. I didn't even glance at the Falconieri High School. I didn't think about waiting for Babi to get out of school or about me waiting for her, about that time we had.

But I'm thinking about it now. Suddenly, like a bolt out of the blue. A memory. That morning. As if it were happening right now. *I was outside her school. I was watching from a distance. I saw her come down the stairs and laugh with her girlfriends, chatting about who knows what. I smiled. Maybe it was about me.*

I waited for her. "Ciao."

"What a nice surprise! You came by to pick me up at school," Babi said.

"Yes, I want you to run away with me."

"Mamma would deserve it. She's never on time to pick me up."

Babi climbed up behind me on my motorcycle. She immediately held on tight.

"Wait, now, let me get this straight. You're not running away with me because you even want to be with me. It's just to punish your mother for being chronically late. You really are a piece of work."

"Okay, but excuse me very much, if I can kill two birds with one stone, isn't that better?"

We went by her sister, who was out front waiting too.

"Dani, tell Mamma I'll be home later. Don't run now, okay?"

A short while later on Via Cola di Rienzo, at the Gastronomia Franchi, we walked out of the delicatessen with one of those vegetable fritters they only make there, and which Babi was in love with. They're fried perfectly, still hot, with a handful of napkins, a bottle of mineral water to split between us, and ravenous appetites. We just gobbled them down. She was sitting on the motorcycle, and I was standing facing her. We weren't talking, just gazing into each other's eyes.

Then, without warning, it started to sleet. It came down heavy, an incredible downpour of frozen slush. So we ran, we ran like crazy, and we managed to find shelter in a doorway, locked but still offering a modicum of space, practically slipping and falling just to get out from under that sleet. There we stood, chilled to the bone, in the shadow of the terrace above. Then the sleet gradually softened into snow. It was snowing in Rome. But practically before touching the ground, that snow melted.

We smiled at each other again for a moment, she took another bite of her fritter, and I tried to kiss her . . .

And then *poof*, as quick as that sleet, this memory

melts away too. There's never a good reason for a memory. It just arrives like that, without warning, without asking permission. And you never know when it will disappear. The only thing that you *do* know, alas, is that it will come back. Usually only for split seconds at a time.

But by now I know how to handle it. The minute the memory arrives, you need to turn and run from it as fast as you can go. Do it immediately, without regrets or second thoughts, make no concessions, don't even focus on it, don't stop to play with it. Don't let it hurt you.

There, that's better. Now it's over. That snow has melted away entirely.

Chapter 15

It's morning, and as Marcantonio and I walk past Da Vanni, it is teeming with people. All of them busy, some well-dressed, or fantastically dressed, or poorly dressed, or even deplorably dressed. A broad range of styles, heterogeneous to the brink of insanity. The useful and useless of the great and sequin-spangled world of television. Inevitably present. One way or another. Always.

"Hi, there, Signor Director," a man says.

"Buongiorno, Dottore," another man says.

"Do you remember me? I didn't want to disturb you, but what ever became of that show?" a woman asks.

"In any case, we absolutely have to make sure that we cast this young woman."

"Why? What's she like? Is she pretty?" another woman asks.

"What does that matter? We just need her on the show," a man answers.

And so on and so forth. Creating, manipulating, earning, greasing, negotiating, extorting, building, generating excitement, producing, and harvesting hours and hours of television. However it goes, with new ideas, old formats, copied and plagiarized here and there, but always, inevitably, broadcasting. In a thousand different ways, through that little household electric appliance we've all known as long as we've been alive. The TV set, our big brother, our multiple sisters, our second mother.

Or really, perhaps, our first and only. It's kept us company, it's loved us dearly, and it's nursed us from generation to generation, with the same milk from the same cathode udder, long-life, high protein, curdled and stale.

"You understand?" Marcantonio asks.

"So that's what you think. And you came here all the way from Verona to create television," I say. "To create images and logos in noble fashion."

Marcantonio looks at me. He smiles. "Good work, you're improving. Aggressive and a bit of a son of a bitch, that's the way I like you."

"I recognize it: *Platoon*."

"You're really starting to amaze me. Come with me. Let's go see how work is progressing on the TdV."

"What's the TdV?" I ask.

"What, you don't know? The Teatro delle Vittorie, RAI's Theater of Victories, the great and historic temple of old-time Italian television."

"Well, if it's a *great and historic temple*, by all means, let's go."

We cross the street. A used-book market occupies the space in the gardens. Young men and women looking more or less intellectual leaf through low-cost books. Then we approach the entrance to the theater.

Marcantonio rapidly lights a Chesterfield and smokes hungrily. "Buongiorno, Tony," he says to the man at the front door.

"Hello, Count. How's it going?"

"Not well since the fall of the Italian monarchy."

Tony bursts out laughing. He's an unassuming door-man and security guard at the Teatro delle Vittorie, and he appears happy to be working there. I suppose that, in his small way, he's found power. He manages the door. He lets in important people, directors, extras, and actors, and he stops others from coming in just because they lack a pass. In other words, a bouncer of the media arts.

"Right you are, Count. At least you could have sent me a team of plebeians to open this emergency door. I called the technicians a week ago. But no one's shown their face."

I think to myself, *The guy is a stickler.* Then he leans forward and confides further details in a low voice. "It's not a minor detail, I use this door to go take a pee in the downstairs restroom. Instead, the other way, I have to go the long way round...a real pain in the ass." And he bursts out laughing.

"Tony, we finally have someone who's going to solve this problem of yours, a matter of top priority."

"And who would that be?"

"Him, Step!"

"And who is he, a member of your court?"

"Don't be ridiculous. In any case, Tony, are you interested in peeing without waiting—or aren't you?"

"I hope so. Hey, Step, if you can do it, I'll owe you a favor."

"Well, you might want to show me where this door is."

"Right you are." Tony serves as our guide. "Come right this way."

Inside the theater, work is proceeding loudly, metal clanging, electric saws, welding sparks. "It's almost finished.

They're just installing the lights," Tony explains almost apologetically. "Here, this is the door. I've tried everything I could think of. Nothing, no good. Not a fucking thing to be done."

I look at it carefully. It's one of those panic-bar doors, and someone must have switched on the internal safety lock. Maybe it was Tony himself, and he no longer remembers or wants to admit that he's pulled this boneheaded move. We need the key. Or else . . . "Do you have a metal bar that's not too thick?"

"Like this one?" And he pulls one out of a crate sitting there on the floor. "Obviously, I tried everything I could think of, okay?"

"Pretty close." I insert the bar in the lock and give it a single hard bang. Not even that hard, actually. "Open, sesame." And the door swings open as if by enchantment. "Et voilà, presto fixed-o."

Tony is overjoyed. He seems like a little boy. "Hey, Step, I don't know how to thank you. You're a magician."

I hand back the metal bar. "Well, let's not exaggerate."

Marcantonio takes the situation in hand. "That's right, let's not exaggerate. Just remember that you owe us one favor apiece, understood?"

"We can do that, we can certainly do that." Tony smiles, and he inaugurates the emergency door by using it to head downstairs for a piss.

Marcantonio gives me a wink and walks ahead of me. "Come on, let me show you the theater."

We walk down to the stage, beyond the seats of the orchestra section and beneath the grand arch of the gallery. And there they are. To the sound of an enveloping wall of music, the dancers. Colorful bodysuits, legwarmers pushed low, hair long or short or else partly razored and designed. Blondes, brunettes, redheads, or hair dyed with unnatural color. Physiques sculpted, taut, skinny, well-defined abs. With muscular legs and rounded buttocks and tight bellies. Ready to explode into the splits at the sound of a high note. Perfect, mistresses of agile and cat-like movements, fatigued and exhausted but unfailingly smiling.

The music at high volume fills the whole stage. And they allow themselves to be carried. They intersect, locking limbs, moving in unison to the beat, falling backward, sliding sideways, slaves to the rhythm.

Huge spotlights elevate them, bathing them in shafts of light. The lights caress their bare legs, their small bosoms, their skimpy outfits.

"Stop! Okay, okay, that's enough!" The music comes to a halt. The choreographer, a little man who appears to be in his forties, smiles, satisfied. "Fine, let's take a break. We can start rehearsing again later."

"This is the dance troupe," Marcantonio says.

"Yes, that much was clear to me."

They file past us, smiling, all in a bit of a hurry, all overheated but still sweet smelling and light. Two of three plant a kiss on Marcantonio's cheek. "Ciao, girls." He seems to know them well.

He glances at me, lifting his right eyebrow. "Dancers... God, I love TV!"

I smile, looking at the last dancer in the line. She's a bit smaller than the others, and she goes out at a run. She'd lingered behind to grab her sweatshirt. Rounded and fast-moving, carrying a little more flesh but all of it in the right places. She smiles at me. "Ciao."

I don't have a chance to answer before she's already flown away. "I'm starting to love them too."

"There you go, that's what I want to hear. So, this is the stage, and *that's* our logo. You see, right there, on the proscenium. *The Great Geniuses.* Modestly speaking, my creation."

"I had no doubt about it, you can tell from the touch." I'm lying shamelessly.

"Wait. What are you doing, mocking me?"

"Are you joking?" I smile.

"Well, that same logo is already in 3D in the graphics. This is the idea behind the program: A series of ordinary people, actual inventors, come up on stage and show us how they solved a small or a large problem afflicting our society with just a simple insight."

"That's a powerful idea."

"We introduce them, we array the dancers around them, we build a show around them, and they show us the idea that they've come up with, along with their prototype, already registered with the patent office. It's a pretty simple program, but I think people will find it interesting. That's not all. The people who present their ideas here with us already have a springboard on TV that can take them who knows where. They can make some real money with their inventions."

"Ah, certainly, if those inventions are interesting and if they actually serve some purpose."

"Oh, they are, and they do. Trust me, this is a great show. It's Romani's idea. If you ask me, it's going to be a big hit, like everything else he does. They say Romani has the Midas touch when it comes to TV."

"Because of how much money he makes?"

"Because of all the hits he churns out. Everything he touches really brings in the viewers."

"Well then, I should be happy to work with him."

"Sure, you started at the top. And here they are."

I see them come in, practically in a procession. Romani is leading the group. Following him are two men about thirty-five years old, one heavyset and completely bald with a pair of sunglasses pushed up on his head, the other one skinny with a slightly receding hairline. Behind them is a guy with long but neatly groomed hair. He has an aquiline nose and a darting gaze. He's wearing a green corduroy suit that no longer has cuffs. The cuffs of his trousers were recently altered, and you can see the dark crease. That certainly gave his legs another inch or two, but at the cost of a portion of sartorial elegance.

"All right, then, where are we?" Romani looks around. "Isn't anyone here?"

A short man with blond hair and blue eyes comes galloping up. "Buongiorno, Maestro. I'm just putting up the last lights. It will all be ready for this evening."

"Bravo, Terrazzi. I always say you're the best."

Terrazzi smiles. "I'll head back to the console to fine-tune the focal points of the lights."

"You go, go on."

The guy with long hair approaches Romani. "You always need to encourage them, don't you? Warm them up so they'll be more productive, am I right?"

Romani narrows his eyes and glares at the man. "Terrazzi

is seriously good at what he does, the best of them. He's been doing lighting since before you were born."

The guy with long hair goes back to his place in line in utter silence.

Actually, now he's at the end of the line. He starts looking around again, pretending to take interest in any old random corner of the set. At last, he goes after his right hand and starts chewing on his nails.

"Those are the writers. Romani is the director too. You remember him, don't you?" he asks me in an ironic tone.

"Of course I do. He's the one who gives us our jobs."

"As for the other two, one stout and the other skinny, they're Sesto and Toscani, one half-bald and the other full bald. People call them the Fox and the Cat, and they're Romani's two longtime slaves. At one point, they tried to do a program of their own. It went off the air after just two episodes, and ever since then, we've renamed them the Cat and the Cat. In that little group, the only real fox is Romani, and he's a sly fox. Then, aside from the Cat and the Cat, you have Renzo Micheli, the Serpent. He's from Salerno, and he's got his hands in operations all over the place. Romani has been carrying him around with him for the past year. They call him the Serpent because he has nothing good to say about anyone, not even Romani, in fact."

"Serpent, nice nickname."

"Step, look out for him. He has lots of friends in powerful positions, and he's always coming on to every woman who enters his line of sight, especially young girls."

"In that case, you're giving the wrong guy advice, Mazzocca, if that's the way things are. In that case, *he's* the one who needs to look out for *me*."

I emerge on the street with some gelato after eating lunch with Marcantonio, and I see Gin. I can't believe it. *Here*, too, of all people. I feel like laughing. I walk over. "Well, well, look who's shown up. Hold on, now I get it. You want me to buy you lunch too."

"What, are you kidding me? Dinner was more than I needed," Gin says. "No, I have a question for you. Namely, what are *you* doing here at Da Vanni? Hold on. Wait. Now I get it, you followed me."

"Calm down, just calm down. Why do you think everything always revolves around you? Can't you see? I'm getting a frozen yogurt with a friend."

"Strange. I've been coming here, like, all my life, and I've never seen you before."

"I very much doubt you've been coming here all your life. Maybe you've been coming here for the past two years while I was out of the country."

Marcantonio weighs in. "Excuse me, I hope you won't object if, while you all explore your biographical details, I go inside. And don't take too long, Step. We have an important appointment."

Marcantonio goes back into Da Vanni shaking his head.

The woman with Gin shrugs. "What a jerk your friend is. He didn't even introduce himself."

I turn to address Gin. "Well, so what's up? What are you two doing around here?"

Gin's friend replies, "We're here to audition." Gin elbows her in the ribs. "Ouch!"

"Don't talk so much. You don't even know this guy, and now you're letting him in on all our private business."

I take a taste of my gelato. "And who would you be, a new band? The Spy Girls?"

"Ha, ha, that's rich. You know, Ele, he's great for his phenomenal wisecracks. The whole problem is figuring out when they're jokes and when they're not."

"Ah, I see."

"Well, that wasn't a joke. Just like last night when you were coming on to me—"

"You didn't tell me about that!" Ele looks at us both in surprise.

Gin smiles as she glances at me. "It was something so unimportant that it slipped my mind completely!"

I take my spoon out of my mouth and peer into the bottom of the cup to see if I can scrape out a little more gelato. "Did you tell her that, at a certain point in the proceedings, you were sighing dreamily?"

"Fuck off, you!"

"I don't remember you saying that last night."

"Well, let me say it to you today, not once but twice: Fuck off and re-fuck off!"

I smile. "I just adore your sophisticated elegance."

"Too bad you're not capable of appreciating it in all its charm. Well, we need to be on our way."

They head off. I watch them as they go. Gin, the tough girl, and her friend, a little shorter. Ele, as she calls her, short for Elena, Eleonora, or who knows what other name. They make me laugh.

Without bothering to turn around, Gin raises her left

hand and, in particular, holds her middle finger up so that it's pointing at the sky.

Marcantonio shows up just in time to see that charming salutation. "She's crazy about you, isn't she?"

"Yes, she melts at the sight of me."

Ele and I continue on our way. Ele seems deeply and seriously annoyed. "You want to tell me why you told me nothing about this?"

"No, I swear to you, Ele. It completely slipped my mind, I mean it."

"Sure, no doubt. I mean, you kiss that incredible babe of a guy, and it slips your mind!"

"For real, you like him so much?" I ask.

"Well, for hot's sake, he's hot, but he's not my type. I like the other guy. He looks like a young Jack Nicholson. If you ask me, he has a lot of filthy thoughts in his head. He seems more like the disreputable type."

"And you like your men disreputable?"

"Yes, but tell me, who *is* that incredible bombshell of a guy?"

"You called him an incredible babe of a guy before."

"Well, okay, whatever. What does he do, where does he live, how did you meet him, did you two seriously kiss, and what's his name?"

"Am I really supposed to answer that machine gun burst of questions?"

"Of course you are. What are you waiting for?"

"All right, then, here we go. I'm answering them all,

okay? I don't know, I don't know, I met him last night, there was one kiss, and his name is Stefano."

"Stefano?"

"Step."

"Step? Step Mancini?" Eleonora bugs her eyes out and stares at me.

"Yes, his name is Step. So what?"

She grabs me by the jacket and shakes me physically back and forth. "I can't believe it. Yahoo! We're going to go down in history. At the very least, when I spread word of this, we'll be featured in *Parioli Pocket*. Step the rebel. He rides a dark blue custom Honda 750, he races like Valentino Rossi, he's traded punches with half the population of Rome, he was a regular fixture at Piazza Euclide, a friend of Hook and Schello, and to stand up for his girlfriend, he even fought with the Sicilian. And who does he decide to date? You!"

"Aside from the fact that we're not dating, number one. And number two, who is this woman of his?"

"Ah, then you *do* like him. You've fallen for him!"

"What are you talking about? I'm just curious."

"He was dating a girl who's older than us, I think, and quite attractive, she used to go to Falconieri High School. She's the sister of Daniela, that chubby thing who was dating Palombi, the guy who used to date..."

"I get it, the guy who used to date Giovanna who was going out with Piero who used to go steady with Alessandra and so on and so forth. Your usual endless network. Okay, well, I don't know any of those people, and what's more I couldn't care less about them. Now let's go do this audition because I could use some money."

Chapter 16

Women are arrayed at the center of the stage. Tall, blond, brunette, the occasional redhead. Elegantly dressed, or casual, or bohemian in a desperate attempt to blend together two things that pretend to match. Gym shoes together with perfect charcoal-gray skirt suits, the latest thing, old platform shoes too tall for a fashion that's forgotten about them. Noses that are straight or crudely fixed, or not yet fixed at all due to a shortage of funds. Some women are relaxed, others are nervous, others still are defiant with a bold piercing they're flaunting, while there are a few timid ones who've done a piercing with a small, understated stud. And then there are tattoos displayed more or less openly, and who can say how many others are concealed. The audition girls.

Gin and Ele sneak in and sit in the back.

"All right, then..."

Romani, the Cat & the Cat, the Serpent, and a few other members of the staff are all seated in the front row, ready for this little show, a minor amusement before the real work begins.

I sit down at the far end of the row, with my gelatos

down to the last two spoonfuls, and I enjoy the show from a distance. Gin doesn't see me. She seems self-confident and relaxed with her hands in her pockets. I don't know what group she belongs to. She strikes me as unique.

Her friend isn't kidding around either. Every now and then, she moves her head in an attempt to swish back her hair.

The choreographer has a microphone in his hand. "All right now, take a step forward, introduce yourselves, first and last name, age, and any work you've already done. Look into the central camera, camera two, the one with the little red light with a man who's going to wave at you now. Wave at them, Pino!"

The guy sitting behind the middle TV camera lets go of the camera for a second, without taking his face away from his monitor, and puts his hand in the air to wave at the women.

"Okay! Is that all clear?"

A few of the women indicate a hesitant yes with their heads. Gin, as I expected, remains motionless.

The choreographer drops his arms in disappointment and then speaks into the microphone. "Hey, ladies, let me hear your beautiful voices. Say something to me. Let me know I exist." A half chorus of yeses, okays, and all rights comes back, even a few smiles.

The choreographer seems to be more satisfied this time. "Fine. Then let's get started."

Marcantonio comes over. "Hey, Step, what are you doing back here? Come on. Let's get seated in the front. We'll get a better view."

"No, I'll enjoy it more from here."

"As you prefer." He sits down beside me. "Wait and see, Romani is going to summon us. On every detail, he's going to want our input."

"Okay, and when he calls us, we can go down."

One at a time, the women pass around the microphone and introduce themselves. "Ciao, I'm Anna Marelli, and I'm nineteen. I've appeared on various shows as a presenter, and I'm studying law. I also had a small part in a film by Ceccherini..."

Renzo Micheli, the Serpent, seems seriously interested. "What part did you play?"

"The prostitute, but it was just a cameo."

"Did you like the role?"

Everyone snickers but tries not to be too obvious. Only Romani remains perfectly impassive.

Anna Marelli replies, "Sure, I like making movies. But I think I have more of a future in television."

"Fine. Let's move on to the next one."

"Buongiorno, I'm Francesca Rotondi, I'm twenty-one years old, and I'm about to take my degree in economics. I've been in..."

Romani turns to his right and left and then cranes his neck around and spots us. "Mazzocca, Mancini, come up front."

Marcantonio stands up and gives me a glance. "What did I tell you?"

"All right, let's go. It seems sort of like being in school, but if it's part of the game..."

The women auditioning have the light full in their faces and they can't see. One young woman after another introduces herself. Then the one next to Gin starts. I wind up sitting in the front row, on the right. She still hasn't seen me. But her friend, Ele, has.

Ele naturally doesn't let the occasion pass unobserved. "Hey, Gin." In a stage whisper. "Look who we have in the front row." Gin raises her hand to shade her eyes from the glare. Then she cranes her neck a little and sees me.

I lift my right hand up to my face and, unobtrusively, wave to her. I'm not interested in bothering her. I know that she's there for work. But nothing doing, she takes it the wrong way and once again, as usual, with her left hand extended at her side, she gives me the finger, telling me to go fuck myself. And that makes three.

"You're next, brunette."

This is her big moment but, because she was distracted, she's caught off guard. "What? Oh, right." She takes the microphone that the woman on her right hands to her. "I'm Ginevra Biro, age nineteen, and I'm studying literature with a focus on theater. I've been in a number of shows as a presenter. *Ta-dah.*" Gin pushes both hands forward and then up, taking a step forward and then performing a small bow. "If I'd been holding the usual envelope, it would have flown away."

Then she steps back to her place in line, and everyone breaks into laughter.

"That one was something."

"Yes, funny and cute too."

"Yeah, nice job."

I sit there, watching her, amused like the others. She glances at me, bold and self-confident, by no means intimidated by being onstage in front of everyone with the spotlights focused on her. In fact, she even makes a face at me.

I lean toward Romani. "Excuse me, Dottor Romani..." and he turns around to look at me. "Would you mind if I asked this young lady a question, you know, just to get to know her better?"

He looks at me, curious now. "Would it be a professional question or are you trying to get her phone number?"

"Absolutely work related."

"Well, then, certainly, that's why we're here."

I sit back down again, I look at her, and I give myself a moment. Then I speak up. "What plans do you have for your future?"

"A husband and lots of little children. If you like, you could be one of the children."

A full knockout, and I'm on the canvas. Everyone laughs hysterically. They laugh harder than they needed to. Even Romani laughs and looks over at me, spreading his hands as if to say, *She got you*. And she did. I feel as if I just went into the ring with Mike Tyson. He wouldn't have hurt me this badly. Okay, as you like it, Gin.

I ignore the others and start up again. "In that case, why are you here auditioning instead of going out in pursuit of this husband?"

Gin looks at me and smiles. She pretends to be a nice, naive young lady and replies with modesty. "Why couldn't my ideal man be right here, on this sound stage? You seem to be concerned, but really you shouldn't worry because you, sir, are naturally ruled out of my search from the outset."

A few more snickers.

"Okay, that's enough," says Romani. "Have we heard from everyone?"

"No, actually, I still haven't introduced myself."

Gin's friend, Ele, takes a step forward, making herself known.

"Fine. Then introduce yourself."

"I'm Eleonora Fiori, twenty years old. I've auditioned for a number of shows without much success, but I'm studying industrial design, where I'm doing very well indeed."

Someone comes out with a stupid wisecrack in a muffled voice. "Then why don't you just stick to industrial design, in that case?"

It must have been Sesto, the guy from the Cat & the Cat. But no one laughs. At that point, Micheli, the Serpent, looks around. Romani pretends he didn't hear. And so, of course, does Micheli. Toscani, the other Cat, laughs for a moment. Then, when it becomes clear that it's not in his best interests, he shuts down the laughter in a sort of faint cough, a fake, improvised hoarse hacking.

"Very good. Thank you, ladies."

Romani approaches the choreographer, looks at the sheet of paper in his hand, and points to certain names with his forefinger. Then he looks up and comes toward us. "Do you have any preferences?"

I look at the sheet of paper. There are checkmarks by certain of the names. Five or six have already been selected. I look down at the end of the list. There she is. Ginevra Biro already has her checkmark. Incredible but true, Romani and I have the same opinion. Sesto and Toscani pick one each, and Romani lets them have their way. The Serpent actually picks two, but Romani only lets him have one.

Then Mazzocca arrives and puts in his recommendation. "Romani, it might seem absurd to you, but there's one we absolutely have to take. You might not like her but, if you think about it, picking her would be a flash of genius."

"Okay, let's hear it. Which one?"

"She'll win the hearts of everyone who's insecure, all those who feel sure they can't measure up. That's the one to pick, Romani."

"*Which* one?"

"The last one."

The Cat & the Cat, followed by the Serpent, pile on, practically in unison. "Booooo." Romani says nothing, and when the three notice his silence, they pipe down.

By now, the Serpent has already taken it too far. He decides to make a fight of it. "But this is ridiculous. What are we doing, a bizarro Miss Italy? You can send the viewers the subtitles with the explanation to their home addresses."

Mazzocca shakes his head. "It's a great idea. You were already thinking about it, weren't you, Romani?"

Romani says nothing for a little while. Then, all of a sudden, a smile spreads across his face. "No, I hadn't thought of it, but you're right, absolutely right. Okay, mark down this one too, Carlo."

The choreographer doesn't appear to have understood a single thing that's happened, but he marks down that last, much-yearned-after checkmark. "Okay, now, ladies..." The choreographer gets up out of the front row and heads to center stage. "Let me start by thanking all those who have participated but weren't selected..."

Ele shrugs and says, "You're welcome."

I elbow her. "Don't always be such a pessimist. Be constructive, be positive, you bring certain jinxes down on yourself."

The choreographer starts to read aloud. "Now then, Calendi, Giasmini, Fedri..." And certain of the young women suddenly brighten, smile, and take a step forward. Others, whose names have already been passed over in the list, look gloomy, once again seeing their chance to shine, if even momentarily on TV, vanishing into the distance. "Bertarello, Solesi, Biro, and Fiori." Ele and I are the last to step forward.

Ele looks at me. "I can't believe it. Now they're probably going to do like in *Chorus Line* and the dancers who take a step forward are the ones they send home, and all the others get to stay."

"All right, now. The women whose names I called will start next Monday. Now, this is important, at noon in the offices to sign your contracts and then at two here in the theater to start rehearsals. Rehearsals go from Monday afternoon to Saturday. Then Saturday evening, we're on the air, live, is that all clear?"

One of the women cast in the show, one of the younger ones with big eyes, raises her hand.

"What's wrong?"

"Actually, I *don't* understand."

"You don't understand what?"

"What you said."

"Oh, we're off to a great start. Here's what you do. Stick close to the dancer with the red hair who's right next to you and just do whatever she does. Did you understand that?"

"Pretty much," says the young woman, annoyed now as the redhead smiles at her, trying to encourage her. Maybe she didn't understand something either.

Ele runs her hand through her hair. "I can't believe it. They actually picked me!"

"Well, believe it. You're done with this whole rejection syndrome," I say.

Ele and I head for the exit.

"I'm going to be a star! Weeee-haw! I can't believe it!" Ele yells.

"Well, I wouldn't get my hopes up too high on that last point."

Tony sees us and waves in amusement. "Well, how did it go?"

"Just great."

"For both of you?"

Ele looks at him, grimacing angrily.

"That's right. They took us both, and before anyone else." And we leave the building, laughing merrily and shoving each other. "Every so often, you need to know how to sell it, right?"

"Holy guacamole, the car!"

"Where is it?"

"It's gone." I look around in concern. "I'd parked it right here. My car . . . Someone stole it. Fucking car thieves!"

⌐

"Hey, don't blame the car thieves," I say, emerging behind them along with Marcantonio. "Who's going to steal that hunk o' junk, anyway?"

"Don't you get started now. I need to go to the police and report the theft."

"It was yours. Now it's their car. I mean, all you have to do is change the name and everything will go back the way it should be!"

"I think all you'll have to do is pay a fine. They probably towed your car, so if you want to blame anyone, blame the traffic cops. And then, if you really want to put the blame where it belongs, which it strikes me is certainly your prerogative, blame yourself."

"Listen, I'm furious right now. What are you talking about?"

"I'm talking about the fact that you parked outside the theater's emergency exit. It's plain as day."

"The gentleman is quite right." A female traffic cop walks past us. She's heard our whole conversation and decides to weigh in. "We had no choice in the matter but to tow it."

"Well, it certainly strikes me as an exaggeration to say that you had no choice in the matter. You could have just waited for a couple of minutes. I was in the theater for work."

The female traffic cop stops smiling. "What, are you trying to dispute the violation?"

"I'm just trying to tell you the way things went."

The traffic cop walks away without another word.

Marcantonio decides to butt in on the fly. "Okay, that'll do. Since we have the whole afternoon free and especially because you two ladies got cast in the show, I'd suggest we go get something to drink and raise a toast, all together." Marcantonio smiles at Ele.

"You're right. Well then, let's go get something to drink," I suggest.

Gin swings around in front of me with great determination. "What is this, another audition?"

I look at her with a smile. "If you like."

"Sorry, then, you can dream on."

Marcantonio gets between us. "Can it seriously be that whatever a person says, you've got to pick a fight? All I said was let's all go get something to drink together. A smidgen of enthusiasm, for Pete's sake!"

Marcantonio shakes his head and then locks arms with Ele. "Come on. Otherwise we'll be standing here until the sun comes up." And he leads her off.

Gin stands there, watching her.

"Ouch, so painful. He took your girlfriend away."

"She's a big girl, and she knows what she's doing. The problem would have been if she'd left with you."

"Why? Would you have been jealous?" I ask.

"Hey, you're pretty sure of yourself! I would have thrown myself off a cliff. Okay, where did you park your motorcycle?"

"Why?"

"You're driving me home."

Chapter 17

When we get to the motorcycle, I climb on and start the engine. Gin tries to get on behind me but I rev it and lurch forward. "Nothing doing, I'm an innovative taxi driver."

"What's that supposed to mean?"

"You have to pay before you start the ride."

"Namely?"

"You have to give me a kiss."

I lean forward and pucker up my lips and shut my eyes. Actually, I keep the right eye just slightly open. I wouldn't want her to take off the way she usually does.

Gin leans in and gives me a disgusting slurp, from down to up, across my lips, as if she were doing an emergency intervention with a half-melted ice cream cone.

"Hey, what was that supposed to be?"

"That's how I kiss! I'm quite an innovative young woman myself." And she hops aboard right behind me. "Come on. With the fare I just paid, at a minimum, you ought to take me to Ostia."

I break into a laugh, and I take off in first gear, lurching into a wheelie, front tire spinning in the air, but Gin is quick as a whip. She wraps both arms tight around my waist and presses her head into my shoulder. "Go, go, go, Step. I love racing on a motorcycle."

I don't have to hear that twice. I tear out of there like a bat out of hell, and Gin squeezes her legs, clamping them tight around me. We feel like one single body on that motorcycle. Right, left, easy leans into each curve, accelerating as we go.

We turn in front of Da Vanni and then continue straight toward the Lungotevere, the Tiber-riverfront boulevard, with a curve to the right at the end. I slow down for a moment at the red light, which almost magically turns green, as if it had noticed us. I roar fast past two stopped cars. To the right, leaning into the curve, to the left, again leaning into the curve, and then here we are next to the Tiber, and off we go, hurtling forward with the wind in our faces.

In the rearview mirror, I glimpse a part of Gin's face. Her eyes, half-shut, her hairline, a faint edge of her white skin. Long dark hair tosses and flails, caressing the sun far behind us as it sets, tinged red, rebelliously battling the wind, but when I accelerate, that hair surrenders and lets itself be caught up in the sheer velocity. Her eyes are still shut.

"Here we are, signorina. We have arrived." I pull up in front of her house, put down the kickstand, and remain seated.

"Holy moshy, that took no time at all."

I look at her in amusement. "Holy moshy? What's that supposed to mean?"

"It's a cross between holy moly and gosh."

I've never heard it before. "Holy moshy. I'll have to start using it myself."

"No you won't. It's mine. I have all rights reserved for Italy."

"No kidding?"

"Certainly. Well, thanks for the ride, I'll have to use your service some other time. I have to say that, as a taxi driver, you're more than acceptable."

"Well then, you ought to invite me upstairs."

"Why would I do that?"

"That way I can give you a loyalty card, and you get a discount on each individual ride."

"Don't worry. I'm more than happy to pay."

This time, Gin thinks she's faster than me and quickly slams the glass street door, convinced she's tricked me.

"Ha ha, no way! I tricked *you*!" I reach into my jeans pocket and pull out her house keys, dangling them right in front of her eyes. "You taught me this trick, didn't you?"

"Okay, give me those keys!"

I look at her, laughing. "I just don't know. I think I might just go take a ride and come back later, maybe a special night fare."

"It wouldn't be worth it. In half an hour's time, I could get all the locks changed."

"But it would cost you more than ten real taxi rides."

"Okay, you want to negotiate?"

"Why of course."

"All right. What do you want in exchange for my keys?"

I look up and shoot her an amused glance.

"Don't even tell me. Let's just go upstairs. It's better to just end on 'let me fix you a nice tall drink,' like in the movies. But first, give me back my keys."

I open the door and keep the keys clutched good and

tight in my right hand. "I'll give you the keys when I get upstairs and inside. I'm just trying to be a responsible chaperone."

Gin smiles in amusement. "Sheesh, you'll never cease to amaze me."

"Because I used a big word?"

"No. Because you left your motorcycle unlocked." And she walks in proud and aloof. I hurry out and put on the steering lock, and a second later, I'm standing in front of her.

I dart into the elevator. "Well, now, does signorina wish to enter in elevator or is signorina afraid and want to walk upstairs?"

She walks in confidently and steps in front of me. Close to me. Very close. Way too close. I'll tell you, she's something. Then she moves away.

"Fine, you trust your chaperone. What floor, signorina?"

Now she's leaning against the wall and looking at me. She has big eyes, completely innocent.

"Fifth floor, thanks." She smiles, clearly amused by the game. I lean forward in her direction, pretending I can't find the button. "Oh, here it is, at last. Fifth floor, there we go." But she stays there, pressed against the elevator wall, made of antique wood worn dull by the continuous up and down, there at the center of that stairwell.

We ride up in silence. There I stand, leaning against her, careful not to press too hard, breathing in her scent. Then I pull away, and we look at each other. Our faces are so close. She bats her eyes for a moment and then continues to hold her gaze on me. Confident, bold, by no means intimidated.

I smile. She looks at me and subtly moves her cheeks, a faint hint of a smile from her too. Then she leans closer and whispers into my ear, warm and sensual. "Hey, chaperone..."

It makes me shiver. "Yes?" I look her in the eyes.

She raises an eyebrow. "We're here." And she slips out through my arms, agile and lightning quick. In an instant, she's out of the elevator. She stops in front of the door. I catch up with her and pull out the keys. "Hey, these are worse than the bunch St. Peter has to use."

"Give them here."

Nearly all us guys use this line about the keys of St. Peter. I feel like a fool for having dragged it out at a moment like this. I dunno, maybe just a way of killing time. Who knows why we even say it. St. Peter must just have one key, or maybe he doesn't even need a key. After all, do you think they're going to lock you out of heaven?

Gin gives the key one last turn. I'm ready to slip my foot in the door and keep it from shutting when she tries to leave me outside. But instead, Gin surprises me. She smiles gleefully and courteously opens the door. "Come on in, and don't make a ruckus." She lets me go by and shuts the door behind me. Then she walks past me and calls out, "Hey, I'm home! Is anyone here?"

The apartment is charming, modest, not overdecorated, and casual. There are photos of relatives above a linen chest, and more photos still on a small half-moon dresser placed against the wall. A tranquil home without excess, no weird paintings and with no excessive profusion of doilies and centerpieces. But above all, at seven p.m., halfway through sunset, no one is at home.

"Hey, you really are lucky, living legend."

"Are you done with this living legend routine? And why am I so lucky? Aside from the fact that if there's anyone in here who's lucky, it's you. Just look at the body God gave you. Shapely, strong, and perfect." I smile as I reach my hand out to touch her.

"Oh, are you done? You'd think you just got out of prison after six years without ever seeing a woman."

"Make that four."

She looks at me, furrowing her brow.

"Four what?"

"I was released recently after four years in prison."

"Oh, really?" She doesn't know whether to believe me or not. She looks at me curiously but must decide to play along. "Aside from the fact that you're surely innocent, what is it you did?"

"I murdered a girl who invited me up to her house at exactly..." I pretend to check the time. "Well, just about this time of day, and decided not to put out."

"Quick, quick! I heard a noise. I think it must be my folks. Darn it!" She pushes me toward an armoire. "Get in here."

"Hey, I'm not even your lover yet, and you aren't married. So what's the problem?"

"Shhh." Gin shuts the door and then runs out of the room. I sit there, in silence, not certain about what to do next. I hear the distant sound of a door opening and then closing. After that, nothing. Then more silence. Five minutes, and still nothing. Eight minutes. Nothing. I look at my watch. Fuck, it's been nearly ten minutes. What should I do? Well, by now I'm sick of this.

I get out. Softly, softly I push open the armoire door. I peer through the crack. A few pieces of furniture and a strange silence, at least strange to me. Then suddenly the corner of a sofa. I push the armoire door open a little farther. A carpet, a vase, and then her leg, crossed over her other leg. Gin is sitting relaxed on the sofa, her head tilted against the sofa back, smoking a cigarette. She's laughing in delight. "Hey, living legend, you sure took your time. What have you been doing, locked up in the armoire? You've been having fun with yourself, haven't you? *Egoïste!*"

Fuck, she tricked me. I lunge out in a single leap and try to catch her. But Gin is faster than me. She's just crushed out her cigarette and she takes off at a run. She slams into the corner of a door, almost slips, and falls on a carpet that crumples beneath her foot, but she recovers in the curve.

Two more leaps and she's in her bedroom. She whips around and tries to get the door shut. But she's not fast enough this time. I'm holding her by the shoulders. Gin tries to resist for a moment and then gives up the effort. She lets go of the door and throws herself onto the bed with both feet raised in my direction. She kicks, laughing like a lunatic. "Okay, sorry, living legend. No, let me make that *epic* Step. In fact, just plain Step, Step and nothing more. Step perfect as he is. Come on, I was just kidding. But at least when I kid around, it's funny, not like you."

"Why?"

"Yours are grim! The story about how you murdered a girl while you were at her house all alone. Come on!"

I stalk around the bed, trying to pierce her web of defense, but she follows me as I go, kicking upward. Quick and alert, she follows my moves, lying on the bed and revolving, never once losing sight of me. Then I dodge to the right, try to feint, and lunge at her. I dart beneath her guard, and she immediately tucks her arms in and raises them in front of her face. "Okay, okay. I give up. Let's make peace."

"Of course we can make peace."

She laughs and presses her cheek against my left shoulder. "Okay..." She gives me a little smile and comes toward me. And then she lets herself be kissed, soft, tender, and warm. And she kisses back, too, sliding and returning up between my lips with attention and care, with dedication, with passion, and with her entire being.

I open my eyes for a moment, and I watch her navigate like that, so close to my face, so caught up, so involved, so determined. No, this time she doesn't have any tricks up her sleeves or concealed in her small pockets.

I shut my eyes again, and I let myself go with her. Together we journey, little surfers on our own same wave, soft tongues, hand in hand, laughing and shoving only to embrace once again. Lips playing like bumper cars, trying to shove their own way in, to fit together properly.

Then Gin starts to shake a little. I continue to kiss her. She shakes a little more. What is this, unrestrained passion? She pulls away from me. "Oh my God, I'm sorry." She bursts out laughing. "I just can't hold it in. You locked in the living room armoire for eleven minutes and thirty-two seconds, I just can't even think about it. Forgive me, please, just forgive me, but it's too rich." And she hops off the bed before I get a chance to get a grip on her. "But you are a good kisser, if that's any consolation."

I lie there, sprawled on the bed. I brace myself on one elbow and continue staring at her. It's rare to find such an attractive young woman who's also funny and fun to be with. In fact, hold on, I got that wrong. So fun, funny, and very pretty. No, I still don't have it right. And so very...beautiful. But I don't tell her that.

"You know what the most incredible thing is? That we're going to be working together every single day for who knows how long, and since things do come back around in this life, *you'll* be there, and *I'll* tease you."

"Oh, isn't that nice. You threaten me. How did you want tonight to go? That I'd show you the apartment, that I'd offer you a drink..." Gin does a falsetto voice. "Would you care for something, Stefano? An aperitif? And some potato chips to go with, perhaps..." And she does a perfect staging of a fake laugh. "Ha, ha!"

I decide not to respond. I look around the room. A few teddy bears and plush dolls, photos of Ele, or at least I think it's her, and then a few other girls and two or three cool-looking guys.

She notices. "Those are advertising models. We worked with them, and nothing more." Gin doesn't miss a trick.

"Who asked you?"

"You were looking a little worried."

"Absolutely not. I don't even know the meaning of the word."

"Oh, of course, I was forgetting what a tough guy you are."

I get up and take a walk around the room. "Do you know that you can figure out everything you want to know about a woman by looking in her closet? Let me see!"

"No!"

"What are you afraid of, a skeleton in the closet? Holy shit, how much clothing do you own? And all of it's brand-new! This stuff still has the price tags on it. And it's all designer stuff. Well, look at you, signorina! Gifted and prosperous and dressed to kill, eh?"

"You see what a fool you are? You don't keep up with the times. This is all stuff I don't have to pay for."

"Yes, there she is, the influencer working for some designer line."

"No. I just use YOOX. I order everything online on this special outlet site. You can find all the leading designer labels. I pick what I want and have it sent to my home. I wear it for a couple of days, taking great care not to damage it. I make sure I keep the tag in place. Then I send it back before ten days is up, informing them that I'm not happy with my purchase, maybe because the size was too big."

I continue sorting through her clothing. There's all sorts of things, tops by Cavalli and Costume National, a Jil Sander long skirt, couture dresses, a couple of D&G hand-bags, a cashmere sweater by Alexander McQueen, a denim Moschino coat, an amusing checked jacket by Vivienne Westwood, a Miu Miu blouse, a pair of Miss Sixty luxury jeans...

She's something else. She's pretty, she's funny, and she's shrewd and ruthless. She knows how to live large. And look at the scam she's come up with. YOOX lets her wear an ever-changing assortment of clothing, always in fashion, without spending a euro. I like it.

"Hold it right there! You have an odd expression on your face. What are you thinking about?" She takes something off the table and holds it up in my direction. "So smile, tough guy!" A Polaroid camera. I raise my eyebrow just as she takes the picture. "Come on. All things considered, you'd look fabulous between those two male models. Certainly, they haven't lived the life you have, but they'd be excited just to spend a little time next to a living legend!"

"Well, sure, like the two thieves on the cross next to Jesus."

"Well, the comparison seems a little exaggerated to me."

"Sure, but they became famous too."

"But they weren't happy, that's for sure!"

I grab the Polaroid camera out of her hand and take a picture of her.

"Hey, hold on there! I look terrible in pictures."

I push the button and then pull off the photo as soon as it emerges from the camera.

"You look terrible in *pictures*? Well, what's your explanation for looking beautiful in real life then?"

"Idiot, moron, give that back." She does her best to grab it out of my hands.

Too late. I slip it into my jacket pocket. "Wait and see. If you don't behave yourself, if you try to tell the story about the armoire, you'll find your face on posters papering half of Rome."

"Well, okay, I was just saying!"

"And what is this chart supposed to be?" I point to a sheet of paper hanging on the wall over the table, perfectly partitioned into days and weeks and months and covered with the names of various gyms and health clubs.

"This? These are the gyms of Rome, you see, one for every day. They're divided up by trainers, lessons, and sections of town. Understood?"

"Well, yes and no."

"Damn, Step, come on, it's easy. A sample gym class in

each gym, each day in a different place, and there are more than five hundred different gyms in the city of Rome, and they aren't even that far apart. You can train and exercise completely free of charge!"

"So, for example, tomorrow..." I look at the grid, and I run my finger across to the date, as if I were playing Battleship. "You could do a lesson at Urbani and not pay a cent."

"And so on! It's a system I invented myself. Not bad, eh?"

"Right. It sort of reminds me of that trick where you use a padlock to fill your gas tank."

"Sure, it's all part of my great big money-saver's manual. Not bad, right? Hey, look how nice your picture came out." The Polaroid is clearer now. "Come on, I'll put it between these two.

"But I've noticed how interested you are in my schedule. Do you want to freeload the same training sessions as me? I'll write up a schedule just for you. I'll offset you by a day, and you can slipstream without problems, and we'll never have to run into each other."

"I don't need it."

"Are you rich?"

"Not at all! It's just that these days the gyms actually want to use me to build up their public image."

"Of course they do, who could doubt it? Well, the guided tour is all done. I'd better walk you to the door because, before long, my folks are going to be home. Or would you rather hide in the armoire again? I mean, now that you know how to do it."

She walks past me to see me to the door and glances back, raising an eyebrow. We remain together like that, in silence, for a moment. Then she starts. "Well, let's not let this farewell drag out too long. Take care of yourself, taxi driver. We'll see you around, right?"

"Of course."

I want to say something else to her but I don't even really know what. Something nice. Sometimes, if you can't think of the words, it's better to just go with your instincts so I pull her close and give her a kiss. Soft like the last time. In fact, even softer. Suddenly, there's someone behind us...

"Excuse me, guys, okay? It's just that you seem determined to say your farewells right outside the door."

It's her brother, Gianluca, who's just stepped out of the elevator. Gin isn't even so much embarrassed. She's annoyed. "You sure have some impeccable timing."

"Oh, so now you're saying it's my fault! My sister is quite something. Listen, Step, would you do me a favor? Between kisses, could you set this girl straight on a few things?" And he makes his way between us on his way through the front door.

Gin takes advantage of the space and gives me a punch to the chest. "I knew it that with you it was bound to be nothing but trouble all day long."

"Ouch! Now you're saying it's my fault."

"Who else? It's also just one more kiss, and another kiss, and one last kiss. What is this, can't you hold out for a minute? Are you already addicted to me, like a pathetic junkie? Sheesh..."

And she shuts the door in my face.

⌐

Gianluca walks into my room. "That Step is really something, but you guys are like a steady couple now, aren't you?"

"What are you talking about? And what do you mean he's really something?"

"Well, the two of you are constantly kissing."

"What's the big deal, just one kiss."

"Two, actually, if I'm counting accurately," Gianluca says.

"Oh, what are you doing anyway? Trying to be the poll watcher around here? Okay, I know that you make a little extra money on the side counting ballots."

"But that's politics."

"I'm guessing that Step is even more of a con artist than any politician."

"Why do you say that?" Gianluca asks.

"Because I don't trust a guy like him, likable and even funny. But who knows what's lurking underneath that glib surface?"

"If you say so."

"I certainly do say so, Luke. From a kiss, you can tell all you need to know. And he's kind of...kind of strange."

"What do you mean by that?"

"He doesn't give of himself, he doesn't trust, and when someone doesn't offer trust, then it means that, first and foremost, he's not deserving of trust."

"Maybe so."

"Definitely so!"

Gianluca exits the room and finally leaves me with a little privacy. That's a relief. Now I want to get my thoughts screwed on straight. I shake my head and fluff up my hair.

Gin, if you can hear me, come back down off whatever

cloud you're on. I can't believe that you've fallen for this hunk of myth, this living legend. Step isn't right for you. Problems, complications, who knows what lurks in his past?

Plus, have you even noticed? Every time you kiss him, just when things are going perfectly, right at the very best—no, let me be more descriptive and precise—right at the most wonderful, the most fantastic, the most super-fabulous and delightful moment, your brother Luke always seems to show up. What's that supposed to mean? Is it a sign of destiny, a saint sent down from heaven to keep you from plummeting straight down to hell, an anchor of salvation? Or is it just standard-issue bad luck?

Gosh darn it, we could go on kissing for hours. The way that Step kisses. A kiss is everything. A kiss is the absolute truth. Without too many flourishes, without any extreme twists and turns, without any highwire acrobatics. It's just natural, the finest thing. He kisses the way I like it. Just plain and simple. Confident, gentle, unhurried, relaxed, having fun, no technique, with taste.

Dare I say it? Lovingly! Oh my God! No, not that!

Chapter 18

Ciao, Paolo."

"Stefano, where have you been all this time? You've gone missing."

"Hey," I reply as I walk past him on my way to my room, "you know what the first rule they teach you in America is?"

"Sure, if you want to survive, mind your own business."

"Very good. How about the second one?"

"That's one I don't know."

"Fuck you!" I go into my room and shut the door behind me.

"So you see? You really did learn a little English. Good work. I hope you know a few other vocabulary words though," Paolo shouts.

I don't bother answering, and I collapse onto my bed. At that very instant, the intercom buzzes from downstairs. I hurry out of my room. Paolo is already in the living room, heading for the intercom.

"I'll get it." I practically snatch the receiver out of his hand.

He stands there, aghast. "Wait, I'm not clear about this.

This is my house, you're my guest, but you've taken control of everything."

I glare at him but then I smile. "Come on, I'm just serving as your butler." It buzzes again. I pick up the receiver. My heart is racing.

"Hello, is Step there?" A female voice. My heart races faster. "It's me, Pallina!"

"Hey, it's me. What are you up to?"

"I wanted to see your new home, and then I was going to drag you on a pub crawl."

"We can negotiate the details on that last item. Okay, come on up. Sixth floor."

I push the button to open the downstairs door. Paolo looks at me and smiles. "Woman?"

I nod.

"Do you need me to leave you the apartment? Should I lock myself in my room and pretend I'm not around?"

My brother. What does he think is going on. What does he really know about me anyway?

"It's Pallina, Pollo's old girlfriend."

He says nothing. Then he seems to grow sad. "I apologize." He heads off to his room in silence. My brother. What a character, a man from another era. In fact, maybe that explains his timing.

Doorbell. I go to answer the door. "Hey!"

"Fuck, Step!" Pallina throws her arms around my neck and holds on tight. "I still can't believe you've finally come back."

"Keep this up, and I'll leave again, eh?"

"Come on, forgive me." Pallina regains her composure. "Show me around the apartment."

"Come with me." I shut the door, and I lead the way, acting as her tour guide.

"This is the living room, light fabrics, window treatments, et cetera et cetera."

I go on talking, describing everything I see. I see her moving along behind me, looking at everything carefully, every once in a while reaching out her hand to get a better understanding, to judge the heft of some object. Pallina, how you've grown, lost weight, gotten a new hair style. Even your makeup looks a little dark, or is it that my memories are just faded?

"And this is the kitchen. Do you want anything?"

"No, no, nothing for now."

"Oh, listen, I can't stand the sight of you being pointlessly polite, okay?"

She bursts out laughing. "No, no, really, nothing for me."

Her laugh hasn't changed a bit. She seems healthy, well rested, and relaxed. If only Pollo could see her now. He would be proud. From the stories I've heard, he was your first man, Pallina. And Pollo never lied to me. He didn't have any reason to. He never needed to exaggerate to make himself look good, to make himself look cool, not to me, his true friend.

Now here she is, in front of me. Pallina is walking tall, confidently. Then, all of a sudden, Pallina changes expression. "Aren't you going to show me the bedroom?"

Suddenly different. Sensual and mischievous. A pang in my heart. Does she have another man? What happened after Pollo? It's been nearly two years, sure, but still, I don't want to hear it. She's a young woman, appealing, attractive . . . I understand that but I don't care. I just don't want to think about it.

"Here, this is one of them." I open a door after tapping lightly. "Can we come in?"

Paolo had been taking his shirt off, but he quickly regains his composure and comes to the door. "Of course. Well, hello, Pallina!"

"Here he is, the decorator responsible for everything you've just seen."

"Ciao."

They shake hands. Pallina smiles with a hint of embarrassment. "Congratulations, it's beautiful, what exquisite taste. I thought a woman had chosen everything."

Paolo starts to reply, but I don't give him time. I quietly shut the door, cutting him out of our house tour.

"Hey, but I meant *your* bedroom." She gives me a flat-handed smack on the shoulder, shoving me forward.

"Oh, there was a misunderstanding then. Here, this is it." I open the door to my room.

"Hey, not bad." Pallina enters and looks around. "A little spartan, perhaps. It needs color."

I realize that the Polaroid of Gin is standing on my bedside table. Without letting her see, I cover it up.

"Well, it has its charm just as it is though. And after all, there's plenty of time to add color," I say.

She looks at me, her curiosity obviously aroused, but at that exact moment, the telephone rings. Pallina pulls hers out of her jacket pocket, looks at it, and then holds it up to her ear. "Hey, it's not my phone."

I pick up my cell phone from the table nearby. "You're right. It's mine!"

I don't recognize the caller's number. "Hello?"

"Welcome back."

I can feel myself blush as I listen to her voice.

"I hope we can see each other, now that you're back in Rome."

"Sure."

"Do you like your new place to live?"

"Sure."

"Did you have a good time overseas?"

"Sure."

I nod. Then I listen to the other things she has to say, always kind, courteous, and full of a delicate love, careful not to shatter that fragile crystal, our past, our secret. I go on answering. I even manage to get out something more than my simple succession of *sure*s.

"So how are *you* doing?" But she goes on talking.

Pallina looks at me but says nothing. She moves her head while silently asking who that is. But I don't give her a chance to ask because I turn away toward the window. I look out, into the distance, while chasing after her voice.

"Yes, it's a promise I'll call you back. I'll come and see you, yes..."

Then a difficult silence as we search for some way of saying goodbye.

"Ciao." And I end the call.

"Hey, who was that? Another one of your women?"

"Well, yes and no."

I smile, pretending to be amused, trying to shake off that difficult phone call. "That was my mother. So, now what? Shall we go out for this pub crawl?"

Chapter 19

We're out in the night on my motorcycle, Pallina and me. I let the 750 unwind. An unhurried velocity, thoughts in the wind.

She holds tight to me, but without overdoing it. Two equivocal human beings, astral conjunctions of a strange destiny. Me, her boyfriend's best friend; she, my ex-girlfriend's best friend. But all that belongs to the past.

I shift gears and race away fast into the refreshing wind, which carries away my thoughts. Ah, I sigh. It's so nice sometimes just not to think. Don't think. Don't think...

Wind, speed, and distant sounds. A series of clubs. Akab is the first stop.

"Come on. I know everyone here. They'll be delighted to see you," Pallina says.

I let her guide me in. We enter the place, and I say hello. I recognize a few faces. "I'll have a rum, thanks."

"Light or dark?"

"Dark."

Another club. The Charro Café. I decide to cut loose. "Another rum, this time with ice and lemon."

And then on to Alpheus. And another rum. Ice and

lemon. Here they've got all kinds of music. Seventies and eighties, hip-hop, rock, and dance.

Then Ketum Bar. I forget where I parked my motorcycle. Who cares? "Another rum. Ice and lemon." We laugh. I say hello to someone. Some guy jumps up and hugs me. "Fuck, Step, you came back! Let's start making a ruckus, what do you say?"

Yes, let's start kicking up a fuss again. But who the fuck even was that guy?

Another club and another glass of rum and then another and yet another. And two more rums. Who was that guy who just jumped on me? Oh, right, Manetta. He'd fallen asleep one time in the mountains. That's right, we were at Pescasseroli. Under the quilt, his feet sticking out. We put some matches between his toes with the heads sticking out and lit them. Fuck, the way he jumped in the air when he woke up with his toes on fire. And we both fell on the floor laughing like lunatics. Me and Pollo. And he was jumping around the room with his toes all burnt, shouting, "Fuck what a nightmare! What a nightmare, fuck!" And we were just falling over laughing so hard that it hurt. Oh, how we laughed. Like crazy.

But Pollo's gone now. A wave of sadness sweeps over me, powerfully.

Another glass of rum, throwing it all back at a single gulp, glug. As I dance with Pallina, his girlfriend, the friend who's no longer there. But I dance, I just dance and laugh, and I laugh with her. I laugh and I think of you. Another glass of rum, and I don't know how, but I'm outside my building.

"Hey, we're here." I get off the motorcycle, a little wobbly. That last rum was one too many.

"Where did you put your vespa?"

"No, I came by car. Now I have a Fiat 500, the new model."

"Ah, cute." Actually, there's no kind of car I hate more. But is it going to help anyone for me to tell her so? No, so I keep quiet.

"Fun night out, huh?" Pallina asks.

"It's been great." I'm not kidding about that. "The clubs in Testaccio have changed."

"Changed how?"

"They're better. Great music, everyone's dancing. Yeah, a great night out."

Pallina rummages through her pockets and in her jacket. "Hey, I think I must have left my keys up at your place."

"No problem. Let's go upstairs."

In the elevator, there's a strange silence. Our eyes meet. We ride without speaking. Pallina smiles. She does it tenderly. I drum my fingers against the metal wall, against the mirror. Fuck, sometimes it just seems like the elevator is never going to reach the floor. Or is it the number of rums I've had that slows down that ride? Or something else entirely?

We've arrived. I open the door to the apartment, and Pallina slips inside. She looks around, before walking over to the table. "Here they are. I found them!" But she's in my line of sight, and I can't see what she has or hasn't found. Were her keys really on the table, did she really forget them, or was that just an excuse to go upstairs? What on earth are you thinking, Step? Too much rum. The keys were on the table; they must have been there.

"Hey, you even have a terrace."

"Yes, I guess there is one. You know I'd never noticed it."

"Oh, come on! You're always so distracted and careless."

I open the French doors, and I step outside. There's a gorgeous moon tonight. Riding high and round, there among the distant buildings, all of them bathed in its pale light. I take a deep breath, and I catch the scent of summer jasmine, the night air of September, distant crickets, and silence all around us.

Pallina comes up behind me. "Here, I brought you another." She hands me a glass. "To finish the night in glory."

I take the glass and raise it to my mouth, sniffing it as I do. "Another rum. And it smells like a good one." Paolo is just surprising me all the time these days. He's improving. I take a sip. This must be a Pampero. No, a Havana Club, viejo de siete años, at least. "Excellent."

I go back to looking into the distance. Then the noise of a car vanishes into the night somewhere.

"You know, Step, I have something I should tell you."

I stand there in silence. I take another sip without turning around.

Pallina continues talking. I hear her behind me, close to my back. "You won't believe this. Since Pollo died, I haven't been with any other guys. Can you believe that?"

"Why shouldn't I believe it?" I still don't turn around.

"Not even a kiss, I swear to you."

"Don't swear. I don't suspect you of lying."

"Well, I did tell you one lie."

I turn around, and I look her in the eyes.

She smiles. "I had the keys, in my jacket."

A light gust of hot wind in the night softly tosses her

dark hair. Pallina, all woman, grown up now. She steps close to me and embraces me. She lays her head on my chest. Kind, sweet-smelling friend. I let her do it.

"You know, Step, I'm so happy that you're here."

I hold my arms out wide, unsure what to do now. Then I set the glass down on the sill and gently put my arms around her.

I can feel her smile. "Welcome back. Please, hold me tight."

I stand there like that, too weak to squeeze her any tighter. I try to apologize. "Listen..."

But it happens in a flash. She lifts her head from my chest and gives me a kiss. She presses against my lips and opens her mouth. Then she tries to move, first to the right and then to the left, searching for the right fit, the right position, the natural progression.

But it's impossible. I'm motionless. I don't know what to do. I don't want to hurt her feelings so I stand there, lips closed, certainly cold, for all I know, stonelike.

Pallina slowly relaxes. Then she lowers her head against my chest again and starts weeping. In silence. Small jerks of her head and then shorter and shorter sobs. She holds me tight, not meeting my gaze.

I gently stroke her hair. Then I whisper into her ear. "Pallina...Pallina, don't do this."

"No, I never should have done it."

"But what did you do? Nothing happened. It was nothing. Everything's all right."

"No. I tried to kiss you."

"Seriously? I didn't even notice it. You know, our friend must surely be up there looking down and laughing at us."

"Maybe, at me."

"He's just mad at me because I wouldn't go for it."

Pallina bursts out laughing. But it's a nervous laugh. She sniffs and wipes her nose on the sleeve of her jacket. She's sort of laughing and still crying at the same time. "Forgive me, Step."

"Oh, this again. But forgive you for what? Listen, if you keep this up, I'll have to take you to bed."

"Yes, that would be nice."

She laughs again, less upset this time. I wave my index finger menacingly in her face. "I mean, put you to bed, to get some sleep. What did you even understand, eh?"

She smiles again. "No, I really am going to bed now, to get some sleep."

And without another word, she heads for the door. She stops for a moment. "Please, Step, forget this ever happened, and call me."

I smile at her, and I nod my head. Then I shut my eyes, and a moment later, Pallina is gone. I stand there like that, in silence, in the living room, and then I look around and see the bottle of rum. I was right. It's a Havana Club. But only three years old. That Paolo. What a cheapskate.

I go out onto the terrace. I look down and just manage to get a glimpse of Pallina's Fiat Cinquecento turning at the end of the street. I drain the last drop of the bottle without bothering to use the glass and stand there. Arms crossed, leaning on the parapet, with the bottle next to me but empty now.

"Fucking hell." I have a rage inside me, and I don't know who to take it out on. Fuck and double fuck. Why? Why? Why? Shit. There's nothing I can do about it. I can't even curse. No, that wouldn't do a bit of good. But I don't want to think about it. I'm really hurting.

I look down. There it is. Thanks. I'm happier now. I take the bottle by the neck, I summon up all my strength, and I hurl it straight down like a boomerang, perfect and fast. Let's just hope I don't see it come hurtling back at me. The bottle spins as it rockets down and boom, hits the windshield of the Renault Twingo dead center, disintegrating it. It was a brand-new, untouched Twingo. Black, I think, or maybe just dark. The epitome of everything I hate. A single shot. Like in *The Deer Hunter*.

Chapter 20

A light breeze wanders around through the cemetery, lost amid the tidy little structures of white and gray marble, with flowers that have just wilted and other flowers that have just been set out. Photographs and dates commemorate people. Loves of the past, lives shattered or else just naturally snipped short. In any case, over. Uprooted. Like the life of my friend. And sometimes all this happens without a reason why and then the pain is just so much worse.

I walk between the vaults. I have a bunch of flowers in one hand, the finest sunflowers I could find. In friendship, as in love, money is no object.

Here I am. I've arrived. "Ciao, Pollo."

I look at that photo, the smile that kept me company so many times. That tiny image, small though his heart was vast and generous.

"I brought you these." As if he couldn't see me, as if he didn't already know.

I bend over and pull the withered flowers out of the little vase. I wonder who brought them and when. Maybe it was Pallina herself. But then I toss the thought far away, exactly like the flowers I've just removed.

I arrange the big sunflowers as best I can. They still seem to quiver with the strength of those fields, healthy from the light of the sun. I arrange them carefully, spacing them carefully. They seem to make themselves comfortable, almost naturally. "There, there we go."

I stand there for a while in silence, as if worried that he might have misunderstood me, that I might have thought some mistaken thought, not pure, the way our friendship always was. "But that's not the way it is, Pollo, and you know it. It wasn't that way for even a second."

And then I practically take up in defense of Pallina. "You have to understand her. She's a young girl, and she misses you. And you know, or maybe you don't know, how important you were to her, what you meant to her, how you made her laugh, how happy you made her. And we can admit this to each other. How much you loved her."

I look around, as if worried that someone might overhear those words spoken in confidence. Far, far away, there's an old woman dressed in black. She's praying. A little farther along, there's a gardener trying to rake up a few yellowing leaves.

I focus back on my friend. And on Pallina. "She's become a beautiful woman. It's incredible the way they transform. You see them once, you run into them again, and it's only taken a short while, a moment, and then there's a completely different woman who's taken their place.

"And I already know the question you would have asked me. No, I haven't seen Babi, and I have no intention of doing it, okay? At least not now. I'm not ready.

"Instead, I wanted to tell you something about this girl, Gin. She's a breath of fresh air. I swear to you, fuck, she's cheerful and likable and intelligent. She's really something. I can't tell you any more than that because, because...I haven't taken her to bed yet."

Just then, the old woman walks past. She's finished all her prayers. She smiles a strange smile. It's not clear whether it's a smile of camaraderie or just one of idle curiosity. The fact remains that she smiles and then moves away.

"Okay, Pollo, I'm going to go now too. I hope I'll be able to tell you some stories soon about Gin, something good."

Not far away a new guest of the cemetery has appeared. A few people get out of their cars in silence. Eyes glistening, fresh flowers, last memories. Words spoken in hushed voices, trying to figure out exactly what to do now. All of it mingled with sorrow and pain.

Then I bend down one last time. I carefully adjust the biggest sunflower. I give it a little more space and a chance to keep my best, my closest, friend company. I'm reminded of something that Walter Winchell once said: "A real friend is one who walks in when the rest of the world walks out." And you, Pollo, you're still there inside of me.

Chapter 21

So what did you get up to?" I ask Ele.

Silence.

I roll my eyes. She's just incorrigible. "Okay, so are you going to tell the story, or not?"

"Well, you know what he did? He invited me over to his house for dinner."

"Who did?"

"Marcantonio, the graphic artist."

"Step's friend!"

"Marcantonio is Marcantonio, and that's all. And you can't imagine how sweet he was, all the work he did, how he made me a wonderful dinner."

⌒

Marcantonio smiles at me. Like someone who knows more than he's telling. Or better, someone who knows it by heart with all the times he's put it into practice.

"All right, Step. For starters, I went downstairs to Da Paolo, the Japanese restaurant on Via Cavour, and I picked up some food. Tempura, sushi, sashimi, passion fruit.

Delightful stuff, with a high erotic content. I brought it all upstairs, I heated the tempura back up, and et voilà, dinner was ready. I set the table with the classic Japanese chopsticks, plus a fork just in case she wasn't used to eating Asian-style..."

"Did you also go by the Moroccan at the stoplight and pick up the usual five-euro bouquet of flowers?"

"Well, certainly, those are ideal, minimum expense for a centerpiece!"

⌒

Ele seems to be enthusiastic about the evening's entertainment.

"Well, so go on. He'd set the table thoughtfully, he chose everything with impeccable taste..."

"Are you ready? Fundamental question: Were there flowers?"

"Certainly! Tiny, beautiful roses. He even played off my surname..."

We both burst out laughing. Then I turn serious again. "Ele, now tell me the truth."

Ele rolls her eyes.

"There, I knew it. So long and we'll talk again next week."

"No, okay, all right, I'll talk, I'll talk."

I look at her with concern. "What have you done?"

"Okay...I gave him a blow job!"

"No, Ele, that's just not done. On a first date! I've never heard of such a thing."

"What are you talking about? Benedetta, the one you thought was such a saint, remember, Paoletti? She was caught at the Piper Club in the bathroom kneeling in blessed oral adoration with a certain Max that she'd met on the dance floor. Time she'd known him? Half a song by Will Young, the cover of the Doors' 'Light My Fire.' After which, sure enough, she was seized indeed by a strange fire. She sang into his microphone, and she was even caught in the act.

"And what about Paola Mazzocchi? You know that they caught her at school in the bathroom with the phys ed teacher, Mariotti? Hah, and don't you know it, after just a week of school. The worshipper of Sicilian cannolis! You remember that that nickname made the rounds of the whole school. And you know why? Because Mariotti might have dyed blond hair, but he's from Catania."

"Yes, but these are urban legends. Mariotti is still teaching. Do you think he would have been caught and then allowed to stay?"

"Oh, I couldn't say. All I know is that Mazzocchi got a C minus in phys ed..."

"What does that have to do with it?"

"Everything to do with it. It means she didn't even know how to give a decent blow job."

⌣

Marcantonio obviously enjoys recounting the details to me.

"I did body art on her."

"What is that supposed to mean?" I ask.

"You come from New York, and you don't know these things, Step? That is, I'd be justified—I've always spent my holidays at Castiglioncello—but you, living there, in the Big Apple, don't even know what we're talking about here?"

I heave a sigh of weariness but smile as I look at him. "I know what it is. But what it means is quite another matter."

"Oh, there you go. I painted her whole body. I stripped her naked, and then I started painting her. Paintbrushes with light, warm tempera, all over her body, up and down, dipping them in the warm water of a flask. I slid over her, giving her pleasure, watching her. And her cheeks took on color without any assistance from me. I painted back onto her the very same panties I'd just taken off of her, then slowly the chiaroscuro of her nipples which, increasingly turgid, seemed to go crazy at those brushstrokes of sheer, warm pleasure."

"And then?"

"Seized by the throes of a chromatic orgasm, she insisted on coloring my paintbrush."

"In translation?"

"She gave me a blow job."

"Phew. And after that?"

"Then, nothing. We just hung out, talking about this and that. We picked at the rest of the Japanese food, and then I took her home."

"Come on, after the blow job, you didn't fuck her?"

"No, she didn't want to."

"No, now explain this to me. A blow job yes, and a full fuck, no. What's the reasoning here?"

"She has quite a philosophy on the subject. Or at least, so she informed me."

"But she didn't tell you anything more?"

"Yes, she told me, 'You have to be happy with what you get.' No wait, it was better than that. She said that 'he who is willing to be happy with what he gets, gets the most pleasure.' And then she started laughing."

⌒

"Wait, Ele, excuse me. In that case, you might as well have gone to bed with him. I mean, sex is just sex."

"What does that mean? Fucking is a different matter, the perfect union. Total involvement. He's inside you, and this could produce a child. You understand? Whereas a blow job is another matter."

"Why, certainly! Of course!"

"Listen, as far as I'm concerned, it's just like a very friendly way of saying goodbye. I don't know, like a handshake."

"A handshake? Tell your parents that."

"Certainly, if it came up in the conversation. Why, what do you think, that they've never done it? We're the ones who don't see how normal sex is. People ought to talk about it like anything else. It's just that we're bourgeois. I mean, for example, just imagine your mother giving a..."

"Ele!"

"Why, does your mother play hard to get?"

⌒

"Well, Step, I have to bid you farewell for the moment. When do we have our next appointment with Romani, the Serpent, and the rest of the sordid demimonde?"

"Tomorrow at eleven. Well, this takes the cake. Now I have to remind you of the appointments."

"Certainly. This is the real job of an assistant. Well then, we'll see you tomorrow at that time, or a few minutes before then."

I watch Marcantonio walk away with a cigarette already in his mouth. After barely taking a single step, he turns around. He looks at me and smiles. "Hey, let me know if there's any news with Biro. I'll be waiting to hear your stories, and don't invent anything. After all, a blow job is easy to beat!"

Chapter 22

In the Prati district, near the headquarters for the national public broadcasting company, RAI, is the Residence Prati, home and hotel to so many starlets of Italian film and television. And just a little farther along is a gym.

I head downstairs because it's a basement facility. You'd never think it, but it's 4,500 square feet easy, if not even bigger, nicely arranged with plenty of mirrors and a perfect ventilation system, a large steel duct that wends its serpentine way overhead, exhaling and inhaling relentlessly.

"Hello, are you looking for someone?" A young woman with short hair smiles at me from her hiding place behind a strange desk. She's hiding a textbook, shut with a pencil as a bookmark and a pair of highlighters beside it. A classic of the first year of university.

"Yes, I'm looking for a young woman I know."

"What's her name? Maybe I know her. Has she been a member for long?"

I'm tempted to laugh, and I'd like to answer her "Since never!" But that would amount to dismissing any chance I might ever have with Gin. Ratting her out in her network of gyms, that would not be a great move.

"No, she just told me that today she'd be doing a trial lesson."

"Tell me her name, and I can call her on the intercom."

"No, thanks." I smile, feigning innocence. "I want to surprise her."

"Okay, as you like."

The young woman goes back to her studies. Criminal law. I was wrong. She must be on her third year at the very least. Then I laugh to myself. Someday she might be my lawyer. It's a good possibility.

There she is now, Gin Biro. She's tirelessly jumping around the boxing bag. Suddenly she reminds me of Hilary Swank when she goes to the gym, all alone, on her birthday. She moves quickly around the bag, and Morgan Freeman decides to give her some pointers on how to punch.

I'd heard rumors that Italian women were obsessed with boxing. But I just assumed they were nothing but that, idle rumors. This, on the other hand, is reality.

"Go on, that's good. Punch from the shoulder." Someone is training her but he doesn't resemble Clint Eastwood.

I look at her, and it seems as if I'm looking at her in a whole new light now. How strange. When you look at a woman from a distance, you notice the slightest details, the way she moves her mouth, how she pouts, the way she bites her lip, how she sighs, the way she does her hair, and, well, lots of other things. Things that you overlook from up close, things that from up close are pushed aside by her eyes.

Gin keeps punching the bag and huffing and puffing.

"Right, left, and down! That's good, start again, right, left, and down... Do it again, just like that..."

She continues to sweat as she punches and tosses her black hair back. I creep closer, careful not to let myself be seen.

"Now try a lunge and down."

Gin throws two left straights and then tries a lunge with her right. I suddenly yank the bag aside and block her right arm. "Boom." I see the look of astonishment on her face, practically aghast. Quickly, I form a fist and tap her lightly on the chin. "Hey, there, Million Dollar Baby."

She wriggles free. "What the heck are you doing here?"

"I just wanted to try out this gym."

"Well, how about that! This one in particular?"

"It just so happens, yes. It's handy, and since I work around here myself—"

"I was picked fairly for that role, and it had nothing to do with you."

"Who said anything different?"

"I know what you were implying."

"You're sick in the head."

"And you're an asshole!"

"Hold on now, you two. Calm down. You're not going to start a fight right here in the gym, are you?" the trainer intervenes. "Plus, excuse me, Ginevra, this is your first trial lesson here, isn't it? You're not a member here at Gymnastic. So how could he have known? There was no way for him to be sure he'd find you here. It was just pure chance."

I look at her and smile. "That's right. It was just pure chance. Life is made up of coincidences. And it seems absurd to go looking for reasons behind what are clearly random events. Right?"

Gin heaves a sigh, hands on her hips, still imprisoned in her boxing gloves. "What *pure chance* are you talking about?"

"Now be nice, Ginevra," says the trainer, redoubling his efforts. "There's too much hostility between you two. It seems as if you hate each other."

"No, it doesn't *seem*. It's the simple truth!"

"Then you need to be careful. You must recently have finished school, and you should remember '*Odi et amo. Quare id faciam, nescio.*'"

Gin rolls her eyes. "Yes, yes, thanks. I read that poem by Catullus in Latin class, so I'm familiar with it. But we have a whole different set of problems here."

"Then you're going to need to solve them outside of the gym."

I look at her with a smile. "True, well put. That's a very good idea. Shall we go?"

"You should be careful. Don't underestimate her. Ginevra is strong, you know?"

"Believe me, I know that. She's even third dan."

"Not really?" The trainer's curiosity is aroused. "I didn't know that. Seriously?"

"Yes, strangely, he's telling the truth for once."

The trainer walks away, shaking his head. "There's hostility, there's hostility. This won't do." Then he comes back, smiling, as if he'd just come up with the solution to world peace. Or at least, peace between me and Gin. "Why don't you have a little match? I mean, it's ideal, a healthy venting of tensions."

Gin raises her hand in the boxing glove in my direction, pointing at me. "Don't be silly. I can bet you this guy hasn't brought a change of clothes."

"No, actually, *this guy* has everything he needs." I grin at her in delight and reach around behind the column and get out my gym bag. "And now, in accordance with your trainer's advice, I'm going to go get changed, right away."

⌒

"Nothing could be better. After all, it seems to me that he's a nice young man, so now you can put into practice some of the punches I explained to you today. In any case, it seems to me that you grasped them perfectly."

"Sure, but do you know who that guy is?" I ask.

The trainer looks at me, perplexed. "No, who is he?"

"He's Step."

He stands there for a moment, lost in thought, with his eyes half-shut. "Step, Step, Step. No, never heard of him."

I look at him while he smiles pleasantly at me. "No, seriously, never heard of him. But don't worry, you'll be able to handle him!"

At that moment, I understand two things. One, he's certainly not a good trainer, and two, for that reason I should start worrying.

⌒

I'm putting on a light T-shirt, shorts, gym socks, and the new Nikes I bought at Nike Town in New York.

"Hey, Step, ciao." In the locker room, I meet someone I know, but I can't remember his name. "What are you doing here? Do you train here?"

"Just for today. I want to take a trial lesson just to get an idea of how things work in this gym."

"They work great, let me tell you! Aside from the fact

that it's full of women. Did you see the one working the heavy bag? A hottie to die for."

"In a few minutes, I'm going to be trading punches with her."

"Don't tell me!" The guy whose name I absolutely can't recall looks at me in surprise and then with a hint of worry. "I didn't make a mistake, did I? Should I not have said it?"

"Said what?"

"That she's a hottie to die for?"

I lock the locker, putting the key in my pocket. "What possible reason? It's just true!" I smile at him and leave.

"All right, third dan, are we ready to start?" I say to Gin.

She looks at me with a fake smile. "Leaving aside the fact that the third dan has nothing to do with it, and you are so incredibly repetitive, can't you come up with anything new?"

I laugh like an idiot and spread my arms wide. "I can't believe it. Here we are about to have a boxing match, a nice serious match, no holds barred, and what do you do? You just start a taunting match."

"A taunting match, nice, I hadn't heard of that."

"You can't use it, in this case *I* hold the rights to it!" And a split second later...Boom. I wasn't expecting that. She hits me right in the face with a fast, sharp right straight.

"Good job, nice work." The trainer jumps in the air. "Right, left lunge, and then get back on guard."

I move my jaw, shifting it right and left. It's slightly numb.

"Nothing broken, I trust?" Gin is jumping in place, looking at me and raising an eyebrow. "If you want, we can get started for real now." Then, jumping, she comes over to me. "This was nothing but a first taste, oh, living legend. Ha, my trainer has never heard of you."

I look at her as I lace up my boxing gloves. "As far as that goes, he hasn't seen the photo I took of you with the Polaroid camera. Certainly, if he did see it..."

"If he did see it?"

"Well, maybe he'd think things over. In that photo, you look so scary that he'd suddenly get over even that itch he has to take you to bed!"

Gin lunges at me like a fury and starts hitting me.

With a laugh, I parry punches that are coming in from all directions, with an open glove, then a closed one, variously wide and narrow. Finally, she catches me with a straight kick.

"Hey..."

Lower belly. She lands the kick there good and solid. I fold over, keening from the pain. I just barely manage to catch my breath. "Ouch! No fair!"

"All's fair with you."

"Okay, Gin, even if I wanted to show you all my love, right here and now I wouldn't be up to it."

"Don't worry. I'll take you at your word."

Damn it to hell, she distracted me, she made me laugh, and then she kicked my balls in. I stand there, folded over at the waist, doing my best to recover.

The trainer comes over. "Problems?" He puts his hand on my shoulder.

"No, no, everything's fine. Or almost."

I stamp my feet, and I put my hands on my hips, breathing deeply as I pull myself upright.

"Okay, you see, now I could finish you off, if I didn't feel pity for you," she says.

"How charitable you are. Shall we move over to the ring?"

"Certainly." Gin smiles at me calmly and walks confidently past me.

The trainer goes over to the side of the ring and raises the ropes, helping us to pass under them. "Hey, pal, listen to me. No low blows and go easy on her, okay? I want to see a nice, fair match."

Gin joins me at the center of the ring. We tap each other's boxing gloves. Both of them at the same time, just like in the movies.

"Are you ready?" I ask her.

"I'm ready for everything. And don't pay any attention to him. He's not my trainer, and you're done for! Let me inform you that all kinds of blows are allowed, especially low ones, illegal ones, and unfair ones, especially from me."

"I'm so afraid!"

In response, she tries to punch me right in the face, but this time I'm ready for her. I parry with my left, and I give her a nice, fat kick in the ass, but without hurting her too badly. "I'm here for the party too, now. Well, shall we get started?"

We bounce up and down, circling around each other, studying each other's moves while the trainer has started the timer on a Swatch chronometer of his. Gin starts punching me and smiles as she does it.

"Hey, are you still enjoying yourself, Gin? Good. Enjoy it while you can because in a minute..." Then a quick, hard straight to the belly takes my breath away for a moment. My friend is fast.

"Save your breath, living legend. You're going to need it. Did I tell you that I've done a fair bit of full-contact boxing too?"

I continue to bounce up and down as I catch my breath. "First rule, you always need to attack after connecting with a punch. Otherwise..."

I start in on her from up close but not too hard, not too fast. Right, then another right, then I dribble her with a left, and then another right. She parries the first three punches perfectly, and then I make it through her defenses with the final right.

When I see Gin absorb the punch, she moves to the left and almost slips and falls. I've hit her too hard. I reach out to steady her before she drops to the canvas.

"Hey, I'm sorry, did I hurt you?" Sincerely concerned. "It's just that—"

Gin responds with an uppercut, catching my chin just off center. She takes the words right out of my mouth. Luckily just the words.

"You didn't hurt me at all." She huffs proudly and whips her head around to toss her hair back and then leaps in to attack with a double scissor kick. Right, left, and with the flat of her foot, she pushes me back and then goes to town. Right, left, and then another right.

Left, right, hook, I parry as best I can, trying to keep from hitting her again. I parry smiling and with some difficulty, truth be told.

Closer and closer. She forces me into the corner and attacks again.

"Hey, take it easy." I cover myself with my gloves, and she continues punching. Then she attempts a right straight, and boom, it happens. I swing a wide left on the fly and manage to reach around her body. I block her right arm under mine, and I hold her tight. "Imprisoned!"

She stands there, blocked like that, with her left slightly farther away.

"If you go at it with too much enthusiasm, you see what happens?"

Gin does everything she can to get loose. She pulls back, she leans on the ropes, she comes at me, she throws herself back again, and she slams against me, trying to wriggle free.

I give her a light punch to the face with my right. "You see what I could do to you?" I continue hitting her. "Boom, boom, boom. Gin as a punching bag. You'd be finished!"

Her only response, as if demented, is to try to hit me with her unhampered left fist. I parry it easily, but she won't give up. Boom, boom, boom. I parry every one of her punches, one after the other. Gin tries an uppercut, then a straight, a hook, another uppercut, then she climbs up on the ropes with one foot and launches from there to add impact to her punch.

None of it does a bit of good. I'm braced against the corner, and I hold her right fist pressed close against me.

Gin is beside herself. "Ah-hooo!" she howls, like an enraged wolf. She tries to knee me, but I quickly lift my own knee and parry that too. She tries to punch me again with a left hook, but it comes in slower this time. Maybe she's starting to run out of steam.

There's the mistake I was looking for. I spread my right arm wide, and I clamp down on her left arm too, pinning her close to me. "So what now?"

She stands there, glaring, in front of me, completely hemmed in. "Now where is Gin, the tiger, supposed to go?" She tries to break free. "Just relax, here in my arms."

She tries to wriggle free once again, but she can't do it. I lean close, and I kiss her, and she seems to respond for a moment. "Ouch!" She just bit me. I quickly let go of her, freeing both her arms. "Fucking hell." I lift my gloves to my mouth to see if I'm spitting blood. "You nearly took my lip off. What about all my other girlfriends? Watch out, they'll beat you up, and there are plenty of them."

"I already told you. I'm not afraid." And in order to re-inforce the point, she whips around to try to hit me with a whirling kick. But I'm too fast for her, I slide to the ground and sweep her legs out from under her so that she drops to the floor next to me.

"It's no good, Gin. It's like when Apollo Creed says in *Rocky IV*, 'I taught you everything you know. Almost everything. Remember, you fight great...but I'm a great fighter!'"

And in just a second, I'm on top of her. I immobilize her body with both legs wrapped around her waist, and with my right hand, I push her tight against the floor, her face pressed against the mat, right there, next to mine.

"Do you know that you're beautiful like that?" I don't know why, but she's making me think of *Lethal Weapon* when Mel Gibson and Rene Russo compare battle scars and then fall to the floor. "Gin, do you want to make love?"

Gin smiles and shakes her head. "Here? Now on the gym floor, in front of the trainer and everyone else that's watching?"

"The trick is just not to think about it."

"What are you talking about, Step? Have you lost your mind? Next thing you know they'll all start chanting, trying to set the rhythm."

"Okay, in that case, let's go back to boxing, if that's what you want. Don't say I didn't give you a chance."

We both get back to our feet. This time, though, I start in first. I force her into the corner and start pummeling her. Obviously, without hitting too hard though.

Gin is quick and tries to dart out from under. I shove her quickly back into the corner. She drops, dodges, tries to get free, but I hem her in. Then she feints to the left but actually swings wide. I launch a lazy, slow punch to her body.

With extreme speed, she closes her arm, locking down my right. Immediately afterward, she does the same thing with great rapidity to my left. "Ta-*dah*. Now I've got you locked in. What now?"

Actually, all it would take is a headbutt to get free, but I decide that's not the move to pull right now.

Gin sighs. "As usual, you're my prisoner. Don't you dare try and bite me though. I swear that if you do, I'll deck you."

She takes and kisses me. I let her do it, sweat and saliva, smooth kisses, lustful and elusive. She plays with my lips while I hold her tight with my boxing gloves. She rubs up against me, shorts and T-shirt, just sweaty enough. Her hair sticks to my face, concealing me from prying eyes.

But the trainer, who's been following us and timing the rounds, certainly can't figure out the rules of this strange boxing match.

"First they try to beat each other silly, and then they

decided to turn it into a party. Young people are so ridiculous." And he walks away, shaking his head.

You think that what we're doing is throwing a party? This
is art, man. Fantastic, refined, mystical, savage, elegant,
primordial art.

We continue kissing in the corner of the ring, indifferent
to everything, now freer in the clinch and excited, aroused,
or at least I am. We're well beyond the timing of any
round . . . way beyond it.

I let my glove slide down, and it winds up, by some twist
of fate, between her legs, but Gin moves aside. And then,
as if that wasn't enough, a couple of guys in their forties get
up into the ring with a pair of harnesses around their necks.
"Sorry, we wouldn't want to interrupt this match. But we'd
like to do some real boxing, if you wouldn't mind clearing
out of here."

"Yes, why don't you go get a room somewhere else?"
They laugh.

I take Gin by her arm, clutching it with the thumb of
my boxing glove, and I help her out of the ring. The bigger
guy of the pair, who still smells of weed, doesn't want to let
her get away without a comment. "Hey, what do you think
you're doing, anyway, fighting with a woman?"

Gin slips out of my hands and darts quickly back under
the rope and starts climbing into the ring. "What does he
think he's doing? Do you want to find out?" And she takes
her stance.

I get in the middle quickly before it all goes to hell.
"Okay, okay. Never mind, we'll leave the ring to you.
Forgive us. The young lady is just a little on edge."

"I'm not on edge."

"Ahem, well anyway, we'd probably better go get a gelato." Softly to Gin, whispering into her ear, "My treat. I'm just begging you to drop the offensive."

Gin spreads her arms wide. "Okay, okay."

"There you go, go get yourselves some gelato, go on."

"Yes, a gelato kiss." They both laugh. They just had to go for the parting joke.

Gin tries to whirl around again, but I push her away forcefully. "Go get changed, get a shower, and then gelato. March, and don't argue."

"Hey, you're scaring me worse than my papà. Just look, I'm shaking all over." And she simulates a sort of butt dance, twerking wildly.

Wow. I smack her on the ass. "Go on, I told you. Go get changed."

And with one last push, I manage to propel her toward the locker room. Phew, that wasn't easy.

Gin slips back out the door to the locker room. "Listen, I'm getting changed strictly because it's eleven, and I'm done with my free hour of gym."

"Yes, certainly."

She looks at me in bafflement for a moment with one eyebrow raised, then she drops it and smiles. "Okay." She understands that I've just let her win. "It'll just take a second. I'll see you down at the gym café, all the way down that hallway."

I go to get changed myself. What a battle. I don't know if she's better in the ring or out of it. I pull out the key to my locker. What is it that's so special about her? I get in the shower. Okay, no doubt, a nice ass, a nice smile...I find a bottle of shampoo someone's left behind and empty it over my head. Sure, she's amusing, a quick wit. But she's exhausting too. True, but how long has it been since I had an affair worthy of the name? Two years.

I dry off, and I put on my pants. I button my shirt, and I grab my gym bag. I arrive at the bar, and I order a Gatorade, not too chilled.

"With what, excuse me?"

"With orange."

I shell out two euros, I twist off the top, and I drink my Gatorade. I look around. A guy dressed up in standard post-training gear is reading *Il Tempo*. He eats mechanically, bent over a bowl of rice, plain, colored here and there by a few scant kernels of corn and a green pepper. At the next table, another muscular guy is chatting up a young girl in an unbearably false tone of voice. He reacts with excessive cheer to anything she says to him. Two young women plan who knows what for a hypothetical vacation they're scheming to go on together. Another is telling her dearest, closest, bestest friend how badly some guy treated her.

A young man at the counter, still sweaty from his work-out, another already changed into street clothes. A young woman drinks a smoothie and then leaves. Another young woman is waiting for who knows what. I search for the face of this second young woman in the mirror facing the counter but she's covered by the young man who's working the bar. Then he serves an order and leaves, unveiling her. Like the card that is dealt you in a hoped-for hand in poker, like the last bounce of the ball in roulette that maybe lands on the number you'd put every penny on...it's her. There she is. Gin looks at me and smiles. Her hair is hanging down right over her freshly made-up eyes, smudged with a light gray. Her lips are pink and faintly pouty.

She turns around and looks at me. "Well, what's up, don't you recognize me?" Gin is wearing a powder-blue skirt suit. On the hem, you can see a pair of small monograms. D&G. I smile. All credit to YOOX. Then a pair of ankle boots in the same color. Extremely elegant. René Caovilla. The pattern of the laces reveals stretches of her ankles. Her toe-nails are painted with a lighter shade of pale blue, peeking out of a faint dusky tan. Chanel sunglasses, again light blue, sit perched atop her head. It's as if a thin layer of honey had been allowed to drip over her bare legs and perfectly molded to her arms and over her smiling face. "Well?"

Well, all my good intentions vanish in a puff of smoke. I try to come up with a word or two. I'm tempted to laugh, and at the same time, my mind darts back to that scene in *Pretty Woman*. Richard Gere looking for Vivian in the hotel bar. Then he sees her. Ready for the opera. Gin is every bit as perfect, or better. I'm in dire straits here.

She picks up her purse and walks toward me. "Are you thinking about something?"

"Yes." I lie. "That the Gatorade was too cold."

Gin smiles and walks past me. "Liar, you were thinking about me."

She heads off, self-confident as she climbs the steps leading out of the gym. Her legs extend below the hem of her skirt, faintly pleated, and then vanish upward, lithe and strong, perhaps just slightly anointed with beauty creams, and taper down into a solid and determined square heel.

She stops at the top of the stairs and turns around. "Well, what are you doing, looking at my legs? Come on. Don't stand there staring. Let's go get an aperitif or whatever you want, and after that, I have lunch with my parents and my uncle. A real pain in the neck. Otherwise, I never would have bothered to get tricked out like this."

Women. You see them at the gym. Skimpy bodysuits, strange, invented leotards, tight short-shorts, and spangly T-shirts. Full-tilt aerobics. Sweaty, their faces without makeup, their hair plastered to their scalps, straggling down their faces. And then, poof. Like something out of Aladdin's magic lamp. They emerge from the locker room, and a miracle has been performed.

"Oh, what are you thinking about?"

"Me?"

"Who else? Nobody here but you and me."

"Nothing."

"There you go again. Well, it must be a very special nothing. You seemed like you were lost in a trance. I guess I must have punched you too hard, huh?"

"Yes, but I think I'm recovering."

"I'll come with my car," Gin says.

"Okay. Just follow me."

I climb aboard my motorcycle, but I can't resist. I position my rearview mirror so I'll be able to watch her get into her car.

I drive past her. I keep her at the center of my line of sight. There she is, she's getting in. Gin leans forward, she seats herself, and then lightly and softly she makes each of her legs fly up off the pavement. Quick and agile, almost simultaneously except for a fleeting instant, that tiny frame of lacey underwear that is like a whole film though. What a sensual flash.

Then I return to the realm of reality. I put the bike in gear and take off.

Gin follows me easily. She drives like an experienced racer. She has no problems in traffic. She swings wide, overtakes, and slides back into line. She honks her horn occasionally to forestall impending drivers' errors. She anticipates the car's oscillations as it enters and follows the curves of the road, her head swaying, I imagine, to the beat of some music. Every so often, she flashes her brights at me when she can see me keeping an eye on her in my rearview mirror, double brights as if to say, *Hey, don't fret, I'm right behind you.*

A few more curves and we're there. I stop. I let her slide past. Then I pull up next to her. "Go on, find a place to park here because you won't be able to get in."

She asks no questions. She just locks her car and climbs on behind me, tugging her skirt high. "Too cool, this motorcycle, I like it. I haven't seen many like it."

"None. They only made one, just for me."

"Sure, no doubt, I believe you. Do you know how much it would cost to make a single model for just one person?"

"Yes, four hundred and fifteen thousand euros."

Gin looks at me sincerely amazed. "So much?"

"And just figure that they gave me a major discount."

She sees me smile in the rearview mirror that I've turned in her direction to catch her gaze. I try to do a little bout of wrestling with our gazes. Then I give in and smile.

She punches me hard on the shoulder. "Oh, come on. What the hell are you talking about? You're such a bullshit artist!" This is something that hasn't happened to me, not since the times of legendary brawls on Piazza Euclide, the raids down the Via Cassia as far as Talenti and back. Step, a bullshit artist. Who had finally dared to say it? This woman, the one riding behind me.

And she's not done. "Leaving aside the cost, I really like this motorcycle. One of these days, you'll have to let me drive it."

Sheer insanity, someone asking to drive my motorcycle, and who asks? The same woman who just called me a bullshit artist! But the truly incredible thing is what I say back to her, "Yes, certainly."

We turn into the park of Villa Borghese, where I drive fast but without undue haste, and I park in front of the little café next to the lake. "Okay, here we are. People don't come here much so it's nice and quiet."

"What's the matter? Don't you need to put in an appearance somewhere for your adoring fans?"

"Hey, are you trying to pick a fight? If I'd known, I would have taken it out on you a little harder at the gym."

"You're lucky you didn't," Gin says.

"Okay, okay, truce, come on. Let's have an aperitif as a peace offering, okay?"

Chapter 23

Gin smiles, and we sit down at a small table. Not far away, an intellectual with a pair of tiny eyeglasses and a book on the table is sipping a cappuccino. Then he picks up an article in *Leggere*, the literary monthly. Farther away, a woman in her early forties with long hair and a small mutt under her chair is languidly smoking a cigarette, sad and nostalgic, perhaps, for all the joints she can't smoke anymore.

"Nice little place, huh?"

Behind me, a waiter has appeared. "Buongiorno, signori." He's about sixty, and he treats us with old-fashioned elegance.

"I'll have an Ace cider," Gin says.

"And I'll have a Coke and a small prosciutto and mozzarella white pizza."

The waiter nods slightly in a nominal bow and then heads off.

"Hey, after the gym, you give yourself a treat, don't you? A small pizza and a Coca-Cola, the diet of athletes!"

"Speaking of athletes, since you're a freeloading athlete, you'll need to let me have your list of your gyms, one for each of the three hundred sixty-five days of the year."

"Why not? I'll give you a copy of it right away."

"My compliments. In any case, it's an excellent idea."

"That's not all, but if you're careful, you can even get the same kind of lesson every week, the only thing is you have to make friends with the instructors because, sooner or later, they're bound to figure it out."

"So what do you do about that?"

"After the lesson, you buy them a couple of Gatorades, you lay out your financial difficulties, and off you sail, free as a bird. It's just wonderful and, really, easy as pie."

"Is there anyone else you know who's using this method?"

The waiter returns. "Here you are, the Ace for the signorina and for you, signore, the small white pizza and the Coca-Cola." The waiter sets it all down at the center of the table, placing a check under the faux-silver tray and walking away.

"No, I don't think so." Gin bites into a large potato chip and eats it. Then, laughing, she covers her mouth with her hand. "At least I hope not." And so we continue chatting, laughing, and trying to figure out what else we have in common.

"Come on, you've never been outside of Europe?" I ask.

"No, Greece, England, France, once even in Germany for the Oktoberfest with a couple of girlfriends."

"I've been to Oktoberfest myself."

"Seriously? When?"

"In 2002," I tell her.

"Me too. But the most absurd thing about the whole trip is that one of my girlfriends was a teetotaler. You can't imagine what she turned into. She ordered a one-liter stein of beer, you know the goblets I'm talking about, brimming over, the ones they wash in those giant basins. She tips back half of it, and before half an hour goes by, she's dancing some sort of tarantella on top of a table. Just a disaster."

I watch her as she drinks the Ace. There was a girl dancing on a table in the beer hall we went to. But that evening I think everybody was dancing on tables at the Oktoberfest. I remember that when I told Babi that I was going to Munich with Pollo and Schello and another carful of friends, she got insanely angry. *"So, you're going to Munich, and what about me?"*

"You're not coming. It's a guy trip."

"Ah, really? We'll see about that."

And then that asshole, Manetta, in the other car, what did he decide to do? He shows up with his girlfriend. And when we get back, furious arguments about it with Babi because, naturally, like everything else, sooner or later, that fact became general knowledge.

"What are you thinking about?"

I lie. "About your friend who danced on the table. You should have filmed her. You would have laughed afterward."

"But we laughed like fools while it was happening. What good is afterward? What matters is now." And she takes another sip of Ace, glancing at me knowingly.

Ouch, what's that supposed to mean? Things look bad. Very bad. Gin wants things "now." But not now, not this instant, not yet. But maybe tomorrow.

"What are you thinking about? Still thinking about my girlfriend dancing on the table? I doubt that. If you ask me, you met someone at the Oktoberfest, and you're thinking back to one of your escapades."

"You're seeing it all wrong."

"I'm seeing it perfectly. I've got twenty-twenty vision."

I look around and I'm in luck. Behind me is the waiter, who smiles. I hadn't noticed him.

"May I?" The waiter leans forward and pulls the check out from under the little faux-silver tray. I hadn't even heard him come up behind me. Odd, that's not like me. Look at that, for the first time, I'm relaxed with Gin. Is that a good thing?

"That will be eleven euros, signore."

I reach into my pocket for my wallet. I open it and smile. "You'll have to pay. I don't have any money."

Gin, so elegant and beaming, perfectly attired and made up, grimaces at me, with faux irony. Then she smiles at the waiter, in apology for the wait. She opens her purse, pulls out her wallet, opens it, and this time she doesn't smile at all. In fact, somewhat awkwardly, she blushes. "You know, signore, I changed clothes for lunch today with my family and, since they're paying, I just didn't think of it."

"That's not good." The waiter changes both tone of voice and expression. That courtesy of his seems to vanish into thin air. Perhaps, a mature and even elderly gentleman like him feels that he's been made a fool of by these two kids.

I take the situation in hand. "Listen, don't worry. Just let me accompany the young lady to her car, I'll get cash from an ATM, and I'll hurry right back here and pay you."

"Sure, of course... and you must take me for a fool rube! Do I look stupid to you? Out with the cash, or I'll call the cops."

I smile at Gin. "Excuse me." I stand up and take the waiter by the arm, courteously at first, and then, in response to his rebellious "What do you think you're doing? Get your hands off of me," I grip a little more tightly and take him farther away. "Okay, signor waiter, we're in a position here, but don't make too big of a deal about it. We have no interest in stealing eleven euros from you. Is that clear?"

"But I..."

I clamp down more firmly, this time in an unmistakably determined way. I see a grimace of pain on his face, and I immediately release him. "Please, I'm asking this as a favor. This is the first time I've gone out with this young lady..."

Perhaps primarily because he's moved and convinced by this last confession of mine, he nods. "Okay, then, I'll expect you later."

We return to the table. I smile at Gin. "Everything's settled." Gin gets up and looks at the waiter with sincere regret. "I'm really so sorry."

"Oh, don't worry about it. These things happen."

I smile at the waiter. He looks at me. I think he's trying to figure out whether or not I'm planning to come back. "Don't come back too late, signore, if you please."

"Don't worry."

And so we leave. With a courteous smile and a crumb of dignity.

Chapter 24

I'm behind Step, on the motorcycle, my thoughts in the wind. Look at this guy. Where have you gotten yourself, Gin? It's absurd. I shake my head, but he notices. I pretend to look in the opposite direction but he tracks me in his rearview mirror and leans back to make himself heard.

"So what's wrong? Did I come off as a jerk?"

"In what way?"

"First date, I don't have the money to pay. I practically ask you to pay for me. Even worse, we come that close to being arrested. I can already imagine what you're thinking." Step smiles and pitches his voice up into a falsetto in imitation of what I must be thinking. "There, I knew, this scoundrel is a good-for-nothing."

I ignore him.

Step smiles and continues, undeterred. "Just look at who I've made the mistake of frequenting. Goodness, if my folks could see me now."

Oh, he's really plumbed all my innermost thoughts. Still, he's likable. I try not to smile, but it's more than I can do.

"I nailed it, didn't I? Come on, tell the truth."

"No, I was just thinking of what my uncle Ardisio would probably have said."

"You see? Well, in that case, there was a smidgen of truth in that smile of yours."

"He would have called you the Prince of Pigs!"

⌒

"Here she comes now! Hey, Gin!"

I wave to them from a distance. What a strange group they are, glimpsed as a collective with different, clashing heights, dressed so very differently. My brother in jeans and a Nike T-shirt, my mother in a dark flowered dress with a navy-blue shoulder cape over it, my father impeccable in blazer and necktie, and my uncle Ardisio in an orange jacket and a black necktie with white polka dots. It's incredible where he manages to come up with certain stuff. Television costume designers, or even Fellini himself, would go crazy for him. With his mussed up, tousled hair, white and unmanageable, framing that funny face and counter-balanced by his little round eyeglasses, what a character my uncle is!

"Ciao," I say, and we all exchange kisses on the cheeks, and Mamma as usual puts her hand on my cheek as she gives me a kiss, as if to impress an extra layer of love on top of that simple, basic kiss, as if she wished to anchor it a tiny bit tighter than any of the other loving greetings. My uncle, on the other hand, overdoes it with his kiss, pulling me forward with thumb and forefinger joined under my chin, forcing me to shake my head right and left.

"Here she is, my little princess." Then he releases me,

leaving me with a lingering pinch of pain. I necessarily have to rub my hand under my chin to smooth it out, and my uncle gets a glance of faint annoyance in return. But it only lasts a second. Then I smile back at his smile. That's just the way my uncle is.

"Well?" This is how our meals always begin. "Who chose this place?"

I shyly raise my hand. "I did, Uncle Ardisio." And I wait for the response. My uncle gives me a look with one eyebrow raised slightly, a somewhat dubious expression. A few too many seconds tick past, and I start to worry.

"Good job. It's a lovely place, young lady, I like it. For real. There was a time when people ate surrounded with art..."

I sigh. Phew. It was acceptable, and even if I don't much care about the title of "young lady," I do love my uncle. I was hoping he'd enjoy eating with all of us at the Caffè dell'Arte near Rome's Viale Bruno Buozzi.

Uncle Ardisio begins one of his stories. "I still remember the time I flew over the encampment, looking down on all my men..." His voice grows slightly hoarse, as if modulated by the pressure of his memories, here and there cracking under the weight of sentimental nostalgia. "And I shouted and shouted to them, 'Study, read.' But they were all too concerned with death. And then I circled around in my twin-engine airplane and came back to report in and landed on the meadow nearby. Bing, bang, boom, all tossed around like a bushel of wheat, I landed in that airplane, which I considered a miracle of modern avation..."

Luke naturally is a stickler for details exactly when he shouldn't be. "*Aviation*, Uncle, aviation with an *i*."

"Which is what I just said, isn't it? Avation, right?"

Luke shakes his head and smiles. Luckily, this time he decides to let it ride.

A young and serious waiter arrives at the table. His hair is short but not excessively so, and he has a naive but clear-eyed gaze. Almost perfect, I'd venture to say, if it weren't that he's pushing a trolley upon which perch an array of glistening champagne flutes, polished to a fine sheen, as well as a bottle already sitting comfortably in an ice bucket, chilling away. It's a Möet & Chandon, a first-rate champagne, and certainly not what we expect, seeing that we're footing the bill.

"Excuse me, eh? But this can't be right. No one ordered a..." I can already see Mamma glancing over at me with a worried look.

The young waiter replies with a smile. "No, signora, this bottle is sent to your table with the compliments of that gentleman across the room."

The waiter, even more serious now, points to a table some distance away, practically at the far end of the restaurant. Framed by the trees depicted in the stained-glass windows behind him, it's Step. He gets up from his table and bows his head, smiling, performing an understated bow. I can't believe it—he's followed me here. And certainly, he wanted to see where I was going, he wanted to see if I was really with my family. But maybe he just wanted to express an apology for the unsuccessful aperitif; after all, he came off looking like a fool in that situation himself.

"This note is for you, signora."

The waiter hands me a slip of paper, and this only further reinforces my belief that my choice is the correct one. I open it, slightly embarrassed, with everyone's eyes focused on me. Before reading it, I blush. Oh, what a pain in the ass. Why now of all times? I read it. *It's wonderful to look at you from a distance, but from up close, it's even better. Can I see you tonight? P.S. Don't worry, I found an ATM, and I've already paid the waiter for our aperitif.*

I fold up the note, and I smile and practically forget that I have everyone's eyes on me. Uncle Ardisio, Papà, Mamma, Luke. They all want to know what the note said, what prompted the delivery of that fine bottle to our table, and naturally the one who is most unbridled, the one whose curiosity is most probing and persistent, is Uncle Ardisio. "All right, then, princess, to what do we owe this bottle?"

"Well. I helped that guy. He didn't know how, he was having trouble, oh, he was just studying for an exam."

"Ardisio, what business is it of yours?" Mamma throws me a lifeline. "We have a nice bottle of champagne here on the table. Let's just raise a toast and drink in peace! No?"

"Right, exactly . . ."

I look at Step, and I smile in his direction. He sees me from a distance, and he's sitting down again. But now what is he doing? Why doesn't he leave? That was nice, and now enough's enough. Go on, beat it, Step. What are you waiting for?

"Excuse me?"

The waiter is looking at me with a smile. He still hasn't opened the bottle.

"Yes?"

"That gentleman told me that he'd appreciate an answer."

"What?"

"I'm not sure, but I imagine an answer to the note."

Everyone looks at me again, even more closely this time than before.

"Why, tell him yes." Then I look at them. "Yes, he just wanted to know if I'd signed him up for the exam."

They all heave a sigh of relief. Except for Mamma, naturally, who stares at me, but I avoid her gaze. Again, I turn back to look at the waiter, who now pulls out another note. "In that case, I'm instructed to give you this, signora."

"Another note?"

Everyone is a little gobsmacked.

"Wait, so this time are you going to tell us what it says?"

"What is this, a treasure hunt?"

I blush again, and I open it. *In that case, at eight o'clock, I'll be outside your house. I'll be expecting you. Don't be late. P.S. Bring money. You never know.*

I smile inwardly.

The waiter has finally popped the cork. He lifts the bottle, quickly fills the champagne flutes, serves them around, and turns to go.

"Excuse me, one more thing . . ."

"Yes?"

He turns on his heel and looks at me.

"But if I'd told you no, did you have another note?"

The waiter smiles and shakes his head. "No, in that case, he told me I was simply to remove the bottle."

Chapter 25

Comfortable and relaxed, I'm well-dressed like never before, or at least I think so. I look at myself in the rearview mirror, and I can't seem to recognize myself. Hair still wet from the shower I've just taken, navy-blue blazer, white dress shirt, and tan linen trousers, with a pair of dark brown leather American shoes. A wide belt with a big buckle, a dark brown leather that matches the shoes. Ah, I almost forgot my shirt buttoned up to the second-to-last button and my cell phone in my pocket. Me with a cell phone. I still can't quite believe it. I can be reached anywhere I go, any time of the day or night, and therefore am never free.

As if by magic, or maybe just bad luck, naturally, it rings. Fuck, now of all times. I open the phone. You want to bet that Gin is running late or can't go out? If that's the case, I don't give a damn. I'll go straight over to her house and wait outside.

"Hello?"

"Step, what a relief. I'm glad you answered."

It's Paolo, but of course, how could I have failed to think of him?

"What's going on?" I ask.

"Step, something awful's happened. Someone stole my car."

"Damn it to hell. You made me think it might have been Mamma or Papà."

"No, they're fine. I went downstairs, and my Audi A4 was just gone. Fuck, how the hell do you think they did it? There's no glass on the floor, so they couldn't have shattered the side window. But the garage was wide open, and no one had pried it open or anything like that. How do you think they could have done it?"

"Hey, Pa, by now car thieves have really perfected their techniques, you know? And garages with remote openers? Nobody uses crowbars on those anymore. They have frequency-hacking devices. They just keep trying new frequencies until the garage opens."

"Oh, right. I hadn't thought of that. Fucking hell!"

I like hearing my brother pissed off like this. It makes him seem alive and, finally, fuck, he gets worked up. But still, worked up over things that don't really matter, like his car. What does that amount to?

"Now of all times they decide to steal it. Last week I paid the final installment on the financing. They could have stolen it a year ago, at least then I'd have saved all that money."

Such a cynic. An accountant, right down to the bottom of his shoes.

"Oh, well, Pa, what are you going to do about it anyway?"

"No, I was just hoping..."

"That I might have stolen it from you?"

"No, what, are you kidding? I mean, the keys and the duplicates are still here."

"Ah, so for just a second there, you did think it, didn't you?"

"No, it's just that, I mean..."

"Oh, no, you went and checked to see whether the duplicates were still there, so that means you thought about it. Only *I* could have stolen your car."

A moment's silence.

"Well, yes, I did think it, just for a moment. But I would have been happy to find out, I mean, you know, it would have been *better* if it was you."

My brother. "Pa, just shut up. You're not doing yourself any favors."

"Why?"

Right, "Why?" he has to ask me. And I'm stupid enough to try to get him to understand.

"Nothing, Pa. Don't think about it. It's fine."

"I just had a question, Step. I mean, as long as you don't take offense, okay?"

"What? Go ahead."

"I mean, I'm just saying that, for better or worse, you must know a bunch of people in those networks. Well, you see, if it's no problem for you... if you could put your ear to the ground and find out if anyone took it."

"Hey, but those people are going to want money, you know? You're not going to ask me to go duke it out with people at that level just for any old car."

"Any old car? It's an Audi A4!"

"Sure, right, for an Audi A4."

"No, no, not that, absolutely not... Sure, I'd already thought that through. I'm willing to shell out as much as forty-three hundred euros."

"And why that exact sum?"

"I just figured that with the deductible and all the rest of it..."

My brother, the great accountant. The very best.

"Okay, Pa, if I can, I'll see what I can do."

"Thanks, Step. I knew I could count on you."

My brother who thinks he can count on me, that really takes the cake.

Two curves and I'm downstairs from her apartment. I go to the intercom, and as I'm about to ring her apartment, I remember that she has a cell phone. I call and let it ring twice to let her know I'm here. Did she understand? In my doubt, I decide to wait a minute. Sooner or later, she'll come down.

Maybe it would be better if I ring the doorbell. Another minute. I give myself another minute of waiting for her. I light a cigarette. There, I'll finish smoking this cigarette, and then I'll go over to the intercom.

The street is quiet. I look around. A few cars go by in the distance. One screeches to a halt because another decided to act tough and cut the first one off. But then the first car takes off, too, and life goes on, quietly and calmly, in this small patch of a much larger city.

What deeply stupid thoughts I'm having. Where am I going to take her this evening? How strange, I've thought about everything *but* that. That was something I ought to have been pondering. I get an idea but then I start to worry. I start to worry about what I'm considering. The idea of me worrying about where to take her to eat? Could I be worrying entirely too much? When you go out with a woman, if you start outlining the evening in advance, that's when things start to go sideways.

And I mean violently, disastrously sideways! No, that won't do. This demands nonchalance, improvisation, whatever happens, happens. Then, suddenly, I have an idea. Fuck though, I like this idea of mine.

One more drag and then I'll press the button on the intercom. But at that very moment, the front door clicks open. Light filters out of the lobby, a faintly orange hue. It lights up the leaves all around in the garden, the distant steps, the parked scooters.

Then an old lady comes out through the door. She is walking slowly, smiling, her legs slightly bent under the weight of the years.

Then, immediately behind the old lady, Gin. Gin let the old lady go first. She's still holding the door open for her, and she's helping her out. She's speaking to her with a smile, nodding in response to some chance question. She's courteous, she's pretty, and she's smiling.

The old lady goes by me, and even though I don't know her, I can't help but say, "Buonasera."

She smiles at me as if she'd known me all her life. "Good evening to you," and she walks off, leaving me alone with Gin.

Gin's hair is pulled back. She's wearing a short leather jacket, covered with zippers and little buckle straps, an amusing light blue 55DSL belt, and low-waisted dark trousers with five pockets and stitching in contrasting shades. With a large fabric Fake London Genius bag. She has style.

Incredible the way you notice all the details when you

like someone. She has a funny face. What am I saying? She has a pretty face.

"Where's your motorcycle? Didn't you come on your motorcycle?"

"No."

"And here I was, all dressed up special for it." She pirouettes in front of me. "Don't I sort of remind you of Marlon Brando in *The Wild One*?"

I smile. "More or less."

"So, then, how did you get here?"

"In this, I just thought you'd be more comfortable."

"An Audi A4! Who did you steal it from?"

"Ah, you underestimate me. It's mine."

"Sure it is, and I'm Julia Roberts."

"Depends on which movie you're thinking of. Oh, I get it, *Pretty Woman*."

"Tsk tsk." Gin heads over to the car door, and as she passes, she gives me a sudden punch in the shoulder.

"Ouch."

"We're not getting off to a good start. I did not like that wisecrack."

"Oh, not that way. I meant *Pretty Woman* in the sense that she's chasing a dream."

"And so?"

"And so, you've found your dream."

"What dream, the Audi A4?"

"No, me." I smile, we get in the car, and I take off out of there, tires screeching.

"More than a dream, this strikes me as a sort of a nightmare. Come on, tell the truth. Who did you steal it from?"

"My brother."

"There, I like that better. It's probably still a lie, but at least now it's believable."

I accelerate slightly, and we disappear into the night. And I think about the copies of the car keys purchased from that guy near the Sorci Verdi bar on Corso Francia, the one who has copies of all the keys of all the cars you could ever want or imagine. I think about Pollo and the first time he took me to see that guy, I think about the pranks we played, I think about my brother worrying and fretting about his stolen car. I think about the evening ahead of us, I think about my idea, and I think about my past. A few rapid thoughts, more powerful than the others.

I drive by the Church of the Assumption of Mary. I want to have some fun and take my mind off things. I turn to look at Gin. She's turned on the radio, and she's singing along with a song and has lit a cigarette. Then she looks at me and smiles. "Well, where are we going?"

"Oh, that's a surprise."

"That's what I was hoping you'd say."

She smiles and tilts her head to one side. She undoes her hair. And at that very moment, it dawns on me that she's the real surprise.

Chapter 26

So what's the surprise? Is it a nice surprise?"

"It's more than one surprise."

"So, tell me what it is."

"No, I can't. Then it wouldn't be a surprise anymore."

I park and get out of the car. A valet parking attendant comes running toward me with his hand already extended. I grab it immediately and clasp it vigorously. "Ciao, buddy."

He laughs. "That'll be two euros."

"No problem. But I'll pay when I get back." I shake hands, and I kind of overdo it with my grip. "That way I can rest assured it will be in perfect condition, right? I'll pay when the service is complete."

He looks at me, worry painted on his face.

"So keep an eye on it for me, I don't want to find any scratches when I get back. Is that clear?"

"But, after midnight I'm going to be..."

"We'll be back before midnight." And I walk away.

"Then I'll wait for you, all right?"

I say nothing and look at Gin.

"Your brother really cares about this car, doesn't he?"

"He's a maniac about it. Right now he's in a state of despair because he's convinced that I stole it from him."

"It's not like the police are going to pull us over and then we'll wind up in jail, is it?"

"He gave me the night to get it back to him."

"And then?"

"And then he'll lodge the criminal complaint. But don't worry, I've already found it for him, right?"

Gin laughs and shakes her head. "Your poor brother, I can just imagine what you've put him through."

"Actually, he may not know it, but I've saved him from plenty of bad situations, all our lives together."

I think about my mother for a moment. I feel like telling her...But this is *our* evening together, hers and mine. And no one else's.

"What are you thinking about?"

"That I'm hungry. Come on!"

And I grab her hand and drag her away. We go to Angel's for an aperitif, a chilled Martini for both of us, shaken not stirred, the way James Bond liked it, and it's a dream on an empty stomach.

Gin laughs and tells me stories. Stories from her past, girlfriends from her childhood, and Ele and how they met and the quarrels and jealousies of her good friend. And then I take her by the hand, and I say so long to a guy with an earring who seems to know me, and I take her into the restroom.

"Hey, what do you think you're up to? This hardly seems the kind of thing."

"No, listen, don't worry." I hand her a twenty-cent piece or maybe it's a fifty-cent piece or maybe a one-euro coin, maybe a two-euro coin, I don't even see them. I put them in her hand. I think about the parking attendant. About when I'll get back there and I'll have to tell him I've run out of coins. "This is the wishing well. You see all the coins at the bottom?"

Gin peers into a sort of well in that restroom decorated with potted plants and colorful carpets, in red and purple and orange. "Okay. Did you make your wish?" She smiles before turning from the well and tosses in the coin I gave her with a wish that's all hers. It lands at the bottom of the well in the hopes that wish will come true.

I follow suit immediately afterward, and I toss my own coin over my shoulder. And down it drops with great aplomb, vanishing into the water, sinking in a strange zigzag pattern and then settling on the bottom amid a thousand other dreams and a few wishes that may even have come true, to some extent.

We leave in silence while a guy hurries in the door, practically slamming into us as he unzips his trousers, but then at the last minute, he changes his mind and lurches over to the sink and vomits into it. We look at each other and burst out laughing, disgusted and shuddering. We shut the door behind us and get out of there.

I leave fifteen euros on the table, and in a flash, we're outside. I run into Angel, who says hello.

"Ciao, Step. It's been a while."

"Yes, yes it has. Later, maybe, I'll swing back by."

His real name is Pier Angelo. I can still remember him back in the day when he sold strange paintings to foreigners on Piazza Navona, improbable pieces of artistic flotsam and jetsam for even more improbable sums of cash, palmed off on a passing German or Japanese or American tourist. He'd spout a strange explanation in less-than-perfect English, butchered and completely invented, and he'd have placed another "package," one more brick in the wall that would allow him to buy his restaurant, Angel's, as in fact he finally did.

"Well? Is that it?" Gin asks.

"Don't worry. I understand, you're not interested in expending effort." I pick her up and throw her over my shoulder.

"No, come on. What are you doing?" She laughs and tries to beat me, but she does it in a jovial fashion.

"I'll carry you. As long as you promise not to ask any more questions."

"Put me down!"

We walk past a small group of young women and men who gaze at us, more-or-less amused, dreamily the girls, embarrassed the boys. At least, that's what I think I can read in their expressions. And we hurry on. Cul de Sac is the name of the next place.

"There, now you can get down. Here we're going to enjoy an aperitif with cheese and wines."

Gin tugs down her jacket, which had hiked up, as well as her T-shirt, which had uncovered her belly, soft but taut and compact without any strange piercings in the belly button.

"What are you doing, peeking? My little belly isn't my best feature."

Beautiful and insecure. "You mean to say there's more?"

Gin huffs.

"I'm magnetically drawn, attracted, inevitably pulled into the maelstrom, and..."

"Yes, yes, okay. I've grasped the concept."

We take a seat at the first table we see, and I place an order with a gentleman who is even wearing a white apron.

"Then we'll have a bitter seasoned goat cheese and two glasses of Traminer."

The guy nods, and I hope that he's actually understood, given his uncertainty.

"Where did you read this thing about Traminer and goat cheese? Did your brother suggest it?"

"No, sorry, I took a personal course with a French sommelier. Actually, a French *lady* sommelier, to be exact. In Epernay, in Champagne country."

The waiter sets down a wooden platter on the table and he nailed it: goat cheese and chilled Traminer. Incredible, and that's not all.

"I brought you some organic honey as well."

"Thanks."

It's nice to see someone who loves his work. But there's nothing nicer than seeing a young woman who's eating with genuine gusto. As Gin is. She smiles and spreads the honey over bread that's still warm, fresh from the oven, lightly toasted, perfectly bronzed, not burned. She sets a chunk of cheese on top and takes a big bite, determined but slow, while with her other hand she wards off the freefall of crazed crumbs. Then she touches her palm with the tips of her fingers and, as if playing a strange little tune, lets the crumbs drop into the little plate, next to what bread's left over, while with her other hand she takes the Traminer and, with a little sip, chases the whole thing down.

It's perfect, I know that. Little tastings and morsels. What it all means I can't say. But in reality, I do know.

The Traminer goes down easy, chilled, with its aftertaste. Icy. One glass after another. And from the thoughts in my head, from the way I trip myself up, I realize that I'm already half-drunk. I wait for her to finish her last bite, I set some money down on the table, and I abduct her. "Come on, let's go."

"Where are we going now?"

"A different place for every single specialty."

And we race away, just like that, a little wine, a little laughter. Surrounded by indiscreet glances, people at the other tables, heads turning in our direction to look at us, observe those two strangers... The two of us, meteors on any ordinary everyday night, in an ordinary everyday club, at a moment that's anything but ordinary and everyday, a moment that belongs to us alone. As does this food tour.

"Hey, Step?"

"Yes?"

"How many places will we be hitting?"

"What does that mean?"

"I mean, seeing that we're going to eat one item in each place, just to understand how many there will be. Otherwise, I'm afraid I might simply burst. Yes, tell me, how many places will we be stopping at?"

"Twenty-one!"

Gin suddenly stops. She halts in the middle of the street and digs in her heels.

"What's going on now?"

She grabs me suddenly by the jacket and pulls me to her with both hands, gripping my lapels.

"Tell me who you stole it from?"

"The Audi, I told you, my brother."

"No, this idea. Eating something different in every single place. Where did you get it?"

I laugh as I shake my head, drunker than ever, high on the fun as much as on the alcohol. "I thought it up myself."

"Do you mean that this was an idea all yours, that you didn't steal it from anyone else? I mean, some stupid book, some romantic film, some urban legend?"

I spread both arms wide, and I shrug my shoulders slightly. "It's all mine. It just occurred to me, like that." I snap my fingers.

Gin is still gripping me by the lapels, and she gazes into my face with a still slightly dubious expression. "And you've never done this with any other girl?"

"No. It's for you and you alone. As far as that goes, I've never even been to any of the places that I selected with any other girl."

She lets go of me all at once, shoving me backward. "Come on! This time you lied!"

I grab her by the lapels and spin her around before she can get too far away. She turns a one-eighty and winds up close to my face.

"Okay, I spouted bullshit. But it was always the bunch of us, in a group. Never alone, the way I am here, now, with you."

"Okay, that's already much better. Now I can believe it."

"You'd better believe it." My voice drops an octave, and I'm as surprised as anybody to hear it sounding so choked and suffocated, almost whispering, into her ears, around her neck, tangled in her hair. I look into her eyes. I smile sincerely. She appreciates that, I think. But I'm determined to put the seal on it. "I swear..."

She smiles back and lets herself go. I kiss her. A soft kiss, a slow kiss, a non-invasive kiss. A Traminer-scented kiss, a light kiss, a kiss that tastes of surf, a kiss that rides the wave, a kiss with a nibble and a bite, a kiss that's an "I want to go further but I can't." An "it's not possible" kiss. A "there's people all around us" kiss…

Chapter 27

I can't believe this. It's me, Gin, here on Via del Governo Vecchio, kissing publicly on the street. People walking past me, people looking at me, people stopping, people staring at me...

And me, right in the middle of the street. Without thinking, without looking, without worrying. Eyes shut. People all around me. In fact, I think that, right this second, there might be someone staring at us kissing from a comfortable vantage point just two inches away from our kiss.

I open my right eye ever so slightly. Nothing to be seen. All quiet on that front. I shut my eye again. Who knows what there might be on the other side...

But I don't give a damn! It's me and Step. That's all I know for sure. I wrap my arms around him even tighter, and we go on kissing like that, without problems, without a single thought in our heads. Then we burst out laughing, who even knows why. I press my right cheek against his shoulder, smiling, leaning sideways against him, letting a shiver run through me. Or maybe it was a burst of desire.

"Come on. Primi della Classe are waiting for us. The Heads of the Class."

"Who are they, some egghead friends of yours?"

"Not at all! It's a place that only serves pasta."

The proprietor introduces himself as a certain Alberto. He says hello, shows us to a table, and suggests we try a "triptych," as he puts it. "Trofie al pesto, tortelloni alla zucca, and rice with shrimp and champagne."

We exchange a glance and nod our heads. Okay, all right, certainly.

"And to drink?"

Step asks if there's some kind of white wine, at least I think he did. But I didn't hear all that well. Avalanchina or something like that.

"Excellent." Alberto, on the other hand, seems to have understood, and he walks away.

I look around the interior of the club. Arches made of age-old bricks, stones protruding from the walls, and white, brown, and red lights aimed at the ceiling. I look down. A perfect, brand-new terra-cotta floor. Not far away is the kitchen. Faux antiques, wrought iron, older items, and a couple of swing doors like an Old West saloon, and sure enough a young man steps through them with a piping hot dish of something but no one shoots at him. In fact, at one table, they wave happily, urging him to come faster. Who knows how long they've been waiting.

"Here is your Falanghina." Alberto brings a bottle of white wine and places it in the middle of the table, uncorking it smoothly. Falanghina, not Avalanchina. I'm out of it. Step takes the bottle and pours some in my glass. Then I wait for him to pour some for himself, and we lift them to drink.

"Hold on. Let's drink a toast," Step says.

I look at him with some concern.

"Let's hear it." I smile. "What are we drinking to?"

"You name it. Each one decides for themselves and then we raise the toast together."

I focus for a second while he looks me in the eyes. Then he extends his glass and clinks it against mine. "Maybe we're making the same wish."

"Maybe someday we'll tell each other."

"If it comes true."

I look at Step, trying to understand. He smiles at me. "Oh, it'll come true. It'll come true."

And I toss it back all at once with the certainty that sooner or later that wish, at least *my* wish, is going to come true. We'll make love...What? Help! What am I saying? Omigod.

I must get distracted. I look around. How different the other couples seem, each dining at their separate tables. Who knows why it is, but we each always believe that we're the best. Or at least, that's how it is with me. Yes, Gin the Conceited One.

"Ahhh!"

"Wait, what are you doing, shouting?" Step looks at me with concern. "You've gone insane."

"No, I'm just happy!" And I shout again while the bored lady at the table stops chewing for a second and stares at me in astonishment, her curiosity piqued. And I, well, I smile at her. I take a morsel of food from the dishes that have just been brought to the table, and I put it in my mouth. "Yum, delicious..."

I twist my forefinger into my cheek, still gazing at my bored neighbor who shakes her head, uncomprehending.

And to think that the man, sitting across from her, hasn't even noticed a thing.

And Step laughs. And he looks at me. And he shakes his head.

And I smile at him. "Hey, aren't you spending too much money?"

"This dinner is my brother's treat. Actually, he's a little tight when it comes to paying for things, but he has plenty of money."

"Great! But why is he doing it?"

"I don't know. Maybe it's just to help me, his little brother who has trouble meeting women."

⌣

And off we go again, laughing. Then we get in the car. I don't know how it is, but I still find two euros in my pocket. I give them to the valet who might have been hoping for something more. But then he appears to think it over, and he's satisfied, and he guides me out of the parking spot. "Come on. Keep coming, sir. You're good, you're good. I guarded your car like a precious little flower."

He gets no answer from me except a curt nod of the head.

Music. 107.1 FM. Radio TMC. The sound of the DJ's voice fades away, replaced by the melody of U2. And Gin, of course, knows the song. "And I miss you when you're not around. I'm getting ready to leave the ground..."

"But you know all of these songs!"

"No. Just the ones that are about the two of us."

The Tiber, racing down the Lungotevere. Then we cross the bridge. A right, then a left, then Piazza Cavour, and Via

Crescenzo. The restaurant Papillon. Mario, the proprietor, greets us. "Hello, just the two of you?"

"Yes, but two very special customers, eh?" I smile at Gin and pull her close.

The guy looks at us. He narrows his eyes a little. He must be thinking, *Wait, do I know this guy? Who is he? Is this someone important?*

But he can't come up with an answer, in part because there is none. "Come right in. Let me put you over here. You'll be more comfortable."

"Thanks."

In his momentary indecision, he's apparently decided to just treat us like two people who, in any case, get the best. Whoever we turn out to be, in other words.

We walk through a dining room with a big tableful of people, most of them women, and good-looking ones too. Blondes, brunettes, redheads, they smile, they laugh, they talk loudly, but they eat politely and with refinement. They share slices of pizza, piping hot and fresh from the oven, served on a single large central tray. Not far away, forks are plunged into slices of prosciutto, just sliced, pink and airy, the offspring of who knows what pig.

Mario has appeared behind Gin. "So, what can I have them make for you?"

"We've come to try your biggest, rarest, most delicious T-bone steaks, sliced and laid out beautifully. We've heard so much about them."

"Perfect." Mario smiles, happy that he's famous for his steaks.

"And please bring us a nice cabernet," I say.

"Will a Piccioni be acceptable?"

"We're in your hands."

"Excellent."

When Mario comes back to set down the two plates of sliced steak in front of us, Gin sets right to work with fork and knife.

And we continue eating, pouring ourselves more cabernet, chewing and savoring slowly, laughing, telling each other insignificant stories and facts that seem, however, compellingly important to us. Bits of our lives, my life or hers, we never took part in. Diverse and euphoric moments with friends from the past that, looked back upon objectively from the present, actually don't seem like such a big thing after all. Or maybe it's the fear of not being sufficiently amusing.

Gin pours me some wine. And the mere fact that it's her doing the pouring already makes me forget everything.

⌒

Mario arrives at our table, looking concerned. "What are you two doing? Are you leaving already? All you ate was a main course. I have a delicious dessert, homemade right here with my own two hands. Actually, truth be told, my wife's two hands."

That last confession catches me off guard. I'm tempted to tell him everything, explain that we're not dissatisfied with his food, but that I've had this great, magnificent idea, a special dish in every place, in each restaurant or café that's famous for the dish in question. And now the cabernet, too, has had its effect and is an invited guest at the party. So I decide to just go for a lie, plain and simple.

"No, we just have an appointment to meet up with our friends, and if we don't go now, they'll leave without us."

Mario seems to accept that explanation with equanimity. "Arrivederci, in that case, but I want to see you back here soon."

"Certainly, certainly."

Gin plays her part too. "The steak was delicious."

"Come on, we still haven't had dessert..."

Gin lets herself be led along. Then, all of a sudden she stops short. She holds me by the hand and moves her lips, puckering up, a funny little duckling, pouting ever so slightly. "Why, are you saying I'm not dessert enough for anyone?"

I try to come up with a response, but she doesn't give me the time. She slips out of my hand and takes off, running fast, chest thrust forward, leaning into it, legs pumping, laughing gleefully at her freedom.

Chapter 28

I catch up to Gin and take her by the hand. There is a night wind, a soft wind, an October wind. A few leaves on the ground, not much more.

"Where are you taking me now?" Gin asks.

"There's still a dessert that we haven't had yet."

"Which means what?"

"Which means you."

I turn up the volume on the car radio so that Gin can't answer me, and I'm in luck. It's Eros Ramazzotti. "Another girl like you, even if I invented her, she wouldn't exist...it seems clear to me that..."

Gin smiles and shakes her head. I manage to take her hand and raise it to my mouth. I kiss it gently. It's soft, it's cool, it's sweet smelling. And I kiss it again. Just lips. Amid her fingers. Rubbing, feeling, sliding, without braking, letting myself go, falling. I see her shut her eyes, let her head fall back on the headrest. Now, even her hair seems to have relaxed.

I turn her hand over, and I kiss her palm. It presses my face, gently, as I breathe into the lines on her palm. Lines of life, fortune, love. I breathe softly, ever so softly. She suddenly opens her eyes and looks at me. Her eyes seem different, as if crystalline, faintly fogged by a slight veil. Of happiness? I couldn't say. They peer at me in the dim light. They seem to smile all on their own.

"Keep your eyes on the road," she scolds me.

I obey, and a short while later, I turn right, down along the river, the waterfront boulevard, the Lungotevere, between the cars, passing everyone else, fast, with the music going and her hand in mine, moving every so often, invited to who knows what dance.

What could she be thinking? And what will be her answer? Yes, or no. It's like a poker game. And she's right there, across the table from me.

I look at her for a moment. Her eyes, faintly downcast, smile at me, sweet and amused. There's nothing left to do but see her cards, ante up and show. It might be a yes. It might be a no. Is it too soon? There's no time for these things, and after all, this isn't a game of poker, there *is* no ante.

"My head is starting to spin," Gin says.

She smiles at me as she says it. Is it a minor justification, just in case anything happens? Or perhaps it's a major justification if she already knows that something *isn't* going to happen. I'm getting tied up in knots with these complex and complicated meanderings.

"My head's spinning too." That's my simple answer. Very simply.

Gin squeezes my hand rather tightly and I, stupidly, take it as a sign. Or not. What the hell. I've had too much to drink.

A curve and then up the Aventine Hill. This car really

runs beautifully. My brother is going to be so happy that I've recovered it for him. I can't help but laugh.

She looks at me, I turn around, and I notice. "What's wrong? What are you thinking about?"

Gin, her brow furrowed, Gin with her somewhat grim gaze, Gin worried. "Oh, nothing, just family matters."

The Janiculum Hill. Botanical Garden. I screech to a halt, pull the handbrake, and get out.

"Hey, where are you going?"

"Nowhere special. Don't worry, I'll be right back."

She locks the door, stretching out over the driver's seat, safely closing herself in.

I look around. Nothing. Perfect, no one in sight. One, two, and . . . three. I climb over the gate, and I'm inside. I walk in silence. Faint perfumes, stronger perfumes, scents that verge on the pungent. Future colognes not yet extant. Distilled in small bottles, costly essences.

Here we are. Behold my prey. I choose it instinctively; I pluck it with care. I uproot it forcefully but without mistreating it.

Now you're mine. Uno, due, tre steps and now I'm outside again. I look around. Nothing. Perfect, no one in sight.

I go back to the car. Gin sees me appear suddenly. She takes fright. Then she opens the door to let me in. "Where did you go? I was starting to get scared."

So now I open my jacket, revealing my gift. Like a spinnaker catching a sudden gust of wind in open waters. And in an instant, its perfume floods the car. An exotic orchid. It appears as if by magic in my hands with a simple gesture, more the presentation of a prestidigitator than that of a clumsy flower thief.

"For you. From one flower to another, straight out of the Rome Botanical Garden."

Gin sniffs it and then dives into the center of that wild orchid to inhale its most intense perfume. I'm reminded of an animated movie. A cartoon. *Bambi*, that's it. Those big eyes, thrilled and glistening, appearing beyond those delicate flower petals. Those eyes, frightened and uncertain, looking out upon the near and impending future. Not just any old future, *her* future.

First gear, second, and then third, and we're traveling again. Small curves and then a steep climb. I steer around a barrier that's supposed to stop us, and then I park a short way farther up. Campidoglio. The Capitoline Hill.

"Come on!" I help her out of the car, and she follows me.

"Wait, listen, you know—"

"Shh! Talk softly. People live here."

"Yes, all right. I just wanted to tell you...Listen, you can't get married here at night. Plus, we haven't even discussed it. But I want a fairy-tale wedding, I've already told you that."

"Namely?"

"Long white gown with a bit of a plunging neckline, flowers mixed with spikes of wheat, and a beautiful church set amidst the greenery. No, wait, make that overlooking the sea." She laughs.

"You see that you're still being indecisive?"

"Why?"

"Amidst the greenery or overlooking the sea?"

"Ah, I thought you meant that I was being indecisive about whether or not to marry you."

"No, as far as that goes, you're stunningly decisive. You'd kill to marry me." I pull her close and try to kiss her.

"You're conceited and not very romantic."

She laughs and then wriggles out of my arms, like a fish leaping out of my net. She runs away, fleet-footed, turning the corner. And I'm after her in the blink of an eye.

We're on the large Piazza del Campidoglio, a vast square on the summit of the Capitoline Hill. A brighter light. A statue at the center of the piazza with a sign fastened to it. We stop nearby, close but separate. Everything is beautiful, especially her.

She peeks out from behind the statue. "Well, what are you doing now? Have you already run out of steam?"

I pretend to leave, and she runs around behind the statue. I dart around the other side and catch her on the run. She shrieks. "No. No, stop it!"

I pick her up and carry her away. Away from the light, away from the center. We wind up beneath the colonnade in the shadows. I set her back down on solid ground, and she adjusts her jacket, tugging it down to cover her stomach. I take her hair and uncover her face, slightly reddened from the recent run. Her chest is heaving up and down, rapidly, and then it slowly calms down.

"Your heart is really racing, isn't it?"

My hand is just above her hip. Under the jacket, beneath the T-shirt, light and gentle, almost like a mere shiver, on her own flesh. She shuts her eyes, and I gently climb up, at the edge, along her hips, up her sides, up up up, behind her back. I open my hand, and I pull her close, squeezing her tight, pressing her against my body, kissing her.

Behind us is an ancient column shorter than the others

and wider in diameter. There, gently, I push her down, letting her lean back, lowering her little by little. And she lets
herself go. Her hair, her back surrendering on that ancient
platform, eaten away by time with its faded marble veins,
so porous and by now seemingly tired. Oh, this column
must have seen things in its many days.

Gin clamps her legs around my hips and sides, fastening
me in a light vise grip, letting her legs rock right and left.
And I let her take me where she will. All the while, my
hands run happily aground, cast away along her belt, her
trousers, her buttons. Without haste, without liberating
anything. Without any excess of desire. For the moment.

Then, all of a sudden, Gin turns to her left and opens
her eyes, and then opens them wider, in alarm. "There's
something over there!"

Frightened, determined, perhaps even slightly annoyed,
I peer into the shadows, still somewhat tipsy from the faint
drunken binge of love. "Oh, it's nothing. Just some bum."

"And you call that nothing? You must be insane."

She sits up, and I take her by the hand to help her down.
Together, we flee, leaving behind us both that ancient
lopped-off column and that vaguely present, lurking figure,
both forgotten in the shadows.

As if in some labyrinth, we make our way through the
hidden greenery and the more-or-less suffuse lights of the
Roman Forum. Beneath us, in the distance, are ancient columns and architraves and monuments. A narrow line winds
up steeply from the Piazza del Campidoglio. Terraces jut
eagerly forward, with gravel on the ground, neatly tended
greenery, and wild, unbridled bushes and shrubs. All around,
in every direction, a precipice. The Tarpeian Rock.

And so, seemingly buoyed up over the emptiness of those ruins, beneath a low wall, in a perfectly sheltered cone of shadow, we find a hidden bench.

Less fearful now, Gin looks around. "No one can see us here."

"You see me."

"But if I choose to, I can just shut my eyes."

She doesn't say no, and she doesn't say yes. She doesn't speak. She breathes into my ear as she lets me undress her. Away with the jacket, away with the T-shirt, and they both fall untidily from the bench, into an even darker pool of gloom.

Away with the shoes, away with the trousers. Each of us strips off the other's garments. Then we stop. And before my eyes, she covers her breasts, embracing herself with both hands crisscrossed over her shoulders, framed by her hair hanging down in the moonlight, and farther down covered by nothing other than her panties. I can't believe it. There she is, Gin.

"Hey, what do you think you're doing, peeping at me?"

"You didn't tell me not to look. And actually, no, you're wrong. My eyes are shut."

Somewhere, streaming out of a club or someone's open window, we hear music from a stereo in the distance.

"What a liar you are." And she spreads her arms wide, letting me look and smiling. Then she leans toward me, her legs half open. She sits there, staring at me. "Listen..."

"Shh...let's not speak." I kiss her and gently, slowly, pull off her panties.

"No, I want to talk. First of all, do you have...uh, you know...what we're going to need?"

"I have it," I reply, with a laugh. "I have it."

"There, I knew it. Do you carry it around in your pocket or in your wallet? Or did you buy it on your way over to pick me up? Because maybe you were pretty sure this is how things would turn out!"

"Actually, no, I couldn't know that this was how things would turn out. It is always up to you."

"Okay, and one other thing..."

"No, that's enough talking for now."

I pull her close. I kiss her neck. She tosses her hair back, and I, like a little vampire, continue to suck on her neck, savoring her, and her scent. My hand seems to travel of its own free will, down her side, her hips, her waist, and between her legs. I hear her breathe slowly, then a little faster, as she squirms in my arms as if dancing, gently, up and down, without any contrived modesty, smiling, opening her eyes, looking at me, with a tranquility and a serenity that only embarrass me. And as if that weren't enough, as I move my hand to reach out and extract our protection...

"No, here, let me. I want to do it."

"But listen, I'm the one who has to wear it."

"I know that, dummy. Do you want to know how many I've put on in my time? Hold on. Let me think..."

"I don't want to know."

"This is the twelfth one I've put on."

"Oh, that's a relief."

"Why?"

"Because if it had been your thirteenth, I would have started worrying. It's bad luck!"

She doesn't give me the satisfaction of laughing at my joke, but she amuses me anyway. She peels it open as if it were an individually wrapped piece of candy, or tries to, first with her fingernails and then popping it into her mouth, and this time grinning at me mischievously.

"Don't worry. I'm not going to eat it."

One sharp tug with her teeth and the condom is in her hands. She turns it over and over again, smiling. "It's a funny thing." And that's all she says. Then she moves her head toward me. "Well?"

Naked, I open my legs, and she caresses me, slowly, gently, up and down, and then she calmly slips the condom on me.

"Was I good?"

"Too good!" But I say nothing more. Now I'm an astronaut in this journey between astral conjunctions beneath a starry sky, with an enchanted woman, amid the ruins of the past, delving deep into the pleasure of the present.

～

I can't believe it. I can't believe I'm doing this. I remain silent, floating, as if listening to my own life flowing over me, beneath me, inside me. In this decisive moment, so important to the rest of my life, unique, once and for all. I will never be able to erase it. My one and only first time.

And I chose it. And I chose you. It almost seems like that song. But it isn't. This is reality. I'm here, me, in this moment.

And so is Step. I see him, I feel him. He's on top of me. I embrace him, I hug him, I hold him tight, and tighter still.

I'm afraid, the way you are any time you do something

unfamiliar. But it's a normal fear, all too normal. Or not? Gosh darn it, Gin, don't let yourself be caught up now in all your obsessions, the films you play in your mind. In other words, obsessed with everything.

I shut my eyes. I breathe, I sigh, but still, I like this. I'm resting on his shoulder, no longer tense, no longer worried. In silence, like this, carried, abandoned, shipwrecked. And I like it. I feel his hands, I can feel him touching me all over, pulling off the last article of clothing on my body, gently. Oh, yes, I practically don't even notice. I don't want to be lying here, thinking, seeing myself from outside, checking on myself, splitting myself into two consciousnesses, having this mind that continues talking and discussing. I want to let myself go. In the cradle of his love, in this sea of desire, slowly letting myself be carried along on its currents. Yes, without another thought. Lost like this in his arms...

Now. There.

～

A louder moan and then she's mine. Mine now, mine for the moment. Mine at this instant, mine and mine alone. I can't help but think it. Mine forever. Maybe. But right this second, certainly. Now it's love, inside her. And more and again and more still, without stopping. Now she smiles, gently.

～

And just at that very moment, I feel him inside me. It happens in the space of an instant. A leap, an inside-out dive. A stabbing pain, like a pierced ear, a tiny tattoo, a lost tooth, a blooming flower, a plucked fruit, a hitched ride, a tumble off your skis... Yes, that's it, a tumble off your skis onto the fresh new snow, cold, white, just fallen, directly out of the sky.

And there you are, face forward, still sliding, laughing, embarrassed, opening your mouth still full of snow. You so clumsy, you laughing helplessly, at your first tumble, your slide in the snow. That very snow, so clean and soft, the same way I feel right at this moment.

Finally. He's inside, I can feel him... How nice though. And I smile. I go back to feeling, to testing, to trying, to savoring the pleasure, one tiny bite, a morsel. I feel good. I like this. I want him. As if his name, on my flesh, but from today forward, etched for all time inside of me.

"Step, I want you."

⌒

Later, I don't know how much later, I'm listening to Gin as she embraces me, sitting on my legs while I slide off the condom. "Wait, you'd never...?"

"No, I'd never made love in my life before, so what's wrong with that? There's a first time for everything, right? Well, this was my first time," Gin says.

I'm left speechless. I have no idea what to say. Maybe because there really is nothing to say.

Gin is putting her clothes back on. She looks at me and smiles, shrugging her shoulders. "So you see how strange? Of all the boys, you were the one. You won't blame yourself, will you? Or brag about it, I hope."

She puts on the T-shirt and the jacket without bothering to put her bra back on. I still haven't been able to utter a word. She slips her bra into one of her jacket pockets.

"And after all, what do I know. It might have just been the evening, but starting tomorrow—now don't get any funny ideas—I need to make up for lost time. Because, really, statistically speaking, I'm four years behind the average. Most girls have already done it by the time they're fifteen."

By now, Gin is completely dressed again, and she's already on the stairs under the streetlamp while I'm still zipping up my jacket.

Then she starts laughing. Confident, relaxed, perfectly at her ease. "But it's also true that nowadays there's something of a return to certain values of the past. So, to sum up, let's just say that I comfortably occupy the middle ground."

A little while later, I'm next to her, and we start to walk. This time, we walk in silence, in part because I've been unable to find anything else to say. Then, at a certain point, she puts her arm around me. I embrace her, pulling her close to me. We continue like that as I breathe her in. Gin, still redolent of her first love. Mine. Mine. Mine.

"You know, Step, I was thinking something . . . "

"What?"

She rests her head on my shoulder. "I had the strangest thought, or really I guess I could say I was curious about something. If you stop to think about it, do you believe that ever since ancient Roman times, right up to the present day, anyone else might ever have done it in this spot?"

"No one. Ever."

"How can you be so sure of it?"

"There's just no two ways about it. There are certain things that you can tell. You feel them, and that's that."

So she rests her head on my shoulder again. This time, I've convinced her of it. Still, I can't even say why, but seriously, I'm convinced of it myself.

Gin starts talking again. "So we've written a piece of history, our history." She smiles at me and gives me a kiss on the lips. Soft. Warm. Loving.

Forget about the twenty euros. I think that, when all is said and done, Gin really robbed me of my heart.

Chapter 29

Stop here. Put on the brakes."

I don't stop to think. I just do as Gin tells me. Suddenly, screeching to a halt, on the fly. It's a good thing there was nobody right behind us. I'd never hear the end of that from my brother. Well, okay, we could always blame it on the car thief.

Gin quickly gets out of the car. "Come with me."

"But where are we going?"

"Just follow me. You really like to ask questions, don't you?"

We're facing the bridge of Ponte Milvio in a small piazza on the Lungotevere, overlooking the river right at the beginning of Via Flaminia, which runs from there to Piazza del Popolo.

Gin runs along the bridge and stops halfway across, at the foot of the third streetlamp. "Here, it's this one right here."

"What is?"

"The third streetlamp. There's a legend about this bridge, Ponte Milvio, or Ponte Mollo—the soft bridge—as the poet Giuseppe Gioachino Belli liked to call it."

"What are you doing now, acting the scholar?"

"But I am quite scholarly! About only a very few things. Like about this, for instance. Do you want to listen or don't you?"

"First, I want a kiss."

"Come on. Just listen. It's a beautiful story." Gin turns around and heaves a sigh of annoyance.

I hug her from behind. We lean against the parapet and look into the distance. Not far away is another bridge. The Corso Francia bridge. I gaze, lost in the view. And no memory comes to disturb me. Are even the ghosts of the past capable of having respect for certain moments? So it would seem.

Gin joins me in a kiss. Beneath us, the Tiber flows, black. The faint light of the streetlamp illuminates us gently. We can hear the slow lapping of the river water along the banks. Its flow is suddenly broken around the columns of the bridge where the water gurgles, rises, seethes, and mutters. Then, past the bridge, the water comes together again and silently continues on its journey to the sea.

"Well, will you tell me the story?"

"This is the third streetlamp facing the other bridge. And do you see this, wrapped around the base?" Gin asks.

"Yes, but it looks to me like someone did a bad job of securing their scooter."

"What a jerk you are. That's not it at all. This is called *the lovers' chain*. You're supposed to fasten a padlock to this chain. Then you lock it, and you throw the key into the Tiber."

"And then?"

"You never break up."

"How do people come up with these stories?"

"I don't know. This story's been around forever, even Trilussa tells it."

"You're just taking advantage because I don't know about it," I say.

"True. It's just that you're afraid to put a lock of our own."

"I'm not scared."

"That's the title of the book by Ammaniti."

"Or the film by Salvatores, depending on how you look at things."

"Anyway, you *are* scared," Gin says.

"I told you I'm not."

"Certainly you're just taking advantage because we don't have a lock of our own."

"Stay here. Don't move." I'm back in a minute or so. With a padlock in my hand.

"So where did you find this one?"

"My brother. He carries a padlock with him, along with a chain, to fasten his steering wheel so no one can steal his car."

"Right, and it just never would have occurred to him that the one who stole it from him would be his own brother."

"Listen, you're as responsible in this matter as I am. Among other things, you still owe me twenty euros."

"What a money grubber."

"What a thief!"

"A thief of what? Oh, what do you want? Money for the padlock? We'll just reckon up at the end, one final payment..."

"You'll owe me too much by that point," I say.

"All right then. Enough's enough. Let's put an end to it here. Well, are you up to this or not?"

"Of course I am." I put the padlock on the chain, I snap it shut, and I turn the key and pull it out. I hold it extended between my fingers while I stare at Gin.

She looks at me, challenging me, and then she smiles and raises an eyebrow. "Well?"

I take the key between thumb and forefinger and dangle it gently in midair, high above the water below, undecided.

She's beautiful. I look at her amused smile, her defiant stance, her clear desire to put me to the test. Could she be my new true love? To fall in love with her, to lose myself... Yes, it would be a nice thing if this legend turned out to be true. A couple puts a padlock on a bridge, and then they're bound together forever. There's no doubt, no uncertainty, no memory of the past, no regrets, no new love story, no reckless impulse. It's just Gin, and nothing else, no one else, ever.

Yes, it would be nice if a relationship worked like that: You snap shut a padlock, you throw away the key, and that's the start of everything. And the love story that begins with that chosen person lasts as long as the steel of the padlock, impervious to any buffeting winds, never undermined by the pouring rain or the passing years. That padlock lasts forever. What if our legend turned out to be true?

Gin's hair tosses gently in the breeze, her gaze, her dark eyes are so curious, so full of life and enthusiasm, so intense and beautiful. She feels so right. So I smile at her. Then, all at once, I drop the key. Down it hurtles, headlong, twisting in the air and then vanishing into the waters of the Tiber.

"You actually did it." Gin gazes at me with a strange, dreamy look, and seems moved as well.

"I told you. I'm not scared."

She lunges at me and jumps on, legs wrapped around me, hugging me, kissing me, shouting with delight. She's crazed, she's insane, she's...she's beautiful.

"Hey, you're way too happy right now. You don't think that this legend actually works, do you?" I ask.

"You jerk!"

And she kisses me again, at length, passionately, and I abandon myself, just settling into that kiss. I lose myself, and for a moment, I breathe in that kiss, and it's as if...as if I were floating. That's it, eyes shut, in a calm, smooth sea. Then when I open my eyes, I see that she's smiling, and we pull apart. "What are you thinking about?"

"Nothing."

"That's impossible."

"All right, then, I'll tell you. Here's what I was thinking. If only you knew..." Gin begins.

"If only I knew what?"

"No, nothing. I'm definitely not going to tell you."

It doesn't matter to me. I pull her close, and I kiss her again. Then she pulls away, cocks her head to one side, and stares at me for a while in silence. Then she says, "Hey, tough guy, you haven't fallen in love with me, have you?"

"Me? Don't be silly. You're not in any danger of that."

"You see? You're afraid. You use the word *danger*. Actually though, it's nice to be in love, melt into the other person, belong to each other. Who knows what it might be like between us."

Then she thinks it over and finally nods. "Yes, when all is said and done, I'd like it with you. I feel as if I've known you all my life."

"Well, I've heard that before."

"Sure, but in my case, it's the truth."

"All right, I'm going to go ahead and believe you." And we go on looking at each other like that, in silence, standing on that bridge, surrounded by people who may just be walking by, or may even be looking at us, but I don't see anyone, or really, I should say, I see only her. And I see her eyes, glistening, emotional. And then I smile at her. "Now, you're the one who's afraid...or are you the one who's fallen in love?"

"Me? Don't be silly. I'm tough. Actually, come to think of it, I ought to just go get a pair of bolt cutters and remove that padlock entirely, in case it turns out that this legend really does work, and I can't shake you loose..."

"Don't you dare...!"

I try to stop her, but she suddenly leans down and breaks loose of my grip and takes off running, laughing and shouting, along the bridge. She encounters a group of gentlemen walking along together. She tugs on the overcoat of the most serious-looking member of the group, spins him around, and almost forces him to dance with her. And then she's off again. Behind her the other men laugh. They good-humoredly shove the serious man, who's red-faced with anger and is trying to scold and berate her.

I walk past the group and spread my arms wide in helpless acknowledgment. They all share in Gin's happiness. Even the most serious gentleman smiles at me in the end. Yes, it's true. She's so full of life that she more or less obliges everyone to rejoice in her presence.

Chapter 30

I can't believe it!" Paolo comes busting into my room in the morning. "It's crazy. I had no doubt. I knew that you're still the same legend. How the heck did you do it?"

I'm befuddled and baffled; all I know is that the right word would have been "fuck." I turn over in the bed and burrow into the pillows.

"Do what?"

"The car, how did you find it, and so fast too? It just took you a single evening. You're unbelievable."

"Oh, right. I made a few phone calls. And I had to spend the money you know about."

"What do I know about? No, I don't know about anything." Paolo sits down on the bed. "What did you have to spend?"

"Hey, don't act like you don't know what I'm talking about. The cash."

"Ah, certainly. But, no, it doesn't really matter, you know, it's worth it. Listen, what did the guy who stole my car look like? Was he an asshole, a tough guy, one of those guys with the face..."

I interrupt this fake hypothesis. "No, I didn't see him. A

guy I know brought me the car, but he had nothing to do with the theft."

"Well, so much the better. 'Cosa fatta, capo ha.' What is done is done."

"What does that mean?"

"Well, it's a quote from Dante. It's just something that people say."

I toss and turn in bed and stick my head under one of the pillows. My brother. He says things, and he doesn't even know what they mean. I can hear him get up from my bed.

"Thanks again, Step."

He starts to leave my room. I sit up. "Paolo..."

"Yes, what is it?"

"The money..."

"Oh, right. How much did we have to pay?"

"How much did *we*? *You* had to pay twenty-three hundred euros. A lot less than you'd expected to pay."

"Still, it's a lot, fucking hell."

When it's about money, sure enough, he can definitely curse like a normal person.

"Those thieves, I'm almost tempted not to pay them."

"Well, actually, I already paid them. But if you want, we can just call the cops and report the theft, after I take the car right back to the thieves."

"No, no, are you kidding? In fact, thanks so much, Step. You don't have anything to do with it. I'll leave you the money on the table."

A little while later, I get out of bed. After all, it's morning and I'm hungry for breakfast. I cross paths with Paolo in the living room. He's sitting there, just finishing writing the check.

"Here you go." He finishes his signature with one last flourish. "I gave you a little extra for your trouble."

I take the check and look at it. Paolo puts on a happy face as if to say, *Well, aren't you satisfied?*

It's made out for twenty-four hundred euros. That is, one hundred euros more than what I was supposed to give to the car thief. A reward of one hundred euros for a guy who knocked himself out to retrieve the man's stolen car. At least, that's what he thinks happened. What a miser! Live life large. Make the check for at least twenty-five hundred euros and be done with it, no? But seeing that, in reality, he's given me an enormous tip to pay for the privilege of "lending me" his car and enjoying a splendid night out, with a magnificent meal and all the rest, I can't really say anything to him but "Thanks, Paolo."

"Don't mention it. I should be thanking you."

These are the kind of pat phrases I detest.

"And another thing. Step, you can't guess what an absurd thing it is, but they also stole a padlock."

"A padlock?" I pretend to be stunned by this development.

"Oh, right, I was so worried about my car that, whenever I parked it, I'd wrap a chain around the steering wheel. It wasn't on the wheel yesterday, but how was I supposed to think they'd be able to steal my car when it was safely parked in the garage? Plus, what is a thief supposed to do with a padlock, anyway?"

"Huh, yeah, what are they going to do with it? You got me."

In response to this question, I really have no idea what answer to give. Try to explain that away.

"And that's not all, Step. Just look."

He tosses it on the table in front of me. I pick it up and examine it closely. Delicate. Simple. I recognize the hook and clasp that I opened last night. A bra. Gin's bra.

"I mean, seriously, these assholes stole my car, and then they went and fucked in it! My only hope is that she, whoever she is, didn't put out for that piece of shit car thief. In fact, I hope that she put a padlock on it."

"Well, if you found that bra in the car, then I don't think things went the way you're hoping."

"Oh, true, you have a point."

I get up and head into the kitchen.

"Wait, what are you doing? You're keeping it?"

I pretend I don't know what he's talking about. "Keeping what?"

"What do you mean? The bra!"

I smile, letting it dangle in front of my face. "Well, why not? I'll do an updated version of Cinderella! Instead of the glass slipper, I'll be looking for the girl who'll fit into this bra."

"Aside from the fact that it'll fit any girl who wears a B cup."

"That's quite a clinical eye you have there. So much the better, that'll make it easier."

Paolo looks at me and raises his eyebrow. "Step, excuse me for this question, but do you see yourself as a sort of Prince Charming?"

"That depends on who's Cinderella this time."

Chapter 31

I've found my Cinderella. Step, what the fuck are you thinking? Mamma mia, you're a wreck. Yet true enough, I like Gin. She's cool, she's likable, she's a lot of fun, and she's beautiful. And she's late.

I'm downstairs from her apartment. I rang her on the cell phone, one ring, and she rang me back, one ring, in response. So she knows I'm down here.

Enough's enough! I'm buzzing her on the intercom. I step over to the entrance, run down the list of names and find *Biro*.

"Step, what do you think you're doing?" Gin asks as she approaches.

"What do you expect? I'm buzzing a late arrival."

"I'm right on time! You rang my phone, and I came straight down. But I thought you'd be coming by in the Audi A4, and instead you're on your motorcycle and I'm wearing a dress."

"Worst case, everyone in the cars around us will be happy. Are you wearing panties under that skirt?"

"Idiot!" She punches me in the same shoulder as always. I probably have a bruise by now.

"I'm sorry, but I had a long negotiation with the car thief. I had to haggle on the price, then I delivered the car back to my brother who's overjoyed."

"Poor guy."

"Poor guy, my ass. Leaving aside the fact that he has plenty of money, he was perfectly willing to spend up to forty-three hundred euros to get his car back. So actually, I saved him money."

"How much?"

"A little over half."

"So, in your opinion, he should be grateful to you?"

"Extremely grateful. Come on, climb aboard."

"Well, he lucked out to have a brother like you."

"You can say that again, loud and clear."

Gin raises her voice. "He lucked out to have a brother like you."

"It was just a manner of speech. I heard you fine the first time."

She plants a kiss on my lips and climbs up behind me, careful to tuck her skirt safely under her legs. "You don't really have much of a sense of humor, do you? It was meant as a joke."

I hand her the helmet. "Oh, listen, I just had an idea. Your brother, how is he fixed for cash?"

"Oh, don't start. Anyway, anyone who touches my family is out, understood?"

Gin gets off the motorcycle and stands brazenly in front of me. "Come on, let's switch things around, immediately!"

"What do you mean by that?"

"That means, get off the motorcycle because *I'm* driving now."

"What?" Gin actually wants to drive my motorcycle? *My* motorcycle. Then I realize how absurd I'm being. "Yes, okay. I'll be interested to see how you do with it."

Still, this is *me*. I can't believe this. Fucking hell. I slide the motorcycle underneath me until I'm riding pillion, leaving room for Gin to get on in front. And, ultimate irony, I actually help her on! Oh, God, I've taken leave of my senses.

"Okay, listen, do you know how to ride a motorcycle?" I ask.

"Of course! Who do you take me for? How do I start this thingie?"

"This thingie is a 750 custom, made by Honda, with a lenticular wheel. It'll do two hundred kilometers per hour like it's standing still, and this is how you start it." I shove forward, grab the handlebars, and squeeze Gin between my arms, as if I were embracing her from behind. Then with my right thumb, I hit the ignition button. I give it a little gas, and I take a deep breath through her hair. Soft and perfumed. I shut my eyes. I'm lost.

"Hey!"

I open my eyes again. "Yes? What is it?"

"If you stay there like that, I'm not going to be able to drive." She smiles.

"Okay, certainly." I move my arms and push back a little. Gin puts on her helmet and lowers her visor. I follow suit.

"All right, Step, are you ready?"

"Yes. So do you know how to shift the gears on this—" I don't get a chance to finish the sentence before Gin has put the bike in gear, twisted the throttle, and shot forward like a bat out of hell. I practically fall off the back of the bike from the jerky start. She caught me off guard. It won't happen again. At least I hope it won't.

I hold on tight to her, grabbing her jacket and passing my arms around her waist. Hey, though, I have to say, she knows how to drive this thing. Incredible. She shifts gears smoothly, playing expertly with the clutch. She really does have experience driving motorcycles. A lot, from the looks of it.

Red light, she brakes at the intersection in too high a gear. Okay, never mind. The engine sputters to a halt, and she almost goes over the handlebars. We fall to the right, and it's just a good thing I got my leg straight in a hurry. I'm holding us both up. Plus the motorcycle.

"Hey, how's it going? Are you sure that you want to drive it?"

"I didn't see that the light was red. That won't happen again." She shifts into neutral.

"Are you sure that—"

"I already told you, it won't happen again. Have you decided where we're going?"

"To the Warner multiplex. It's got lots of theaters, and they're showing—"

She doesn't let me finish. "Okay, great. That way I can let this thing unwind on the beltway." And she takes off fast in first gear, surprising me once again.

Warner Village. Fourteen movie theaters, or more, different movies starting at different times. Two restaurants, a pub, and lots of people.

"Hey, Gin, I didn't think we were going to make it."

"Why? Were you worried about having enough gas or finding Warner Village?"

"Let's just say that my concerns were a little more basic, whether we were going to get here alive!"

"Ha ha! Aren't you satisfied with the way I brought you all the way here? And on your own motorcycle too. Didn't I simultaneously thrill you and reassure you?"

I remain silent as we head for the entrance.

"Come on, buck up! Buy the tickets, and I'll go get the popcorn."

"Sure, but which theater?"

"How should I know?"

"Okay, fine, but which movie do you want to see? A comedy, a rom-com, or a horror flick?"

"Why don't you decide? I mean, I brought you all the way here, now I'm supposed to pick the movies too? Why don't you do something around here? Contribute."

Two girls ahead of me laugh, and Gin walks away shaking her head. I can't help but laugh either. Gin, the first woman who ever drove my motorcycle. The whole way around the beltway, at night, in a skirt, shifting gears in her fancy shoes, in the cold, with fast cars on all sides.

Then it's my turn. I snap to attention, buy my tickets, and I have no doubts about my choice.

Gin is standing at the entrance to the theater with two big tubs of popcorn in her arms and a Coca-Cola sitting on a bucket nearby, with two straws poking out.

I take the Coke, I sip from a straw, and I walk around her. "Come on, let's go."

Gin follows me, taking care not to spill the popcorn. "Do you mind telling me which movie you picked?"

"Why? Even if I tell you, you'll have something to say about it."

"Me? I don't know why you see things that way. It isn't true. I'm someone who adapts." Gin punches me in the shoulder. "Plus, I haven't seen any of these movies. Neither the comedy, nor the rom-com, and not even the horror flick. They would all have gone perfectly."

"Come on, the film is starting. Let's go get our seats," I say. And in an instant, we're in the theater where they're showing films from previous seasons. This is a new feature at the Warner multiplex.

Gin leans close to me and watches the film with one hand over her mouth. She's curled up, chewing on her fingernails, and she cuddles close to me again. *Message in a Bottle.* Kevin Costner's wife is dead, and he doesn't want to date anyone new. He doesn't want to resume his life. He writes letters and seals them in bottles that he tosses into the ocean, one after another.

Then someone finds that message in a bottle. A female journalist. The letter stirs her emotions, and it becomes a big topic of public interest.

The lights go up. Intermission, end of the first half. Gin laughs, sniffing loudly and covering her face with her hair to keep anyone from seeing her. She turns away and looks at me and then bursts out laughing again and sniffs some more.

"You were crying!" I say, pointing to the culprit.

"Well, so what? I don't have to be ashamed of it."

"Okay, but it's just a movie."

"Yes, and you're just an insensitive clod."

"Oh, I knew it. As usual, I'm to blame!"

Gin punches me in the shoulder. "You see, you're not even trying to understand. Such a jerk! But I—"

"Shhh! Enough, the movie's starting up again!"

And Gin slides back down in her seat, hugging me and laughing as she grabs my hand, which was wandering off in search of some other distraction.

Later, over a beer, "Did you enjoy it?" I ask.

"It was just beautiful. I'm still an emotional wreck."

"But Gin, it's too much!"

"Oh, what can I do about it? It's just the way I am. Certainly, if he hadn't drowned with the boat and all the rest...Now, just as he'd finally begun to be able to love again, just as he'd fallen in love with the journalist. Screen-writers are so mean."

"No, why? It's perfect! Now it's going to be the journal-ist who writes love letters and puts them in the bottles, that way another guy will find them and the whole story starts over again. Or else she could put a lead weight in the bottles, that way they'll wind up on the bottom of the sea, and Kevin Costner can read them."

"*Mamma mia.* You certainly are macabre!"

"I'm just trying to take some of the emotion out of this stark drama you're experiencing."

"Well, Step, have you ever thought about..."

"About what?"

"About, I don't know, writing a note or a poem..."

Actually, I *had* tried to write something for Babi. It was Christmas. I can remember it like it was yesterday. The sheets of paper crumpled under my desk. Desperate attempts to find the right words. Attempts suitable to someone drowning in a pool of desperation. Namely, me as I feverishly chased the impossible dream of winning back a love that was slipping through my fingers.

And then running into Babi with another guy and not being able to come up with even the simplest words. I don't know, like, *Ciao. Ciao, how are you doing? Ciao, it sure is cold. Ciao, it's Christmas. Ciao, Merry Christmas.* Or even worse, *Ciao, I love you.* What does any of that have to do with anything? Nothing, at least not anymore.

"No. I've never written anything. Not even a Christmas card," I lie.

"Wait, you never even tried?"

"No. Never."

She gives me the side-eye. "Hmmm..." And then she starts all over again. "Well, that's too bad. If you ask me, it would be wonderful!"

"What would?"

"To get something written by you. I'd like a poem. A beautiful poem."

"Oh, it's not enough for me to write. It also has to be beautiful."

"Well, it especially has to be beautiful! It doesn't have to be long. A beautiful and heartfelt poem, filled with love...ideally written to win forgiveness!"

"That was the last thing we needed. I haven't even written the poem yet, and already I'm in trouble for something."

"Why? Didn't you lie to me earlier?" She smiles, lifts an eyebrow, and stands up, leaving me at the table.

I finish my last sip of beer, and in the blink of an eye, I'm over next to her. "Hey, tell me the truth. How could you tell?" I ask, confirming for her that she'd been spot on.

"Your eyes, Step. Sorry, but your eyes say it all."

"What do you mean?"

"They made it clear to me that at least once you tried to

write a letter or a poem for someone else. I don't know who, but you do."

We walk along, side by side, in silence, toward the motor-cycle. One thing is certain. I need to wear glasses more often. Dark glasses. Maybe even wear sunglasses at night.

Chapter 32

Wo-o-o-ow! The first episode went great. I didn't screw up anything. Not that I should have. I had only one walk-on at the end of the episode where all I had to do was bring out an envelope containing the winner's name. What could I get wrong? Well, I could have tripped and fallen, I guess.

But Ele was fantastic. She was supposed to make an entrance in the middle of the episode to deliver the envelope with the provisional rankings. She didn't trip and fall. No, she was perfect. She came on, walked right up to the moderator at the exact right time, at the exact right place, only . . . she forgot to bring the envelope! Legendary! Ele is always Ele.

But everyone laughed, the moderator made a funny joke, and now everybody likes Ele! In the end, instead of getting angry with her, everyone just clapped and laughed. There were a few people who even said that she did it on purpose. With Ele, not on your life. That's showbiz.

November 5

By now, I'm doing great! They've made me one of the extra dancers on the troupe. And I was keeping up during rehearsals! It's so easy to get something wrong when you're on live, and then your mistake goes straight into the houses of everyone in the country. I don't want to think about it.

My own mother would see it. She doesn't miss a show I've been on. She watches them from start to finish, and she always manages to spot me. The last time she told me, "I saw you tonight!"

"You couldn't have, Mamma. I didn't do a thing."

"Of course you did! You came on for the finale when the whole cast said good night. You were the last one on the right, way in the back of the stage." My mother!

You can't hide anything from her. Or almost.

December 24

We rehearsed until 6:00, and then everyone went home for Christmas! We've decided to do something supercool, me and Step. First, everyone at their own home with their parents for the big dinner and then, after midnight, everyone at Step's house, or really, his brother's house, to open presents. Ele and Marcantonio are coming, too, and strangely they're still a couple! In any case, from what little I know about him, I never would have expected him to last this long. Go figure! Maybe they really have implemented the open relationship plan. Who can say? So much the better for them.

I reread what I've written, and I see that it's riddled with who-can-says, maybes, and go-figures... have I become too uncertain? Who can say, maybe, go figure! One thing is certain. In life, the best thing is not to be too sure of anything. For now, things are going well with Step. And it's going tremendously well!

December 25

I woke up at noon, and I enjoyed a fantastic breakfast, nothing but panettone and cappuccino! Lots of people say that the Christmas holidays are depressing, but personally, I love them. The tree with the strings of lights, the manger scene, everyone together for the big Christmas dinner, and all the good food. Sure, I might put on a few pounds, but what's so sad about that? You can always shed those pounds again. And with Step, you get plenty of exercise. You can shed all the pounds you want. How are you going to get fat? That's like a bad joke! Let's just hope nobody ever finds this diary. And if by some chance, you are the one who stole it, and you're reading it now... you're making a terrible mistake! You understand, you damned thief and/or busybody! Anyway, I don't want to think about it.

Last night was fabulous! At half-past midnight, we were all at Step's brother's house. Except Paolo wasn't there. He'd gone to celebrate at his girlfriend's house, a woman called Fabiola. So we were on our own.

Marcantonio brought a wonderful CD. It was a Café Del Mar complication (or something like that), and he put it on. A perfect atmosphere, sentimental without overdoing it. And I was daring, very daring! Rum, brandy, and champagne, I tried it all. I took two sips of Step's rum, and I was already drunk!

We played spin the bottle to see who would be the first to go off by themselves. It came to rest on Marcantonio so it was those two who left the room. Only Marcantonio took advantage of the spin the bottle game and, "reminiscent," as he said, "of the good old days" when it was only thanks to that bottle that we were able to overcome our shyness ... he lunged at Ele. I mean, he wrapped himself around her like an octopus. He kissed her, slathering her with saliva, and Ele laughed and laughed. The two of them are great together! I'm happy for Ele.

Nice gifts, all around, really cute. Ele, who always overdoes it, gave him a very special graphics program sent all the way from America at enormous cost. (That's what Step told me because he'd used it when he was living down there.) When Marcantonio saw it, he literally lost his mind. He threw his arms around her and started shouting, "You're the woman of my dreams. I've finally found you!"

I ripped open the gift that Step gave me. "No! I can't believe it. I'm speechless."

"What's wrong, didn't you like it?" Step asked.

I looked at him, and I smiled. "Open yours."

Step started to open his gift but the whole time he's saying, "Listen, we can return it if it's too small for you, okay? Or is the color you don't like?"

"Get busy, open your package," I told him.

"No!" Step cried. "I can't believe it!" He said the exact same words I said, but that wasn't the only thing that he copied. We

gave each other two identical navy-blue Napapijri jackets.
Mamma mia, I was speechless. But I laughed and laughed!

A beautiful end to the evening. Music, nougat torroncini,
chatting idly for a while, and then Marcantonio and Ele
left. I take off my boots, I stretch out on the sofa, I snuggle
up against Step, put my feet under a cushion, nice and
warm. A totally dreamy position. We talk and talk and
talk. Or maybe I should say, I talk and talk and talk.
I told him about the earrings my folks gave me, my gifts
from Uncle Ardisio, my aunts, my grandmother, and so on
and so forth.

Then, when I ask him how his Christmas went, I felt him
tense up. I persist and, in the end, with great effort, I manage
to drag out of him the information that he and Paolo had
dinner with his father and his father's new girlfriend. Step
tells me that he got a pair of very nice black shoes from his
brother and a green sweater from his father, the only color he
can't stand, as he informed me (Good to know!). Step really
emphasizes the fact that his father had his new girlfriend
sign the card on the gift he gave him. I try to justify it as
understandable, but Step has no doubt about it. Would you
want a present from someone you don't even know? Looking
at it from that point of view, he's not entirely wrong. Then,
the most absurd thing of all, he told me (after I pestered him
for a long time) that he had also received a gift from his
mother, but that he hadn't opened it. And when I kiddingly
told him, "Well, you do know your mother, don't you?" I
realized I really put my foot in it. "I thought I knew her."
Oh my God. I've ruined his Christmas. Luckily, I'm able to
recover. Sweetly, calmly, passionately, over time. But he still
refused to open his mother's Christmas present.

Chapter 33

I arrive home from work, enter the apartment, and set down my bag. I take off my jacket, and as I do, I hear Paolo in the other room, chattering away. Is he with someone or is that the television?

Paolo comes in, smiling at me. "Ciao. There's a surprise." It's not the television. Someone's here. Then, all of a sudden, she appears. Framed by the jamb of the living room door, with a glow of light from the window backlighting her, making her outline just a little more blurry and out of focus to my eyes, like some delicate vision. It's my mother.

"I made something to eat if you're hungry, Step," says Paolo, taking his heavy jacket out of the armoire and putting it on. "It's all there on the table, if you're hungry," he goes on, clearly concerned about that situation. I don't know if he's more concerned about the idea that I might not be hungry or that he might have served me a dish I didn't happen to want just now. Namely, encountering Mamma.

Maybe he hadn't planned for it to happen, maybe he'd thought it through and maybe he hadn't. But it's over in a flash. Paolo has exited the apartment, leaving us alone together. Alone the way we've always been ever since *that* day.

Or at least that's how I've been. Alone and without her. Without the mother that I had sketched for myself, drawing a picture of her based on all the stories she'd told me, from the fairy tales she'd read me when I was small and all the stories that she'd told me, sitting next to my bed where I lay with a mild fever, delighting in cuddling in that warmth, the warmth of the blankets and the warmth of my mother. Knowing that she was there, beside me, reading to me, holding my hand, pressing her hand against my forehead to feel my temperature, bringing me a glass of water. How many times, just to bring her close for another second, right on the verge of falling asleep, had I asked her for that final favor, just so I could see her return to my bedroom one last time, appearing in the frame of another door, another apartment, another piece of history.

And that whole beautiful tapestry, created by none other than her, filled with love, fairy tales, dreams, enchantment, light, and sunshine, puff, gone up in smoke in the blink of an eye. To have discovered her there, in bed with another man.

"Ciao, Mamma." Any guy, a stranger, a man other than my father, in bed with my own mother, and since that day: darkness. Utter darkness.

I feel ill. I sit down at the table, where the dishes have already been laid out. I don't even look at the food that's been prepared, but at the mere idea of eating, I feel like throwing up. But it's my only escape route. Keep calm, Step. This will pass. It all will pass.

No, not everything. With her, the pain and grief and sorrow still hasn't passed. Calm down, Step. You're a big boy now. I drink a glass of water.

"So, I hear that you have a job. Are you happy?" Happy? Coming from her lips, that word makes me feel like laughing. But I don't laugh. I manage to get out an answer, as I then do with all her other questions. "How did you like living in America? Did you have any problems? Are there lots of other Italians? Are you thinking of going back?"

I answer. I answer everything, reasonably well, I believe, doing my best to smile, to be kind and courteous. The way she taught me. With good manners.

"Look, I brought you these." And she pulls something out of a bag, not the one I gave her that time for Christmas or for her birthday—exactly when it was I can't recall. But I do remember that I found that bag on the armchair in that apartment. In the living room where in the bedroom another man was offering comfort to her, my mother. That's enough, Step. Stop it, just stop it.

"Do you recognize them? These are the morselletti you used to like so much."

Yes. I did used to love them. I loved everything about you, Mamma. And now, for the first time, after looking at her so many times, I see her again. My mother. She smiles with this little plastic bag in her hands. She sets it down lightly on the table and smiles at me again, tilting her head to one side. My mother. Her hair is lighter now. Even her skin seems fairer. She, delicate as always, seems even more fragile. She's lost weight. That's right, she seems thinner, and her skin seems faintly ruffled, as if by a light breeze. And her eyes. Her eyes seem a little hazed over, as if they were emanating a little less light. It's as if someone, who had it in for me, had decided to turn down the switch a little, casting our love into the shadows. My love.

I take another drink of water. "Yes, I remember them. I used to love them."

And I use the past tense without meaning to, without knowing, with the fear that even those simple cookies might have lost the flavor that I once loved so utterly.

"Did you open my present?"

"No, Mamma." Even now, I can't seem to tell her a lie. And it's not just the fear of being caught out in a lie. I'm reminded of Gin, and what she said about eyes. For a moment, I feel like smiling. And it's a good thing. "I haven't opened it."

"That's not good manners, and you know it."

But she doesn't wait for me to ask her forgiveness, no apology is needed. Her smile makes it clear to me that everything's all right, it's all water under the bridge, and she's not going to hold it against me. "It's a book, and I really wish that you'd read it. Do you have it here?"

"Yes."

"Then go get it."

And the way she asks is so kind and courteous that I can't help it, I get to my feet, I go to my room, and I come straight back with that present. I set it down on the table, and I unwrap it.

"There. It's by Irwin Shaw. *Lucy Crown*. It's a very beautiful story. I just happened upon this book. It made quite an impression on me. If you have time, I hope you'll read it."

"Yes, Mamma. If I have time, I'll read it."

We sit there for a little while in silence, and even though it's just a short time, it seems to go on forever. I look down, but not even the book cover can help me to make that infinite span of time progress forward. I fold up the wrapping paper, but even that only increases the weight of the seconds that creep by, never seeming to get anywhere.

My mother smiles. At last, she helps me to get over this small, short chunk of eternity. "My mother used to fold up the wrapping paper from all the gifts she received too. Your grandmother." She laughs. "Maybe you got that from her." She stands up. "Well, I'd better get going."

I stand up too.

"Let me walk you out."

"No, don't go to the trouble." She gives me a light kiss on the cheek. "I'll be fine. I have my car parked right downstairs."

She goes to the door and walks out, her back to me, without once turning around. She seems tired, and I'm utterly drained. And I no longer feel all the strength that I'd always felt I possessed. Maybe, then, that kiss wasn't as light as it first seemed.

Chapter 34

Oh, I was just thinking about you. We're simpatico! Seriously, I was about to call you." Gin is disarming in her constant and inevitable cheerfulness. "Where are you?"

"Right downstairs. Will you let me in?" I ask.

"But I've just finished eating, and my uncle is still here. Plus, what are you doing? Do you want to come to my house, introduce yourself to my parents, and take advantage of the fact that my uncle is here to ask me *something*?" She laughs cheerfully.

"Come on, Gin. Invent some excuse. I don't know. Say that you have to take in the laundry that's hanging on the line out on the terrace, that you have to go pick up something from your girlfriend who lives upstairs, that you need to elope with me, tell them *that* if you want, but just get free. I want you."

"You didn't just say that you wanted to see me, right? You actually said *I want you*?"

"Yes, I did."

Gin takes a long pause. Too long. Maybe I gave the wrong answer. "I want you too."

She says nothing more, and I hear the front door click

open. I don't bother taking the elevator. I climb the stairs like a bolt of lightning, all the way to the top floor without stopping once, actually taking the steps four at a time. And when I get there, the elevator door opens. It's Gin. Simpatico in this too.

I plunge into her lips and search for my breath there. Kissing her uninterruptedly, not even letting her breathe. I steal away her strength, her taste, her lips, and I even steal her words. A silence made up of sighs, her blouse falling open, her bra hook popping undone, our trousers falling to the floor, the banister moving, her laughing and telling me "Shhh" lest we be overhead. And strange positions in that elaborate tangle of legs, trapped in that denim that just excites me more, that captivates me, that is killing me right now.

Stopping for a moment and, down on my knees on the cold marble of the landing, kissing her between her legs. She, Gin, a strangely out-of-control cowgirl, feigns a rodeo all her own to keep from falling away from my lips. And then I mount her again and we race, together, we stupid, savage, impassioned, enamored horses, kept here on earth by a wrought-iron railing. It vibrates in silence just like our passion.

For a moment, we are suspended over the void. Distant noises. The sounds of a building. A drop of water in a sink. An armoire being shut. Footsteps. Then nothing. Us. Just us. Her head thrown backward, her hair hanging loose, abandoned, dangling over the stairwell. Her hair moves frantically, as if getting ready to leap into the void, just like our desire.

But a last kiss makes us both come down to earth together, setting foot on solid ground just as someone, somewhere, summons the elevator. "Shhh." She laughs, collapsing to the floor. Exhausted, sweaty, wet and not just with sweat. Her hair plastered to her face, laughing with her.

We embrace, joined together, like a couple of punch-drunk boxers, wrung dry, exhausted, squatting on the ground, defeated. While we await an unnecessary verdict: it's a draw, on points.

Smiling, we kiss. "Shhh," she says again. "Shhh." She delights in that silence.

The elevator stops one floor down. Our hearts race, and certainly not out of fear. I hide in her hair. I rest my face on her soft neck. I relax, unflustered and calm. My lips, tired, happy, satisfied, in search of nothing but an ultimate answer.

"Gin…"

"Yes?"

"Don't leave me."

And I don't know why but I say it. And I almost regret it. And Gin remains silent for a little while. Then she pulls away from me, and she observes me, curiously. Then she tells me, softly, practically whispering it, "You threw the padlock key into the river."

Softly she holds my head in her hands and looks at me. It's not a question. Then she gives me a kiss and then another and yet another still. And she says nothing. She just keeps kissing me.

And I smile. And I willingly accept that answer.

Chapter 35

It's a warm afternoon, strangely hot for December. The blue sky is as intense as those days in the mountains when you can't wait to go swimming. But I have to work. It's the last episode, or really I should say, the last day of rehearsals before filming the last episode. And yet it seems like a very particular day. I can feel something strange, and I don't know why. Sixth sense, possibly. But I never could have imagined.

"Buongiorno, Tony."

"Buongiorno, Step."

I hastily enter the theater. A group of photographers, all relatively down at the heels, with a strangely motley array of cameras, as mismatched as their clothing, blocks my path. They certainly aren't like those very precise groups of Japanese tourists with their cameras that you'll encounter in the piazzas of Rome. There is no image they've ever missed out on.

"That way, she went that way. Get moving, and we'll catch her."

I stop, baffled, and Tony, naturally, doesn't miss that.

"They're trying to track down Claudia Schiffer. She got

here early because she wants to rehearse walking out onto the stage. I mean, what is there to rehearse? It's just a short walk. There aren't even stairs. Maybe it's partly to justify the money she makes, goddamn her to hell."

Oh, of course *she's* around. Tony adds, "Listen, if you're looking for Gin, she went right up to the dressing room next to Schiffer's. One of the writers asked her to come up. Maybe they'll have her come on with Schiffer. Wait and see. If she learns to walk well, too, she'll start pulling down the big money too."

Tony laughs chaotically, stumbling over a strange cough, all cigarette smoke and unhealthy lungs. In spite of that, he immediately lights up another MS, discarding the empty pack. Is that the one I brought him yesterday or a new one, already smoked through? What does it matter if it doesn't matter to him?

Well, I'd better go see how Marcantonio is doing and how our work is coming along. Here he is, sitting in front of the computer, concentrating. I watch him from a distance, through the door that stands ajar. Then he smiles to himself and pushes a button, printing the pages, and in a burst of satisfaction, he lights a cigarette just as he sees me come in. "Hey, Step, you want one?" Well, at least he, unlike Tony, offers you a cigarette, and he doesn't seem sick, or not seriously.

"No, thanks."

He shuts the cigarette pack. "More for me!" He tucks it into his jacket pocket and smooths back what little hair persists on either side of his head. "I did it. I managed to lay it all out the way they want it."

"Ah, fine." I notice that he takes special care to avoid

saying, *the way the writers want it*, but I see no purpose pointing that out to him. If for no reason other than the fact that he's offered me a cigarette.

We stand there for a moment in silence, watching the sheets of paper being spewed out of the printer. Vrrr. Vrrr. One after another. Precise, clean, and tidy. Clear, light colors, perfectly legible, exactly as they wanted them, I have to imagine.

Marcantonio waits for the last sheet to appear. Then he picks them up, delicately, from the printer and blows lightly on them to dry off the last layer of freshly printed ink. "All done. They seem perfect."

He looks at me in search of approval. "Yes, they seem fine."

It's not as if I'm all that sure of it. Seeing those sheets of paper thrown into Marcantonio's face has completely made me forget even what the source of the argument was in the first place.

"Yes, perfect!" I limit myself to saying, trying to get out of that awkward situation. But it's not enough.

"Listen, Step, will you do me a favor? Can you take these upstairs to the writers?"

He's finally managed to utter that word. But is that a victory of some kind, what's the word for it again, oh, right, a *Pyrrhic* victory! Because in any case, it's up to me to confront them. What a pain in the ass! But Marcantonio, my mentor, has asked me to do it as a favor. How can I say no?

"Certainly, happy to."

He looks at me, relieved. He hands me the sheets of paper, and as I leave the room, he flings himself backward in his chair, crushes out his cigarette, and immediately lights another one. There's only one thing I know for sure. That man smokes too much.

Well, I've got to do this. I gallop up the stairs. There they are. The photographers are all sitting or, to be more accurate, sprawled on low, faded settees. They're waiting for the diva to emerge. A strange profession.

When I arrive, they understandably give me not so much as a first, much less a second, glance. So much the better. Already, it's a burden to be carrying these sheets of paper. No doubt the writers will have comments to share.

I look around, trying to determine where they might be. SCHIFFER. The name, perfectly printed in large letters by a LaserWriter, stands out clearly against the first door. The second door has nothing written on it. So I knock. I hear no answer. I wait a few seconds and then I open the door. Nothing. Silence. But then I notice a narrow hallway. At the end of it, another door. Same format, same color. I proceed through it, my hands full of paper. Maybe they're down there. In that other room. Well, as long as I'm here, I might as well give it a shot.

But as I approach, I hear a sound. A strange sound. A few muffled laughs. Then a series of chaotic, dull, rebellious movements. Like the flailing kicks of a child lifted into the air, trying to kick a ball beneath its feet. So I open the door without knocking. Bad manners, plain and simple. But it just comes spontaneously to me, and what I see strikes me as surreal. Toscani is holding Gin from behind, both arms wrapped around her. Sesto is leaning on a table with the usual toothpick in his mouth and smiling in amusement at the scene, while Micheli is in front of Gin, moving to a strange tempo.

Then, all at once, I manage to focus more clearly on the scene. Gin's blouse is torn. Her breasts are bare, uncovered by a bra twisted aside. There's a length of packing tape covering her mouth. Toscani is licking her neck with his rough tongue. Micheli, the Serpent, has his trousers unzipped in front, his dick out, and he's masturbating.

Gin, her hair soaked with sweat from her struggle, suddenly turns to look at me. She's desperate. She sees me. She heaves a sigh. She seems to experience a moment of relief.

Toscani locks eyes with me and stops licking her neck. His tongue hangs out in midair, as does his sagging jaw. Sesto isn't much better. He wears a stunned expression, and his mouth falls open too. His stupid toothpick therefore hangs dangling in midair, stuck to his lower lip.

Finally, those sheets of paper come in handy for some real purpose. It only takes a split second. I hurl the papers forcefully into Sesto's face, the only one who might intervene quickly. I catch him full in the face. He tries to dodge the blow. He slides off the table and winds up on the floor.

Micheli, the Serpent, doesn't have a chance to turn around fast enough. I hit him with a punch from right to left, open-handed as if trying to push him away. But I catch him right in the trachea. He flies backward, landing with both legs in the air and a strange moan. His timid little dick retracts instantly.

Toscani stops embracing Gin. In an instant, I'm on them. I free her, pulling the packing tape off her lips. "Are you okay?"

She moves her head up and down as if to say yes, with tears in her eyes and her brow furrowed. Her lips tremble in a desperate attempt to speak. "Shhh," I tell her. I gently lead her toward the exit. I can tell that she's putting her bra back in place and straightening her blouse. Getting her thoughts in order, to the extent that it's possible. She's trying to find a place for her grief and pain. She's trying to cry. But she can't seem to do it. In any case, she doesn't turn around. She just walks away. Unsteady on her feet, her footsteps wandering as she walks, lost in thought about what to do next.

But as for me, I have not a shadow of a doubt. Boom. I whip around and hit Toscani with a violence I didn't even know I possessed. I punch him full in the face from below, my fist taking in lip, nose, and forehead, basically a sliding impact, but putting all my weight and all my rage into that blow.

He slams against the wall, and no sooner does he come to that sudden halt, than I am all over him again. Straight into his belly with my right foot, taking his breath away, giving him just enough time to hit the floor before I pull that same foot back, a short windup for a powerful kick, smashing into him like a ricocheting ball. Right in the face. Like a penalty kick, like the finest work of Christian Vieri, or Giuseppe Signori, or Cristiano Ronaldo. With a bellowing shout and a threat, it's a penalty kick I have no intention of getting wrong.

Boom. Again. Against the wall. I shatter his cheek, and there's a spurt of blood. I climb over Micheli who's still gasping and trying to catch his breath. I smile at him involuntarily. I'm savoring the fact that he's starting to recover. He needs to be in better shape for what I naturally intend to save for last as the grand finale.

But now I'm on Sesto. He covers his face with both hands, hoping for a miracle that never happens. Boom! I hit him with a right straight, wide, handsome, tense, and open. From right to left with all the weight in my body. Again! Right there, on his ear, with a violence so overwhelming that I'm surprised it doesn't pop off the side of his head. But then I quiet down. In the end, he's bleeding. And he stupidly, in his surprise, still incredulous, takes his hands off his face and holds them out in front of his eyes. He looks at them, unable to believe it, searching for who knows what absurd explanation for that pain, that blood, and that noise.

But he's not fast enough to realize anything. Boom! Now his face is uncovered. Boom. One after the other I land a series of blows to his face. One after the other, faster and faster, faster and faster, like a lunatic. The only thing holding him up are my fists, supporting that face as it slowly disintegrates. Boom! Boom! Boom! And I feel no pain and I feel no pity and I feel nothing at all.

I smile. I stop. I take a breath. Smash. A chair hits me from behind. It catches me in full on the back of the neck but all I hear is the blow. I turn around. Micheli is standing in front of me. He's finally caught his breath.

I open my eyes wide, trying to regain focus after the blow I just took. And just in time, I see the chair arrive again. I bend down instinctively as it swings over my head. All it takes is just a split second and I feel a faint gust just over my hair. Dodged it.

I pop up again, blocking his arm, gripping his wrist and making him drop the chair. Then I pull him toward me, slamming my head forward to meet him. A perfect headbutt, right to his nose, breaking it.

Behind him, all those photographers have appeared. They voraciously wave their cameras in the air, inundating us with dazzling flashes. They must have seen Gin leave. They must have seen her, traumatized, her blouse torn, in tears. But they saw her. And that offers me some comfort.

Chapter 36

I don't have time to go downstairs. The news has arrived before I can. A strange agitation has created a feverish situation throughout the theater. It feels like being caught in an unexpected live broadcast. Everyone's running in this direction or that. Curious, crazed, shouting, urgently demanding more information, already confident masters of some variant of the story. They color it as they best prefer, adding tidbits, blowing details out of proportion, altering the beginning or the end. "Have you heard?" "Wait what happened?" "A brawl...a security guard fired his gun." "Is anyone hurt?" "Everyone is!"

I ask about Gin. One young woman tells me that she's gone home. So much the better. I head for the exit. Tony comes to meet me. He seems agitated too. He must seriously be upset given that he doesn't have the usual cigarette in his mouth.

"Get out of here, Step. The police are on their way."

He seems to be the only one to have understood anything. "However it turns out, you did the right thing. I've always cordially disliked those three."

I head for my motorcycle. I hear my name being called. "Step, Step!" It's Marcantonio, and he's running straight toward me. "Everything okay?" For a moment, I look at my bloodied hands, and without meaning to, I massage them. Strange. They don't even hurt.

Marcantonio notices. I reassure him. "Yes, everything's fine."

"Okay. So much the better. Then you get on home. I'll stay here. We can talk later, and I'll fill you in on everything. Is Gin all right?"

"I don't know. She went home."

Then he tries to defuse the high drama. "Well, for this last episode, it can air practically without changes now, right?"

"Yes, I think so. You're just going to have to reprint those sheets. The ones I took upstairs got a little messed up."

"The sheets of paper, huh? From what I've heard, the guys themselves are ruined, and I don't just mean physically. It's a grim story. You'll see, you'll come out of this the winner."

I start my motorcycle. "Thanks, Marcantonio. We'll be in touch."

I put it in first and pull away. A winner? In what? I sincerely give not a damn about it. Gin is all I care about.

A little later, I'm at home, and I call her. We talk on the telephone. She's still in a state of shock. She's talked with her folks. She's told them everything. She speaks softly. She hasn't fully regained her strength. I can hear her speaking an octave lower than usual. But she's able to tell her side of the story.

I continue listening to her, as calm as I can be for her.

"They told me to file a criminal complaint. You'll be my witness, won't you?"

"Yes, certainly." I find it odd to have changed my role in this. "Sure, from defendant to eyewitness. And on the part of right and justice. I'll take that."

I listen to her for another little while. Then I recommend that she drink a nice cup of chamomile tea and try to get some rest. Because I don't know what else to say. No sooner do I hang up than the phone starts ringing off the hook. I don't much feel like answering, and after all, Paolo is here, maybe it's for him.

"Should I take that?" He seems happy to answer.

"Certainly." He walks past me. I nod and decide to go take a shower. As I'm undressing, I realize it wasn't for him. I can hear him talking in the living room. "What? And how are they? You say critical condition? Ah, serious but not critical. You were starting to worry me. But how did it happen? What? You want to invite him to appear with Mentana? Ah, with Costanzo? But there must have been a reason..."

From his tone, I can tell that he's trying to save me. "Well, that's just the way he is...Ah...Wait, you're saying you want to present him as a hero? Ah, a sort of knight in shining armor, a workplace vigilante. Well, I can't speak for him. No, I'm not his agent. I'm just his brother."

I can't help but laugh, and I climb into the shower.

The following day, starting at seven in the morning, the telephone starts ringing again. After my shower yesterday evening, Paolo wanted to know every detail about what happened. He held me captive for more than an hour in a sort of interrogation session, though he offered me, instead of the usual glaring lamp in the face, a delicious bowl of spaghetti. My brother is actually a very good cook. There was even a nice, ice-cold beer to go with it. I needed it too.

I'm eating breakfast and watching him now. He's on the phone. He's taking notes and answering questions. My brother. He'd definitely be a first-rate agent.

"Ciao, Pa, I'm going out."

Paolo stands there with the telephone held up in one hand and his mouth hanging half-open.

"Don't worry, I'm going to see how Gin is doing."

And he seems to understand on that point. "Yes, of course, certainly." I see him immediately hurl himself at his sheet of paper. He does a rapid calculation of all his hypothetical earnings. Then he looks at me. And in a split second, he sees it all go up in smoke.

Chapter 37

Gin is feeling better. Her eyes are still a little red, she's a little beat up, but I assure her that she's going to be okay. She's set aside her torn blouse and her bra, put away in a bag. As evidence, she says. I don't want to look at them. It hurts just to think back on that scene.

I give her a light kiss. I don't want to meet her folks. I wouldn't know what to say to them. But they know who I am. "The guy who sent over the bottle of champagne," Gin told her folks, to help them understand. "They'd like to thank you."

"Yes, I understand. Just tell them that I have some things to take care of. I have to go home. I mean, tell them whatever you want."

I don't want to listen to their thank-yous. Sometimes *thanks* can be such an annoying word. There are things I don't want to be thanked for. There are things that just never should have happened. I try to make that clear to them, with courtesy.

Later, I'm at home. Paolo senses that he needs to just let me be. He says nothing to me about appointments or the whole idea of easy money. He doesn't try to get me to talk to Papà or Mamma. Pictures appeared in several news-papers, and a bunch of people called to say hello. To express their solidarity.

But I don't want to talk to anyone. I just want to watch the episode. There. It's ten after nine. The theme music starts up. After just two panels showing the usual credits comes the surprise. The first and last names of the three writers no longer appear. The dancers continue to dance perfectly, smiling and relaxed in spite of everything that's happened. And anyway, as we all know, the show must go on.

And to think that it's the last episode. There's no way it's not going to air. Market considerations. I have learned a few things. The credits continue to roll. The girls dance. The music is the same. The audience smiles. There's another surprise. My credit is still there.

My cell phone rings. I see the number. It's Gin. I answer.

"So you saw your name? I was right. I thought so, but I didn't tell you. It's like it means you won't be in trouble. I'm happy for you."

She's happy for me. She *would* be happy for me. She's incredible. She always manages to surprise me. I say good-bye to her. "Let's talk later, after it's over." I hang up.

I open a beer, and at that exact moment, the cell phone rings. An undisclosed number. I shouldn't take the risk but, who knows why, I feel like it, and I go ahead and answer. It's Romani. I recognize his voice. I shoot a glance at the TV. In fact, they're showing a commercial. The first commercial break of the show, almost always at 9:45. I look at the clock. They're running a few minutes early. Who knows who even made up the schedule. Maybe those three had already completed it.

But I forget about all those thoughts. I try to understand what he's saying and, as I listen, I'm surprised.

"So what I wanted to tell you, Stefano, is that I'm sorry. I didn't know. I could never have imagined such a thing."

And he continues with his customary tranquility, with his effortless elegance, with his calm, firm voice, so resounding. A voice that instills confidence. I listen in silence, and I remain speechless, even if I had wanted to say anything. Two other young women have now reported the same thing, an occurrence dating back some time. They'd lacked the courage to speak up for fear of losing their job or worse. And maybe there are others.

"And after what you did, Stefano, they're gaining confidence. It wouldn't have been uncovered for who knows how much longer, and possibly never. So, Stefano, I feel guilty for having put you into a situation like this one. And of all people, your girlfriend..."

I shake my head. There's nothing to be done about it. Romani knows it too.

"So please accept my apologies and thank you. Seriously, thank you very much, Stefano." Again, a thank-you. The one word I never would have wanted to hear.

"Well, now, I bid you farewell, I have to go back to work on the episode. Come see me though. I have something for you. It's a gift. After all, I can't use it. I have another show that starts in just two months, so I can't even get away."

He tries not to put too much emphasis on his generous gesture. No two ways about it, he's really something.

"That way, you two can get some peace of mind. Then, if you like, we can work together again. He pauses. "If you like. But it would certainly make me happy. I'll wait to hear from you...Stefano?"

I still haven't said a thing but I end it nicely. "Yes, Romani, all right. I'll swing by tomorrow. Thanks."

As if by magic, the commercial ends, and the show starts up again. I drain my beer. Well, at least I managed to say one thank-you myself.

Chapter 38

At the TdV theater, they're already breaking down the set. Bits of scenery and stage decoration are being hauled off, one after the other. A team of demolishers laugh among themselves. They almost seem to take pleasure in their destruction.

"It's easier to destroy than to build..."

Romani's voice catches me by surprise, coming from behind me. But it's still reassuring. I smile and shake his hand. He's been the most interesting person to get to know. The most unexpected, the one with the complex personality. The true winner of the rat race, which has proved disappointing and worrisome in so many ways, in the end even manages to make you appreciate it.

We walk together while tiny bits of stage dressing continue falling from above. Constantly and necessarily moving forward, the importance and the stupidity of success, the narcotic that is success, the beauty of success. To believe for a fleeting moment that you won't be forgotten. But don't worry, you *will* be forgotten.

"Here." He hands me an envelope. "These are the

contracts for you and for Ginevra for the next broadcast I do. If you like, you're both already on staff. In March, a game involving music. A broadcast that will be super easy to put together, already tested in various European countries. It has more than thirty-five percent ratings in Spain.

"Marcantonio will be working on it, so will the same choreographer. I signed up some of the same dancers. I got rid of other members of the staff..." He smiles, clearly alluding to the three writers. "In part because I honestly don't think they'll ever work in this town again.

"All right, then, I hope that you and Ginevra will accept this contract. I've raised your salaries, both of you." Then he remains silent. "Well, think it over..."

"Listen, Romani, can I ask you something?"

"Certainly."

I look at him for a moment. What the hell. I just go ahead and ask him. "Why do you always wear one of your collar buttons unfastened?"

He looks at me. Then he smiles. "It's very simple. To understand the character of the people I'm dealing with. Everyone wonders the same thing, everyone wants to ask me, to figure it out. But people are split into two groups: those who don't dare to ask me that simple question and those who do. The first group will never know the answer to their curiosity. The second, on the other hand, will learn the reason for this idiotic detail!"

We laugh. I don't know if it's the truth. But I really like it as an explanation, and I decide to accept it at face value.

"This, on the other hand, is an envelope from me. An excellent place to go and think over the contract.

The occasional beach in a hot place can help you get to *yes*."

And he smiles allusively at all those hypothetical *yeses* that we'll be able to get to. Then he strides quickly away. But by doing so, he's beaten me to the punch. This time I didn't get a chance to thank him.

Chapter 39

I can't believe it. Gin said yes. She had to invent a story that, aside from me, there are going to be three or four other people on the trip, but her parents said she could go.

That's not all. They even threw in a reassuring phrase. "After all, as long as he's there..." That "he" would be me. Which is just absurd. For the first time in history, there are parents who imagine that their daughter is safe if she's with me. Yes, Gin is safe in my arms.

It's a dream come true. We're flying first class. Thailand, Vietnam, and Malaysia. All expenses paid. The best flights. The best bungalows. The most beautiful beaches. The sun, the sea, and a contract waiting for us when we come back, ours to accept or reject. And freedom. The freedom to say *yes* every minute of the day if we feel like doing something, or else *no*, without commitments, without unexpected phone calls, without problems, without meetings with people you don't want to meet. We board the airplane, free and relaxed.

A young female flight attendant shows us to our seats. I smile at her. She's very courteous. And also very cute. She offers us drinks. When she turns to go, Gin gives me an elbow to the ribs.

"Ouch!"

"I want to see you being rude and abrupt with the flight attendants."

"Certainly, I've always been like that." I smile. I take a drink from the glass that the young lady from Thai Airways has courteously offered us. Then I kiss Gin rapidly. A light champagne hue colors our lips. I make it last for a while. The airplane is starting to roll down the runway. Gin holds tight to me, and we're in the air.

Rat-a-tat. The wheels fold away into the belly of the aircraft. The airplane reaches altitude. It climbs into the clouds. A closer sunset caresses us through the window. Gin relaxes her embrace and rests her head on me. "Do you mind if I lean on you like this?" I don't have time to reply. I sense her drop into slumber, abandoning all the latest tensions, letting herself relax in my arms, aboard an airplane in flight, scudding lightly above our clouds. She must feel safe.

Tenderly, I try to move her as little as possible. I reach into the bag I have lying nearby and extract *Lucy Crown*, the book my mother gave me, and I start to read. I like the way it's written. At least, for the first few pages, it's not painful. Not yet.

Suddenly. I hear music. I realize that I've fallen asleep. The book is propped up on the tray table. Gin is next to me, looking at me and smiling. She has a small camera in her hands. "I took some pictures of you while you were sleeping."

I hug her, pulling her close. We kiss. Then we notice the presence of a person. We pull apart, and Gin blushes. It's the flight attendant from before, with two glasses in her hands. "These are for you. It's almost time."

Curiously, we take them. The petite flight attendant heads off, just as quickly as she appeared.

"It's true, I hadn't thought about it. It's December thirty-first..."

Gin looks at her watch. "It's just a few seconds to midnight."

A strange countdown with an American accent starts up from the cockpit. "Three, two, one...Happy New Year!"

The music gets louder. Gin gives me a kiss. "Happy New Year, Step."

We raise a toast with the two glasses of champagne delivered just in the nick of time. Then we exchange another kiss. And another. And yet another. With no more fear of being interrupted. Everyone on the airplane is singing and happily celebrating the year that's just ended or the one that's about to start, the fact that they're starting their vacation or returning home. In either case, they're happy. With their champagne. With their heads, and the rest of their bodies, in the clouds.

The airplane drops to a slightly lower altitude, and there's a good reason. "Look," says Gin, pointing out the window. In some country down below us, they're celebrating. Fireworks are leaving earth, coming up to greet us. To celebrate our arrival and departure. They open up beneath us like newly blooming flowers. A thousand unexpected colors. With a thousand carefully crafted patterns. Charges of gunpowder, perfectly crowded together, free themselves into the sky, catching fire in midair. One after another. One inside another. For the first time ever, we see them from above. Gin and me, embracing, with our faces framed in the window, see the end of the year, the part that has always been hidden, always seen only by the stars, the clouds, and the sky.

Gin looks ecstatically at the fireworks. "Gorgeous!" Distant lights manage to depict her face. Delicate brushstrokes of luminous color caress her cheeks.

We continue looking out the window. And the music continues. And the airplane, fast and secure, continues on its way. It flies through the sky, over the happiness and high hopes of who knows how many countries. And we, drunk with happiness and some other influence, wish each other Happy New Year over and over again. We drink toast after toast for that same New Year's, with only one great certainty. "Let this be a year of happiness."

Thailand, the island of Koh Samui

We wake up on the beach. And it almost seems as if we're dreaming again in the presence of that sea, that crystal-clear, perennially warm water, that sun.

"So you see, Step, it's the same as the postcards I used to receive. I always believed that some strange counterfeiter might have dummied them up on a computer. Even if I'd worked on it, I never could have dreamed of a place like this."

"Certainly, God has some imagination. And He created this out of nothing. What a great artist."

And so she gets out of the water, leaving me soaking amid a thousand colorful fish.

Vietnam, the island of Phú Quốc

Still in the water, embracing now, splashing each other, fighting a minor skirmish on the sand before the amused eyes of children whose curiosity is aroused by these two strange tourists who first do battle and then hug and kiss! And we continue like that. Kissing a little more, lulled by the sun, wet with desire, we hurry into our bungalow.

A shower. Curtains lowered, dancing to the rhythm of the wind but without unveiling the windowpanes and ruining our privacy.

Waves break on the rocks, and we, not far away, follow the rhythm of the waves.

I let Gin set the pace. She climbs on top of me, throwing her leg over me, and takes me in her hand, and slides me into her, softly and decisively. Confidently. She continues kissing me. Bent over me, she holds my arms wide and shoves her hips down hard at me, taking me in all the way, into her most remote being.

She grips my wrists tight, and for a moment, she abandons her kiss. She opens her mouth. She remains suspended over my lips. She sighs repeatedly and then utters that fantastic phrase. "I'm coming." She says it softly, slowly, enunciating each tiny letter, in a low voice. A voice of unrivaled eroticism...

And a split second later, I come too. Gin throws back her hair, pushes her hips toward me another two or three times and then stops and opens her eyes. As if she had suddenly returned. "So you came inside me?"

"Of course, there was no one else here but you and me."

"Sorry, but I'm not taking anything. I'm not taking the pill."

"Really? Am I getting confused? I mixed you up with another girl!"

"You...complete knucklehead!" She climbs back on top of me and starts hitting me.

"Ouch! Ouch! That's enough, Gin, I was just kidding."

She calms down. "I understand, but were you just kidding when you said that you came?"

"No, not about that! Certainly not about that."

"What do you mean?"

"That it was such a beautiful, unique, fantastic moment, that it seemed to me to be stupid to interrupt it."

She throws herself down on the bed next to me again, plunging headfirst into the pillow. "You're crazy, and what are we going to do now?"

"Well, we'll do whatever you want to do."

"Where are we going to find a morning-after pill in Vietnam? It seems absurd. We'll never find it! I guess there's no reason to bother looking for it."

"What?"

"If we'll never find it, then there's no point in looking for it, is there?"

I kiss her. She's stunned for a moment but she lets me kiss her. She doesn't participate all that much. I pull away and look at her. "Well?"

She has a funny face. She's surprised and perplexed at the same time.

"I'll just rest up for a second, and then we can get started again."

Gin shakes her head and smiles, as crazy as I am, and

kisses me. She caresses me and kisses me again. And we both get our breath back quickly. And this time, I decide to lead, without haste. And as the sunset once again plays hide-and-seek, we come again, this time without hiding, laughing, united, like before, but more than before. Embracing our love. And embracing everything that might be next.

Later, in a strange pub named Apocalypse Now by its ironic Vietnamese owners, we're drinking beer. Gin writes furiously in her diary.

"Hey, do you mind telling me what kind of Divine Comedy you're putting down there? You haven't stopped writing ever since we sat down, so what does that do to our conversation? A couple is also made up of communication, you know that right?"

"Shhh! I'm capturing the moment."

Gin writes one last thing quickly and then closes her diary.

"All done! I'm better than Bridget Jones. This will be a worldwide bestseller!"

"What have you written?"

"Everything we've done."

"And you take this long to describe two people fucking?"

"You jerk! You want to know what I wrote? Everything! Not just how we made love, but everything that happened. It's a piece of our destiny. Maybe it was thanks to that instant that we'll have a child. We'll be together forever."

Malaysia, the islands of Perhentian and Tioman

Golden, healthy, and slightly toasted by a sun that just never quits, we walk. The afternoon of any given day. The same as all days when you're on vacation.

We stop by a painter stretched out comfortably in the shade of a palm tree and select our canvas without haste. "There, that one!"

One of the many paintings set in the sand like giant colorful seashells, left to dry in the open air. We choose it together, amused to notice that we were both captured by the same one.

"We certainly are simpatico, aren't we, Step?"

"Yeah."

I pay the man five dollars, he rolls it up, and we carry it home with us to our bungalow at a slow and leisurely walk.

"I'm worried."

"Why? About your belly? It's early for that."

"You jerk! It just seems strange to me. It's been ten days, and we haven't fought once! All day, every day together, and we haven't had a single quarrel."

"Well, then, wouldn't it have been better to say: 'All night, every night together and we've always, unfailingly...'"

Gin whips around. She gives me a tough, grim expression.

"Made love! Don't get mad at me. There's no reason to glare at me! That's exactly what I was about to say. All night, every night together and we've always, unfailingly made love."

"Yes...yes...certainly."

"Even though..." We continue walking. "Sorry, Gin. But 'we've always, unfailingly fucked' just seems to me to be a more accurate description."

I start running. "You jerk. Then just say it, that you want a quarrel!"

She starts running after me, trying to catch me. I quickly

open the front door to the bungalow and slip inside. She arrives a short while later.

"All right then...you're really looking for a fight."

"No, look..." and I point to the window, "it's almost dark. It's late now, and if we're going to fight, we fight in daylight!" I pull her close to me. "Because at night..."

"At night?" Gin replies.

"At night we make love, okay? We can say it however you prefer."

"Okay."

She smiles. I kiss her. She's beautiful. I hold her a little distance away from my face. I smile back at her. "But now let's fuck!" She hits me again. But it only lasts a moment, we get lost between cool sheets that smell wonderfully of the sea. And we make love, fucking.

⌒

We've spent a number of days on the island. And it's true, we've never once quarreled. Quite the opposite. We've had our fair share of fun. I'd never have thought it could be like this, and with someone like her...The other evening, I found myself lost amid the ocean waves. They seemed so sweet, warm and soft, in that shallow water, without strong currents. Or maybe it was all because of the beauty and simplicity of that kiss we exchanged. Just like that, in silence, looking into each other's eyes, embracing in the moonlight, going that far and no further. We laughed, we chatted, we remained in that embrace. The beautiful thing about an island like this one is that you have no appointments. Everything you do, you do purely because you feel like it, never because you have to. Every night, we eat dinner in a little restaurant. The whole place is made of wood, and it's right by the water's edge, I mean, you walk down three steps and you're already in the water. We read the menu without any real idea of what's actually written on it. In the end, we always ask them to explain. The people who work there are all very courteous, and they smile a lot. And after listening to their explanations, generally pretty easy to understand, consisting of hand gestures and lots of laughter, we decide to try a different dish for each meal. Maybe it's because we want to try them all, more or less, because we're hoping that, sooner or later, we'll like at least one. But especially because we're happy.

"And listen, this is important, without any strange sauces, without anything on it. Nothing, nothing..."

When they hear us talking like that, they always nod their heads. Invariably. Even when we say absurd things to them. In the end, we never know what they're really going to bring us. Sometimes it goes well, sometimes, not so well.

I try to give Gin some advice. "Anyway, if you go for roasted 'pescado' you'll never be sorry."

She laughs. "My God, you're already an old man. The fun of it is to try lots of new things, to try everything."

I look around. There's practically no one else on this island. At a small table some distance away, another couple is dining. They're older and quieter than us. Is it normal that as you grow older, you have less and less to say? I don't know, and I don't want to know. I'm in no hurry. I'll find out when the time comes.

Gin, on the other hand, just talks and talks, about this and that, about amusing and interesting things of all sorts. She makes me aware of aspects of life that I would never have known about, much less even imagined, if it hadn't been for her. And I listen to her, as I gaze into her eyes, without ever losing track of each other. Plus, she always has a thousand ideas about what to do next.

"Listen, I just have a wonderful idea. Tomorrow, let's go to an island just across the water, no, even better, let's rent a boat and go out fishing, no, no, better still, let's do some trekking on the interior of the island...Huh, what do you say?"

I smile. I don't tell her that the island has a total diameter of barely a kilometer. "Certainly, a wonderful idea."

"But which one? I just made three separate suggestions!"

"All three of them are wonderful."

"Sometimes I really think you're making fun of me."

"Why do you say that? You're beautiful."

"You see, you're making fun of me."

I sit down beside her, and I give her a kiss. A long kiss. An impossibly long one. Eyes shut. A totally liberated kiss. And the wind tries to whisk between our lips, our smile, our cheeks, our hair...Nothing, it's no good, it can't get through. Nothing separates us. All I can hear are little waves breaking beneath us, the respiration of the sea, which echoes our own breaths, which taste of salt and brine...And of her. And for an instant I'm afraid. Am I trying to lose myself again like with Babi? And what will happen then? Who knows? I let myself go. Because it's a fear that I like, a healthy fear.

Gin suddenly pulls away from me, steps away, and stares

at me. "Hey, why are you looking at me like that? What are you thinking about?"

I gather her hair, pushed forward by the wind. Then I pull it back, uncovering her face, which is lovelier than ever. "I want to make love with you."

Gin stands up. She picks up her jacket. For a moment, she seems angry. Then she turns around and gives me a dazzling smile. "I'm over my hunger. Shall we go?"

I stand up, set some money down on the table, and join her. We start walking along at the water's edge. I put my arm around her. The night. The moon. An even gentler breeze. Boats far off, in the open water. White sails luff. They seem like handkerchiefs, fluttering in our direction. But no, we're not leaving. Not yet. Small waves from the sea caress our ankles, making only subdued sounds. They're warm, slow, and silent. They're respectful. They seem like a prelude to a kiss that wants to venture further. They're almost afraid to make themselves felt.

A waiter arrives with a trayful of plates at our table but we're no longer there waiting for him. Then he sees us. Far away now. He calls after us. "Tomorrow, you'll eat tomorrow." The waiter shakes his head and smiles. Yes, this island is beautiful. Here everyone is respectful of love.

Chapter 40

W hen I was little and I came home from the holidays, Rome always seemed different to me. Cleaner, more orderly, with fewer cars, with a direction of travel that had suddenly changed, with an extra traffic light or two. This time, it seems identical to what it was when I left.

It's Gin who seems different to me. I look at her, and she doesn't notice. She waits obediently in line for our turn to catch a taxi. She moves her hair now and then, thrusting it back, pushing it away from her face, and her hair, still redolent of the sea, complies. No, not different. Simply more of a woman.

She holds her duffel bag between her legs and a backpack, not too heavy, slung over her right shoulder. Austere and erect, but soft featured. She turns, looks at me, and smiles. Is she a mother now? Omigod, is she actually expecting a baby? I must have lost my mind. She looks at me curiously, perhaps trying to divine my thoughts. I look at her instead, trying to divine her belly. Are there already two of her?

I remember a TV show I saw when I was just a kid. The story of Ligabue. But not the singer. The painter. Looking at one of his models, painting her on a canvas, Ligabue

realizes, by a change in the light of her eyes, from the soft
features of her body, that she's pregnant. But I'm not a
painter. Even if I may be even crazier than Ligabue.

"May I ask what you're thinking about?"

"It might strike you as absurd, but Ligabue."

"Oh, seriously? You can't imagine how much I like him,
both as a singer and as a man."

She sings a few bars from several songs, cheerfully and
perfectly in tune. She knows all the words to "Certe notti"
but she hasn't guessed one of my thoughts. Luckily. At least
not this time. "Hey! You know something? I like Ligabue
as a director too. Have you seen *Radiofreccia*?"

"No."

Our turn has come. We put our luggage in the trunk and
get in the taxi.

"Too bad, at a certain point in that movie there's a great
line... 'I think I have a hole inside of me, but one that
rock and roll, a few girlfriends, soccer, the satisfaction from
my job, and fucking around with my friends, well, every so
often, that's enough to fill that hole.'"

"Sounds great. You certainly do remember a lot of the
lines, don't you?"

Gin persists. "How about *Da dieci a zero*?"

"Nope, not that either."

"But are you sure you were thinking of the singer, and
not Ligabue the painter?"

She looks at me, curiosity piqued and mocking. I tell the
taxi driver the address of Gin's house, and he nods his head
and takes off. I put on my sunglasses.

Gin laughs. "I caught you red-handed, didn't I? Or don't
you know who that is either?"

She doesn't expect an answer. She decides to leave me be. She leans on my shoulder the way she did during all our flights on the various airplanes. Like all the nights of the past few weeks. I see her reflection in the cab driver's rearview mirror. She shuts her eyes. She seems to be resting, but then she opens them again. She meets my gaze, even through the sunglasses. She smiles. Maybe she's figured it all out.

One last farewell. "Ciao. Well, see you around." With her backpack on her shoulder and her duffel bag in her hand, Gin goes through the front door. I see her leave like that, without being allowed to lend a hand. She refused to let me.

"I don't want to be helped and most of all, I hate long goodbyes. Now get out of here!"

Gin is too cool. I get back in the taxi, and I give the driver my address. He nods his head. He knows that one too.

In a moment, my mind is filled with so many different moments of our trip. It's like a scrapbook flipped through quickly. So I choose the nicest pictures. The timeless chats, the timeless love, the timeless reawakenings. And now? I'm worried, and it's not just jet lag. Leaving her at her house after a trip is like setting back out on another trip, but without knowing where I'm going and especially not knowing with whom. I'm traveling alone now. And I miss Gin already.

"We're here, sir."

Luckily, I have the cabbie to bring me back in touch with reality. I get out. I don't wait for the change, I get my things, and I go inside.

"Is anybody home?" Silence. So much the better. I need to return, quietly, on tiptoe, without too much noise or upset, without too many questions, to my ordinary, everyday life. I unpack my bag, I put my dirty laundry in the hamper in the bathroom, and I take a shower. I can't feel the impact of the jet lag but luckily, I do hear my cell phone. I get out of the shower. I grab it just in time. I dry off for a minute before picking up the phone. It's Gin.

"Hey, I just turned my phone on a second ago before getting in the shower. I knew you couldn't resist."

"Just think that I'd called you to see how you were holding up. You're not banging your head against the wall, are you? Are you like a junkie going through withdrawal... from love?"

"Me?"

"Start thinking about what you're going to say to my folks, you'll have to come meet them in the next few days."

"What?"

"Well, since *it* hasn't shown up, it would be better for you to swing by, right?"

"What?"

"Time is up, and *it* hasn't given a sign of arriving, that means I'm pregnant! Get ready to ask me to marry you, apologize to my parents, and all the rest of it."

"But I thought all I was going to have to do was pick the name."

"Why, certainly. The easiest part! No, don't worry, I'll take care of that. You just worry about all the rest. Do you know what my mother always likes to say? 'So you wanted the bicycle? Well, now pedal!'"

"If it's a girl, we could call her Bicycle. She'd certainly be a very athletic young woman, and then I don't know what else, maybe in honor of your mother."

"That's a relief. I thought you'd slipped into a state of depression. Instead you're still capable of coming out with idiotic jokes."

"Yes, but they're the last ones. You know that when it comes time to be a father, I'll be much more serious."

"I miss you..."

We go on talking without really even knowing what we're talking about, much less why. Then we decide to end the call, promising to talk again tomorrow. It's a pointless promise because we would have done it anyway.

When you're wasting time on the telephone; when the minutes hurry past without you even noticing; when the words don't even make sense; when you realize that, if anyone else was listening in, they'd think you were crazy; when neither of the two of you wants to hang up; when you check, after she's hung up, to make sure she really has; then you're really in trouble.

Or maybe I should say, then you're really in love.

Chapter 41

The following days in Rome slowly go back to normal. The hours return to their proper stations. It turns cold again. Everyone is holed up in their own home. The sea withdraws to a respectable distance. As does our memory of it. All that we're left with now are the photos of that magnificent journey. They wind up in some drawer somewhere, and before long, they too have been forgotten.

Romani seemed happy to see us, and even happier to see us accept his employment contract again. Paolo and Fabiola seem to be getting along. Paolo has abandoned the idea of becoming an agent and gone back to being an accountant. According to the stories Paolo tells, my father and his girl-friend are cooing and lovey-dovey all the time. Concerning Mamma's current dating record, on the other hand, Paolo knows nothing. Or at least, he tells me nothing. But he is worried about her state of health. He's seen her undergo a number of exams at the hospital. Here, too, however, Paolo knows nothing for certain. Or perhaps in this case, too, he prefers to keep a tight lid on it. I read the book that Mamma gave me, a story similar to ours, but with a happy ending. But after all, that's a story.

In the gym, I say hello to several people. Then I start working out.

"Hey, welcome back." It's Guido Balestri, skinny and smiling as usual. With a crimson tracksuit, a designer brand like everything else he wears. That, too, the same as always.

"Ciao. Are you here to work out?"

"No. I came to the gym in the fond hope of running into you," he says.

"I don't have a lira to lend you."

He laughs in amusement, perhaps because we both know perfectly well that that's the last thing he'd ever need to have.

"All right then, all kidding aside, what can I do for you?"

"No, I'm the one who can do something for *you*. I'll swing by and pick you up at nine o'clock for a party, Step. You up for it?"

The idea of enjoying a get-together with old friends agrees with me. It's been too long. I think about Pollo, and somehow it doesn't hurt. A nice swim in a pool full of people is exactly what I need. Slaps on the back from people I haven't seen in far too long a time. Hearing some good old stories about way back when from the truest friends there are.

"Why not?"

"Okay, then give me the address." We say farewell. "See you at nine! Be ready to go."

Chapter 42

I'm in the car with Balestri. He's driving cheerfully and fast, and possibly not just because of the beer that I brought him. "Here we go. We've arrived."

Via di Grottarossa. We get out. There are a few cars parked in front of the villa but none that I recognize. He buzzes at an intercom. CORSI. I don't recognize that last name either. Guido looks at me curiously. He seems amused.

"Oh, Guido, you didn't come to the wrong place, did you? I don't see anyone's motorcycle. And who's Corsi? I've never heard the name."

"This is the villa, trust me. There's at least one person here that I'm certain you know."

The gate buzzes and swings open. We go in. The villa is very nice with big windows covered by colorful awnings that look out on the vast garden. A half-empty swimming pool reposes not far away, waiting for the beginning of May, and close to the pool, there's a tennis court, red clay, no less, and the net, stretched taut, seems to be standing guard.

A smiling butler awaits us at the door. He steps aside and lets us in. Then he shuts the door behind us.

Guido says hello to the butler. They seem to know each other. "Is Carola here?"

"Certainly, she's in the other room. Come this way." He leads us down a hallway with paintings illuminated by small spotlights and past an impeccable library, surrounded by antique books, softly colored Chinese vases, and crystal objects.

We arrive in a large drawing room. The butler steps aside. A young woman hurries to greet us. "Ciao." She hugs Guido, giving him an affectionate peck on the cheek. This must be Carola.

She observes me attentively, as if evaluating me. She squints her eyes, narrowing them as if she can't believe that I am *me*.

"But this is him? It's really him?"

Guido smiles. "Yes, it's him."

"Yes, I actually think I'm really me. Usually people call me Stefano, Step to my friends. Could you tell me what's going on here?"

And suddenly, through a door standing ajar, out of that drawing room filled with strangers, I hear a laugh. *Her* laugh. The one I missed, the one I searched for, the one I've been dreaming of for a thousand nights. Babi.

She is sitting on a sofa in the middle of the drawing room, holding court, recounting an anecdote, and she laughs and the whole room laughs with her. While I, alone, remain silent. How many times in America, rummaging through my memories, have I dug down, all the way to the bottom, in search of that smile? And now, here it is, right in front of me.

And suddenly I find myself running headlong through a

labyrinth made up of moments: our first meeting, our first kiss, our first time. And in a flash, I remember everything I never got a chance to tell her, everything that I'd so wanted her to know, the depth of my love. That's what I'd have wished I could show her. I, a mere courtier allowed into the presence of her court, bowing down before her simplest smile, in the grandeur of her reign, I would have wanted to show her what I had to offer. On a silver platter, spreading my arms in an endless bow, displaying my gift before her, the feelings I had for her: a boundless love.

Here, my lady, you see, this is my love for you. Beyond the sea and all the way over the horizon. And even farther, Babi, beyond the sky and beyond the stars, and still farther, beyond the moon and beyond everything that is hidden and concealed. And even more. Because this is only the mere pittance that is given to us mere mortals to know. I love you beyond all that which we are not given to see, beyond all that which we are not given to know.

This is what I'd dreamed of telling you but I never got the chance. And now what? What could I say now to that young woman sitting on the sofa? I look at you, and you're no longer there. What ever became of you? Where is the smile that left me shipwrecked, stranded, castaway, shorn of all certainty but so sure of happiness?

I'd like to run away, but there is no time, no more time. Here you are.

Babi slowly turns in my direction. "Step! I can't believe it. What a surprise." She leaps to her feet and runs to meet me. She hugs me, holding me tight and kissing me gently on the cheek.

Then she pulls away but she doesn't go far. She looks into

my eyes and smiles. "I'm so happy to see you. What are you doing here though?"

But she doesn't give me time to reply. She laughs and talks, she talks and laughs. She seems to know all about me. She knows where I've been, what I did in America, what I studied, the new job I have.

"And then you got back to Italy at the beginning of September. On the third, I think, to be exact. And you didn't even call to wish me a happy birthday. You didn't remember, did you? Oh, that's okay, I forgive you."

And so Babi continues, laughing. September 6 was her birthday, and I remembered that day perfectly, as always. Just like every year, even in America, like every other thing that had anything to do with her, the finest things and the most painful ones.

"And then you worked on a television show, and then I saw the articles in the newspapers. With those photos. All to save that young woman. What was her name? Well, right now, I can't remember. Anyway, I tried to reach out to you, but..."

Luckily, she goes on. Without asking her name again. Ginevra. I ought to call her. I need to call her. I told her that we'd talk later on.

I turn off my cell phone. I turn around—I do it instinctively—and I see Guido smiling at me. He sees me looking at him, and he gives me a wink. He's the treacherous Candlewick, and I'm the stupid Pinocchio in the hands of a Blue Fairy. Good or wicked? And I watch him turn and leave, shutting the door behind him and leaving me all alone. Alone with her, with Babi, alone with my past.

Babi takes my hand. "Come with me. Let me introduce

you to my friends." And she drags me along, more of a woman, more confident, more mature.

"Okay, so this is Giovanni Franceschini, the proprietor of Caminetto Blu. Now this is Giorgio Maggi. Come on, you must have heard of him. He owns that big real estate firm that works in commercial and home transactions throughout Rome. You know the one, it's going great guns. It's called Casa Dolce Casa."

"No, I don't know it. I'm sorry." And I smile and shake hands as if I cared anything about all this. And then there are other names, other stories. Business titles of young pseudo-noblemen of this society where titles have been abolished. At least, as far as I'm concerned.

"And then this is Smeralda, my best and closest friend!" Babi approaches me, like a purring cat and then suggests in a warm voice, speaking right into my ear, "Let's just say that she's taken Pallina's place."

And she laughs. All I can think about is the smell of her Caron perfume. I look at her, and I'm tempted to ask her, "So who's taken my place?" But I remain silent.

I watch her as she continues this strange dance of introductions. And she laughs and tosses her head back, and then there are billowing waves of hair and perfume and again her laugh.

And I feel every last ounce of my grief and sorrow. Everything I don't know, everything I didn't experience, everything I now lack. And always will. How many arms embraced you to make you who you are?

I go back to watch that black-and-white movie of us that lasted for two years. A lifetime. Far away, long ago. Outside on the balcony, smoking a cigarette, carving my cheeks with my fingernails, calling to the stars for help. Then following that smoke as it rises into the sky, high, higher, and beyond...

How many times was I lost in that dark blue sky, carried up there by the fumes of the alcohol, by the hope of encountering her again? Up and down, ceaselessly. Along the constellations of Hydra, Perseus, and Andromeda... And on down all the way to Cassiopeia. First star to the right and straight on till morning.

And every star I met, I would ask, "Have you seen her? I beg of you. I've lost my star. Where could she be now? What can she be doing? And with whom?" And all around me, the silence of all those stars, embarrassed for me. The irritating noise of all my despairing tears. And I, too stupid to stop searching, to stop hoping for an answer. Give me a reason why, a simple reason why.

What a fool I am. This is known. When a love ends, you can find anything, anything but the reason why.

Chapter 43

Hey, Step, are you listening to me?" Babi asks.

"Certainly," I lie.

"I'm so happy to see you but why didn't you call me when you got back?"

"Well, I didn't know..."

"What didn't you know?" She laughs, covering her mouth. "Whether I was alone?" She looks at me. Now her eyes are more intense.

"I want something to drink." And I quickly manage to find a bottle of rum. A Pampero, the finest. I pour myself a glass and toss it back.

I go back to her, and we sit together on a sofa. She looks at me and laughs. "You've had a lot to drink, haven't you?"

"Yes, I've had something to drink."

And time passes. I don't know how much time. And she tells me everything, everything she decides to tell me. And before I can ask her how many arms embraced her to make her who she is, the evening is over. Finished just like my bottle of rum. "Ciao, Carola. Ciao, guys."

And everyone says good night, kisses are exchanged, appointments are made, and people remind each other of future plans. And then we're standing in front of the main door. Alone, just minutes later.

"What are you doing now?"

"Ah, nothing. I came in my friend Guido's car, but he's already left."

"Don't worry, I have mine here. I'll give you a ride, okay?"

And I get into a dark blue Mini Cooper, the latest model, with stereo and CD player. "Funny, isn't it?" She glances over at me as she drives. "We first met with a ride on a motorcycle where I got up behind you, and this time we meet again, where we ride in a car but I'm driving and you get in."

"Yes, funny." I don't know what else to say. I just wonder whether Guido had imagined that this would happen too. An impeccable Candlewick with a clever, brilliant mind. I see his smile again in my mind's eye, the wink and his perfect exit, stage left, like a great puppeteer of other people's fates. But why mine?

"Here." Babi hands me her scarf.

"Thanks. But I'm not cold!"

She laughs. "Silly." Now she gives me a more serious look. "Put it over your eyes. You're not supposed to see. You remember, don't you? Now it's my turn. And you're going to have to go along with the game."

Without a word, I tie the scarf around my head, the way she did back then. That time on the motorcycle behind me. She and her eyes, blindfolded, flying away fearlessly, letting herself be swept away toward that house in Ansedonia, that night, her first time. Now I can feel her driving, calmly, turning up the stereo a little, letting myself be carried along by the music, by her, by that bottle of rum sloshing around inside of me.

"Okay, we're here."

I take off my blindfold, and in the dim light, I glimpse it. The Tower.

"Do you remember? That time you fell asleep?"

How could I forget? Then, when we woke up, we quarreled, and after that, made peace. The way that lovers make peace. And before I even know what's happening, I find her in my arms. And yet, we haven't quarreled. No, not this time.

She kisses me. Softly, without shame, she smiles in the half light. And she continues that way, caressing me. "I've missed you, you know that?"

I feel foolish, what can I say? Is it even true? Why is she telling me that? I want to remain silent above all but a simple "Yes?" escapes my lips.

"Seriously." She smiles. Then she unbuttons my shirt and goes even further. Without haste, but determined, confident, far more confident than before, if I remember the way I last saw her.

"Come on. Get out." Babi practically shoves me out of the car, and she laughs. She takes off her blouse and undoes her bra, uncovering her breasts. She lets the rain run over her and off her skin, caressed by the raindrops and then by me, as I run my tongue over her flesh, over her wet nipples. With confident hands, she undoes my belt, unzips my trousers and lets them fall down my legs, and then inserts her hand and whispers in my ear, "Hello, here he is. Ciao. It's been a while."

Bold and daring in a way she'd never been before. Or at least, never with me. Then she kisses me on the chest while raindrops keep pouring out of the sky. And Babi slides down, letting herself be carried by those drops until she finds me. And I let myself go, carried along by the rum, the rain falling out of the sky, and by *her*, kneeling so low. And the pleasure is killing me, and I'm suffering just admitting it.

By now, wet all over as she sucks me off, practically angrily, I let myself be carried away. All that time gone by. All that pain under the bridge. All that I lost.

I raise my head to the sky. Suddenly I see those raindrops, caressed by that shaft of light from a distant moon. I'd like to match my actions to Battisti's song. "But I said no, and now I'm coming back to you with all my miseries, with my hopes stillborn, that I no longer have the courage to paint with life…"

But instead, I remain. And she goes on like that, not stopping, faster and faster, with her mouth greedily seeking out everything that belongs to me.

Then she pulls away, stands up, and hauls me down to the ground with her, and I let myself fall. I stretch out beside her in the falling rain. And she climbs up onto me and hikes her skirt, and by now, she's wearing no panties underneath. Wet all over, she spreads my hands wide and is on top of me.

The rain keeps falling. I hold on to the ground with my hands as my head spins; I've had too much to drink. From above me, Babi smiles down and takes her pleasure and looks at me, lustful and sensual. And for a moment, I just wish I wasn't there. How could I wish that? That smile of hers, that long-beloved smile, wasn't that what I came back for?

And suddenly a flash. No light, just awareness. Like a

nocturnal bird, a flutter of wings, thunderous in its delicacy. Gin's voice.

"Will you call me later?"

"Yes, maybe I'll call you."

"No maybe about it. Let's talk later! And don't say you'll call me, say you love me!"

And then, like pixels in an overexposed photo, an out-of-focus image on a Polaroid, suddenly the picture forms with great clarity in my mind. Sweet Gin, tender Gin, funny Gin, innocent Gin. She appears before me, entirely, in all her beauty. And the distant moon seems to present me with a new face, hers. Crushed, heartbroken, disappointed, betrayed. And in that lunar pallor, I see everything I wish I'd never seen.

As if by enchantment, the rain falls harder, and the fumes of all the alcohol I swigged begin to disperse. And I, suddenly lucid, try to squirm out from under Babi. But she clutches me tighter, rising and falling above me with an intensity practically verging on rage. No, she won't let me escape. As if spurred on by the fact that I'm trying to get away, she leaves me no breathing room, no truce, no respite. More, and more, and more. She only dismounts at the last moment when I'm in the throes of my orgasm and I come. And satisfied, placated, by now satiated, she collapses on top of me. She abandons herself like that, leaving my semen and my guilt lying somewhere on the ground.

Then she gives me a light kiss, and all I know is that I just feel so much the guiltier. And she smiles, beneath the rain, more driven than ever, more woman than before. Different. A funhouse mirror image of what I once loved so deeply.

"You know, Step, there's something I need to tell you . . ."

As I get dressed again under the streaming water that I so dearly hope might somehow bring me a cleansing wash, a form of purification, beneath the dark, low clouds that glare at me, inquisitorial beneath that moon that has so indignantly turned her face away from me, Babi continues. "I just hope you won't get mad."

I look at her. How could I get mad at her?

She puts both hands up, pulling her wet hair back. Then she tilts her head to one side, trying for a moment to turn into a little girl again. But it's no longer possible. She can't pull it off.

"Well...I wanted to tell you. In a few months, I'm getting married."

Chapter 44

Yes, hello?"

"Hey, what happened to you yesterday evening?" Gin asks. "I called and called you, but first it wouldn't go through, and then it said the phone was turned off."

I feel like dying.

"Oh, yeah. We went with Guido to eat in a place, but I didn't notice that the reception was bad. It was under..."

I don't know what else to say. I feel like vomiting.

And the absurd thing is that Gin comes to my rescue. "Yes, underground. I tried for a while, and then I fell asleep. I can't see you today. I have to go with my mother to visit an aunt outside of Rome. What a bore! Do you want to talk later? I won't turn my phone off, okay? I'm just kidding! A nice kiss to you, and later, when you're awake, an even nicer one!"

And she hangs up. With all her cheer, Gin with her love of life. Gin with her beauty. Gin with her purity. I feel like an absolute piece of shit. It might be the rum, or it might be all the rest. Could the amount I drank be taken as a justification? No, it's not enough. I knew the difference between right and wrong. I knew I should have said no at the outset. I should have turned down the offer of a ride, I should have refused to blindfold myself with that scarf, and I shouldn't have kissed Babi.

What if I just dreamed it? I get out of bed. The clothing hanging over the chair is all still wet from the rain, those shoes caked with mud leaving no room for doubt. It was no dream. It's a nightmare. Guilty beyond any and all reasonable doubt.

I sift through my memories in search of a phrase, words I can cling to. I'm reminded of something a teacher of mine said in high school in a philosophy lesson: "A weak man has doubts before a decision; a strong man has them afterwards." I think it must have been Karl Kraus. So, in his opinion, I would be a strong man. And yet I feel so weak.

And so, stupid mastermind behind my own condemnation, I drag myself into the kitchen. Some coffee should help. A day will pass and then another and then another after that. And eventually all this will be forgotten because it will be part of the past.

I pour myself some coffee that's already made, sitting in the pot. It's still hot. Paolo must have left it out before going to work. I sit down at the table. I drink some of the coffee, and I eat a cookie.

Then I see a note. I recognize Paolo's handwriting. Usually perfect and neat. This time, however, it seems ever so slightly wobbly. Maybe he was tired and he wrote it in a rush. I read it. *I went with Papà to Umberto I Hospital. Mamma has been admitted there. Come as soon as you can, please.*

Now I understand the handwriting. I leave the coffee on the table and hurry to get a shower. Yes, now I remember.

Paolo had told me about Mamma, but he hadn't struck me as especially worried.

I dry off, get dressed, and minutes later, I'm already on my motorcycle. A blast of wind in my face brings me back to full consciousness immediately. Everything's going to be all right.

Chapter 45

Excuse me, I'm looking for Signora Mancini. I believe she was admitted here earlier today."

A male nurse sets down an issue of *Corriere dello Sport*, opened to an article about who knows what soccer star purchased by a team, and takes a bored look at the computer in front of him. "Mancini, you said?"

"Yes."

Then it occurs to me that she might have used her maiden name. "Or she might be under Scauri."

"Scauri? Yes, here she is. Bed 114."

"Thanks."

I turn to go search for her in the ward. But as soon as I pass his workstation, the bored male nurse seems to come wide awake, and he stands in my way. "No, you can't go." He looks at the clock behind him. "Visiting hours start in about an hour."

"Yes, I know that, but she's my mother..."

"I don't give a damn if she's your mother. At three p.m., the same as for everyone."

And in a flash, I glimpse Paolo's note. *Come as soon as you can, please.*

And then I just suddenly see red. "I have to see my mother. Now. Right this second. I'm not trying to create an incident. Don't try to stop me. Please..."

And so I head off, moving fast, trying to get out of there before he can catch me, before he can say or do something that would be justified and right but which, at this moment in time, would seem so terribly wrong to me.

Beds 120, 119. Right and left. So I move through the beds, past lives abandoned on the threshold of a more-or-less happy abyss. A toothless old man gives me the faint echo of a smile. I try to smile back but it doesn't turn out especially well.

Bed 116. Bed 115. Bed 114. Here it is. I'm almost afraid to step closer. My mother. I see her there, lying between the sheets, pale and small as I've never seen her before. My mother seems to have sensed something, a faint noise, but one I certainly hadn't made. Maybe it was just a slight quickening of my pulse, a racing heartbeat at finding her like this.

She turns to look at me and smiles. She shifts in the bed, raising herself on her elbows, pushing her back up against the bed. But a sudden twinge of pain splashes across her face. And so she flops back, collapsing onto the pillow.

I quickly hurry to her side. I lift her delicately from below her shoulders and move her slowly toward the head of the bed. I help her, taking great care not to get tangled up with any of the tubes hanging down with who knows what medicines, disappearing into her arms. Her face is creased by a grimace, painted with suffering. But it only lasts for a moment. It's over now.

She smiles at me as I bring over an empty chair from a

nearby bed and set it down beside her so that she doesn't have to raise her voice to make herself heard, to keep from tiring her out, at least no more than she already is.

"Ciao."

She tries to speak but I tell her, "Shhh," lifting my finger to my lips. And so we remain in silence for a few seconds.

Then she seems to feel better. "How are you, Stefano?"

It's absurd. She's asking *me* how I feel. She gives me a delicate smile. She looks at me, seeking an answer.

I try to talk, but the words won't come out. "Fine." I manage to get that word out before it happens. A slightly longer word would have cracked between my lips, like a fragile crystal glass. My pain would have shattered into a thousand pieces, into smithereens, like an incredibly thin, brittle mirror carrying a reflection of our entire lives, mine and my mother's. Our life together. Her words, her stories, her laughter, her little jokes and pranks, her errands and chores, her lectures and dressings down. Her cooking, her makeup, and the way she dressed up.

Now they all slide away, impossible to restrain, like drops of water on the windshield of a speeding car, on the window of an airplane during takeoff, falling unrestrained from a shower at the beach, left running and buffeted by gusts of wind. Mamma.

The way she did so many times with me, growing up, it comes natural to me now, I take her hand. She squeezes mine in response. I can feel her hands, skinnier now, some of her rings turning freely, the skin hanging almost randomly on those tiny bones. I lift her hand to my mouth, and I kiss it.

She laughs softly. "What's that, the kiss of forgiveness?"

"Shhh." I don't want to talk. I can't bring myself to speak. "Shhh." I press my cheek against the back of her hand. She lets me rest, untroubled, on that small human pillow, so filled with love. My love, her love? I couldn't say. I lie there, resting, eyes shut, heart at peace, tears suspended, in silence.

She strokes my head with her other hand and toys a little with my hair. "Did you read the book I gave you?"

I nod my head, moving it lightly against her hand. I feel her smile.

"So now do you understand how it can happen? Your Mamma is a woman, a woman like any other. Maybe more fragile than most."

I remain silent. I look for some kind of help, anything. I can't handle this. I bite my lower lip, and I choke back my tears. Who will help me? Mamma mia, help me.

"I made a mistake, it's true, and the Good Lord chose to have you of all people catch me. But that was too harsh a punishment. To lose my son on account of that mistake."

I leap to my feet and manage to give her a smile, calm and powerful, the way she wants me, the way she made me, my mamma. "You haven't lost me. I'm right here."

She manages to extend her arm and caress me on the cheek. "Then I found you again. I got you back."

I nod my head.

"And now I'll lose you again."

"But why should you lose me? No. You'll see, everything will turn out all right."

Mamma shuts her eyes and shakes her head. "No. They told me. I'm going to lose you again."

She pauses and looks at me. Then, gently and slowly, she

smiles. I can see in her face the sheer happiness of having me at her side and then, instead, the pain that comes from inside her. Suddenly. A small grimace. She closes her eyes. A little later, she opens them again, once again serene. The pain has passed.

She looks at me and smiles. "But this time, it won't be my fault."

I remain silent. I'd like to find something to say, go back to before, get another chance. Apologize for all that lost time. I wish I'd never gone through that door, never seen her with another man, never intruded on her, never suffered for it. I wish I'd been quicker to understand, to accept, to forgive. But that's not how it went.

I can't seem to speak. I can't do anything but hold her hand lightly, afraid that everything could break again, shatter into pieces. But she saves me. She reaches out to help me, once again. After all, she's my mother. "Let's talk about what separated us."

She catches me off guard. I say nothing.

"Let's not pretend nothing happened. I think there's nothing worse than pretending that nothing's happened. If you're here, that means that somehow, to some extent, you're over it now."

Nothing, I say nothing.

"Well, I don't think in any case that it was my fault that you went all the way to America, was it?" She smiles. And that smile makes everything easier.

"I just wanted some time off."

"Two years? You certainly took your time. Anyway, I'm sorry for what happened. Your brother didn't understand any of it. Your father, on the other hand, refused to understand. He ought to have been there in your place. Things happened between us..." And she stops. Suddenly a stab of pain cuts through her smile. Like a slight wave arriving from who knows where. Then it vanishes again, and my mother opens her eyes. And she struggles to find that smile again. She finds it.

"You see, I shouldn't try to talk. Better not to. At least that way, you'll always have a good memory of him. I'm the guilty one, the wicked witch who ruined everything, and it's only right that I should pay." Another stab of pain. It seems to be stronger this time.

I step closer to her. "Mamma..."

"It's nothing. I'm fine. Thanks." She takes a long breath. "They give me these medicines, and they're so powerful. Sometimes it's as though I'm not even here. I dream while I'm wide awake. I don't feel anything at all. It's nice. Now I understand why you young people like to take drugs so much. They make you forget all your pain."

"I've never taken any though."

"I know. You've learned to live with your pain. But now enough is enough. Don't give that pain any more leeway. Make it give you back your life."

We remain in silence for a while.

"I missed you, Mamma."

She lays her hand on mine and squeezes. She tries to squeeze hard, but I can sense how weak, how fragile she is. I look at her hand. It's skinny. She's lost so much of that life, a life that she so generously gave to me. Then she lets go.

"Anyway, Stefano, I didn't want to talk about me."

"What do you want to know?"

"I remember that when I was very young, younger than

you are now, I had a boyfriend I really, really liked a lot. I was certain I was going to spend the rest of my life with him. Instead, he wound up with my best friend, and I sort of lost my mind. You should have seen my poor parents. In the end, I resigned myself to it. And right after that, I met your father. You see, I was happy that my first time should have been with him in particular. Well, something that at a certain moment seems so perfect to us might not seem that way with the passing of time. Maybe we realize that it wasn't so perfect after all, and even if we've lost something, that doesn't necessarily mean that we can't find it again, or even find something better."

She lies there for a while in silence, and then she smiles at me. She wants me to be happy. I so much want to be. In part, for her sake.

"I've met a young woman."

"There, that's what I wanted to hear you say. Will you tell me what she's like?"

"She's funny, she's pretty, she's strange. She's...very particular."

My mother laughs. "What about her...three-meters-above-the-sky girl...what does she have to say about it?"

"I saw her yesterday."

"What do you mean you saw her yesterday? I mean, sorry, aren't you dating that other girl?"

I remain silent. Mamma spreads her arms.

"Well, certainly, now that I stop to think about it, I'm the last person on earth to preach about it, right?"

We look at each other. Then suddenly we both burst out laughing.

"I don't know what you've done, but do you want some

advice? Don't tell the other girl anything. Not even that you've seen this one. Let your mistake pass in silence. I hope that what I did previously isn't something hereditary, otherwise I'd have to feel guilty about your mistakes as well as my own."

"No, Mamma, don't worry about it, I already feel guilty enough as it is. I wanted to see her again so badly. I thought about it day and night. I constantly imagined that moment, the way it would be..."

"And how was it?"

"You and me, three meters under the ground!"

"It's just that sometimes we do incredibly stupid things. And not when we're in love, but when we think we are." My mother remains silent for a few moments. "Well, so much the better. At least you cleared one thing up. What's over is over. History. Done. You couldn't avoid it, I think."

"As if that's not enough... she's getting married."

"Ah, from bad to worse. Is that why you were so upset?"

"No. The absurd thing is that I didn't care one bit. She seemed like a different person, someone who had nothing to do with me. With everything I remembered, she was no longer the same young woman I'd missed so badly, for whom I'd suffered so deeply. And the absurd thing is that she told me after everything had already happened. It only made me feel worse, a greater burden of guilt."

"Because of what she told you?"

"No, because of the other young woman. Because of how different she is from her, and because of how deeply she didn't deserve this."

My mother looks at me. Then she smiles. And she goes back to being exactly the Mamma I'd been missing so badly for so long. "Stefano, there are things that just have to happen, and you know why? Because if it had happened later, then it would no longer have been possible to put right. Unfortunately, I'm certain of that fact."

We just remain there for a while like that, in silence.

"Well, I'd better go." I give her a kiss on the cheek.

"Come visit me again."

"Of course I will, Mamma."

I walk to the door and turn around to say goodbye. She smiles at me from a distance and raises her hand. She winks at me too. Maybe to make it seem as if she's stronger. "Stefano..."

"Yes, Mamma, what is it? Do you need something?"

"No, thanks. I have all I need. Welcome back."

Chapter 46

By now it's sunset. I ring the buzzer. A voice comes out of the intercom in response.

"Excuse me, is Ginevra there?"

"No. She's in church, nearby, at San Bellarmino. Who's asking about her?"

I turn and leave. I don't feel like answering. Rude for this once. I hope you'll forgive me too.

I enter the church in silence. I don't know what to say, what to do, whether to pray, and if so, for what. Not now. Now I don't want to think about it.

A number of elderly women are on their knees, facing the altar. They're all holding rosaries. They move those rosaries from time to time, twitching in their hands, uttering words directed at the Lord, prayers that they hope He can grant. And He can, no doubt about it. But who knows if He'll feel like it. Who knows if He'll consider it just, that is, if there is any such thing as justice.

But I have other things to worry about. I have my sin. There she is. I see Gin from behind. She isn't down on her knees, but she's praying. Or she's saying something, anyway, and she too is certainly speaking to the Lord.

I quietly make my way toward her. "Gin?"

She turns. "Ciao. What a lovely surprise. I was just thanking the Lord. You know..." She smiles at me. "I was so worried. That is, it's not like I didn't want a baby...But just not right now. Such an important thing, and such a beautiful one, to have a child."

"Shhh," I tell her. I give her a light kiss on the cheek while I process the news that I am not going to be father after all. I am reluctant to ruin the feeling of relief in this moment but I lean and whisper into her ear, all in a single burst, without waiting, without fear, taking that fatal leap. I tell her everything, I whisper my sin to her, slowly, hoping that she might understand, that she can grasp it, that she can find it within her to forgive me.

I'm finished. I pull away. She looks at me in silence. I look at her. She doesn't believe me.

"Is this a joke?" She tries to smile.

I shake my head. "No. Forgive me, Gin."

She starts hitting me, furiously, with both fists, sobbing, shouting, forgetting that she's in church, or perhaps feeling all the more justified in consideration of that fact. "Why? Tell me why? Why did you do it? Why?"

And she goes on like that, in despair, falling to her knees and continuing to weep, searching for an answer that I can't give her. Then she turns and runs away, leaving me standing there in that church, even emptier now, before the eyes of all those ancient women who, for a fleeting moment, have forgotten about their prayers and are now fully focused on me.

They turn back to the altar and silently resume their prayers. Maybe they've forgiven me. With Gin, it's not going to be that easy.

Chapter 47

Mamma, I'm going out."

"All right, Gin. Call me though if you're going to be late. I need to know if you'll be here for dinner. I want to make you that pizza you like so much."

She goes on but I don't even hear what she says. "Yes, thanks, Mamma."

I put on a sweatshirt and decide to go out, to just get lost, without any sense of time. Only I can understand. I so deeply wished for all of this. And now? Now I have nothing. Now I find myself empty-handed, deprived of my dream. But was everything I dreamed of for so long even real? I don't feel like thinking about it. I'm in such bad shape.

Sheesh, there's nothing worse than finding yourself in a situation like this. You can talk and talk about it, from an outsider's perspective, when you hear about all these absurd situations that concern other people, I don't know why but you always assume that nothing of the kind could possibly happen to you, but instead, bam, there you are, right in the middle of it! It happens to you, it concerns you directly, as if you'd jinxed yourself, cast your own hex on your personal fate.

Christ, Gin, you need to face some kind of reckoning with your pride and your determination to go on being with Step. But I'm yearning for him, all the same.

I'm at the Ponte Milvio. I stop my car and get out. I remember that night, those kisses, my first time. And then here, on this bridge. I stop in front of the third lamppost. I see our padlock. I remember when he tossed the key into the Tiber. That was a promise, Step. Was it really that hard a promise to keep? I start crying. For a minute, I wish I had brought something with me to break that padlock. I hate you.

I get back in the car and leave. I drive around like this, without any clear idea of where to go now for a good, long while. I don't know how long. All I know is that now I'm walking by the sea. Lost in the wind, distracted by the sing-song of the maritime currents. But I feel so damned stupid. I can't believe it, this just can't be. I miss that asshole so bad that it's killing me. I miss everything I dreamed of.

Yes, I know someone might perfectly well say to me, *But Gin, what were you expecting? Step left for America to try to forget how upset he was over breaking up with Babi. It's just normal that he'd fall for her again.* Oh, is it? I don't feel that way, and what's more, I don't give a damn about what's normal. Because I'm crazy! That's right, I'm crazy about him, and crazy about everything I dreamed of. You can't even begin to imagine how much I've wanted him.

Chapter 48

The male nurse on duty is sitting in front of a monitor. He's the same one as always. He finishes typing something on the computer and then sees me come in. He recognizes me.

I walk down the corridor. From the rooms lining the hallway, I hear labored, pained breathing. All around is a smell of cleanliness and lavender. But also a certain something, a sense of falsehood. A man drags himself along in pajamas with whiskers unshaven and eyes dull and lifeless. Under one arm, he's carrying the sports daily, the *Gazzetta dello Sport*, pink and crumpled. Maybe the team he roots for might purchase a new player, and such an event might somehow bring a sparkle to his gaze. Who knows. In pain, even the simplest and most ordinary things take on an unexpected importance. Everything becomes a way of grasping on to life, an interest that can in some sense help to distract us.

There she is. She's resting. Lost in a pillow much larger than her small face. She sees me and smiles. "Ciao, Stefano."

I pull up a chair that's sitting nearby, and I put it at the foot of her bed.

"Well?" She looks at me quizzically. I already know what she's referring to.

"No good, I couldn't do it. I'm sorry. I told her."

"And how did that go?"

"She punched me."

"Oh, finally, a girl who's willing to hit you. You've chosen the hardest path there is. Is she a very special young woman?"

I describe her.

"And I have a photo."

I show it to her. She's curious. Small wrinkles appear on her face. Then a smile of surprise. Then, again, a grimace of pain somewhere in her body, tucked away, well concealed. Unfortunately.

"I have something to tell you."

This worries me, and she notices it. "No, Stefano. It's not important. That is, it's important, but it's not something for you to worry about."

She lies there in silence for a moment, apparently uncertain about whether or not to tell me. We seem to have gone back in time to long, long ago, when I was small and she was hale and healthy. She would play little tricks on me, hide things from me, tease me, and we'd laugh together. Now I feel like crying. I don't want to think about it. "Well, Mamma, will you tell me?"

"I know her, this Ginevra."

"You know her?"

"Yes, you have excellent taste. In other words, she's the one who chose you, and you're the one who messed everything up."

"But how on earth do you know her? I mean, how did you manage to pull that off?"

"How did *I* pull it off? No, she was the one who wanted

to get to know *me*. I always saw this young woman waiting downstairs outside the building. At first, I just assumed she was waiting for someone who lived in the building. But then, whenever I drove away, I saw her leave."

"And then?"

"Then one day, I spotted her at the supermarket, and we ran into each other. I can't say if it was a coincidence. We made friends. We started talking." She coughs. Then she looks at me, and her eyes are full of love.

"Okay, will you tell me the whole story?"

"Yes. We made friends. She didn't know that I'd already seen her waiting outside. Well, come to think of it, I'm not so sure of that anymore. The fact remains that I talked to her, told her a few things about me, about Papà, about Paolo, and about you."

"What did you tell her about me?"

"That I love you, that I missed you, that you'd left the country, that you'd be coming back. In the end, she seemed especially curious to know more about us. And she was always asking whether you'd called, if I'd heard from you."

"And what did you say?"

"What could I tell her? That I never got any news of you. Then I heard that you were going to return that same day, when Paolo told me that he was going to pick you up at the airport. And so when Ginevra and I talked on the phone..."

"Wait, what do you mean, when you talked on the phone? Did you have phone conversations too?"

"Yes, we'd exchanged phone numbers. What's so strange about that, excuse me very much? We'd sort of become friends."

I can't believe it. It all seems so very strange.

"Well?"

"Well, what?"

"Nothing, I just told her."

"And what did she say?"

"Oh, she went on chatting as if it were the most inconsequential thing, of no importance, just mentioning that she'd joined the pool and was going to swim regularly. Oh, also, she made me laugh because she asked if I wanted to go with her, but now that I think about it, there is one strange thing..."

"What?"

"Since you've come back, I've gone to the supermarket many times."

"And so?"

"Well, since you returned, I've never once run into her."

I look at her. I remain silent. Then I nod and smile. She tries to smile back, but another wave of pain makes her shut her eyes. Longer this time. I take her hand. She squeezes hard on my hand, an unexpected show of strength. Then she releases her grip and opens her eyes, weary, wearier than before, and she makes a faint stab at a smile.

"Stefano...please..." She points to a glass on the side table. "Would you bring me some water, please?"

I take the glass and stand up. I take a few steps but then I hear her call me again. "Stefano..."

I turn around. "Yes?"

"This friend of mine, Gin...would you send her some flowers, some beautiful flowers?" She sits up on her pillow and smiles at me.

"Yes, Mamma, certainly."

I leave the ward, and I find the bathroom. After letting the tap run for a while, the way my mother had taught me, I fill the glass with water, just a little more than halfway full. I return to the ward. It's a short walk, just a few steps. I see her there, peaceful, in repose. In Bed 114. With a faint smile on her face and her eyes shut, exactly as I'd left her. But she's decided not to wait for my return. Mamma always hated saying goodbye. And I don't know why, but I'm reminded of the time that I took the train on my first school field trip to Florence. The other mothers were all there, waving their handkerchiefs, variously white or colorful, saying farewell to the kids crowding the windows of the train compartments. I stuck my head out. I scanned the crowd packed along the platform under the canopy, a teeming mass of waving mothers, but she was gone. She was already gone. Just like right now. She'd already departed. Oh, Mamma.

I set the glass of water down on the side table next to her. *I brought you your water, Mamma. I filled it just the way you taught me. Mamma.* The only woman I'll never stop loving. The one woman I wish I'd never lost. But whom I lost twice. Forgive me.

And so I leave the ward in silence, walking past numbered beds, amid strangers. Distracted by their pain, they ignore my pain.

An alarm sounds in the distance. Two male nurses go running past me. One of them slams into me unintentionally, but I pay them no mind. They're going to tend to my mother. Stupid fools, they don't know that she's already left. Don't bother her. That's just the way she is. She doesn't like saying goodbye, she doesn't look back, she doesn't wave farewell. Mamma. I'll miss you, more than I've already missed you in all these years. "If what wounded me also wounded you, I think of you in a field of strawberries, I think of you happy there, dancing, lightly, so beautiful, so free..." The words of an old song surface in my mind. For you, Mamma, only for you. Carry them with you, hold them tight wherever you're going now. Dance, beautiful one, in that field of strawberries, finally free from whatever it was that had imprisoned you here.

I'm crying now. I go downstairs. The male nurse isn't there at the workstation. There's a woman, instead. She looks at me, curious for a moment, but says nothing. She must have seen people leave that ward, unable to conceal their brutal grief. She doesn't even notice it anymore. We all seem the same to her, she's practically bored by now with all our stupid tears that can do nothing.

I leave. It's afternoon by now. The sun is still high, the sky is clear and blue. A day like any other, but different from all other days, and forever. I see my father and my brother arriving. They're far away. They're chatting, relaxed, with smiles on their faces. Who knows what they're talking about. I don't know and I don't want to know. Lucky souls, who don't know yet. Let them go on enjoying it. Still carefree and happy, blithe in their ignorance.

I change direction and head off. I let myself drift; I wander in the wind. I'd like to let my grief become light and airy. But that's not what happens.

Then I think about Mamma, her last words, her advice. I smile. Yes, Mamma. And obedient as I've never been before, like the son I so wished I could have been, I enter the closest flower shop.

Chapter 49

Ginevra, may I come in?" Gin opens the door to her room and speaks to her mother. "What is it, Mamma?"

"This afternoon they delivered this for you."

Peering through a large bouquet of red roses, her mother peeks into the bedroom and smiles at her as she lays them on the bed.

"You see how beautiful? And just look. There's a white rose in the middle. You know what that means, don't you?"

"No, what does it mean?"

"It's a way of asking for forgiveness, a floral apology. Is there someone who's done something wrong, someone who's sorry for something?"

"No, Mamma. Everything's fine." But mothers never miss a thing. There's no doubt her mother observes Gin's reddened, bloodshot eyes.

"Here." She hands Gin a handkerchief and smiles at her.

"Whenever you like, dinner is on the table."

"Thanks, Mamma, but I don't feel like eating right now."

"All right. But don't take it too hard. It's not worth it."

Gin smiles at her mother. "Maybe it isn't."

Before she leaves the room, Gin's mother gives her a

card. "Here, this was in among the roses. Maybe it's an explanation of that white rose."

Gin's mother exits the room, leaving her alone with her sorrow, alone with her flowers, alone with her card. Gin opens it. Curiously, she reads the beginning.

You've asked me to do this so many times, but I've always said no. However, I was planning to do it for you on your birthday, or for Christmas, or just any special occasion. But never as a way of asking your forgiveness. But if it does any good, even if it's not enough, even if I have to write another thousand and then another thousand and then yet another thousand more, I'd gladly do that because I can't live without you.

And Gin continues reading. *Here is what you wanted. My poetry.* She slides through the words, tears coming to her eyes, she sniffs, and she laughs again.

She gets up and continues reading. About their moments, their passion, the trip, the excitement. And she continues smiling, sniffing again, wiping at her eyes, smearing one of the words with a runaway tear.

And she goes on like that, all the way to the end. *I'll wait for you. And I'll go on waiting. And I'll go on waiting even longer. To see you, to have you, to feel happy again. Happy as the sky at sunset.*

Then she has a sudden, strange sensation. She turns around rapidly and looks at her desk. There in the corner where she has always kept them, hidden. And suddenly she understands. And she feels herself die a little bit inside.

She jumps and runs into the other room. "Mamma! Did you let him come into my room?"

"Why, it was that nice boy, the one who sent us the champagne, no? He seemed so kind and respectable. And after all, he'd brought those beautiful flowers. I couldn't tell him no. It would have seemed rude."

"Mamma, you have no idea what you've done."

Chapter 50

I'm sitting in my room. I feel like a thief. And actually, I am one. But I'm just too curious. When I saw them sitting on Gin's desk, I couldn't believe my eyes. Three diaries, one for each year.

I start leafing through the first one. She's written an unbelievable amount, all of it amusing. I wonder who this Francesco is. Or Fra, as she calls him. And then all these little hearts.

She is the way she is. Unique. She has a strength, a drive, a sheer determination... And she laughs and always has a joke handy...

Gin, I'm so sorry for what happened. But the situation with Babi just got out of control. I didn't know what I was doing; I'd had too much to drink. Sometimes you're just looking for love but don't realize that the woman you loved so much has disappeared. Was it you who invented her in the first place? You're seeking in that kiss the desperate flavor of what you once tasted and experienced so deeply, so intensely but which no longer exists.

But sometimes memories are best left undisturbed. Enough is enough. Gin will understand. She has to understand. If I hadn't done it, I'd have always lived in hiding. I'd never have come out into the open, coming back into the light of love.

She'll understand. She has to understand.

I start to read.

Yesterday the most incredible thing of my whole life happened. I was at a party at Roberta Micchi's house—she's an older girl, a senior who thinks she's the bomb. I'd crashed the party with two other friends of mine (Ele and Simo), and we were having the time of our lives when they showed up, the party crashers themselves, the Budokans.

I found out that that's what they were called while they were throwing the birthday girl's cake and hit Giò (the goofball who was coming on to Ele) right in the face! What aim. Anyway, I'm completely head over heels for this guy. He knocked into me first thing, as soon as they came in. But he apologized, and to keep from knocking me to the floor, he caught me and held me up, his arms around me. Damn! There we were, our faces a millimeter apart, and that's when I lost it. Who knows if he realized it. All I know is that his name is Step!

Jesus, are you telling me that at the same party where I first met Babi, Gin was there too? I don't remember her. And I go on reading as if in a frenzy, crazed, surprised, indignant at having been played. My eyes rush over the lines, back and forth. And there it is.

I saw him! It's 2:30 in the morning, and I can't sleep. I was out on the Via Olimpica, and he was there with his friend.

Pollo is his name, I think. Step even won a race! I'm just crazy about him, but I can see that he's constantly kidding around with that high school senior, Babi Gervasi. Gosh darn it, Step, if you wind up dating that girl you lose a lot of points in my book. That girl is a complete dope. In fact, I don't even know what she was doing there, but then she even rode as a chamomile! Oh, you transform them, Step. You must have some kind of magic touch, and I couldn't tell you what it is. Hey, magical prince, sooner or later you're going to have to notice me too. TRANSFORM ME. Otherwise I'll have to cast a spell on you. Well, I'm going to Sleepy Town.

I'm speechless, and I read on. I leaf through the pages, and I realize that she never once let her sights waver. She was focused on me the whole time. Page after page. Gin, you wrote it all down. You were always there.

I can't believe it! But it's actually true. Ele called me to give me the news. I even went all the way over there to see if it was true. There it is, on that bridge, and it's beautiful:
*   YOU AND ME...THREE METERS ABOVE THE SKY!*

And there's more.

His friend Pollo died. I was there in the church. I wished I could put my arms around him. I prayed for him, for his love. But he needs her right now. Not me.

And I continue reading in silence, sorting through those pages and reading fragments of my own life. Seeing them

again through her writing, her colorful notes, her under-
lined sentences.

*They broke up! Silvia told me. It's true! I'm sorry. I know
I should never be so overjoyed about someone else's misfortune.
But overjoyed is the only word for it. I want to make you
happy myself, Step. I want to make you feel loved. Please,
just give me that chance.*

I continue through giddily cheerful pages and bits of
her life that concern only her. But she's talking about
me again.

*I'm a wreck. I'm so miserable. I heard that he's leaving the
country. He's going away. Damn it, that must have been
some crush he had on Babi if he made up his mind to do
that. Still, I remember something that my mother always
used to say, it's a really great phrase, "You can change the
sky overhead but you can't change the soul inside." Will it
do him any good to leave? All I know is that I'll wait
for you, Step.*

It's true. Sometimes it does no good to live under a
different sky. The things you need to resolve are still there,
inside of you, wherever you might go.

I read about Gin befriending Mamma. Mamma had
figured it out. She never misses a thing.

*What the hell? I got everything mixed up. I arrived at
8:30 in the morning. I didn't realize you were arriving at
8:30 that evening! I went to the airport and waited for*

twelve hours, and I still didn't have the courage to do any-thing! That is, Step at a certain point turned around, and I had to scramble and hide behind a column, and for all I know, he actually saw me! Jesus, he could tell that someone was watching! He must have eyes in the back of his head. But he's just too cute. He's lost weight. He looks older. He is . . . what he is!

She even came to the airport. And there's more.

Tonight I'm going to get him, I'm sure of it. I've already figured out a perfect plan. I went down into the garage in the afternoon, and I opened the little tube that connects the gas tank to the engine which will mean he's run out of gas. I overheard at the gym what he was going to be doing, so he only has two options: either he goes to the gas station on the Via Flaminia or else the one on Corso Francia. But when a guy is done at the gym, he wants to take off fast. I think he'll go to the gas station that's farther away. He wants to feel the wind in his hair, someone like him who loves motorcycles so much.

I can't believe what I'm reading. I turn a page.

Yahoooo! I passed the audition at the TdV theater, where he works. I really wasn't hoping for it to go so well. But the most absurd thing is that Ele passed too! Step, are you bringing me good luck? There's only one thing I know for sure. From now on I'm going to see him every day. So how are you going to run from me now?

Suddenly I hear a bang. I whip around. Gin is at the door
to my room.

Paolo is right behind her. "Sorry, Step, I couldn't stop
her. She came running into the house like a slingshot and
then—"

I raise my hand. Paolo understands. He stops. He just
stands there, motionless in the doorway while Gin walks
into my room. She looks at me but her gaze seems to
penetrate right through me. Her eyes are sad. Glistening.
Beautiful. And I feel a pang in my heart. "Gin...I..."

"Shhh," she says to me. She lifts her forefinger to her
lips, like a sweet little girl. She shuts her eyes and shakes
her head. "Don't say anything, please." She takes back her
diaries, one after another, and puts them in her bag. And
she leaves, without looking back, in silence.

Chapter 51

A church. Bare walls, unadorned. A hundred or so mourners. Some standing, others seated, some of them leaning against those massive, ancient columns, withstanding the passage of time, the many prayers overhead, the wishes invoked, the grief suffered. By them. By the many. By others.

And then there's my own grief. The sorrow of not having known how to be the protagonist of my own life, not fully, of having just wasted the time that was given to me. And to do what with it? I just judged my mother. And I can't seem to figure out how I failed to understand it at the time.

Only now do I clearly see how badly I failed in my simplest, most straightforward task. No one wanted anything more from me, literally nothing, but my silence. Just to refrain from opening my mouth. But instead, stubborn, muleheaded, egotistical, blind, I insisted on raising myself up as judge.

And then the thing that's even worse. Not merely arrogate to oneself the right to forgive, but then to fail to know how to do it. Fail to forgive. There, that's the thing.

I look around. My father, my brother, their girlfriends.

Even Pallina, Lucone, Balestri, and my other friends. There are some faces I don't see, names that are missing. There are others who really shouldn't be here at all. But I hardly feel like thinking about it. Not today.

All around me, so many people whose names I don't even know. Distant relatives, cousins, uncles, and aunts. People I remember only from faded photographs, confused memories of parties, of various moments in the past, variously happy or less so, from who knows when, how many years ago.

A priest reads out a portion of scripture. Now he's saying something. He's trying to make me understand how everything that is happening right now is a positive good for us all. But I can't follow his line of thought. No, I'm lost right now. My grief is overwhelming. I can't think, understand, accept, or agree. He says things, he tells stories, he makes promises, but he can't convince me. There's only one thing of which I'm certain. My mother is no longer here among us. And that's all I need to know.

Or actually, it's not enough for me at all. Mamma, I miss you. I miss the time I wanted to live with you again, to be able to tell you what I now understand. And I utter it inwardly, in silence. But still, you hear me.

An organ starts to play. From the back of the church, I see Gin arrive. She's dressed in black, and she proceeds down the arcades, staying out of the line of sight of most, but not out of *my* line of sight. Then she gently places a wreath at the foot of the altar and looks at me. From a distance. She makes no gesture, no signal of any kind. Not a smile, nor a scowl. Nothing. A gaze as clear and clean as only hers could be.

A last glance. Then I see her leave, heading out to the far

end of the church. A short while later, it's all over. At the entrance, I look around for her, but she's gone now. I've lost her. People cluster around me, hug me, say things to me, clasp my hand. But I can't seem to hear them, to understand. I try to smile, to thank them, to keep from weeping.

Yes, more than anything else, I try to keep from weeping. But I fail. And I'm not ashamed of that. Mamma, I'm crying now. It's a venting, a liberation, it's the desire to be a child again, to be loved, to go back in time, to refuse to grow up, the abiding need for your pure love.

Someone embraces me, puts her arm around my shoulders, hugs me. But that's not you, Mamma. That can't be you. And I lean against the wall, folding over slightly. I conceal my face and my tears. And I wish it hadn't all come so late. Mamma, forgive me.

Chapter 52

A few days later, I don't even know how many because that sorrow and pain fills you. The grief, and you can't even figure out where it's coming from. It tumbles you over, knocks you down like a huge wave you never saw coming, that caught you from behind, that cartwheels you under, taking your breath away, scraping you along the wet sand, back over those steps that seemed so almighty certain in your life. But, instead, no. They weren't certain at all. Or they aren't anymore.

I've been going past Gin's front door for days now. I've been watching her come out that door for days now, looking so many different ways. Pretty. Beautiful. Messy, tangled, fancy. Hair pulled back, hair loose in the breeze, hanging down, crazed, ungovernable. Tied into two ponytails. In a flowered dress, in overalls, with one strap undone, in an impeccable skirt suit, in a light blue blouse with the collar turned up and a navy-blue skirt beneath it. Wearing light blue jeans, or capri shorts, or distressed denim jeans with heavy stitching in a different, clashing, eye-catching color. The powerful imagination that allows her to reinvent her look every day. It's just the way she is.

Gin emerges constantly from that apartment building entrance, every time looking different. But there's one thing I've seen every time that never changes. Her eyes. Her expression. Like a beautiful dream cut in half by a brutal shaft of sunlight from a raised curtain. Like the persistent sound of a cell phone mistakenly left turned on and allowed to go on ringing by someone calling the wrong number. Like a car alarm set off by an inept would-be car thief who's already made his escape into the night. A distracted teeming world of life out there has inadvertently slammed its elbow into her happiness. And that elbow belonged to me. I can't hide. I have no excuse. I can only hope somehow to win her forgiveness.

There she is. I see Gin come out the door. I watch her go by. She's in her car. And for the first time after so many days, hiding in the shadows, I take a step forward and lock gazes with her for a moment. And tenderly and awkwardly, I smile. With my eyes, I speak and explain and recount and do my best to keep her from turning and leaving. All with a glance.

And her eyes seem to listen in silence, nod, grasp, and seriously accept everything. Then, that silence made up of a thousand words, intense like never before, is snapped off. Gin looks down. In search of something. When she looks up and back at me again, she gently shakes her head. Her cheek dimples slightly; a faint grimace appears on her face, trending almost into a smile, perhaps a hint of possibility. As if to say, *No, not yet, it's too soon.* At least that's what I choose to read into it.

And so she heads off, in what direction and with what destination I have no way of knowing, toward the life that's waiting for her. Perhaps toward a new dream, certainly a better one than the dream that I've just robbed her of.

And she's right. She deserves better. So I stand there in silence. I light a cigarette. I take just a couple of drags and then flick it away. I don't want anything. Then I realize that's not true. So I reach into my motorcycle's red box and pull out what I need.

⌐

Far, far away in that same city, cars are on the move, horns honking. Rina, the Gervasi family housekeeper, walks out of the Stellari apartment complex. She waves a greeting to the receptionist with her usual smile, and she continues briskly and without hesitation toward the dumpster. She lifts the lid, pushing down hard with one foot on the metal pedal. With a perfect arching throw, better than a basketball player lofting a three-pointer, she tosses in the black trash bag. The dumpster shuts its maw, like an ax lopping off a head, wielded by an indifferent executioner. But the lid can't complete its trajectory entirely. It's thwarted by a rolled-up poster sticking out of a corner of the bag. On it is a blown-up photo of Step and Babi astride a motorcycle popping a wheelie. The rebel yell of that fleeting moment of happiness, of that love long since dissolved by the passage of time. It's all past now. And as so often happens, it has now been tossed onto the ash heap of history.

⌐

Pallina goes running out her front door. Cheerful and determined, elegant like never before, she gets into his car and kisses Dema, laughing. She wants to take back control of her life. "Well, where are we going?"

"Anywhere you want."

Pallina looks at him and smiles. She's decided to plunge back into the swim of things. And he's the right person to swim with. "All right then, you decide. We can just go random places for one night out."

And Dema doesn't have to be told a second time. He puts the car in gear and gently pulls out, vanishing into the light traffic. Then he turns up the volume on the stereo and smiles.

⌒

Babi is in her bedroom. She happily checks the guest list. It won't be long now. Sheesh, Mamma, how could you? You invited the Pentestis, and you know I can't stand them, and also some cousins we've never even met. Mamma and her rules. Then, for a moment, she decides that that idea would please her enormously. Yes, it would be an incredible idea. Invite Step to her wedding. It would be so cool.

⌒

Paolo and my father have decided to go out for dinner at the Chinese restaurant on Via Valadier. They sit down at a table. They laugh and joke, accompanied by their girl-friends. They've ordered a vast assortment of dishes, from fried seaweed to the inevitable spring rolls, from sweet and sour pork to Peking duck. And that's not to mention crispy beef, both steamed and fried dumplings, and the combo platter. They've shared each other's dishes, and they've stuffed themselves silly, trying every type of sauce on the lazy susan at the center of the table. Then Paolo and my father grab the check out of each other's hands, both insistent on paying.

⌒

Not far away, in a place where, sooner or later, we'll all wind up. Without any need for deeds or mortgages, without clever investments or lucky windfalls. Where everyone is just naturally a guest. In the one place where it no longer matters how much you earn, but only how much you've been capable of giving. The graveyard.

In the silence of all those manicured lawns, all the names and all the posed photographs in the world aren't enough to tell the essence of all those lives. But the faces, the smiles, the sorrow of their visitors, *those* tell the story in a flash of the beauty of everything they were and the degree to which they're missed.

For some time now, Pollo is no longer alone. Now there's another piece of Step's life to keep him company: Step's mother. Both of them now have beautiful flowers, still fresh and brimming over with life and love. The love that Step never had a chance to demonstrate fully. Because love should never be lost or neglected.

⌒

When I get on my motorcycle, the sun is already setting. And that's exactly when I see Gin returning home. Driving fast, so like her. She follows the curve with her head, she sings the song she's listening to just then under her breath. I wonder what song it is. But she seems to be back in a cheery mood. Like before. The way I last saw her. Beautiful with that smile, the life that abounds in her, the dreams that she pursues, the limitations she refuses to acknowledge. Free.

And so I leave, pulling away, seeing her amazement, seeing her smile. And I'm happy. In a way I haven't been in such a long time. Guilty only of that graffiti. Scrawled on that wall. Immense. Across the whole façade of the facing building. Splendid, direct, and true.

And now I have no more doubts. I have no regrets. I no longer have a past. All I have is a deep and abiding desire to start over again. And to be happy. With you, Gin. I'm sure of it.

You see it up there? I wrote it for you. *I want you.*

Acknowledgments

I'd like to extend my thanks to all those who, for better or worse, and above all, without even realizing it, gave me a leg up or an idea to use. After all, that's the great thing about life, the fact that it doesn't all depend on you. I want to thank all those who, intentionally, helped me.

Thanks to Giulia and her excellent advice. But especially for the beautiful moments she gave me. I've hidden a few of them in this book to keep them from being forgotten.

Thanks to Riccardo Tozzi and his niece Margherita, to Francesca Longardi and to the whole staff of Cattleya because, without them, this second book of mine would never have seen the light of day.

Thanks to Ked (Kylee Doust), for her enthusiasm, the pleasure of listening to her memories, which, in the end, match up with mine and became invaluable advice.

Thanks to Inge and Carlo Feltrinelli and all my friends from the sales team who physically carried my book on a grand tour of Italy.

Thanks to Maddy who edits me, teaches me so much, and in exchange laughs and enjoys herself as she learns a little healthy "Romanesco" slang.

Thanks to Giulia Maldifassi, Valeria Pagani, and all my friends in the press office, who introduced me and helped me tour all of Italy.

Thanks to Alberto Rollo, who in a stern but pleasurable fashion always finds a way to show me the best way to write and to whom I naturally always listen.

Thanks to the Budokans, my friends, my real friends, the ones who are always there, not only in my pages and my memories.

Thanks to all my relatives who root for me and share with me the "sofa of their thoughts."

Thanks to Carlantoine, the source of noble inspiration.

Thanks to my "Brother" Mimmo. When I read him what I've written, he shuts his eyes. Then he smiles and nods, as if to say, *Yes, that's good.* He does the same thing, out on the open water, when he chooses currents and winds.

Thanks to Luce and her morselletti, which I love more and more with every day that passes.

Last of all, my friend Giuseppe always gives me suggestions. He stays close to me, listens, and in the end, he laughs with me. I have to admit, he's often right. And so, thanks also to you.

About the Author

Federico Moccia is one of Italy's publishing phenomenons, and his emotional stories have been compared to the works of Nicholas Sparks and John Green. The first two Babi and Step books were blockbuster bestsellers in Italy, spending three full consecutive years on the Nielsen bestseller list. His books have been published in fifteen languages worldwide and have sold over ten million copies, and there are feature films in Italian and Spanish based on the first two books in the trilogy.

Learn more at: FedericoMoccia.es
Twitter @FedericoMoccia
Facebook.com/FedericoMocciaOfficial

Antony Shugaar is a translator and writer who lived for many years in Italy, France, and Spain. He has received two translation fellowships from the National Endowment for the Arts. He has translated close to forty books for Europa Editions and has worked for many of the most prestigious publishers, trade and academic, in the US and the UK. He has translated extensively for the *New York Review of Books* and has written for the *New York Times*, the *Times of London*, and many other publications.